Critical Acclaim for
Dean Koontz and *The Silent Corner*

"FBI agent Jane Hawk goes rogue. . . . She's capable of taking on the opposition single-handedly, with or without her trusty Heckler & Koch handgun. . . . A proven specialist in action scenes, Koontz pulls off some doozies here. . . . The book is full of neat touches. . . . And the prose, as always in a Koontz novel, is first-rate. Perhaps Koontz's leanest, meanest thriller, this initial entry in a new series introduces a smart, appealing heroine who can outthink as well as outshoot the baddest of bad dudes." —*Kirkus Reviews* (starred review)

"Gripping . . . The paranoia and mystery increase as the story unfolds. . . . Koontz has created such a wonderful character in Jane Hawk [that] readers will clamor for more tales involving Hawk and her quest for justice. Koontz rocks it again." —Associated Press

"The latest page-turner by Dean Koontz introduces readers to Jane Hawk . . . an inspired choice for a protagonist, by far the strongest part of a reliably entertaining book by the perennial bestselling author. . . . Action, zippy dialogue and a winning character at the center of the book, part of a new series by Koontz."
—Minneapolis *Star-Tribune*

"Bestselling novelist Dean Koontz is back with a fierce new main character named Jane Hawk. But what's really scary in *The Silent Corner* is Mr. Koontz's chilling villain. . . . In this era of stingy text-message prose, Mr. Koontz is practically Shakespeare. . . . Readers who appreciate heightened expression and super dramatic similes will be thrilled by Mr. Koontz's choices. His authorial individualism continues with a blend of vintage and trendy. . . . But Mr. Koontz is ultra-contemporary, too. . . . [He] makes several points about Jane's antagonists that more than apply to the times in which we are living. . . . *The Silent Corner* brims with both action and emotion." —Pittsburgh *Post-Gazette*

THE
SILENT CORNER

BY DEAN KOONTZ

The Silent Corner • Ashley Bell • The City
Innocence • 77 Shadow Street • What the Night Knows
Breathless • Relentless • Your Heart Belongs to Me
The Darkest Evening of the Year • The Good Guy
The Husband • Velocity • Life Expectancy
The Taking • The Face • By the Light of the Moon
One Door Away From Heaven • From the Corner of His Eye
False Memory • Seize the Night • Fear Nothing
Mr. Murder • Dragon Tears • Hideaway • Cold Fire
The Bad Place • Midnight • Lightning • Watchers
Strangers • Twilight Eyes • Darkfall • Phantoms
Whispers • The Mask • The Vision • The Face of Fear
Night Chills • Shattered • The Voice of the Night
The Servants of Twilight • The House of Thunder
The Key to Midnight • The Eyes of Darkness
Shadowfires • Winter Moon • The Door to December
Dark Rivers of the Heart • Icebound • Strange Highways
Intensity • Sole Survivor • Ticktock
The Funhouse • Demon Seed

ODD THOMAS

Odd Thomas • Forever Odd • Brother Odd • Odd Hours
Odd Interlude • Odd Apocalypse • Deeply Odd • Saint Odd

FRANKENSTEIN

Prodigal Son • City of Night • Dead and Alive
Lost Souls • The Dead Town

A Big Little Life: A Memoir of a Joyful Dog Named Trixie

DEAN KOONTZ

Bantam Books | New York

THE
SILENT
CORNER

A Novel of Suspense

2017 Bantam Books Mass Market Edition

Copyright © 2017 by Dean Koontz
Excerpt from *The Whispering Room*
by Dean Koontz copyright © 2017 by Dean Koontz

Published in the United States by Bantam Books, an imprint of
Random House, a division of Random House LLC,
a Penguin Random House Company, New York.

BANTAM BOOKS and the HOUSE colophon are
registered trademarks of Random House LLC.

Originally published in hardcover in the United States
by Bantam Books, an imprint of Random House, a division of
Random House LLC, in 2017.

A signed, limited edition has been privately produced by
Charnel House.
charnelhouse.com

This book contains an excerpt from the forthcoming book
The Whispering Room by Dean Koontz. This excerpt has been set
for this edition only and may not reflect the final content of
the forthcoming edition.

ISBN 978-0-345-54679-1
Ebook ISBN 978-0-345-54678-4
International edition ISBN 978-1-524-79912-0

Cover design: Scott Biel
Cover image of woman: © Mohamad Itani/Trevillion Images
Stepback image of woman: © Anne Costello/Arcangel

Printed in the United States of America

randomhousebooks.com

2   4   6   8   9   7   5   3   1

Bantam Books mass market edition: November 2017

To Gerda. You rock me.

The major advances in civilization . . .
all but wreck the societies in which they occur.
— ALFRED NORTH WHITEHEAD

I look down into all that wasp-nest or bee-hive
. . . and witness their wax-laying and honey-making,
and poison-brewing, and choking by sulphur.
— THOMAS CARLYLE, *Sartor Resartus*

THE
SILENT CORNER

The Silent Corner: *Those who are truly off the grid and cannot be tracked by any technology, yet are able to move about freely and use the Internet, are said to be in* the silent corner.

PART ONE

ROCK ME

1

JANE HAWK WOKE IN THE COOL dark and for a moment could not remember where she had gone to sleep, only that as always she was in a queen- or king-size bed and that her pistol lay under the pillow on which the head of a companion would have rested had she not been traveling alone. Diesel growl and friction drone of eighteen tires on asphalt reminded her that she was in a motel, near the interstate, and it was . . . Monday.

With a soft-green numerical glow, the bedside clock reported the bad but not uncommon news that it was 4:15 in the morning, too early for her to have gotten eight hours of sack time, too late to imagine that she might fall back to sleep.

She lay for a while, thinking about what had been lost. She had promised herself to stop dwelling on the bitter past. She spent less time on it now than before, which would have counted as progress if recently she hadn't turned to thoughts of what was yet to be lost.

She took a change of clothes and the pistol into the bathroom. She shut the door and braced it with a straight-backed chair that she had moved from the bedroom upon checking in the previous night.

Such was the maid service that in the corner above the sink, the radials and spirals of a spider's architecture extended across an area larger than her hand. When she had gone to bed at eleven o'clock, the only provision hanging in the web had been a struggling moth. During the night, the moth had become but the husk of a moth, the hollow body translucent, the wings shorn of their velvet dust, brittle and fractured. The plump spider now watched over a pair of captured silverfish, leaner fare, though another morsel would soon find its way into the gossamer abattoir.

Outside, the light from a security lamp gilded the frosted glass in the small crank-out bathroom window, which was not large enough to allow even a child to gain entrance. Its dimensions would also preclude her from escaping through it in a crisis.

Jane put the pistol on the closed lid of the toilet and left the vinyl curtain open while she took a shower. The water was hotter than she expected from a two-star operation, melting accumulated soreness out of muscle and bone, but she didn't linger in the spray as long as she would have liked.

2

HER SHOULDER RIG FEATURED a holster with swivel connectors, a spare-magazine carrier, and a suede harness. The weapon hung just behind her left arm, a deep position that allowed unparalleled concealment beneath her specially tailored sport coats.

In addition to the spare magazine clipped to the rig, she kept two others in the pockets of the jacket, a total of forty rounds, counting those in the pistol.

The day might come when forty was not enough. She had no backup anymore, no team in a van around the corner if everything went to shit. Those days were over for the time being, if not forever. She couldn't arm herself for infinite combat. In any situation, if forty rounds proved not enough, neither would eighty or eight hundred. She did not delude herself regarding her skills or endurance.

She carried her two suitcases out to the Ford Escape, raised the tailgate, loaded the bags, and locked the vehicle.

The sun that had not yet risen must have been producing a solar flare or two. The bright silver moon declining in the west reflected so much light that the shadows of its craters had blurred away. It looked not like a solid object but instead like a hole in the night sky, pure and dangerous light shining through from another universe.

In the motel office, she returned the room key. Behind the front desk, a guy with a shaved head and a chin beard asked if everything had been to her satisfaction, almost as if he genuinely cared. She nearly said, *With all the bugs, I imagine a lot of your guests are entomologists.* But she didn't want to leave him with a more memorable image of her than the one he got from picturing her naked. She said, "Yeah, fine," and walked out of there.

At check-in, she had paid cash in advance and used one of her counterfeit driver's licenses to provide the required ID, according to which Lucy Aimes of Sacramento had just left the building.

Early-spring flying beetles of some kind clicked in the metal cones of the lamps mounted to the ceiling of the covered walkway, and their exaggerated spriggy-legged shadows jigged on the spotlit concrete underfoot.

As she walked to the diner next door, which was part of the motel operation, she was aware of the security cameras but didn't look directly at any of them. Surveillance had become inescapable.

The only cameras that could undo her, however, were those in airports, train stations, and other key facilities that were linked to computers running real-time state-of-the-art facial-recognition software. Her flying days were over. She went everywhere by car.

When all this started, she'd been a natural blonde with long hair. Now she was a brunette with a shorter cut. Changes of that kind could not foil facial recognition if you were being hunted. Short of spackling herself with an obvious disguise that would also draw unwanted attention, she could not have done much to change the shape of her face or the many unique details of her features to escape this mechanized detection.

3

A THREE-EGG CHEESE OMELET, a double rasher of bacon, sausage, extra butter for the toast, hold the home fries, coffee instead of orange juice: She thrived on protein, but too many carbs made her feel sluggish and slow-witted. She didn't worry about fat, because she'd have to live another two decades to develop arteriosclerosis.

The waitress brought refill coffee. She was thirty-ish, pretty in a faded-flower way, too pale and too thin, as if life whittled and bleached her day by day. "You hear about Philadelphia?"

"What now?"

"Some crazies crashed this private jet plane straight into four lanes of bumper-to-bumper morning traffic. TV says there must've been a full load of fuel. Almost a mile of highway on fire, this bridge collapsed totally, cars and trucks blowing up, those poor people trapped in it. Horrible. We got a TV in the kitchen. It's too awful to look. Makes you sick to watch it. They say they do it for God, but it's the devil in them. What are we ever gonna do?"

"I don't know," Jane said.

"I don't think anybody knows."

"I don't think so, either."

The waitress returned to the kitchen, and Jane finished eating breakfast. If you let the news spoil your appetite, there wouldn't be a day you could eat.

4

THE BLACK FORD ESCAPE APpeared to be Detroit-lite, but this one had secrets under the hood and the power to outrun anything with the words TO SERVE AND PROTECT on its front doors.

Two weeks earlier, Jane had paid cash for the Ford in Nogales, Arizona, which was directly across the international border from Nogales, Mexico. The car had been stolen in the United States, given new engine-block numbers and more horsepower in Mexico, and returned to the States for sale. The dealer's showrooms were a series of barns on a former horse ranch; he never advertised his inventory, never issued a receipt or paid taxes. Upon request, he provided Canadian license plates and a guaranteed-legitimate registration card from the Department of Motor Vehicles for the province of British Columbia.

When dawn came, she was still in Arizona, racing westward on Interstate 8. The night paled. As the sun slowly cleared the horizon in her wake, the high feathery cirrus clouds ahead of her pinked before darkening to coralline, and the sky waxed through shades of increasingly intense blue.

Sometimes on long drives, she wanted music. Bach, Beethoven, Brahms, Mozart, Chopin, Liszt. This morning she preferred silence. In her current mood, even the best of music would sound discordant.

Forty miles past sunrise, she crossed the state line into southernmost California. During the following hour, the high white fleecy clouds lowered and congested and grayed into woolpack. After another hour, the sky had grown darker, swollen, malign.

Near the western periphery of the Cleveland National Forest, she exited the interstate at the town of Alpine, where General Gordon Lambert had lived with his wife. The previous evening, Jane had consulted one of her old but useful Thomas Guides, a spiral-bound book of maps. She was sure she knew how to find the house.

In addition to other modifications made to the Ford Escape in Mexico, the entire GPS had been removed, including the transponder that allowed its position to be tracked continuously by satellite and other means. There was no point in being off the grid if the vehicle you drove was Wi-Fied to it with every turn of the wheels.

Although rain was as natural as sunshine, although Nature functioned without intentions, Jane saw malice in the coming storm. Lately, her love of the natural world had at times been tested by a perception, perhaps irrational but deeply felt, that Nature was colluding with humanity in enterprises wicked and destructive.

5

FOURTEEN THOUSAND SOULS lived in Alpine, a percentage of them sure to believe in fate. Fewer than three hundred were from the Viejas Band of Kumeyaay Indians, who operated the Viejas Casino. Jane had no interest in games of chance. Minute by minute, life was a continuous rolling of the dice, and that was as much gambling as she could handle.

Graced with pines and live oaks, the central business district was frontier-town quaint. Certain buildings actually dated to the Old West, but others of more recent construction aped that style with varying degrees of success. The number of antiques stores, galleries, gift shops, and restaurants suggested year-round tourism that predated the casino.

San Diego, the eighth largest city in the country, was less than thirty miles and eighteen hundred feet of elevation away. Wherever at least a million people lived in close proximity to one another, a significant portion needed, on any given day, to flee the hive for a place of less busy buzzing.

The white-clapboard black-shuttered Lambert residence stood on the farther outskirts of Alpine, on approximately half an acre of land, the front yard picket-fenced, the porch furnished with wicker chairs. The flag was at full mast on a pole at the northeast corner of the house, the red-and-white fly billowing gently in the breeze, the fifty-star canton pulled taut in full display against the curdled, brooding sky.

The twenty-five-mile-per-hour speed limit allowed Jane to cruise past slowly without appearing to be canvassing the place. She saw nothing out of the ordinary. But if they suspected that she might come here because of the bond she shared with Gwyneth Lambert, they would be circumspect almost to the point of invisibility.

She passed four other houses before the street came to a dead end. There, she turned and parked the Escape on the shoulder of the lane, facing back the way she had come.

These homes stood on the brow of a hill with a view of El Capitan Lake. Jane followed a dirt path down through an open woods and then along a treeless slope green with maiden grass that would be as gold as wheat by midsummer. At the shore, she walked south, surveying the lake, which looked both placid and disarranged because the rumpled-laundry clouds were reflected in the serene mirrored surface. She gave equal attention to the houses on her left, gazing up as if admiring each.

Fences indicated that the properties occupied only the scalped-flat lots at the top of the hill. The white pickets at the front of the Lambert house were repeated all the way around.

She walked behind two more residences before returning to the Lambert place and climbing the slope. The back gate featured a simple gravity latch.

Closing the gate behind her, she considered the windows, from which the draperies had been drawn aside and the blinds raised to admit as much of the day's dreary light as possible. She could see no one gazing out at the lake—or on the watch for her.

Committed now, she followed the pickets around the side of the house. As the clouds lowered and the flag rustled in a breeze that smelled faintly of either the rain to come or the waters of the lake, she climbed the porch steps and rang the bell.

A moment later, a slim, attractive, fiftyish woman opened the door. She wore jeans, a sweater, and a knee-length apron decorated with needlepoint strawberries.

"Mrs. Lambert?" Jane asked.

"Yes?"

"We have a bond that I hope I can call upon."

Gwyneth Lambert raised a half smile and her eyebrows.

Jane said, "We both married Marines."

"That's a bond, all right. How can I help you?"

"We're also both widows. And I believe we have the same people to blame for that."

6

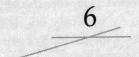

THE KITCHEN SMELLED OF OR-
anges. Gwyn Lambert was baking mandarin-
chocolate muffins in such quantity and with such
industry that it was impossible not to suppose that
she was busying herself as a defense against the
sharper edges of her grief.

On the counters were nine plates, each holding
half a dozen fully cooled muffins already covered
in plastic wrap, destined for her neighbors and
friends. A tenth plate of still-warm treats stood on
the dinette table, and another batch was rising to
perfection in the oven.

Gwyn was one of those impressive kitchen masters who produced culinary wonders with no apparent aftermath. No dirty mixing bowls or dishes
in the sink. No flour dusting the counters. No
crumbs or other debris on the floor.

Having declined a muffin, Jane accepted a mug
of strong black coffee. She and her hostess sat across
the table from each other, fragrant steam rising lan-
guidly off the rich brew.

"Did you say your Nick was a lieutenant colonel?" Gwyn asked.

Jane had used her real name. The bond between
her and Gwyn required this visit be kept secret.
Under these circumstances, if she couldn't trust a
Marine wife, she couldn't trust anyone.

"Full colonel," Jane corrected. "He wore the silver eagle."

"At only thirty-two? A boy with that kind of pep in his step would've gotten stars in time."

Gwyn's husband, Gordon, had been a lieutenant general, three stars, one rank below the highest officers in the corps.

Jane said, "Nick was awarded the Navy Cross and a DDS plus an entire chest full of other stuff." The Navy Cross was one step below the Medal of Honor. Innately modest, Nick had never spoken of his medals and commendations, but sometimes Jane felt the need to brag about him, to confirm that he had existed and that his existence had made the world a better place. "I lost him four months ago. We were married six years."

"Honey," said Gwyn, "you must have been a true child bride."

"Far from it. Twenty-one. The wedding was the week after I graduated Quantico and made the Bureau."

Gwyn looked surprised. "You're FBI?"

"If I ever go back. I'm on a leave of absence now. We met when Nick was on assignment to the Corps Combat Development Command at Quantico. He didn't come on to me. I had to come on to him. He was the most beautiful thing I'd ever seen, and I'm mule-stubborn about getting what I want." She surprised herself when her heart clutched and her voice broke. "These four months sometimes feel like four years . . . then like just four hours." Her thoughtless-ness at once dismayed her. "Damn, I'm sorry. Your loss is fresher than mine."

Waving off the apology, unshed tears in her eyes, Gwyn said, "A year after we were married—'83 it was—Gordie was in Beirut when terrorists blew up the Marine barracks, killed two hundred twenty. He was so often somewhere bad, I imagined him dead a thousand times. I thought all that imagining would prepare me to handle it if one day someone in dress blues knocked on the door with a KIA notice. But I wasn't prepared for . . . for the way it happened."

According to news stories, on a Saturday little more than two weeks earlier, when his wife had been at the supermarket, Gordon let himself out the back gate in the picket fence and walked down the hill to the lake shore. He carried a short-barrel pistol-grip pump-action shotgun. He sat near the water, his back against a grassy bank. Because of the short barrel, he was able to reach the trigger. Boaters on the lake sat witness as he shot himself in the mouth. When Gwyn came home from shopping, she found the street filled with sheriff's cruisers, her front door standing open, and her life forever changed.

Jane said, "Do you mind my asking . . ."

"I'm hurting bad, but I'm not broken. Ask."

"Any chance he went to the lake in the company of someone?"

"No, none. The woman next door saw him going down there alone, carrying something, but she didn't realize it was a gun."

"The boaters who witnessed it—have they all been cleared?"

Gwyn looked puzzled. "Cleared of what?"

"Maybe your husband was to meet someone. Maybe he took the shotgun for protection."

"And maybe it was murder? Couldn't have been. There were four boats in the area. At least half a dozen people witnessed it."

Jane didn't want to ask the next question because it could seem to be an accusation that the Lamberts' marriage had been in trouble. "Was your husband . . . was Gordon at all depressed?"

"Not ever. Some people throw hope away. Gordie was chained to it all his life, an optimist's optimist."

"Sounds like Nick," Jane said. "Every problem that came his way was just a challenge, and he loved challenges."

"How did it happen, honey? How did you lose him?"

"I was making dinner. He went to the john. When he didn't come back, I found him fully clothed, sitting in the bathtub. He'd used his combat knife, the Ka-Bar, to cut his neck so deeply that he severed his left carotid artery."

7

THIS HAD BEEN A WET EL NIÑO winter, the second in the past half decade, with normal rain in the intervening years, a climate anomaly that had ended the state's drought. Now the morning light at the windows dimmed as though dusk must be descending. Once glass-smooth, the lake below lay stippled with white, a breeze scaling it as if it were a great serpent slumbering in the shadow of the pending storm.

While Gwyn took the finished muffins out of the oven and put the pan on the drainboard to cool, the ticking of the wall clock seemed to grow louder. During the past month, timepieces of all kinds had periodically tormented Jane. Now and then she thought she could hear her wristwatch ticking faintly; it became so aggravating that she took it off and put it away in the car's glove box or, if she was in a motel, carried it across the room to bury it under the cushion of an armchair until she needed it. If time was running out for her, she didn't want to be insistently reminded of that fact.

As Gwyn poured fresh coffee for the two of them, Jane wondered, "Did Gordon leave a note?"

"Not a note, not a text message, not a voice mail. I don't know whether I wish he had or should be glad he didn't." She returned the pot to the coffeemaker and settled in her chair once more.

Jane tried to ignore the clock, the louder ticking no doubt imaginary. "I keep a notepad and pen in my bedroom vanity drawer. Nick used them to write a final good-bye, if you can bend your mind to think of it that way." The eeriness of those four sentences frosted the chambers of her heart every time she considered them. She quoted, " 'Something is wrong with me. I need. I very much need. I very much need to be dead.' "

Gwyn had picked up her coffee cup. She put it down without drinking from it. "That's damn strange, isn't it?"

"I thought so. The police and medical examiner seemed to think so, too. The first sentence was in his tight, meticulous cursive, but the quality of the others steadily deteriorated, as if he had to struggle to control his hand."

They stared out at the darkening day, sharing a silence, and then Gwyn said, "How awful for you—to be the one to find him."

That observation didn't need a reply.

Staring into her coffee cup as though her future might be read in the patterns of reflected light made by the ceiling fixture, Jane said, "The U.S. suicide rate dropped to about ten and a half per hundred thousand people late in the last century. But the last two decades, it's returned to the historic norm of twelve and a half. Until last April, when it began to climb. By the end of the year, the annual tally was fourteen per hundred thousand. At the normal rate, that's over thirty-eight thousand cases. The higher rate is more than *another* forty-five hundred suicides. And from what I'm able to tell, the first three months of this year, it's running at fifteen and a half, which by December thirty-first will be almost eighty-four hundred cases above the historic norm."

As she recited the numbers for Gwyn, she puzzled over them yet again, but she still had no idea what to make of them or why they seemed germane to Nick's death. When she looked up, she saw Gwyn regarding her with rather more intensity than before.

"Honey, are you telling me you're doing research? Damn right you are. So there's more to this than you've said. Isn't there?"

There was a great deal more, but Jane wouldn't share too much and possibly put the widow Lambert in jeopardy.

Gwyn pressed her. "Don't tell me we're back in some cold war with all its dirty tricks. Are there a lot of military men in those extra eighty-four hundred suicides?"

"Quite a few, but not a disproportionate share. It's equally distributed across professions. Doctors, lawyers, teachers, police, journalists . . . But they're unusual suicides. Successful and well-adjusted people with no history of depression or emotional problems or financial crisis. They don't fit any of the standard profiles of those with suicidal tendencies."

A gust of wind pummeled the house, rattling the back door as if someone insistently tried the knob to see if the lock was engaged.

Hope pinked the woman's face and brought a liveliness to her eyes that Jane had not seen before. "Are you saying maybe Gordie was—what?—drugged or something? He didn't know what he was doing when he took the shotgun down there? Is there a possibility . . . ?"

"I don't know, Gwyn. I've found the littlest bits of things to piece together, and I can't see what they mean yet, if they mean anything at all." She tried the coffee but had drunk enough of it. "Was there any time in the past year when Gordon wasn't feeling well?"

"Maybe a cold once. An abscessed tooth and a root canal."

"Spells of vertigo? Mental confusion? Headaches?"

"Gordie wasn't a man for headaches. Or for anything that slowed him down."

"This would've been memorable, a real hardcore migraine, with the characteristic twinkling lights that mess with your vision." She saw this resonated with the widow Lambert. "When was it, Gwyn?"

"At the WIC, the What If Conference, last September in Vegas."

"What's the What If?"

"The Gernsback Institute brings together a panel of futurists and science-fiction writers for four days. It challenges them to think outside the box about national defense. What threats are we not concentrating on that might turn out to be bigger than we think a year from now, ten years, twenty years?"

She put one hand to her mouth, and her brow furrowed.

"Something wrong?" Jane asked.

Gwyn shrugged. "No. Just for a second, I wondered if I should be talking about it. But it's not a big secret or anything. It's gotten a lot of press attention over the years. See, the institute invites four hundred of the most forward-thinking people—military officers from every branch of service, key scientists, and engineers from major defense contractors—to listen to the panels and ask questions. It's quite a thing. Spouses are welcome. We women attend the dinners and social events, but not the sessions. And it's not any kind of bribe, by the way."

"I didn't think it was."

"The institute is an apolitical nonprofit. It doesn't have any ties to defense contractors. And when you receive an invitation, you have to pay your own travel and lodging. Gordie took me with him to three conferences. He just loved them."

"But last year he had a bad migraine at the event?"

"His only one ever. The third day, in the morning, for almost six hours he was flat in bed. I kept after him to call the front desk and find a doctor. But Gordie figured anything less than a bullet wound was best dealt with by letting it work itself out. You know how men are always having to prove things to themselves."

Jane warmed to a memory. "Nick was woodworking, gouged his hand when a chisel slipped. It probably needed four or five stitches. But he cleaned the wound himself, packed it full of Neosporin, and bound it tight with duct tape. I thought he'd die of blood poisoning or lose his hand, and he thought my concern was so cute. *Cute!* I wanted so bad to smack him. In fact, I *did* smack him."

Gwyn smiled. "Good for you. Anyway, the migraine went away by lunchtime, and Gordie missed only one session. When I wasn't able to persuade him to see a doctor, I went to the spa and spent a bundle for a massage. But how did you know about the migraine?"

"One of the other people I've interviewed, this widower in Chicago, his wife had her first and last migraine two months before she hung herself in their garage."

"Was she at the What If Conference?"

"No. I only wish it was that simple. I can't find links like that between a significant number of them. Just fragile threads, tenuous connections. That woman was the CEO of a nonprofit serving people with disabilities. By all accounts she was happy, productive, and beloved by virtually everyone."

"Did your Nick have a one-and-only migraine?"

"Not that he mentioned. The suspicious suicides that interest me . . . in the months before they died, some complained of a few brief spells of vertigo. Or strange, intense dreams. Or essential tremors of the mouth and the left hand that resolved after just a week or two. Some experienced a bitter taste that came and went. Different things and mostly minor.

But Nick didn't have any unusual symptoms. Zero, zip, nada."

"You've interviewed these people's loved ones."

"Yes."

"How many?"

"Twenty-two so far, including you." Reading Gwyn's expression, Jane said, "Yeah, I know, it's an obsession. Maybe it's a fool's errand."

"You're nobody's fool, honey. Sometimes it's just . . . hard to move on. Where will you go from here?"

"There's someone near San Diego I'd like to talk to." She leaned back in her chair. "But this What If event in Vegas still intrigues me. Do you have anything from the conference, a brochure, especially a program for those four days?"

"There's probably something in Gordon's study upstairs. I'll go look. More coffee?"

"No, thanks. I had a lot with breakfast. What I *do* need is a bathroom."

"There's a half bath off the hall. Come along, I'll show you."

A couple of minutes later, in the spiderless, spotless powder bath, as Jane washed her hands at the sink, she met her reflection eye-to-eye. Not for the first time, she wondered if by setting out on this crusade two months earlier, she'd done the very worst of wrong things.

She had so much to lose, and not just her life. Least of all her life.

From the roof, by way of the bathroom-vent duct, the growing wind spoke down through the second floor to the first, like some troll that had moved from under his traditional bridge to a home with a view.

As she stepped out of the bathroom, a gunshot barked upstairs.

8

JANE DREW HER PISTOL, HELD it in both hands, muzzle pointed to her right, at the floor. It was not her FBI gun. She wasn't allowed that weapon while on leave. She liked this one as much, maybe even better: a Heckler & Koch Combat Competition Mark 23, chambered for .45 ACP.

The noise had been a gunshot. Unmistakable. No scream before it, no scream after it, no footsteps.

She knew she hadn't been followed from Arizona. If somebody had already been waiting here for her, he would have taken her when she was sitting at the kitchen table, widow to widow, her defenses down.

Maybe the guy was holding Gwyn captive and fired one round to draw Jane to the second floor. That didn't make sense, but then most bad guys were emotion-driven, short on logic and reason.

She thought of another possibility, but she didn't want to go there yet.

If the house had back stairs, they would likely be in the kitchen. She hadn't noticed them. There had been two closed doors. A pantry, of course. The other was most likely the door to the garage. Or to a laundry room. Okay, the front stairs were the only stairs.

She didn't like the stairs. Nowhere to dodge left or right. No possibility of retreat, because she'd be turning her back on the shooter. Once she committed, she could go only up, each of the two narrow flights like a close-range shooting gallery.

At the landing between flights, she stayed low, slipped fast around the newel post. Nobody at the top. Heart knocking like a parade drum. Bite on the fear. She knew what to do. She'd done it before. One of her instructors had said it was ballet without tights and tutus, you just needed to know the moves, exactly where to make them, and at the end of the performance, they would throw flowers at your feet, metaphorically speaking.

The last flight. This was where a professional should try to take her. Aiming down, his gun would be just below eye level; aiming up, hers would be in her line of sight, giving him the surer shot.

Top of the stairs and still alive.

Stay crouched and close to the wall. Both hands on the pistol. Arms extended. Stop and listen. No one in the upstairs hall.

Now it was all about clearing doorways, which sucked nearly as much as the stairs. Crossing a threshold, she could be hosed, right here at the end of it.

Gwyn Lambert occupied an armchair in the master bedroom, head rolled to the left. Her right arm had fallen into her lap, the gun still loosely held. The bullet had entered her right temple, tunneled her brain, and broken out the left temple, spattering the carpet with chunks of bone and twists of hair and worse.

9

THE SCENE DIDN'T APPEAR TO have been staged. It was a true suicide. No scream before the gunshot, no footsteps or other sound afterward. Only the motion and the act, and terror or relief or regret in the instant between them. A nightstand drawer hung open, where the home-defense weapon might have been kept.

Although Jane hadn't known Gwyneth long enough to be wrenched with grief, dull but awful sadness and sharp anger afflicted her, the latter because this was no ordinary suicide, no consequence of anguish or depression. For a woman only two weeks from the loss of her husband, Gwyn had been coping as well as anyone might. Baking muffins, soon to take them to family and friends who had supported her in the current darkness, looking to the future. Besides, of the little she had learned about this military wife, one thing she knew beyond doubt was that Gwyn would not have tormented another grieving widow by putting her in the position of having to be the first to discover yet another suicide.

A sudden beeping caused her to pivot from the dead woman and bring her pistol up. No one. The sound issued from an adjacent room. She approached the open doorway with caution until she recognized the tone as the AT&T signal alerting its customer that a phone had been left off the hook.

She crossed the threshold into Gordon Lambert's study. On the walls were photographs of him as a younger man in combat gear with brother Marines in exotic places. Gordon in dress blues, tall and handsome, pictured posing with a president. A framed flag that had flown in battle.

Trailing on its coiled cord, the handset of the desk phone lay on the carpet. From a jacket pocket, she fished a cotton handkerchief that she carried for no purpose other than fingerprint avoidance, and she cradled the handset, wondering with whom Gwyn might have spoken before making her mortal decision. She lifted the phone and entered the automatic call-back code but got nothing.

Gwyn had ostensibly come upstairs to find a brochure or program from the What If Conference. Jane went to the desk, opened a drawer.

The phone rang. She was not surprised. There was no caller ID.

She picked up the receiver but said nothing. Her discretion was matched by the person on the farther end of the line. It was neither a phantom call initiated by a system glitch nor a wrong number. She heard music in the background, an old song by America, recorded before she'd been born: "A Horse with No Name."

She hung up first. Considering the large properties in this neighborhood, it was unlikely the single shot had been heard. But she had urgent work to do.

10

MAYBE SOMEONE WAS COMing. Or maybe they had no agent in this vicinity, but prudence required that she expect hostile visitors. She had no time to search the general's office.

On the ground floor, she wiped everything that she remembered touching. She quickly washed and put away the coffee mugs and spoons. Although no one could hear, she performed each task quietly. Week by week she had grown quieter in all things, as though she was preparing soon to be a ghost and silent forever.

In the half bath, the mirror captured her attention briefly. Such was the fantastic nature of the mission she had set out upon, so strange were the discoveries she was making, sometimes it seemed reasonable to think that the impossible might be possible—in this instance that, when she left the room, her image would remain in the mirror to incriminate her.

When she departed the house by the front door, she felt not unlike the angel of Death. She came, a woman died, she left. Some said that one day there would be no death. If they were right, Death, too, could die.

As she walked past the neighbors' houses, she saw no one at a window, no one on a porch, no child at play in risk of the pending storm. The only sounds were those that the inconstant wind stirred from the materials of the day, as though humanity had been expunged, its constructions intact but now to be erased by eons of weather.

She drove to the end of the block, where she could either turn left or continue straight. She motored ahead half a mile, made a right turn and soon a left, with no immediate destination in mind, glancing repeatedly at her rearview mirror. Confident that she had no tail hanging at a distance, she found the interstate and drove west toward San Diego.

The day might come when the earth fell under such precise and continuous observation that vehicles without transponders were no less trackable than those lawfully equipped. In such a world, she would never have made it to the Lambert house in the first place.

11

ONE NIGHT THE PREVIOUS NO-
vember, six days before Nick's death, while she'd
been waiting in bed for him as he brushed his teeth,
she had seen a story on the TV news that intrigued
her and that lately had circled back again and again
in her memory, as though it must be pertinent to
what she was currently enduring.

The piece had been about scientists who were developing brain implants using light-sensitive proteins and fiber-optics. They said that we had a
ceaseless conversation with our brains: our senses
"writing in" information, our brains interpreting it
and "reading out" instructions. Experiments were
being done in which cerebral implants could take
the brain's instructions and transmit them past
points of communication breakdown, such as stroke
and spinal-nerve damage, making it possible for a
paraplegic to operate prosthetic limbs just by thinking about moving them. People with certain motor
neuron diseases that locked them in their bodies,
even denying them the ability to speak, might be
able, with such implants, to *think* their side of a
conversation and hear it spoken. Their thoughts,
translated into luminous pulses by light-sensitive
proteins, would be processed by software and rendered into speech by a computer.

At the time, Jane had marveled that everything

was changing so rapidly, that ahead seemed to be fast coming a world of miracles and wonders.

Now she was trapped in a world of violence and horror to which that old news story seemed to have no relevance. And yet she kept recalling it, as if it mattered profoundly.

Maybe she remembered the story not because of anything in it, but because of what Nick had said to her shortly thereafter. He came to bed exhausted from a hard day, as she also was exhausted. Neither had the energy to make love, but they enjoyed lying side by side, holding hands and talking. Just before she fell asleep, he raised her hand to his lips, kissed it, and said, "You rock me." His words followed her into the most lovely dreams, where they were spoken in a variety of whimsical situations, always with great tenderness.

12

IN BENNY'S AT THE BEACH, THE attack on Philadelphia commuters was as commanding of the clientele as would have been the Stanley Cup. Twenty-four/seven, there was enough TV sports coverage, live and replay, to satiate any fan, but on this lunch hour, the two bar screens were tuned to cable news, the bottom crawl devoted to death counts and statements of outrage from politicians rather than to past victories and player stats.

Benny's was not in fact at the beach, but two blocks from the sound of lapping surf, and if it had been a San Diego favorite for fifty years, as its sign claimed, it most likely was no longer owned by someone named Benny, if it had ever been. The customers appeared to be middle-class, a shrinking demographic during the past decade. At this hour, none had drunk enough to bluster in the face of horror, though Jane found almost tangible the anger, fear, and need for community that had brought them to their barstools and chairs.

She ate in the last booth, which was narrower than the others, made for two instead of four. The laminated-granite tabletop had surely been Formica when Benny ruled the room. The tables and the designer fabric on the booth-bench cushions and the barstools, along with a marble-tile floor in a harlequin pattern, laid a claim to prosperity and status never quite fulfilled but so American that Jane found it surprisingly poignant.

Among the customers, a columnist for the local newspaper was having lunch and a beer or two, though he could not restrain his reportorial instincts. She watched him moving through the long room with notebook, pen, and bottle of Heineken, passing out his card and engaging patrons in discussions of the latest act of terrorism.

He was about forty, with good hair that looked as if he spent more on styling than an accountant would have advised. He was proud of his tush, wearing his jeans the slightest bit too tight. He liked his manly forearms as well, and wore his shirt-sleeves rolled up on a day not warm enough for that.

He came to her booth as both a reporter and a man, with the calculation in his eye that some women found offensive but that she did not. He wasn't boorish, and he had no way of knowing she'd taken herself out of the game. She was well aware that men noticed her in any circumstance, and she knew that if she refused a three-minute interview, whether politely or dismissively, she would linger longer and more vividly in his memory.

His name was Kelsey, and she said her name was Mary, and at her invitation he sat across the table from her. "Terrible day."

"One of them."

"Do you have friends or family in Philadelphia?"

"Just fellow citizens."

"Yeah. It still hurts, doesn't it?"

"It should."

"What do you think we ought to do about it?"

"You and I?"

"All of us."

"Realize it's part of a bigger problem."

"Which is?"

"Ideas shouldn't matter more than people."

He raised an eyebrow. "That's interesting. Explain a little."

By way of explanation, she reversed the order of

two words and eliminated a contraction: "People should matter more than ideas."

He waited for her to continue. When instead she took the next-to-last bite of her burger, he said, "My column's not political, it's human-interest stuff. But if you had to put a political label on yourself, what would it say?"

"Disgusted."

He laughed, making notes. "Might be the biggest political party of all. Where are you from?"

"Miami," she lied. "You know a story you should look into?"

"What's that?"

"The increasing rate of suicide."

"Is it increasing?"

"Check it out."

He watched her even as he tipped back his bottle of beer and drank. "Why would a girl like you have such a morbid interest?"

"I'm a sociologist," she lied. "You ever suspect that shit like this Philadelphia attack gets used?"

Although he wrote a column of human-interest stories, he had police-reporter eyes that didn't just look at things, that flensed them layer by layer. "Gets used how?"

She gestured toward the nearer TV. "That story they give like a minute to every hour, between bouts of Philly coverage."

A former governor of Georgia had shot and killed his wife, a wealthy contributor to his campaigns, and himself.

"You mean the Atlanta atrocity," Kelsey said, which was the tabloid title already slapped on that case. "Hideous thing."

"If it happened yesterday, it would be the big story. But it happens same day as Philly, and no one remembers by next week."

He didn't seem to get her implication. "They say the wife and the deep-pockets donor were having an affair."

Having finished her burger, she wiped her hands on a napkin. "There you have one of the greatest mysteries of our time."

"Which is?"

"Who the hell 'they' are that we're always hearing about."

He smiled, indicated her empty bottle. "Buy you a Dos Equis?"

"Thanks, but one's my limit. You know the murder rate has also been going up?"

"We've done stories on that, sure."

The waitress appeared, and Jane asked for the check. Leaning across the table toward Kelsey, she whispered, "It's a good bet what numbers will be up next."

Leaning toward her, taking her intimacy for some kind of invitation, he said, "Tell me."

"Murder-suicides. The governor might be an indication of things to come. The next phase, so to speak."

"The next phase of what?"

Having been sincere to this point, she played it deadpan when she slipped into fantasy that would send him on his way. "Of what started at Roswell."

He was too practiced a journalist to let his smile freeze or his eyes glaze over. "Roswell, New Mexico?"

"That's where they first landed. You're not a UFO denier?"

"Not at all," he said. "The universe is infinite. No thinking person would believe we're alone in it."

But by the time the waitress brought the check, Kelsey had declined to take the bait when she asked if he believed in alien abductions, had thanked Jane—or Mary from Miami—for sharing, and moved on to another interview.

After paying cash and wending through the lunchtime crowd, she glanced back, perhaps intuitively, and saw the columnist staring at her. As he looked away, he brought a cell phone to his ear.

He was just a guy who had come on to her, a guy whom she had turned away rather cleverly, just a guy who still liked what he saw. The phone was a coincidence; it had nothing to do with her.

Nevertheless, once outside, she moved fast.

13

WHITE KITES AGAINST THE LOOM-
ing storm's volcanic-dark plumes, gulls swooped in
from the sea and scalloped down the sky to safe
roosts in the eaves of the buildings and among the
fronds of phoenix palms.

Jane could have parked in the restaurant lot.
She had not. She had left the Ford at a meter around
the corner and two blocks away.

She approached the vehicle from the farther side
of the street, seeming to have no interest in it, all
the while surveying the scene to determine if the
Ford might be staked out.

Not for the first time, she told herself that this
was how fully formed paranoids jittered their way
through life, but she still believed in her sanity.

Although she saw no surveillance, she walked a
block past the Escape before crossing the street and
approaching it from behind.

The reporter had thanked her for sharing, and in
fact she had always been a sharing person in the
sense that she had been open with others regarding
her feelings, hopes, intentions, and beliefs. Her current isolation, therefore, proved that much harder to
bear. Because friendship required sharing, she had
to forgo seeing old friends and making new ones for
the duration. Sharing might be the death of her or of
those with whom she shared.

When she'd sold her house, when she'd converted everything she owned into cash and stashed it where it could not easily be found, she had thought "the duration" might be six months. Now, two months into this journey and almost three thousand miles from where it had begun, she no longer had the false confidence to put a tentative end date to the mission.

She pulled away from the curb, inserting the Ford into a river of vehicles. In nearly every case, each car and SUV and truck and bus was continuously signaling its position for the benefit of commercial collectors of megadata, police agencies—and whoever owned the future.

14

THE NEW SAN DIEGO CENTRAL Library—either a postmodern triumph or a regrettable hodgepodge, depending on your taste—had nearly half a million square feet spread over nine floors, making it too big for Jane's purposes. Its spaces were too thoroughly surveilled for her comfort, and too difficult to exit with alacrity and stealth in an emergency. She went in search of an older branch library.

She had disposed of her laptop weeks earlier. These days, they served as locaters no less than did a vehicle's GPS. Her preferred computer source was a public library, wherever she might be. Even then, depending on the information she sought and reviewed online, she didn't linger long at any location.

She found a branch in the Spanish-mission style, derivative but honest architecture with a barrel-tile roof, palest-yellow stucco walls, windows with bronze frames and muntins. Thriving banana palms sculled the air with their large paddlelike fronds, as if to row the building backward in time to a more serene era.

The parking area serving the library also abutted a park with winding paths, a picnic area, and a playground. As had become her habit, Jane drove past her destination and curbed the car on a side street a block and a half away. After removing a small notebook, a pen, and a wallet, she tucked her purse under the seat before she got out and locked the doors.

Inside the branch library, there were many more aisles of books than there were of computers. She chose a workstation two removed from one occupied by a surly-looking street person whose presence assured that other patrons would avoid that entire quadrant of computers.

Wild witches' broom of dark hair, street-corner-prophet beard bristling and woven through with a white streak as though stiffened and selectively bleached by a lightning bolt, wearing lace-up boots and camouflage pants and green flannel shirt and voluminous black quilted-nylon jacket, the hulking man had apparently defeated the library's block on obscene websites and was watching pornography with the sound off.

He didn't so much as glance at Jane, and he didn't fondle himself. He sat with his hands on the table-top, and he considered the action on the screen with something like boredom and with what seemed to be puzzlement. There were drugs, such as Ecstasy, that if taken in too great a quantity for too long caused the brain to stop producing natural endorphins, so that you could no longer experience rapture, joy, or a sense of well-being without chemical assistance. Perhaps that might be his condition, because his sun-seared and weathered face remained without expression as he stared with the stillness and apparent incomprehension of a sculpture of a man.

Online, Jane searched for and found the Gernsback Institute, which produced the annual What If Conference, among other events. Its stated purpose was to "inspire the imagination of leaders in business, science, government, and the arts for the purpose of encouraging informed speculation in search of outside-the-box solutions to significant problems facing humanity."

Do-gooders. For people with malicious intentions, no better cover existed than a nonprofit organization dedicated to bettering the human condition. Most of the people at the institute might in fact mean well and be doing good, but that didn't mean they grasped the hidden intentions of its founders or their core mission.

In the notebook, she recorded data that seemed most pertinent to her investigation. She used numerical and alphabetical codes of her own devising, so that this information was in a form that no one but she would be able to read. Now she entered the coded names of the officers and nine board members of the institute, only one of which—David James Michael—rang in her memory.

David James Michael. The man with three first names. He was somewhere else in this compilation of names, dates, and places. She would pore through it later to find him.

Having bumped out of the porn site, the homeless man now watched dog videos on YouTube, again with the speakers muted, his hands resting on each side of the keyboard, his time-beaten face as expressionless as a clock.

After she logged off and pocketed her notebook and pen, Jane got to her feet, moved nearer to the guy, and put a pair of twenty-dollar bills on the table beside his computer. "Thank you for your service to the country."

He looked up at her as if she had spoken in a language unknown to him. His eyes were not bloodshot, neither were they bleary from booze, but gray and clear and keenly observant.

When he said nothing, she indicated the tattoo on the back of his right hand: a blue spearhead as background, within which was a complete raised sword in gold bisected by three golden lightning bolts, the insignia of Army Special Forces Airborne, and under that the letters DDT. "Can't have been light duty."

Nodding toward the forty dollars, he said, "There's them who need it more than me." He had the voice of a bear with strep throat.

"But I don't know them," she said. "I'd be grateful if you gave it to them for me."

"I can do that." He did not pick up the money, but turned his attention once more to the dog videos. "There's a free kitchen near here that can always use donations."

Jane didn't know if she had done the right thing, but it was the only thing she could have done.

As she left the alcove where the computers were arrayed, she glanced back, but he was not looking at her.

15

STILL, THE STORM HAD NOT broken. The sky over San Diego loomed heavy with midday dark, as if all the water weight and potential thunder stored over distant Alpine had in the last few hours slid unspent toward the city, to add pressure to the coastal deluge that was coming. Sometimes both weather and history broke far too slowly for those who were impatient for what came next.

In the park adjacent to the library, following a winding path, she saw ahead a fountain surrounded by a reflecting pool, and she walked to it and sat on one of the benches facing the water that flowered up in numerous thin streams, petaling the air with silver droplets.

The park was sparsely populated for the hour, only half a dozen people in sight, two of them walking dogs less leisurely than they might have under a more benevolent sky.

Jane took her case notebook from an inner sportcoat pocket, paged to the growing list of names, and found a previous entry for David James Michael. He was the man who, as she'd discovered in her recent library session, sat on the board of the Gernsback Institute that organized the invitation-only What If Conference attended by Gordon and Gwyn Lambert, now both dead by their own hands.

The notation after the first listing for Michael referred her to the suicide of a T. Quinn Eubanks in Traverse City, Michigan. Eubanks, a man of inherited wealth and considerable personal achievement, had sat on the board of directors of three charitable foundations, including the Seedling Fund, where one of his fellow directors was David James Michael.

Her next line of inquiry was now clear, or as clear as anything got in this case.

First, however, she had to make a call to Chicago.

At all times she carried a disposable phone with prepaid minutes. As far as she knew, disposables had never been trackable. Even if such bargain models now emitted identifying signals, she always bought them with cash and needed no ID to activate service.

A bevy of uniformed schoolgirls hurried past in response to the mother-quail urgings of a nun in a contemporary habit, who seemed to think the storm would break at any moment.

The air was yet too still. Like tectonic plates, a mass of cool air and a warmer mass would strike-slip and throw down a sudden rush of wind, and the downpour would come a minute or two after that.

Confident of her atmospheric intuition—and not wanting to use the phone while in the car, where she could be trapped in the event that she was wrong about the security of a disposable cell—Jane extracted her current phone from an interior jacket pocket and entered the number for Sidney Root's direct line.

Sidney's wife, Eileen, had been the Chicago-based advocate for the rights of people with disabilities about whom Jane had told Gwyneth Lambert. Eileen Root suffered a first and last migraine headache while away from home at a seminar, and three weeks later hung herself in the garage of the family home.

Like Jane's husband, Sidney's wife left a note before killing herself, an even more disturbing, cryptic message than Nick's: *Sweet Sayso says he's lonely all these years, why did Leenie stop needing him, he was always there for Leenie, now I need to be there for him.*

Neither Sidney nor his and Eileen's—Leenie's— three children, who were all in their twenties, had ever heard of a man named Sayso.

Jane had traveled to Chicago and met with Sidney Root soon after being granted leave from the Bureau, early in her unofficial investigation, before she discovered that because of such inquiries, she would be targeted by a mysterious conspiracy as elusive as a confederacy of ghosts. She had used her real name then; and of necessity she used it now when he answered on the third ring.

"Oh, yes, I tried to call you a few days ago," he said, "but the number you gave me was out of service."

"I moved, went through a lot of changes," she said, which was as much explanation as she would give him. "But I've still got this monkey on my back, you know, still looking for an explanation, and I hoped you might spare me a few minutes."

"Sure. Just let me close my office door." He was an architect in a large practice with four partners. He put her on hold, and a few seconds later returned. "Okay. What can I do for you?"

"I know the world of nonprofits is enormous, and it was your wife who moved in those circles, not you so much, but do you recall Eileen talking about something called the Gernsback Institute?"

He thought a moment but then said, "Means nothing."

"What about the Seedling Fund?"

"That neither."

"Now a couple of names. David James Michael?"

"Mmmmm . . . sorry, no."

"Quinn Eubanks?"

"I'm not always good with names."

"The seminar in Boston where Eileen had the migraine—you said that event was a presentation of Harvard University."

"Yes. You can look it up."

"I did. But I'm wondering if she attended any other conference shortly before or after that one."

"Eileen was passionate about her work. She had a busy schedule. I can't recall, but I could find out for you."

"I'd be grateful, Sidney. Say by this time tomorrow?"

"You really do still have that monkey on your back."

"Don't forget those suicide statistics I gave you."

"I remember. But as I told you at the time—look around at all the craziness in the world, all the violence and hatred these days, the economic crises, and you don't need any other explanation for why more people would be more depressed than ever."

"Except that Eileen wasn't depressed."

"Well, no. But—"

"And neither was Nick."

"She wasn't depressed," Sidney said, "but that's what I tried to call you about the other day. You remember the note she left?"

Jane quoted the opening of it from memory: " 'Sweet Sayso says he's lonely all these years. . . .' "

"We didn't share the contents widely at first," Sidney said, "because . . . well, because it was so strange, not like Eileen. We didn't want people to remember her as . . . mentally ill, I guess. Recently, her only living aunt, Faye, found out about the note and solved the mystery. Sort of. For a while when Eileen was four and five, she had an imaginary friend named Sayso. She talked to him, made up stories about him. Like that kind of thing always does, it passed. Who knows why at the end she would flash back to that?"

Jane shivered at the idea of a long-forgotten imaginary friend calling a fifty-year-old woman to join him in death, though if she'd been asked to explain the chill, she couldn't have done so.

"How are you doing?" Sidney asked.

"Good enough. I don't sleep well."

"Me neither. Sometimes, if I snore myself awake, I apologize to her for the noise. I mean out loud. I forget she's not there."

"I've been traveling a lot, staying in motels," she said, "and I can't sleep in a double bed. Nick was a big guy. So it has to be queen- or king-size. Otherwise, it's like admitting he's gone, and I don't sleep at all."

"Are you still on leave from the Bureau?"

"Yeah."

"Take my advice, go back to work. Real work, instead of chasing an explanation for something that can't ever be fully explained."

"Maybe I will," she lied.

"I don't mean to noodge, but work has helped me."

"Maybe I will," she lied again.

"Give me your new phone number so I can call you when I find out if Eileen was at another conference around that time."

"I'll call you tomorrow," she said. "Thanks, Sidney. You're a peach."

When she hung up, she appeared to be the only person remaining in the park. The lawns and pathways were deserted to the limits of vision. Not one pigeon strutting. Not one scurrying squirrel.

At the wrong time, in the wrong place, a city could be as isolate as the Arctic.

On the flanking streets to the north and south, traffic passed: grumble of engines, swish of tires, hiss of air brakes, occasional bleat of horn, rattle of a loosely fit manhole cover. Even as she stepped away from the sizzle of the spritzing fountain, the traffic noise seemed curiously muffled, as if the park were enclosed with insulated dual-pane glass.

The air remained calm under pressure, the sky full of iron-dark mountains that would soon collapse in a deluge, the city expectant, the windows of buildings shimmering with light that normally would be faded by the sun at this hour, drivers switching on headlights, the vehicles gliding through the faux dusk like submersibles following undersea lanes.

Jane had taken only a few steps from the fountain when she detected a buzz like swarming wasps. At first it seemed to come from above her, and then from behind, but when she turned in a circle and faced again the grove of palms toward which she had been moving, she saw the source hovering twenty feet away: a drone.

16

THE HIGH-END CIVILIAN-MODEL quadcopter drone, a small fraction of the size of any military version, resembled a miniature unmanned moon lander combined with an insect. It appeared similar to the DJI Inspire 1 Pro, though somewhat larger, about seven thousand dollars' worth of aeronautics. These were used by real-estate companies to film for-sale properties and were increasingly put to work by many other commercial enterprises. They were also favored by well-heeled hobbyists who ranged from legitimate drone enthusiasts to the contemporary equivalent of Peeping Toms.

Hovering only eight or ten feet off the ground, in the shadows under the cascading crowns of the phoenix palms, it was an effigy of the feared machine god of a thousand movies and stories, a lighter-than-air menace with heavy-as-a-sledgehammer impact that sent a jolt of fear through her. The craft was in violation of all the rules applying to civilian drone use, at least as Jane knew them.

She didn't imagine that its presence here could be a mere coincidence. Its three-axis gimbaled camera remained trained on her.

Somehow she'd given them her location. What her mistake might have been did not matter right now; she could work that out later.

If a backup battery provided the craft with twice the flight time of an Inspire 1 Pro, it could remain in the air for half an hour to forty minutes. Which meant it must have been launched from somewhere in the vicinity, most likely from a surveillance van.

The drone operator would monitor her until enough officers arrived to arrest her. Or maybe they weren't from a legitimate law-enforcement agency, in which case there would be no officers, and they would just . . . take her. *They* were after her. The omnipotent, almost mystical *They*. But she had no idea who *They* might be.

In any case, they were already near.

The park still appeared deserted. Not for long.

She didn't try to run at once, but instead moved toward the drone when she saw something about it that required taking a better look. Her boldness allowed her to detect, sooner than she would have otherwise, that this either was not a civilian model or had been radically customized in the aftermarket. Maybe the storm light and the shadows misled her, although she knew they didn't, and maybe in her paranoia she conjured out of innocent shapes the presence of a sound suppressor wrapping the narrow bore of a muzzle, but she knew that paranoia had nothing to do with it.

The drone had been weaponized.

As the machine drifted toward her, she dodged to one side, behind the thick bole of a phoenix palm. Had she turned and run at once, she would have been shot in the back.

In that brief and desperate moment of cover, she drew the Heckler & Koch from her shoulder rig.

Her mind raced, trying to grasp the threat to its fullest nature. The problem of weight mitigated against a civilian-style drone being converted to a weapon with a high-capacity magazine. Without a gun, the average craft—with camera and battery— weighed about eight pounds. The weight of artillery and ammo would affect stability and greatly reduce flight time. So it would have to be a low-caliber weapon loaded with but a few rounds, and she doubted it would be accurate.

Of course it only needed to be on target once.

She expected the remote-control assassin to sweep into view from her left. Then she heard it circumnavigating the massive old palm from the *right*.

Before the camera could find her, she eased away from it. With her back to the three-foot-diameter trunk of the immense phoenix, she followed in the wake of the drone as it circled toward her.

The firing mechanism wouldn't be a full handgun. No grip, no standard magazine. Just the bare essentials. A .22-caliber weapon. Something like a miniature belt feed with, say, four rounds.

She had the advantage of hearing. The drone had an eye but not an ear. The remote operator was essentially deaf.

But copper-jacketed hollow-point rounds, even just .22s, could kill at close range.

She stopped trying to hide. Stepped away from the tree, quickly around it, boldly closing behind the drone.

The operator had maybe a 70-degree field of view. He must have sensed a threat in his blind zone. With an angry-hornet noise, the drone suddenly began to rotate in hover mode.

With her pistol in a two-hand grip, at point-blank range, Jane squeezed off three, four, five rounds, the roar of each shot banking like a cue ball off every palm bole in the grove. The freaking machine was all landing legs and propellers, with a narrow fuselage, the camera suspended on a gimbal ring, not much of a target, so that she wished her pistol had been a shotgun. On the other hand, this grandmother of the Terminator wasn't armored or to any extent designed to withstand incoming fire. Whether she hit it with one round or five, it spat off pieces of itself, reeled through the air, ricocheted off another palm, and clattered across the grass, thousands of dollars in value reduced to pennies in salvage.

She didn't realize there was a second drone until she saw it coming fast from the area of the fountain.

17

TWO DRONES, A SURVEILLANCE van from which they were launched, surely a quad or more of guys on foot about to appear from somewhere soon: They had resources, and they wanted her, maybe even with more intensity than she had imagined.

When she pivoted to run from the second machine, the massive old phoenix palm blocked her. Before she could juke around the tree, a quiver of slender steel needles stippled it in a vertical line, missing her by a few inches.

Should have known. An eight- or ten-pound airborne drone could not take the recoil of even a .22 and maintain accuracy. This was a low-recoil compressed-air weapon, firing darts. Not darts exactly, these were without fins, so they were technically miniature versions of the quarrels used by crossbows. Poison? Tranquilizer? Probably the latter. They would want to interrogate her—so from her point of view, poison might be preferable.

Out of sight from the street, Jane wove among the palms and the machine buzzed in pursuit as birds racketed out of the protection of the overhead cascading fronds, shrieking and nattering their dismay at being chased back into the pending storm. The big crowns of the palms ensured the boles were farther apart than she needed them to be, forcing her to spend too much time in the open. Weaving, duck-ing, she counted on the drone not being able to click on her, but as she urgently sought cover, she real-ized there was no option except continued frantic evasion. The machine could fly at maybe twenty meters per second in calm air, much faster than she could run. She couldn't evade it for long. And she would never again get away with the circling-the-tree trick that worked before; the drone might be mindless, but its remote operator was not.

The gunfire would draw police, but that wasn't necessarily a good thing. Two months earlier, when all this started, she learned that not all cops were on the side of the righteous, that in this dangerous time when shadows cast shadows of their own, when darkness often passed for light, the just and the un-just wore the same face.

Weaving tree to tree in an obstacle-course mara-thon that she could only lose, in a dream-strange showdown among the phoenixes from which she would not rise phoenixlike if she were killed, Jane felt a tugging at her right sleeve. Dodging around another palm, she saw three thin quarrels pinned through the slack material of her sport coat, having missed her flesh by a fraction of an inch.

In the early gloaming of the shrouded afternoon, a sudden brightness flashed apocalyptic, flaring across the park as if to incinerate all it touched and bespeak a world of ashes soon to come, so that all the shadows either leaped back into the things that cast them or quaked across the lawns and walks like spirits dispossessed and seeking new anchorage. She didn't realize the sky had thrown down lightning that had struck nearby until a second after the flare, when thunder shook the day so hard that she could feel it tremble the ground under her running feet.

One of the many lessons she'd been taught at Quantico was to live by her training, to do what was known to work for a thousand times a thousand other lawmen, but also to recognize when by-the-book would result in a eulogy and a postmortem commendation, and then to trust the intuition that was truer than anything learned. In the wake of the blinding light, the tide of banished shadows rushed back in answer to the thunder's call. As the day darkened around her, she dropped to the ground, rolled onto her back, as vulnerable as an offering on an Aztec altar, the airborne executioner looming as if to the call of sacrificial blood. She saw the hovering drone adjust the barrel of its gimbaled weapon, and she thrust the pistol toward it, squeezing off the remaining five rounds in the handgun.

A glitter of steel flicked past her face, stitching the earth, as the machine fired a misaimed burst. Hit, the drone shuddered up and back, as if to gain altitude and retreat. Instead, having lost one of its rotary wings, it dipped and swayed, bobbled as it strove to execute a turn, accelerated in a cant toward a gap in the trees, and collided with a palm bole at maybe ten meters per second, coming apart like a hurled egg.

Jane was on her feet without remembering how she'd gotten up. She ejected the empty magazine, pocketed it, snapped a full ten rounds into the Heckler & Koch, holstered the weapon, and ran.

18

OUT OF THE PALM GROVE, IN the open near the fountain, she saw them coming at last. Two guys hurried this way from the library lot, which was west of her, and three others sprinted in from the street on the north side of the park, none in uniform, though they were surely not citizens out for the exercise.

The Ford Escape stood at a meter a block to the south of the park, but she didn't want to lead them toward the car if it might be still unknown to them.

She fled east, into the longest sward of this green zone, glad that she had been avoiding carbs, doing stretching exercises every evening, and running regularly.

Even at a distance, she could tell that the five on her tail were formidable enough to have qualified for the NFL at defensive positions: huge guys, big muscles, serious stamina. But she weighed a hundred fifteen pounds, and each of her pursuers bulked twice her size; greater weight required additional energy to move it. She was lean and fleet, and her motivation—survival—gave her a more powerful motor than anything that might be driving them.

She did not glance back. To do so would slow her. She would be caught or not, and the race was more often won by the quarry that had confidence in its endurance.

The second lightning bolt seared the sky, brighter than the first, and cleaved to the heart the tallest tree in sight, a nearby live oak, from which foamed showers of fiery splinters, incandescent chips of bark. A slab calved from the main trunk, bearing a limb of intricate branches like some fantastic microwave mast receiving signals from uncountable worlds.

Although the toppling mass crashed short of her, Jane raised one arm across her face, protecting her eyes from the shrapnel of shattered branches, twigs, and crisp brown oval leaves set afire and swarming like a pestilence of beetles.

As the last of the debris fell behind her and the crash of thunder rolled away through the city, as she came to the east end of the park, the once-dark sky paled, abruptly glaucous, and cataracts of rain fell hard, fat droplets hissing through the trees and grass, snapping off the pavement, plinking the metal hoods on trash cans, carrying with them the faint bleachy odor of ozone, a form of oxygen created by lightning's alchemy.

The torrents of silver rain were suddenly threaded through with red skeins as brake lights revealed drivers reacting to the abrupt drop in visibility.

Without hesitation, she leaped off the sidewalk, into the street, blacktop glistering underfoot, and plunged into the mid-block traffic, greeted by the blare of horns and the banshee shriek of brakes. She briefly glimpsed some startled and some angry faces in the wake of thumping windshield wipers before they blurred behind the fresh rain sluicing down the glass.

Arriving on the farther sidewalk intact, she turned south and ran flat out, dodging among other pedestrians who might have been annoyed but not surprised to see a young woman, sans umbrella, in a hurry to find shelter. She turned north at the corner, sprinted half a block before trading the street for an alleyway, then the alleyway for a narrow service passage between buildings, suitable only for foot traffic.

Halfway along that claustrophobic accessway, she at last risked a look back. She saw none of the five bulls from the park, but she knew she couldn't have shaken off all of them. They were in the area, and likely to cross her path by surprise.

She paused only to drop her disposable cell phone through the bars of a drainage grille. Even above the chorus of the rain, she could hear it splash into dark water below, and then she ran once more.

19

FROM THE NARROW ACCESS-way, she entered a new street mid-block. She was about to cross it when she noticed, fifty or sixty yards to her left, on the opposite side of the avenue, a large man in dark clothing, soaked as she was, standing oblivious to the bustling pedestrians around him. He might have been anybody, nobody, looking for some-body else, but intuition cautioned her to back off toward the passageway from which she had a moment earlier departed.

Just before she would have ducked out of sight, she saw him see her. He raised his head and stiff-ened, as an attack dog will freeze for just an instant when it catches the scent of quarry.

She retreated to the three-foot-wide accessway and ran, blinking rain from her eyes, dispirited by the sound of her labored openmouthed breathing. Throat hot and getting raw. Heart knocking. A thin acid refluxing into the back of her throat.

Insane, this womanhunt in broad daylight, in a busy city. Insane and incredible, but no more incred-ible than Nick killing himself with his Ka-Bar, than Eileen Root hanging herself in the garage, than ji-hadists crashing a plane into hundreds of cars, trucks, and buses on a crowded expressway.

Bursting into the alley she had traveled previ-ously, acutely aware that she didn't have time to reach either end of the block before her pursuer arrived, she saw a truck parked at the back of a restaurant, the logo of a bakery emblazoned on its flank. Delivering bread or pastries or both, the driver wore a yellow rain slicker as he finished stacking four large rainproof plastic cases on a hand truck, which he rolled into the receiving room or kitchen of his customer.

She darted to the driver's door, glanced into the cab through glass partly clouded by interior condensation, saw only that no one occupied it, and hurried to the back of the vehicle. She decided against the cargo area, where the driver had left one of the two doors ajar, most likely because he had more goods to offload. She boarded the front of the truck on the starboard side, pulling the cab's passenger door shut behind her, and she slid below window level, as far into the footwell as she could go.

Rain streamed across the windshield, and the windows in both side doors were partially obscured by condensation. The interior cab light was off, the dashboard dark. As long as she stayed low, she probably would not be seen—unless her pursuer yanked open a door. But he was more likely to think she'd found an unlocked entrance to one of the businesses that backed up to the alley, most obviously the restaurant.

As she tried to quiet her breathing, she heard sounds outside. She couldn't make much of them over the rataplan of rain.

Then came the distinctive crackle of a voice transmitted on a walkie-talkie, the words not quite discernible.

The man holding the walkie-talkie was close, too close. He must have been standing beside the bakery truck. His voice was deep and muffled, but just clear enough. "Half a block east of your position. Behind some joint called Donnatina's Restaurant."

The far voice crackled, and again Jane couldn't understand it.

"All right," said the nearer man. "You two in the front. Sweep the joint hard, restrooms, everything, drive her to me."

His voice faded as he stepped away from the truck toward the back entrance of Donnatina's.

Jane thought of drawing her pistol. But curled in the footwell, with her back wedged between the seat and the passenger door, facing the steering wheel, she wouldn't be able to take a smart shot at anyone if it came to that.

Anyway, they wouldn't give her a reason to shoot first. Whether they were remotely a legitimate authority of any kind or a totally rogue group, they would want to take her away for interrogation.

They.

Although she might not be able to name them now, she would know their identity one day. That was what she'd promised Nick, and even though it was a promise made after he was weeks in the grave, she would damn well keep it as if it had been made to the living man, hold it as sacred as she had held their wedding vows.

A couple of minutes passed before the driver opened the cargo-box door that he had left ajar when he'd taken the first part of his delivery into the restaurant.

The pass-through slider between the cab and the back of the truck had been left open. She heard the guy with the walkie-talkie, his voice no longer muffled, querying the driver. "You see a woman, brunette, five-six, a looker but half drowned like me?"

"Seen her where?"

"Here, the alley. Maybe going in this joint?"

"When was this?"

"Since you got here."

"I been delivering."

"So you haven't seen her."

"In this shitty weather, wearing a hood, keeping my head down?"

A different male voice entered the conversation. "The bitch is slick, Frank. She's somewhere else."

Frank said, "I've got a real hate-on for the pig."

"Get in line. Who's this plastic banana?"

The driver in his yellow raingear said, "I've made deliveries here five years, never saw what you'd call a looker."

To the new arrival, Frank said, "Bakery guy. He's got nothing."

"What I've got is work to do in this shitty rain. What're you guys, anyway—cops or something?"

"Better you don't know," Frank said.

"Better I don't," said the driver, and he began to

offload more waterproof plastic boxes of baked goods.

Jane waited, listened, expecting a face at a window, steam-blurred and menacing like a face in a dream.

Hard rain drumming the truck. No more lightning or thunder. Rain in California was seldom accompanied by extended pyrotechnics.

Soon the driver returned. She heard him lifting the dolly into the truck. He slammed the back door without speaking to anyone.

Jane almost eeled up from the footwell to scramble out of the truck—but then she heard the tinny, static-speckled voice of someone on the walkie-talkie, which had been turned louder to compensate for poor reception.

The driver's door opened, and the deliveryman swung in behind the wheel before he startled at the sight of her.

"Please don't," she whispered.

20

THE DRIVER WAS ABOUT JANE'S age. His broad and pleasant face, sprayed with freckles and capped with rust-red eyebrows, suggested red hair under his bright-yellow cowl.

He pulled his door shut, started the engine,

switched on the windshield wipers, and drove away from the restaurant. Before they reached the end of the block, he said, "All right, they're behind us. You can get up now."

"I'd rather stay down here for a little ways. Then you can let me out, maybe at your next stop."

"I could do that."

"Thank you."

He braked at the end of the block. "But if there's somewhere in particular you want to go, I could also do that."

She considered him as he turned right into the street. "What's your name?"

"Believe it or not, Ethan Hunt."

"Why wouldn't I believe it?"

"Well, Ethan Hunt—like Tom Cruise in those *Mission: Impossible* movies."

"Ah. You get kidded about that, do you?"

"Not by anyone who knows the truth about bakery delivery. I disarm suitcase nukes and save the world about once a month."

"Once a month, huh?"

"Well, every six weeks."

She liked his smile. There was neither snark nor megalomania in it, as characterized so many smiles these days.

"I need to get to my car." She told him where it was parked. "But if you see any of those goons, drive right on by."

She squirmed out of the footwell and sat upright in the passenger seat.

Rain sheeted through the streets and gutters brimmed. The haloed headlights of approaching vehicles made the falling rain look like sleet and seemed to pave the blacktop with ice.

"Probably I better not ask your name," Ethan Hunt said.

"That might be safer for you."

"Don't you believe in umbrellas?"

She said, "The drowned-rat look is so becoming."

"Any drowned rat looked half as good as you, I'd marry it."

"Thanks. I think."

"I'm taking a roundabout route just to be sure it's safe."

"I figured that's what you were doing."

"Plus I want to keep this going a little while."

"Been too long since a suitcase nuke, huh?"

"Seems forever. Those were some bad dudes back there."

"Yes, I'm aware."

"You sure you can handle them yourself?"

"Are you volunteering?"

"No way. They'd squash me like a bug. Just saying."

"I'll be okay."

"It'd make me sick to think you wouldn't." He stopped beside her Ford Escape. "No goons in sight."

"You're a sweet man, Ethan Hunt. Thank you."

"Guess there's no way this could ever lead to a date."

"Trust me, Ethan, I'd be the date from Hell."

She got out into the rain, and as she closed the door, she heard him say, "But you wouldn't be boring."

21

THOSE WHO SEEMED TO UNderstand what lay behind the increase in suicides, who might even have engineered it, were clearly connected root and branch with as-yet-unidentified government agencies. Jane could only assume they would also have influence with authorities at the state level, including the California Highway Patrol.

Leaving the city, she avoided freeways because that was where the CHP patrols could be found in the greatest numbers. There were chokepoints at which traffic could be easily halted or slowed for close inspection. The drones had transmitted video of her, and the men from whom she'd escaped in the foot chase had seen that her long blond hair was now shorter and brown. A new description of her would already be in the hands of the searchers.

She had meant to head up-coast only a few miles to La Jolla, to see a man that evening and put a question to him that, depending on his answer, might decide her future. Instead, she followed a series of rain-sluiced surface streets toward the coast, circled the town of La Jolla, and found her way to Torrey Pines State Reserve.

There she connected with County Highway S12. This coastal route served a number of picturesque beach cities from Del Mar and Solano Beach north to Oceanside.

At Torrey Pines State Beach, she drove into the parking lot, which was deserted in this weather. From under the passenger seat, she fished a small tool kit and took from it a screwdriver.

She got out into the storm. The tall pines soughed. The driven rain danced on the pavement, raising from it a hissing like the threats of a thousand angry serpents.

Her wet fingers slipped on the screwdriver, but she managed to remove the front and rear license plates, all unobserved, as far as she could tell.

If there had been traffic cameras near where she had left the car before walking to the library, as there were nearly everywhere in metropolitan areas these days, agents would soon be reviewing time-stamped video from all the streets that radiated away from the park where she had nearly been apprehended. Even with clarity diminished by the rain, they would hope to find video of her leaving the car and returning to it. She had to assume both that they knew she was driving a black Ford Escape and that it had Canadian plates.

In California, a car without license plates didn't often excite police interest, because dealerships didn't provide temporary plates for new purchases.

Better that she proceed without tags than go cruising with a pair that might be on every cop's hot sheet within an hour or two.

She put the plates under the driver's seat, got behind the wheel, and started the engine. Sopping wet again, she clicked the heater up a few degrees and accelerated the blower.

When the wipers swept the blearing rain from the windshield, she saw the nearby Pacific, storm-lashed and misted, rolling toward shore less like water than like a sea of gray smoke pouring off the fires of some vast nuclear holocaust.

22

AFTER STOPPING IN CARDIFF-by-the-Sea to refuel, she left the coastal highway for Interstate 5. She was more than twenty miles from the San Diego city limits, and the superhighway was worth the risk for the greater speed that it allowed.

She drove out of the storm just north of Oceanside, where the coastal plain was flat and scrub-covered and forbidding in the hard clear end-of-winter light.

During the drive, with time to think, she decided that her first mistake had been to answer Gwyn Lambert's question, *Where will you go from here?* She'd said she had someone to see near San Diego.

The bond between Jane and Gwyn had deserved

her trust. Marine wives. Marine widows. The three-strand bond of service, duty, and grief. She'd liked the woman. She'd had no reason to suspect that Gwyn was somehow compromised and on an emotional precipice.

Who had Gwyn spoken to on the phone before killing herself? Why had she spoken to anyone? To tell him that Jane was headed next to San Diego? If they—the octopuslike *They*—had no agent near enough to apprehend her in Alpine, knowing her next destination narrowed their search parameters.

But "near San Diego" encompassed perhaps a hundred square miles and as many as a million and a half people. Maybe that narrowed the search, but it certainly didn't pinpoint her whereabouts.

In recent weeks, her pursuers had to have figured out that she was using library computers to do her Internet searches. There were numerous libraries in the greater San Diego area, however, including many in colleges and universities. They might anticipate that she'd want to know more about the What If Conference and the Gernsback Institute, after learning about them from Gwyn. But to find her, they would have been required to mount a watch on those websites, with the capability of identifying in real time every query from a San Diego–area library; they would then have needed to be able to immediately track-to-source the query and identify the unique signature of the workstation.

If the searchers were closing in on her even as she concluded her task in the branch library and as she gave forty dollars to the homeless veteran, her second mistake had been to dally in the park next door and make a phone call to Sidney Root in Chicago. If they knew every one of the twenty-two individuals from whom she'd gathered evidence to date, they might expect her to contact one or more of them again. Monitoring real-time phone traffic for that many people, on multiple telecom platforms, would be an enormous task, one that she wasn't even sure current technology allowed.

Supposing all of that was possible, they would also have to trace her call, raveling backward through the microwave maze of millions of current calls to the particular transmissions from the disposable phone, and then somehow use that signal in a GPS search to locate her in the park.

All within minutes.

With only a few hours' notice from the time Gwyn had called them, they would have needed to place teams of agents at strategic points throughout the city, so if Jane's position was determined, at least one team had a chance of reaching her within minutes.

Maybe they had been lucky. But in any case, lucky or not, the entity on her trail suddenly seemed ubiquitous, of greater power and reach than any one law-enforcement organization, more efficient than any of the government agencies with which she was familiar, all but omnipresent and omniscient.

Even if they had identified her vehicle, she would

hope to use it for a while yet. Her financial resources were not unlimited, and this was her second set of wheels since this odyssey had begun.

At San Juan Capistrano, she left Interstate 5 for State Highway 74. As the Escape climbed the rugged chaparral-cloaked hills of the Cleveland National Forest, Jane's mood darkened faster than did the slowly waning day. Greener in this season than it would be later in the year, the borderline-desert landscape was prized by hikers and nature enthusiasts, thought beautiful by some. To her it appeared inhospitable, even bleak, as if beyond the windows of the Ford lay a stricken planet struggling under a dying sun.

Descending then to Lake Elsinore and beyond. A rural world that seemed isolate. Lush meadows and valley scrub. Private graveled-and-oiled lanes leading to properties tucked back from the state route. Small and separate groves of cottonwoods and conifers testifying to an aquifer under land that would have been otherwise hardscrabble.

The remoteness was an illusion, because the hive of Southern California remained quickly accessible to the west, and even in this less bustling inland empire, "small" towns like Perris and Hemet boasted seventy or eighty thousand residents each.

She came to a private lane flanked by live oaks, turned right, and stopped at a plank gate painted white and infilled with wire. She put down her window and reached to the call box. She didn't need to announce herself. She had a personal five-digit code that she entered on the keypad, and the gate swung open.

Beyond lay, for her, the most important place in the world.

23

THE WHITE CLAPBOARD HOUSE was a modest residence but for the luxury of a deep veranda that encircled it entirely.

Duke and Queenie were lying on that porch, among the wicker chairs, and they sprang to their feet as the Ford reached the end of the long driveway. Two German shepherds, superb specimens with deep chests and well-sprung ribs and straight backs, they were both family pets and also guard dogs that had been well trained.

Jane pulled to a stop behind Gavin's prized apple-green '48 Ford pickup that he had chopped and channeled and sectioned himself, adding '37 La Salle fenders and a highly customized La Salle nose section with stainless-steel grillwork, making it a street rod of singular style.

The dogs knew her because she had left her driver's window down to ensure they caught her scent even before she got out of the Ford.

They padded down the porch steps and sprinted

to her, tails lashing the air in delight. Had she been a stranger, their approach would have been far different, circling and wary and full of menace.

Dropping to one knee, she gave each dog its share of affection. They lavished their tongues on her hands, a friendly greeting that might have repelled some people but that she received happily. They were guardians of her treasure, and she slept better knowing they were here.

As much as she loved the dogs and admired the discipline that Gavin had instilled in them, she had not come here primarily to see them. After a minute, she rose to her feet and moved toward the house, the shepherds gamboling at her sides.

With the fluid springy step of a double amputee whose knee-down prosthetics ended in bladelike feet that allowed her to be a tough competitor in a 10K run, Jessica came through the front door and onto the veranda. Jet-black hair. Cherokee complexion. Blessed with beauty that came from the headwaters of her gene pool, she was as always a striking figure.

She'd lost her legs nine years earlier, when she'd been twenty-three, serving in Afghanistan. She'd been an Army noncombatant, but roadside IEDs didn't distinguish between armed troops and support services. Although she'd lost limbs in that godforsaken country, she found Gavin there—a combatant who had seen much hot action but had come through untouched. They had been married for eight years.

Jane bounded up the steps before Jess could

spring down them, and they hugged fiercely there on the veranda as around them the dogs whidded this way and that, whacking the wicker chairs with their tails, whimpering with pleasure at this unexpected reunion.

"Why didn't you call?" Jess asked.

"Tell you later."

She had three spare disposable phones, all activated. Each had been purchased from a different retailer, in three widely separated towns. She had not yet used any of them, there was no way her pursuers could have a trace on them, but events in San Diego had so spooked her that she didn't want to risk calling this special place, this haven in a world that was otherwise increasingly a jungle of hazard and chaos.

"You look good," Jess said.

"You lie like a rug, girlfriend."

"He talks about you all the time."

"I *think* about him all the time."

"God, it's good to see you."

The boy stepped through the front door. His blue eyes shone with excitement, but he was shy, standing there in the shade of the veranda, at the moment indifferent to the dogs with which he usually frolicked. She had seen him only once before in the past two months, and on that occasion—as seemed to be the case now—he had been half afraid to speak or to hurry to her, fearful that she might evaporate as she did in his dreams.

Only five, Travis was already the image of his father. Nick's tousled hair. Nick's fine nose, strong chin. The intensity of his presence and the aura of intelligence that, at least to his mother, radiated from his eyes were uncannily reminiscent of Nick.

He whispered, "It's really you."

Jane dropped to her knees, not merely to be at his level, but also because her legs suddenly grew weak and failed her. He came into her arms, and she held him as if someone might at any moment try to tear him from her. She couldn't stop touching him, kissing his face. The smell of his hair was intoxicating, the softness of his sweet young skin.

When she had begun her search for the truth, she never imagined that she would find herself in conflict with people so powerful and merciless that the first threat they leveled at her would be to kill her only child, the only one she might ever have, this boy who was the living testament to the extraordinary love that she'd known with his special father.

She knew of nowhere else where she might have hidden him with as much hope and peace of mind as she had felt when she'd brought him here. Jessica and Gavin had been strangers to him two months earlier, but they were family now.

Passionate about clearing Nick's name, about proving that he had not committed suicide in any meaningful interpretation of the word, she had unknowingly set out on a path from which there could be no retreat. Those she sought to expose would not allow her to walk away and live even in the deep humiliation of defeat. They had brought something new and terrible into the world, with what purpose she still didn't understand, and they intended to see their plan, whatever it might be, fulfilled at any cost. There was already much murder in it; two more killings—a mother and her son—would be to them not even so much as an inconvenience. She knew little, but she knew too much, and she suspected more, and there would be no one to whom she could risk turning for help until she knew it all.

The boy held fast to her. "I love you, Mom."

She said, "I love you, too. So much. You rock me, kid."

PART TWO

RABBIT HOLE

1

IN THE GOLDEN LIGHT OF LATE afternoon, under scattered white clouds with gilded edges, Travis took his mother to visit the horses.

The stable stood in the deep shade of live oaks that shed their small oval leaves all year.

The surrounding ground was raked clean a few times a week. The swirls of parallel lines scored into the soft soil by the tines of the leaf rake resembled patterns that certain ancient shamans carved in stone to represent the mysterious turnings of fate, the endless cycles of a universe inscrutable in spite of its apparent design.

Bella and Sampson, mare and stallion, were housed side by side, facing two empty stalls, one of which had been fitted with a lower door to accommodate a pony not yet in residence.

The horses craned their necks over their stall doors to watch their visitors approach, and nickered in welcome.

In a paper cup, Travis carried a quartered apple, two pieces for each horse. With their soft lips, the animals finessed the treats from his small fingers.

He said, "Gavin hasn't found the right pony yet."

A month earlier, Jane had approved her son's desire to learn to ride and Gavin's preference that the child begin with a small mount.

"I couldn't ride Sampson yet, but I'm pretty sure I could ride Bella if you guys would let me. She's real gentle."

"And like fifteen times your size. Anyway, Sampson might be jealous if anyone but Jess rode her. He's the only guy for Bella."

"Do horses get jealous?"

"Oh, they do. Like Duke and Queenie get jealous if you pet the one a lot more than the other. Horses and dogs have shared their lives with people so long, they've come to have some of the same feelings we do."

Bella lowered her head so far over the half door that Travis could reach high enough to stroke her cheeks, a ministration for which she had a special fondness.

"But I bet I could ride Bella if it was okay with Sampson."

"Maybe you could, cowboy. But nobody becomes a master horseman if he's not patient and willing to learn one step at a time."

"Master horseman. That would be too cool."

"Your dad was raised on a ranch, did some rodeo by the time he was seventeen. It's in your blood. But so is common sense, so you be a good boy and listen to your common sense."

"I will."

"I know you will."

She smoothed one hand along Sampson's muscular neck, along that indentation called the jugular groove, and felt the power of his pulse against her palm.

The boy said, "Are you still looking for ... the killer?"

"Yes. Every day."

She hadn't told him that his father committed suicide, and she never would. Anyone who ever repeated that lie to Travis would earn her enmity forever.

"Is it scary?" he asked.

"Not scary," she lied. And then some truth: "A little dangerous sometimes, but you know I've been doing this for years and never even stubbed a toe."

When not on leave, she provided investigation support for Behavioral Analysis Units 3 and 4, specifically dealing with mass murderers and serial killers.

"Not even a toe?"

"Not even."

" 'Cause you have common sense, huh?"

"That's right."

Sampson fixed her with his limpid, liquid gaze. Not for the first time, Jane felt that horses, like dogs, with their heightened five senses—or even with a sixth—could read people far better than people could read them. In the stallion's dark and steady stare, there seemed to be an awareness of the fear she denied and of her double grief at the loss of a husband and the necessary separation from this child.

2

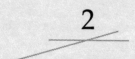

AFTER DINNER, AFTER A PLAY session in the early dark with a glowing Frisbee and the two dogs, after Jane read to Travis from the storybook that Jessica had started three days earlier, after he fell asleep, and after she stood over him for some time, enchanted by his face, in which she saw both Nick and herself, she went to the family room off the kitchen.

Jess and Gavin sat in armchairs and the dogs dozed near the hearth. The only light issued from the fireplace, in which logs crackled and popped and flared briefly each time the flames opened a new vein of sap.

There was an armchair for her, a glass of cabernet on the small table beside it. She was grateful for both.

The TV was off, and the music somewhat surprised Jane. Windham Hill did not seem to be a genre first in the heart of either Gavin or Jess. This was an anthology album featuring Liz Story and

George Winston piano solos, Will Ackerman solos on acoustic guitar.

The elegant simplicity of the music worked a peace upon the room as surely as did the fireplace.

She realized why only the firelight, why the music, when the first thing she thought to say after sipping her wine was "What's the latest from Philadelphia?"

"Three hundred and forty confirmed dead," Gavin said.

Jess said, "It'll go a hundred higher, maybe more. And so many injured, burned, disfigured."

Gavin sat with one hand fisted on the arm of his chair, the other around a wineglass. "It's all over the TV. If you try to watch anything else, you feel . . . like you've lost your humanity."

"Damn if we'll watch it," Jess said. "It's not tragedy, the way they report it, not horror, certainly not *war* reporting. It's all spectacle, and once you let yourself see it that way, your soul begins to turn to dust."

3

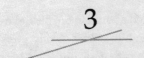

SHE AND NICK HAD MET GAVIN and Jessica Washington fourteen months earlier, at a weekend-long fundraiser for Wounded Warriors, in Virginia. Competing in the 5K race, not in a division for those with disabilities but among the whole-body athletes, Jess's time was less than a minute longer than Jane took to cross the finish line.

The four of them had recognized kindred spirits without long discussions about the state of the world, merely from nuances of speech and gesture and facial expressions, as much from things not said as from things said.

They had spent time together at a second event four months later, and it was as if they had been friends from childhood. Their ease with one another seemed like that of close siblings.

Gavin earned a living writing military nonfiction and more recently a series of novels with a cast of Special Forces ops. He hadn't enjoyed a bestseller yet, but he had a mainstream publisher and a growing reputation that surprised him, considering that he'd fallen into writing rather than planning his career.

Working as a busy volunteer for veterans' causes, Jess proved to have keen organizational skills and a knack for getting others to donate time and money without guilting them.

Of the qualities Jane liked about Gavin, his devotion to Jess spoke most highly of him. Many guys would have professed love for Jess until her legs were gone from the knees down, then would have vanished as if they were nothing more than ghostly manifestations of men. Gavin had never known her *without* prosthetics, which he seemed to regard as no more disabling than a need for reading glasses.

As one who had turned a few heads in her time, Jane had seen desires in men's eyes that they didn't hope to fulfill but that they couldn't conceal. When Gavin looked at her, however, he might have been a monk or a brother of the more conventional kind, for there was no quickening in him, no desire for more than friendship.

She and Nick had planned to meet the Washingtons for a three-day weekend in Vegas in early December—but Nick hadn't lived that long.

By mid-January, Jane's insistent denial that her husband's death was what it appeared to be, her inquiries into other peculiar suicides, and her research brought her to the attention of people who regarded her with pure venomous contempt. Nameless, faceless, they delivered such a convincing threat against Travis that even if she obeyed them and gave up her investigation, she knew that she and the boy would remain at risk.

Besides, she would not bend to them, not then, not ever.

Travis would not have been safe with family or with friends of long acquaintance. If the wrong people had wanted to find him, he would have been found in short order.

Jess and Gavin Washington did not live off the grid, but they weren't given to swimming in social media. Like Jane and Nick, they didn't have a Facebook page or a Twitter account, perhaps because the experienced warrior in all of them intuitively recognized the danger in throwing off camouflage to strut in sunlight. An online search wouldn't link their names. Their friendship was conducted face-to-face, by snail-mail letters that didn't leave the indelible history of text messaging, and by telephone. Even if someone scanned phone records, the number of calls between them wasn't sufficient to raise a suspicion that their relationship might be deep enough for Jane to entrust her son to them.

Once she realized that her days of living an aboveground life were behind her, she'd gotten her first car without GPS, an ancient Chevy purchased off a used-car lot, not yet a stolen vehicle repurposed and souped-up in Mexico. With Travis, she'd driven cross-country, from Virginia to California, employing her law-enforcement training to be sure they were never tailed and that they left no trail to follow, paying cash and keeping a low profile.

She had not called ahead to the Washingtons, neither from a pay phone nor with a disposable cell, telling herself that even such a tenuous lead was too much to risk, though in fact her true fear was that Jess and Gavin would decline to take responsibility for Travis. In that case, she would be at a cliff's edge without options.

They hadn't refused. Indeed, they agreed without hesitation.

In her heart, Jane knew that she had always read them right and that they could be depended on in a crisis. Yet their willingness had moved her to tears, though in the days following Nick's funeral, she had sworn off tears, had forbid herself all expressions of doubt and weakness until she'd brought this business to an end.

Leaving the boy in California had cleaved her. When not in his company, she felt as if an essential limb was missing.

In Virginia again, she sold the house, liquidated investments, and salted the money where only she could draw on it. Her enemies seemed to have interpreted her hiatus from the investigation as abject surrender. When they realized that she was on their trail again, they sought her relentlessly.

4

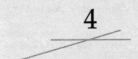

TO THE MUSIC OF WINDHAM Hill and the snoring of contented dogs in firelight, two hours passed with wine and conversation, but with no further talk of Philadelphia, before she returned to Travis's room for the night. Jessica wanted to make up the bed in the spare room, but Jane couldn't abide that distance from the boy, for she would too soon be on the road again, alone.

She didn't want to wake him by joining him on the bed. She sat in an armchair, legs propped on a footstool, wrapped in a blanket, watching him sleep in the low lamplight.

She had nothing to live for now except vengeance

and this precious boy. She would revel in the vengeance, but if she died for either cause, the only good death would be to die for him.

For a while she couldn't sleep, because she remembered. . . .

5

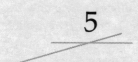

SHE IS AT HOME THAT DAY IN *January, at her computer, collecting yet more stories of unlikely suicides from local newspapers coast to coast, because many of the strangest deaths have not been reported by the national media.*

Travis is in his room, building with his LEGO blocks. He has not been much interested in play since Nick's death, and his recent obsession with building LEGO forts is either a first step back toward a normal childhood or a quiet expression of his fear and his sense of being defenseless in a world that took his father from him.

Appearing in the doorway of her study, bright-eyed and earnest, Travis says, "Mommy, what does it mean?"

She turns from her computer. "What does what mean?"

"Nat sat. What does it mean?"

"Well, I guess it means that somebody named Nat sat down on something."

Giggling, he races away, footsteps pounding along the hall to his room.

Jane is mystified but also charmed and hopeful, because this is the first she's heard him laugh in weeks.

A minute later, he returns. "No, that's wrong. Natsat is one word. Can I have some milk plus?"

"Milk plus what, kiddo?"

"I don't know. Wait. I'll find out." *Giggling as before, he runs to his room once more.*

Natsat, milk plus . . . Jane's mind is busy with the details of unlikely suicides, puzzled by the disturbing and cryptic notes left by some of those who took their own lives, but slowly a memory rises from a time that now seems as long gone as Caesar's Rome, from her college years.

She is getting up from her office chair when the boy appears once more, his enthusiasm in full bloom. "Mr. Droog says you know what milk plus is."

Yes, she remembers now. Nineteen and in her last year of an accelerated college schedule, she is impressed by Anthony Burgess's novel A Clockwork Orange. *The story is of a future society rapidly descending into disorder and brutal violence, and it influences her toward a career in law enforcement.*

In the book, natsat is a dialect spoken by young British thugs, cobbled together from Romany and Russian and baby talk, spoken with Gypsy rhythms. Milk bars serve milk with a variety of drugs. The drug-crazed, ultraviolent thugs call themselves droogs.

By the time she rises from the chair in her study, Jane is fully alarmed.

In the doorway, Travis stands in a state of innocent

delight, unaware that his next words spawn in her a shrinking, anxious dread.

"Mr. Droog says me and him will have some milk plus and then play a really fun game called rape."

"Honey, when did you talk to this Mr. Droog?"

"He's in my room, he's really funny." As he speaks, the boy spins away from her.

"Travis, no! Come back here!"

He doesn't heed her. Off into the hall and gone. His footsteps thundering away.

The average time for police response to a 911 call in her area is three minutes. In this instance, there is no difference between three minutes and eternity.

She yanks open a desk drawer, retrieves the pistol that she put there when she sat down to work.

Natsat, milk plus, droog . . .

This is no ordinary home invasion. Someone has done background on her. Intimately. All the way back to college.

In that instant, she realizes she's been expecting blowback of some kind, a response to her persistent research into the national plague of suicides. Blowback, but not as bold and vicious as this.

All search-and-clear rules forgotten, as panicked as anyone who had never graduated the Academy in Quantico, she later will have no memory of getting from her office to her son's bedroom. She recalls only being there, finding him standing in mild bewilderment, saying, "Where'd he go?"

The closet door is closed. Standing to one side, she pulls-throws it open with her left hand, gun in her right, crossed over her left arm, to take him down, kill him, if he lunges. But he isn't in the closet.

"Stay behind me, close to me, quiet and close," she whispers.

"You're not gonna shoot him, are you?"

"Quiet and close!" she repeats, and there is steel in her voice that he has never heard aimed at him before.

The last thing she wants to do is clear the house with a child in tow. A thousand ways things could go wrong. But she can't leave him there, doesn't dare, because maybe he won't be there when she gets back, won't be anywhere that she will ever find him.

He stays close, quiet, being the good boy that he is. He's scared, she's frightened him, but that's good, that means he's got some small idea, at least, of what is at stake.

Her own fear is so great that with it comes nausea, but she chokes it back, masters it.

In the kitchen, on the table, lies a copy of A Clockwork Orange. A gift and a warning.

The back door stands open. It had been locked. Too many people are foolish about locks. She knows the value of them, keeps them engaged on windows and exterior doors at all hours, day and night.

"Did you let him in?" she whispers.

"No, never, no," the boy assures her, and she believes him.

The telephone rings. It hangs on the wall near the sink. She stares at it, not wanting the distraction. She has been taking calls, and her voice mail is not engaged.

The phone rings, rings, rings. No caller would wait through so many rings unless he knows that she is home.

At last she picks up the handset but says nothing.

"He is a wonderfully trusting child," the caller says, "and so very tender."

No reply she makes will matter. But anything this man says might inadvertently give her a lead.

"Sheerly for the fun of it, we could pack the little bugger off to some Third World snake pit, turn him over to a group like ISIS or Boko Haram, where they have no slightest qualms about keeping sex slaves."

There are two qualities that make his voice memorable. First, he affects the faintest imitation of a British accent, has done so for so long that it is natural to him now. She has heard others who do this, often certain graduates of Ivy League universities who will inform you unasked of their alma mater, of the generations of their family who have attended it, and who wish you to know that they have been overeducated and are of an elite intellect. Second, it's a mid-tenor voice that, when he puts too much emphasis on a word, now and then shades toward alto, as with trusting and fun.

When she says nothing, the caller presses her. "Do you hear me? I want to know you hear me, Jane."

"Yes. I hear you."

"Some of those badasses over there are terribly fond of little boys as much as they are of little girls. He might even be passed around until he's ten or eleven before some barbarian tires of him and finally cuts off his pretty little head."

The words terribly *and* barbarian *sliding toward alto.*

She grips the telephone receiver so tightly that her hand aches and the plastic is slippery with her sweat.

"Do you understand why this was necessary, Jane?"

"Yes."

"Good. We knew you would. You are a bright girl. You're more to my taste than your son, but I wouldn't hesitate to pack you off with him and let those Boko boys who swing both ways have a twofer. Tend to your own business instead of ours, and all will be well."

He hung up.

As she racked the handset, Travis clung to her. "I'm sorry, Mommy. But he was nice."

She went to one knee and held him—but she did not let go of the pistol. "No, honey, he wasn't nice."

"He seemed nice, and he was funny."

"Bad people can pretend to be nice, and it's hard to tell when they're pretending."

She keeps him with her as she goes to the back door, closes it, locks it.

That day she buys the ancient Chevy from the used-car dealer.

That night she sets out with Travis for Gavin and Jess Washington's place in California.

6

HE WHIMPERED, AND SHE GOT up from the armchair to stand over him. His eyes moved rapidly under his closed and shadowed lids, and he grimaced, deep in sleep and dreaming.

She put a hand to his forehead to be sure that he didn't have a fever, and of course he did not. She smoothed his hair off his brow, which seemed to smooth away the bad dream as well. He didn't wake, but his face relaxed and he stopped whimpering.

The day Mr. Droog paid a visit, Jane had known that whoever wanted her to forget about a plague of suicide must have government associations. They were not necessarily a federal operation, but they had connections.

Her back door had been fitted with two Schlage deadbolts, the best locks available. No yaleman ever born could pop them open with the standard set of pick tools. To have disengaged both locks with little noise and quickly, Mr. Droog must have possessed a LockAid lock-release gun, an automatic pick sold only to law-enforcement agencies. For obvious reasons, LockAids were themselves kept under lock and key, and any officer who had a legitimate use for one would be required to sign it out from equipment inventory after presenting a court-issued search warrant limiting its use to a specific street address.

Maybe *They* weren't law enforcement themselves, maybe they were not even government employees of any kind—most likely they were not—but they had serious sources in both of those official worlds.

She deduced this also for two other reasons.

They could have faked a carjacking or a burglary and shot her in the head. They could have staged an accident, a house fire or a gas-line explosion, and taken out both her and Travis. Murder caused them no twinge of compunction, certainly not remorse. Instead of simply killing her, they warned her off, and she could think of no explanation for receiving mercy from merciless people other than that, in recognition of her status as an FBI agent, they were extending her professional courtesy, either on their own hook or because someone in the Bureau or elsewhere in government had asked them to do so.

In addition, the warning they had given her was both over-the-top vicious and delivered with unnerving confidence that they could fulfill the threat and convey the boy into the embrace of the most savage murderers and worst child molesters on the planet, half a world away. Such transport wasn't something the standard malevolent banker or wicked businessman, so familiar in modern fiction, would in real life be able to pull off. Mr. Droog was letting her know that he had connections, perhaps corrupt people in the intelligence services or the State Department, who could and would convey Travis into a new life far from home, a life of brutal rape and endless humiliation, just to keep her silent or to spite her if she would not be silenced.

The problem with such a vile threat, however, was that it convinced her of the perfection of their evil. You couldn't make deals with the devil, because the devil had no honor and would never adhere to the terms of the contract. If the warning dissuaded her from seeking the truth, if it reduced her to the purest cowardice, they would eventually reward her by killing her and Travis anyway, when in time she felt safe and let her guard down.

She was left with one role to play: David to their Goliath. She had no illusions that she could bring them down with one stone and a slingshot. They were not one giant. They were an *army* of Goliaths, as far as she knew, and her chances of coming out of this triumphant and alive were a decimal point away from zero.

Nevertheless, you played the cards you were dealt, and if jokers were wild, you hoped to get one before the game was done.

Now she returned to the armchair and put her legs up on the footstool. She drew the blanket over herself.

She could see the bedside clock—11:36.

Her eyes at last grew heavy, and on the backs of her lids were projected faint constellations of stars that in their turning made her pleasantly dizzy and spiraled her toward sleep.

7

SOMETIME IN THE NIGHT, SHE half woke to the sound of one of the dogs snuffling along the threshold of the closed bedroom door.

Gavin claimed that when he and Jess went to bed, the dogs rarely both slept at the same time, but spelled each other, taking turns on patrol of the house. They had not been trained to do this, but an instinct to assume guard duty was in shepherd genes.

Whether this was Duke or Queenie, the dog satisfied itself that Travis remained abed and all was well. Its nails clicked faintly on the mahogany floor as it continued on its rounds.

As Jane fell into sleep again, she also fell into the past and was a child, cozy in blankets, snow falling past the windows, dogs nearby to keep her safe. This wasn't the truth of her childhood, but a fantasy version, for she'd had no dogs or sense of safety.

8

JANE SET THE COFFEE TO BREW-
ing, toasted the bread and buttered it. Gavin cracked
the eggs and scrambled them, and tended to the
skillet of cottage fries. Jess fried sliced ham with
slivers of yellow peppers and onions, piled it on a
warming platter.

Although they had been fed first, the dogs remained alert and hopeful, though they did not get
underfoot.

As they had busied themselves with the cooking,
making it seem more of a task than it had really
been, making of it a distraction from the fact of
Jane's impending departure, so they also made
much of eating, as if they were all starving. And the
conversation was a little too loud, too fast, some of
the laughter forced.

Travis talked of what they could do with their
day, as if his mother would be there for all of it, including dinner and a game of glowing Frisbee in the
dusk. He suggested names for the pony, spoke about
saddling it for the first time as if Jane would see him
take his inaugural ride days from now. She let him
talk, joined him in the pony naming, because he
knew that for all their talk, she would be leaving;
this was only heartfelt wishing, while there was still
time to wish away the day that must be and hope to
conjure in its place the day that ought to be.

When the time came, after she'd said good-bye to Jess and Gavin, the boy alone accompanied her to the Ford Escape. He thought the car was cool, and he sat in it with her for a while, as they recalled for each other moments of the drive they had made across the country back in January, in a less reliable car.

When he sensed that there would be no more delay, he turned his face away from her, toward the side window, and knuckled his eyes. He put one salty knuckle in his mouth to bite on it. She could see that he bit hard, biting back more tears.

She didn't patronize him by telling him not to cry. His self-control would mean more to him if he managed it on his own.

Neither did she assure him that everything would be all right in the end. She could not lie to him. He would know a lie at once, and it would frighten him that she felt the need to pretend things must be better than they were.

"You're safe here," she said.

"I know."

"Do you *feel* safe here?"

"Yeah."

"And you've always wanted dogs."

"They're good dogs."

"They are. They're special."

"When can you arrest somebody?"

"I'm making progress."

"You're FBI. You can arrest them."

"Gathering evidence comes first," she said, wondering if she would ever unravel enough of it. "You know evidence?"

"Proof," he said.

"That's right. You're a regular FBI kid, knowing all this cop stuff."

He looked at her again. His eyes were red, but his lashes were not beaded with fresh tears. He was something, this little toughie.

From a pocket of his jeans, he withdrew part of a broken cameo locket: a woman's face in profile, carved of soapstone and embedded in a silver oval. Half a hinge was fixed to one side of it. Perhaps a lock of a loved one's hair had been kept in the small case when it had been intact and hanging on a silver chain.

"Last time you came here, like after you left, I found this down at the creek, washed up on some stones. She looks like you."

There was no remarkable resemblance, but Jane said, "She sort of does, doesn't she?"

"I knew right away it was good luck."

"Like finding a shiny new penny."

"Bigger luck. You came back and all." He was solemn when he held the cameo out to her. "So you've got to have it."

She understood the necessity of matching his solemnity. She accepted the charm. "I'll always keep it in my pocket."

"You gotta sleep with it, too."

"I will."

"Every night."

"Every night," she agreed.

The idea of one last kiss, one last touch, seemed too much for him. He opened the door, scrambled from the car, closed the door, and waved good-bye.

She gave him a thumbs-up and then drove off. As she followed the long graveled driveway to the state route, he was always there in the rearview mirror, watching after her, a small figure becoming quickly smaller, until the lane curved and the colonnade of oak trees intervened between them.

9

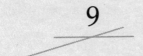

DURING THE PREVIOUS NIGHT, the valley had come to seem remote to her, as she wished it to be, a refuge beyond the horizon of the modern world, where the civilization of the mechanized hive did not encroach, where each individual could exist unto himself or herself, free from the forced intimacy of the digital collective—therefore safe.

As she drove west once more, she soon ascended on an undulant ribbon of blacktop, through the chaparral-stubbled hills that were as they had been ten thousand years earlier. In the hard clear light of morning, the borderline desert landscape did not seem natural, appeared instead to be devastated, as

if the final war at world's end had raged across this
terrain long ago.

The consequences of that conflict were to be
found in the endless busy cities of the coast, and as
she came within sight of them, the truth of the
valley's—and her child's—proximity to all the dan-
gers of this troubled age couldn't be denied.

She could only hope that Travis would be safe
there until she might be able to understand the nature and intent of the conspiracy behind the country's escalating suicides and obtain enough evidence
to break the story to the public. Even in the darkest
darkness, hope was a lifeline, though sometimes as
thin as a thread.

10

FROM CAPISTRANO BEACH, JANE
followed the Coast Highway north to Newport
Beach, and then headed inland to the city of Santa
Ana.

Although the Ford Escape was less likely to catch
the eye of a passing cop now that the Canadian
plates had been stripped off, the vehicle would draw
even less attention if it wore California tags.

Stealing plates wasn't an option. If the victim
filed a police report, the number would be on a na-
tionwide hot sheet in an hour.

The National Crime Information Center database maintained continuously updated lists of wanted persons with outstanding arrest warrants in all fifty states; missing persons; and stolen property that included cars, trucks, boats, aircraft, securities, guns, and license plates. Local, state, and national law-enforcement officers had access to the NCIC and used it regularly.

She intended to buy rather than steal plates. A seller was more likely to be found in Santa Ana than elsewhere in Orange County.

This once-prosperous city had long been in decline before recently undergoing some gentrification. In spite of the best efforts of those who would bring Santa Ana back to its glory days, there were many deteriorated neighborhoods, some of them dangerous.

Wherever decay and poverty flourished, there tended to be less money for public services. Where the police were not properly funded—and often disrespected—gangs thrived like mushrooms in any moist, dark place, and it was easier to obtain whatever you might want.

She cruised until she found a manufacturing district beaten down by foreign competition, bad economic policy, and regulators who acted with the best of intentions but never walked the streets where their destruction was manifest. Abandoned plants with stained and spalling stucco walls. Rusted metal roofs. Shattered windows.

Once filled with employees' cars, parking lots

stood empty, the blacktop swaled with depressions reminiscent of grave sites that sank when coffins and their contents moldered away.

A long building of slumpstone and corrugated steel had been divided into twelve double-wide garages, over which a roof-mounted sign offered SECURE GARAGE AND WORK SPACES FOR RENT. Five of the big doors were rolled up, and men were working on cars either inside those units or on the concrete apron in front of them.

They appeared to be young, mostly in their twenties, and Jane assumed that some of them were operating small car-repair shops without business licenses. Others might have been working on their own vehicles: all-stops-pulled street rods, low-riders with engines on steroids, and ordinary flash wheels.

She parked out of the way and chose a young Hispanic man who was kneeling on Velcroed joint protectors, using gel wax and a power buffer on a pearl-gray '60 Cadillac convertible that had been fully restored and lightly customized. As she approached him, he switched off the buffer and got to his feet.

The guys at other units had turned from their work to watch her. Maybe because she looked good. Mostly because she didn't look as though she belonged there, and people who looked as though they came from outside the neighborhood could be trouble.

The man with the Caddy had close-cropped hair and a Zapata mustache. He wore engineer boots, jeans, a tank tee, and an expression as impassive as a slab of concrete.

His muscular arms were sleeved with vivid tattoos, but the images weren't prison work in either subject or style. On his right arm, a flight of angels swarmed up from the back of his hand to his biceps, where they gathered around a radiant depiction of the Holy Mother with child. An exquisitely depicted tiger climbed his left arm, its head turned at the top to look back; its fangs were not bared in a snarl, but its golden eyes conveyed a pointed warning.

"Sweet car," she said, indicating the Caddy.

He said nothing.

"Those are Dayton wire wheels, huh? And radial tires made to look like bias ply, right for the period."

His brown eyes with faint yellow striations had been flint on the verge of striking a spark. The threat of fire went out of them.

He said, "Coker Excelsior sport radials."

"Your car?"

"I don't steal."

"That wasn't my implication."

"Stupid to think you could score anything in this place."

"I don't do drugs. And I don't think everyone with Mexico in his family deals them."

After a silence while he considered the flint in *her* eyes, he said of the car, "Yeah, she's mine."

"Beautiful job."

When he didn't reply, she looked around at the other guys, who were pretending to get back to work, then at the Caddy owner again. "I'm jammed in a corner. I can pay my way out. But I need help."

He held her stare. "What do I smell?"

"You smell cop."

"You're a psychic lady, huh?"

She sensed that a pure lie would shut him down, that she needed to blend some truth in it. "I'm FBI on suspension."

"Why'd they suspend you?"

"To pull my teeth while they set me up for a rap I didn't do."

"Maybe I'm the one bein' set up."

"Why you in all the world? No need to trick dudes to keep the prisons full when a million assholes are volunteering for a cell."

After another silence during which they maintained eye contact, he said, "So I got to grope you."

"I understand."

He led her into the garage, to the shadowed back of the place.

He started at her ankles and worked his way up both legs, patting her down, searching for a wire. Inner thighs, buttocks, belt line, up the back, around the breasts, his strong hands exploring without apology, his face impassive and his manner businesslike.

When he found the pistol, he pulled aside her sport coat to examine rig and weapon, but he didn't draw the .45 from the holster.

Taking a step back from her, he said, "So what is it?"

"I'll give you five hundred for the license plates from the Caddy, and you don't report them stolen for a week."

He thought about it. "A thousand."

Earlier, she had folded five hundred-dollar bills into each front pocket of her jeans. "Six hundred."

"A thousand."

"Seven hundred."

"A thousand."

"You're cutting my throat here."

"I didn't come to you. You came to me."

"Because you didn't look like a pirate. Eight hundred."

He considered and then said, "Count it out."

She put eight bills in his open palm.

"I'll bring my lady into the first bay. You pull your Ford into the second. We'll do the swap in here."

"Those guys out there are interested and hawk-eyed," she said. "When I leave, they'll see your plates on my wheels."

"I'm not worried about them. They're solid. But we don't know who's passin' in the street."

After the vehicles were in the garage, the big segmented door powered down, closing out fresh air, so the oil-grease-rubber odor intensified.

Jane felt isolated, wary but not alarmed.

When the owner of the Caddy switched the plates and the door groaned and rattled upward, he came to her. "I'll keep her in here, drive my regular bucket instead. You want one week, I'll give you two before I tell the cops the plates were ripped off."

"Suddenly you're generous, but I wonder . . ."

"I don't lie about things this serious."

"That wasn't my implication. What I meant is, I know you can count to seven, but I'm not sure about fourteen."

A surprised laugh escaped him. "*Bonita chica,* if I knew where they make them like you, I'd move there tomorrow."

11

THE SALESGIRL IN THE WIG shop on Santa Monica Boulevard in trendy West Hollywood thought the midnight-purple number with the Chinese-red swags was a perfect comple-ment to Jane's complexion. "But then, anything would be with your great skin."

They had a makeup section with midnight-purple lip gloss and glittery eye shadow. The sales-girl was excited that Jane was going from fade to flash. "The young-attorney look doesn't do you jus-tice. Your stuff is stashed in the right places, so might as well put it on parade before the long slide starts. What'll they say at work?"

"I came into some money," Jane said. "I don't need to work anymore. I'm quitting tomorrow."

"So you're gonna—what?—go in there one last time, flash the hot new you, and tell 'em to screw themselves?"

"Exactly."

"Sensational."

"Isn't it?"

"Beat them into the dirt with it."

"I will," Jane said, though she wasn't sure what that meant.

Across the street and half a block farther east, in a boutique where the salesgirls looked like highly attractive cyborgs from the future, Jane bought a pair of Buffalo Inka flare jeans with a higher rise that gave them a retro look, and a lambskin biker's jacket that, according to the girls, was a perfect knockoff of one by Comptoir des Cotonniers, whoever the hell that was.

She also chose snakeskin high-heeled platform shoes with ankle straps. They were said to be a drop-dead knockoff of a pair by Salvatore Ferragamo, of whom she believed she had heard, though she had been under the impression he was a hockey or soccer star.

Finally, she purchased a pair of black-silk wrist-length gloves with silver stitching. Without them, her working-cop fingernails would belie her flash-girl image. Besides, she was going where she didn't want to leave fingerprints.

She had little patience for shopping, especially because, when trying on clothes, she had to leave her rig and pistol under the driver's seat in the locked Ford. From wig selection to gloves, she felt naked.

Out of West Hollywood, she drove into less glamorous precincts.

For decades, the northwest suburbs of Los Angeles, on the other side of the Santa Monica Mountains, had thrived and expanded. But too many parts of Van Nuys, Reseda, Canoga Park, and other communities were showing signs of the state's decline.

The sparkling coastal communities remained mostly luxe, but here in the western half of the San Fernando Valley, seediness was creeping in everywhere.

Jane passed by a few motels that had gone to the rats and roaches, that appeared to rent by the week to crack junkies who lived four to a double room.

In a better neighborhood, a national-chain motel still looked family friendly. She checked in, paying cash and presenting false ID, confident she wouldn't have to get up in the middle of the night to break up a grudge match between a meth freak and a freebaser.

She began her fade-to-flash transformation.

12

THERE WERE JOBS IN THE AREA, some of them high-paying, and the central commercial district was trying hard to be cutting-edge hip, youth-oriented, the Place to Be if you were one of those who thought there was such a thing as the Place to Be. A few empty storefronts put the lie to full prosperity, but vacancies were not an epidemic.

For every three shops or restaurants that looked as if they might have had a poster of Che Guevara somewhere on the premises, there was one stubborn Jurassic retailer offering knit suits for older women or an Italian restaurant that offered all-you-can-eat garlic bread and didn't call itself a trattoria.

Jane was interested solely in a shop where the sign over the door said VINYL, just that one word, because it was meant to suggest an ongoing business without attracting the annoyance of too many customers. There was no indication of what product or service the place might be hawking. The big windows were painted green, neither displaying merchandise nor providing a glimpse of the interior.

Driving behind the shop, she saw no indications of active surveillance from the buildings on the other side of the alleyway.

After parking a block from Vinyl and around the corner, she walked the south side of the street, tall in her platforms, feeling out-there but not out of place.

She had never been comfortable with undercover work.

She stopped at an ill-conceived hole-in-the-wall take-out business that was trying to be a juice bar, a hip purveyor of chai tea and like beverages, and a gelato shop peddling exotic flavors, all in a space so small that grade-school entrepreneurs would be reluctant to set up a lemonade stand.

She paid for a bottle of coconut water, which tasted like palm-tree piss, if there had been such a thing. She drank it anyway as she strolled that block and the next, pretending to window-shop.

After crossing to the north side of the street, she slowly worked her way back to Vinyl. None of the vehicles parked in the area seemed to be conducting surveillance of the place.

When she went through the painted-glass door, chimes announced her. Rows of record bins divided the front room into aisles. They were filled with phonograph albums and even more ancient 78-rpm platters from the era before the compact disc and digitized music.

On the walls hung framed one-sheets, concert playbills, and posters ranging from Bing Crosby to the Beatles. Vinyl catered to audiophiles, black-wax geeks who preferred authentic recordings that hadn't been engineered to soulless perfection. Such was its apparent purpose, anyway.

On a stool behind the counter sat a long-faced girl with big eyes and ringletted sable-black hair to her shoulders. She sported a small tattoo of a skull in the hollow of her throat, and she must have spent a thousand hours in front of a mirror, perfecting her look of ennui.

Spinning on a turntable near her, an album by Kansas offered their biggest hit, "Dust in the Wind," and it was easy to suppose that this girl played nothing else all day.

Jane placed an index card on the counter. With a felt-tip pen, she had earlier printed this on it: THE FBI HAS AN OPEN-END COURT ORDER ALLOWING THEM TO RECORD EVERY WORD SPOKEN IN THIS PLACE.

Instead of reading the card, the clerk said, "What—you're a deaf mute or something? We don't make contributions."

Jane raised a black-gloved middle finger to her and then with the same digit tapped the index card.

The girl deigned to read the message, and if she understood it, she maintained an admirable deadpan expression.

On the second index card was this: IF JIMMY RADBURN DOESN'T WANT TO SPEND 20 YEARS IN PRISON, HE NEEDS TO TALK TO ME NOW.

The skull tattoo in the hollow of the clerk's throat seemed to widen its lipless grin when she swallowed hard.

She plucked the two cards off the counter, swung off the stool, went to a door on her side of the sales counter, and stepped into a back room.

Jimmy Radburn deserved to spend the rest of his life being some gang thug's main squeeze in Leavenworth or the equivalent.

But Jane needed him. It sickened her to have to turn to him. A lot of things sickened her these days, and yet she didn't spend any time throwing up.

Kansas finished decrying the bleakness of the human condition and moved on to another cut.

13

AFTER A COUPLE OF MINUTES, the salesgirl returned with a guy in his twenties. Tall, rangy. A two-day beard. Brown hair cropped close on the sides, longer on top. His gray T-shirt featured one word in black letters: MALWARE. He wore drawstring sweatpants that were too short and Nikes without socks.

Coming through a gate at the end of the counter, he looked Jane up and down but said nothing. He went to the front door, locked it.

Having settled on her stool, the salesgirl took the Kansas platter off the turntable. She slid another album onto the spindle.

The guy returned to Jane and stared at her as if waiting for her to prove something.

She said softly, "Jimmy Radburn?"

In respect of her claim that every word was being recorded, he tapped his chest with a forefinger, pointing to himself.

In fact, he wasn't Jimmy Radburn, looked nothing like the man. If he was stupid enough to assume she had only the name to go on, he was likely to do something else stupid.

He made a come-with-me gesture and led the way to the gate in the counter.

Once more wearing her expression of exquisite boredom, the girl on the stool set the needle down not on the lead-in groove of the record but instead at the start of a deeper cut. It was Elton John's "Funeral for a Friend," and whether she had chosen the song with a snarky purpose or not was impossible to know.

Jane followed Malware into the shop's back room. Unlabeled cardboard boxes and rectangular plastic tubs full of phonograph records stood on deep wall shelves, on tables, and under tables, with no apparent order to them. In one corner stood a cleaning station where the collectible platters could be lovingly swabbed with appropriate chemicals. Nobody was working there.

Yawning as though the salesgirl's world-weariness might be contagious, Malware closed the door to the front room—and then abruptly pivoted, grabbed Jane by the crotch, by the throat, and rammed her backward into the wall beside the door.

He should have body-slammed her, pinning her tight against him, and in the same instant should have reached under her open biker's jacket to feel whether she was carrying; but he didn't take her seriously enough yet. And he wanted to do that crotch grab, he very much wanted that, because his fingers squeezed and probed through the denim as he lowered his face toward hers with one foolish intention or another.

When she raised her right leg, he thought she meant to knee him in his package, but it was too easy for him to block that move, so it wasn't what she had in mind. The hard edge of the platform sole of her Ferragamo knockoffs struck down across his exposed left shin, shredding the skin and gouging the flesh and bruising the sharp edge of the tibia, from the hem of his too-short sweatpants to the tongue of his Nikes, which might make him think twice about not wearing socks in the future.

The shin, a nerve-rich portion of the lower leg, was webbed with venules returning deoxygenated blood to the small saphenous vein. The pain was immediate and intense, and he could surely feel warm blood running down his leg, a scary sensation if you weren't trained to ignore it. For a man, Malware achieved a remarkable soprano shriek. He lost his grip on her. He staggered back a step as he bent forward to clutch his shin, whereupon she drove a knee hard into the underside of his chin and heard his teeth clack and stepped aside as he collapsed onto the floor.

The door flew open, and Ms. Ennui appeared vividly engaged with the world for the first time. She froze on the threshold, however, because Jane had already drawn her Heckler & Koch, giving the girl's big dark eyes an intimate view of the muzzle.

"Go back to your stool," Jane said. "Put on some happy music. Elton's recorded a lot of it."

14

BEHIND A DOOR, STAIRS LED UP to the second floor, where the real work at Vinyl got done, and Jane wanted Malware to ascend in front of her. These people weren't dangerous in a gangland sense, and they certainly were not as bloodthirsty and twisted as the homicidal sociopaths whom she had spent the last six years tracking down. But if they were all as lacking in common sense as this one, blood could be spilled unnecessarily. She needed to use this humbled assailant for a shield, coming behind him with her pistol ready to perform the ultimate spinal tap, thereby giving the people on the second floor time to rein in their heebie-jeebies.

Malware found it painful to stand up straight, but he was no good to her if he humped up the stairs like a troll. The thought of the gun in his back put some starch in him. He needed the handrail, and he limped step by step, but he ascended at his full height. He cursed her at first, spitting blood because he'd bitten his tongue. Then he realized the point of her wanting a shield, and belatedly he took it upon himself to call out, "I'm in front, Jimmy, I'm in front of her, it's me in front, Jimmy!"

There was one long steep flight of stairs, no door above. As they got close to the top, she pressed the muzzle of the pistol into his spine, just in case he got his macho back when he came eye-to-eye with his friends.

Past Malware, as they rose into the second floor, Jane saw a large room the length of the building, windows boarded over, mellow down-lighting, stained-concrete floor. Maybe ten workstations, each computer with its own printers, scanners, miscellaneous black boxes, support tech. An elevated, circular central desk provided a platform from which the entire room could be overwatched.

Seven guys were standing at various points, looking toward the stairs, all in their twenties and early thirties. Some were stick-thin, some fat, some bearded and some not. All were pale, not out of fear, but due to a lack of interest in activities conducted in sunlight. Each of the seven fit within the spectrum of computer-geek style.

Only one of the seven, Jimmy Radburn, was packing, though in spite of the gun he looked no more dangerous than a kitten. His stance was wrong, his left foot behind him and his weight too much on it instead of evenly distributed. His primary criterion when he'd bought the weapon must have been its intimidating appearance. Maybe a Colt Anaconda, .44 Magnum, with a ridiculous eight-inch barrel. Probably fifty-six ounces, heavier than a large brick. He held it in one hand, arm extended, because maybe Clint Eastwood had done that in a Dirty Harry movie. If he ever squeezed the trigger, the recoil would stagger him backward, he'd blow out some expensive overhead lights—and he'd probably be so startled, he'd drop the revolver.

When it came to firearms, Jane preferred facing experienced gunmen, because if you died in the confrontation, at least it wouldn't be a cartoonish death.

In his free hand, Jimmy was holding the two index cards on which she had printed messages to him.

Jane pushed Malware away from her, but not toward Jimmy Radburn. "Get in a chair."

Cursing her once more, Malware hobbled to an office chair.

Maybe Jimmy spooked easily, but he wasn't a stupid man. He had read the index cards. She'd given him information that could keep him out of prison if he acted properly on it. Even if what she'd told him turned out to be bogus—which it wouldn't—it couldn't be construed as a hostile act.

Counting on him to have more common sense than the guy whose shin she had raked to the bone, she holstered her pistol. While he continued to point the cannon at her face, she fished another index card from a jacket pocket and held it out to him.

For a moment, he couldn't decide what to do, and his crew of six stood tense and expectant, as if this was a spaghetti Western moment if ever there had been one. Then Jimmy lowered the revolver.

With his left hand, he motioned her toward him, and he took the third card that she offered.

On it, she had written this: SOME OF YOUR PHONE LINES HAVE BEEN SLEEVED WITH INFINITY TRANSMITTERS.

The infinity transmitter couldn't be called cutting-edge technology. It was older than Jimmy, who was thirty, perhaps even older than his mother, but it worked as slick as anything. Maybe it wasn't the first threat Mrs. Radburn's baby boy considered when he thought about spending a large part of his life eating prison food, but Jane counted on him having heard of it.

He put the index cards and the revolver on the round elevated desk and said to his crew, "Log off and shut down," and at once they returned to their workstations to do as he instructed.

Once an infinity transmitter had been hooked into a phone, it hibernated until an activating call was placed from an outside line. As the final digit of the number was entered, the caller at the same moment triggered an electronic whistle into the mouthpiece. This instantly switched on the infinity transmitter, which prevented the target phone from ringing but activated its microphone. The people in the room, this room, would be unaware that every conversation among them was being transmitted to a law-enforcement agency, which was recording everything. With an open-end court order granted for national-security reasons, the FBI was most likely eavesdropping on the Radburn operation frequently but not continuously, though there was no reason they couldn't record 24/7 if they wished.

When all the computers had been shut down, Jimmy went to a tall metal cabinet in the northeast corner of the long room. It contained the switching system for a business with a couple dozen phone lines. He fiddled in there for a minute, and when he closed the cabinet door, Jane assumed he had shut off his entire telecom package.

When he returned to her, he said, "What's with the wig?"

She pointed toward the boarded windows at the south end of the room. "There are so many traffic cameras anymore, people stop seeing them. You've got one mid-block, in front of your store, but it's not a traffic camera."

"That sucks."

"It looks as if it's shooting west to east, but it's aimed at your front door."

"Orwellian bastards."

Of which you are one, unrealized, Jane thought.

She said, "It clicks every two seconds and transmits high-resolution images of everyone who goes in or out of Vinyl. That's why the wig. And the massive eye shadow. At least, the last I knew, the camera isn't twinned with facial-recognition software."

"What's your name?"

For the hell of it, she said, "Ethan Hunt," borrowing it from the bakery delivery guy in San Diego.

"Funny name for a girl."

"I'm not your usual girl."

15

JIMMY RADBURN SENT Malware—whose name was Felix—downstairs to get first aid from Ms. Ennui, also known as Britta. He dispatched the other six guys in his crew to wait in the shop for instructions. They thundered down the steep stairs, and he shouted, "Close the door behind you," which someone did.

He led Jane to a table covered with boxes of cookies, packages of candy, bags of potato chips, pretzels, corn chips, cans and jars of nuts—enough munchables to satisfy a legion of potheads during an around-the-clock smoke-in. The complexity and delicacy of the tasks undertaken by Vinyl's blackhat hacker crew ruled out weed before or during—and pretty much after—work, but evidently either a salted-carb rush or a sugar high was thought to contribute to productivity.

They pulled out a couple chairs and sat facing each other.

Jimmy Radburn looked like an adult Kewpie doll—pleasantly rounded but not truly fat, his face smooth and unlined and nearly beardless. He was well barbered, freshly scrubbed, and had the most perfectly manicured hands of any man Jane had seen.

He said, "How'd you get your information, the stuff on the index cards? Which, anyway, is probably all gubbish."

"Doesn't matter how I got it. And it isn't garbage."

She wasn't going to tell him that she was an FBI agent on leave. He couldn't testify in court to what he didn't know.

She said, "They came at you with grandpa tech, and you missed it during your sweeps because you're always running straight-line analysis, looking for breaches where you expect them. When you're developing products—apps, whatever—or trying to crack a network, you want straight-line progress, but you know you also need to take a drunkard's walk."

"Respect randomness," he agreed. "Drunkard's walk. Brownian movement. Random and undirected progress."

"So you should apply it to security sweeps as well."

"I'm a genius *and* an idiot." With his smile, he tried to project self-deprecation, but it was a smile borrowed from a baby rattlesnake. "So how screwed am I? Should I flush this place today?"

"They're paying out line to you, letting you run with the hook, building files on the other fish you swim with. So you've got time. Maybe a few months, maybe a year. But if I were you, I'd melt out of here over a couple of nights, using the back entrance, and leave this an empty room by next week."

"So it's a pessimal situation."

"Opposite of optimal," she agreed. "I won't tell

you how I know any of this, but if you want, I can tell you how they tripped over your tracks."

As she talked, he had extracted an Oreo from a bag of cookies. He popped the entire thing into his mouth, as though it was the size of a Cheez-It, and chewed vigorously. After swallowing, he said, "I guess I need to know. So tell me."

"You remember a client named Carl Bessemer?"

"I make a point of not remembering clients."

"One of your apps allows even tech idiots to perform super-easy spoofing from any smartphone. The call or text message gets routed through a Canadian exchange before it bounces back to the States, where it bounces some more before going to the recipient with fake caller/sender ID."

"I'm proud of that one. My winnitude went off the charts with that one."

His smug expression abraded Jane's nerves. She said, "Plus, the call escapes the phone-company billing system, there's no evidence afterward that it was ever made."

"Spank me now. I'm a bad boy." He plucked another Oreo from the bag. "In my defense, I must say we try to make an effort to identify potential terrorists and not sell to them."

"How does that work?"

Crunching the cookie, he said, "Not as well as I'd like."

"You also sold Bessemer a clever voice synthesizer with an interface that allowed it to be used with his smartphone. Feed the synthesizer a one-minute sample of anyone's voice, which you could record by making a phone call, and the damn thing can change your speech to mimic the other person's so well that a wife would think she's talking to her husband, or a child to her mother, when in fact it was Bessemer."

"Another Radburn top-of-the-charts product." As he spoke, he celebrated himself by bumping one fist against the other.

His thick-fingered hands were pale pink and utterly hairless, as were his wrists to his shirt cuffs, smooth as rubber, seemingly boneless, repellent. Like the hands of some android bred in a vat.

"What's bad for you is, Carl Bessemer wasn't an ordinary phone phreaker trying to stiff AT&T. He wasn't even an ordinary criminal."

"In my experience," Jimmy said, "there isn't such a thing as an ordinary criminal. It's a community of entirely unique individuals."

"Pretending to be who he wasn't, Bessemer lured young women to lonely places, then raped and killed them."

"You can't blame General Motors for selling cars to guys who get drunk and drive."

Jane loathed him, but she needed him. "Understand, I'm not judging you, only telling you how the Feds stumbled onto you."

"Don't worry your pretty purple head. I've got a nose for character. I can smell it. Your character has the same scent as mine. You're not the judgmental type."

"Bessemer wasn't his real name."

"A lot of our clients' names aren't their real names, Ethan Hunt. Anonymity is essential to privacy, and privacy is a right."

"His real name was Floyd Sutter."

"Ah," he said, getting the full picture. "Sutter the Cutter. The star of tabloids and TV news. What— fifteen, sixteen kills?"

"Nineteen." She had been the one to cripple Sutter with a leg shot and secure him with cable zips of the kind he used to bind his victims on first disabling them. "Your bad luck was that they didn't kill him in the process of capturing him. Floyd is a chatterbox. He didn't know your physical address—"

"None of our clients do. We're strictly a Dark Web business."

"But with what he *did* know, with your app and the synthesizer, the FBI had enough to find you."

"They've found Jimmy Radburn, not me." He allowed himself another Oreo, but turned it between thumb and forefinger instead of eating it. "Jimmy's not the real me any more than Carl Bessemer was the real him. When I flush this place, I'll flush Jimmy." He studied her for half a minute, and she allowed herself to be studied, and he said, "You don't worry for a second that I might flush you, too."

"I saw how you handled that blunderbuss. There's no killing in you. You don't care if anyone gets whacked as collateral damage to your business, but you don't have a taste for it yourself."

He smiled and nodded. "I'm a lover, not a killer." He leaned forward in his chair. "Do my excellent winnitude and intelligence turn you on?"

"No."

"Some girls are turned on by that."

"I'm just here to get what I need. I gave you a chance to skip arrest, court, and jail. You owe me."

"I always pay my debts. It's just good business." He stopped turning the cookie between thumb and forefinger, popped it into his mouth, made a production of consuming it with much lip licking, and said, "I could eat you up like a bag of Oreos. I leave the offer on the table. Now, what is it you want?"

16

THE MAN CURRENTLY KNOWN as Jimmy Radburn had no self-esteem deficit and an excess of self-confidence. He always knew what he wanted and how to get it, and there wasn't a problem for which he couldn't find a solution. If he'd ever had doubts about his chosen career, he apparently vaporized them long ago. If anything had ever puzzled him previously, he seemed to have erased the experience from memory, because the intense puzzlement that he expressed over Jane's requests was like that of a precocious child encountering for the first time something that bewildered him.

Paging through the list she'd given him, he said, "Thirty-two coroners?"

"That's right."

"City, county, small-town coroners?"

"Yes."

"Why so many?"

"There's no need for you to know why anything. I could've given you ten times thirty-two. It doesn't matter."

"It's weird, that's all. It's creepy. You've got to admit it's creepy. It's bizarre."

"I've given you their names and websites. Work your way in from there, or however you do it."

"Just suicides. Why just suicides?"

She answered him with a look.

"All right, okay. My interest is epsilon."

"Good."

He put the pages on the snack table and with a pen made notes. "All suicides during the past year in these jurisdictions. A full coroner's report on each. You want details of brain examinations if they went that far. All this stuff is public record, isn't it?"

"Yeah, but there are privacy issues. And using the Freedom of Information Act can take months— years, even. Besides, there are some difficult people who won't like this being looked into. I don't want to draw their attention."

He raised an eyebrow. "Difficult meaning bad-ass?"

"Don't worry about it."

"If you're worried about it, maybe I should be, too."

"I'm not a hacker, you are."

"The word *cracker* is more accurate. Derived from *safe-cracker*. It just never caught on."

"Cracker, hacker, whatever. If I go poking around, they know it. You can slip in, slip out with what I want, and they never know you've been there."

"This is a lot of work."

"Put your entire crew on it. I want it all by noon tomorrow."

"You're one demanding bitch. I kind of like that."

His gray eyes were as pellucid and direct as those of a small and innocent child. If he had made a career of conning elderly women out of their life savings, his victims would have been charmed by his eyes, though Jane saw in them the sharp intention of a predator.

She said, "Don't flirt. You're not good at it. I really mean noon sharp."

"I heard. Okay, you're the big dog right now. We'll tool it till it's done. What's this name on the last page?"

"David James Michael. He serves on the boards of those two nonprofits. I want to know everything about him, all the way down to bank-account numbers, shoe size, whether he suffers constipation."

"If you want a stool sample, you'll have to get that yourself. I'll have the rest by noon, but we'll need to pull an all-nighter."

She rose from her chair. Jimmy remained seated.

She said, "Don't hand it to me on a thumb drive. I've gone primitive. I need printouts."

He grimaced. "There goes a forest. Besides, we don't do volume printouts, 'cause we don't have a mumble line or a foo switch."

"Do you think I'm an idiot?"

"It was worth a try. All right, no thumb drive. Come around noon, we'll have your package."

"You'll deliver it to me in Santa Monica. You yourself. Alone."

"You're a woman accustomed to a lot of personal service. I'm the ace of personal service."

"But you suck at double entendres. Santa Monica. Palisades Park. Somewhere between Broadway and California Avenue. Get one of those helium-filled metallic balloons. Easiest place to find one is a florist. Tie it to your wrist so I can see you coming from a distance. You won't have to find me. I'll find you."

Jane went to the circular desk on the platform. She retrieved the Colt Anaconda .44 Magnum that he had put there.

"Hey, what're you doing?" Jimmy rose from his chair, alarmed.

"Relax. When I leave, I'll put it on the floor by the front door. I don't want it here to tempt you when I turn my back."

"You're the one who said there's no killing in me," Jimmy reminded her.

"Once in a great while I'm wrong."

She walked to the head of the stairs and turned to

him. He was still standing at his chair, but she could see how badly he wanted to come after her, nail her. Although he had seemed not to be stung by the needles that she'd stuck in him during their conversation, Jimmy didn't take commands or mockery from a woman without at least fantasizing revenge.

"If instead of doing this job for me, you try to melt out of here tonight, I have someone watching the place," she lied. "I'll call the local FBI office, do my civic duty. You won't get ten percent of your operation in a truck before they drop a rapid-mobilization unit on you."

"You'll get what you want," he assured her.

"Good. And don't forget the balloon."

With the .44 Magnum in a two-hand grip, she crabbed down the stairs sideways, back against the wall that lacked a railing. Her attention was largely on the door at the bottom, but she glanced repeatedly toward the second floor, just in case the Colt hadn't been the only gun Jimmy kept up there.

At the ground floor, she opened the door and saw no one in the back room, just the boxes full of old phonograph records.

The door stood open to the front room. No music. She could hear Jimmy's crew talking animatedly, which they wouldn't be doing if they were lying in wait for her.

She didn't make a production of clearing the doorway, though neither did she amble through it unconcerned.

They were all gathered toward the farther end of

the sales counter. On this side, Felix sat on Britta's stool. The girl was on her knees, dressing his scraped shin with a roll of gauze. Another member of the crew stood with them. The remaining five were on the customer side of the counter.

As Jane went through the gate, they watched her in silence, like a gaggle of undisciplined and petulant children who had been temporarily put in their place by an adult against whom they were conspiring to commit all manner of wickedness.

She unlocked the front door, put the Colt on the floor, and stepped outside, surprised to find it still daylight after that realm of boarded- and painted-over windows.

17

IN HER CAR ONCE MORE, A FEW blocks from Vinyl, Jane stopped at a traffic light. A young woman, crossing the street hand-in-hand with a little boy, approached from the left.

The child might have been six or seven. He bore no resemblance whatsoever to Travis, but Jane could not stop looking at him.

As woman and child passed in front of the Ford, the boy cupped a hand over his mouth as though shielding a cough. By the time they reached the sidewalk at the nearer corner, he seemed to be wheezing. His worried mother ushered him to a bus-stop bench and rummaged through her purse. She withdrew an inhaler of the kind used by asthmatics, and the boy accepted it eagerly.

The traffic light had changed to green without Jane realizing it. The driver of the Chevrolet crew-cab pickup behind her tapped his horn to inform her.

As she put down the driver's window and waved the truck around her, she kept staring at the breathless boy, wanting to know he was all right. But the guy in the crew cab evidently had to be somewhere yesterday, and after only two seconds, he laid on his horn as if she should regard it as a siren and clear the way.

The mother had one arm around the boy's shoulders, and when he took the inhaler out of his mouth, he didn't have the throttled look that had contorted his features when he'd first sat on the bench.

In three seconds, Jane would have shifted her foot from brake to accelerator, but the guy in the pickup, with his hand *still* on the horn, eased his vehicle forward until it gently bumped the back of the Ford Escape. A bump, a tap, not hard enough to cause even the slightest damage. But the pickup was jacked high on oversize tires, the Chevy emblem centered in the bottom third of her rear window, and there was no reason—no damn excuse—for him to bully with his monster truck. She put her car in park and set the emergency brake and opened the driver's door and got out into the street.

There were two men in the crew cab, both in the front seat. The driver let up on the horn as she got out of the car, then blasted her again. She stood staring up at him, in the grip not of personal anger but of fierce indignation.

She wondered how it could be possible that this jackass could be capable of such petty impatience hardly more than a day after the grisly horror on the Philadelphia expressway, one day after hundreds of fellow Americans had been torn limb from limb by the crashing jet and burned alive on their morning commute. She started walking toward the pickup.

The driver reversed, shifted into drive, swung the pickup into the adjacent lane, and accelerated around her as the specimen in the passenger seat called her stupid and shouted the C word and thrust his middle finger at her as if to curse her with some mortal blight.

Jane walked behind her Ford to the mother and child on the bus-stop bench. She said, "Is he okay?"

Wide-eyed and clearly shaken, the woman said, "What? Benny, you mean? Yes, he's all right. Benny's okay. He'll be fine."

Jane realized that the mother's current anxiety was not so much related to her son's condition as to the altercation that had taken place in front of her. These days, no one could know with certainty whether such a minor incident might escalate into real and terrible violence, with collateral damage. Perhaps as much as the driver of the pickup, Jane shared responsibility for this woman's fear.

She said, "I'm sorry. That shouldn't have happened. I'm sorry. It's just that . . ." But she could find no way to explain her own anguish at Travis's vulnerability and the distance that separated her from him. "I'm sorry," she repeated, and returned to the car.

Two blocks later, she pulled off the street and parked in the lot of a strip center with ten or twelve shops.

Her brief loss of control troubled her. No one enduring long-term stress and under a death threat could be faulted for letting the gears slip now and then, but she expected more of herself.

Part of her problem was sleep deprivation. She hadn't slept more than six hours a night, sometimes four, in the past week.

The busiest enterprise in the strip center was the packaged-liquor store. She wasn't much of a drinker. A little red wine now and then. She had only turned to vodka since being on the run, and only when too many bad nights piled up one after another; sometimes she needed sleep even at the expense of sobriety.

She went to the liquor store and bought a pint of Belvedere for later, after dinner, if the dark would not descend when she closed her eyes, if even behind lowered lids, memories of Nick bloomed as bright and full of motion as if they were events of the moment, if Travis was there in brightness as well, in a sun-seared place where slavery yet lived and children were sold into unthinkable service.

18

JANE DROVE WEST, THROUGH suburb after suburb, until she was far from the community in which she had earlier taken a motel room. It was unlikely that the people looking for her would be able to get a fix on her while she conducted these next bits of business. But if they located her, when their search team turned up, she would be clear of the area, and they would be nowhere near the motel where she had gone to ground.

She curbed the car under a street tree, near the Canoga Park Senior Citizen Center, and switched off the engine.

Less than two hours of daylight remained. The air was dry, and the sunshine seemed to splinter down through it, bright slivers piercing polished surfaces.

In addition to a pair of disposable cell phones in her luggage back at the motel, she had two in the car's glove box. They had been purchased on different days in different towns. All of them had been previously activated; none had yet been used.

She took a phone from the glove box and called Sidney Root's cell in Chicago. He answered on the third ring.

She had asked him to review his wife's schedule to see if Eileen had attended any other conference or overnight event shortly before she had been at the

Harvard conference where she had suffered the migraine.

"I don't see how it could mean anything," Sidney said, "but a week before the Harvard conference, she was two days in Menlo Park, interviewing Shenneck for a newsletter her nonprofit publishes."

"Menlo Park, California?"

"Yes. Shenneck's laboratories are there. You've heard of him?"

"No."

"Bertold Shenneck. He's racked up just about every important science prize except the Nobel."

"Would you spell his name for me?"

Sidney spelled it. "He's on the cutting edge—he *is* the cutting edge—when it comes to designing brain implants to eventually help people with motor neuron diseases, like later-stage ALS patients with locked-in syndrome. Amyotrophic lateral sclerosis."

"Lou Gehrig's disease," she said.

"That's right. Eileen was quite impressed with him."

The green tongues of the overhanging tree trembled in a mild breeze, and shadows licked at the scattered morsels of sunlight that glimmered on the windshield.

"The two nights—where did Eileen stay?"

"I thought you might ask. I've become accustomed to your FBI way of thinking, though it seems unduly suspicious. She stayed at the Stanford Park Hotel. About half a mile from Stanford University. I've been there once myself. It's a lovely place."

"You've visited Dr. Shenneck's lab?"

"No, this was a few years ago. I was in the area to present a bid on an architectural project."

"Do you know where your wife ate dinner?"

"The first night at the Menlo Grill, which is in the hotel. I ate there myself and recommended it to her."

"And the second night?"

"Along with a few other people, she was a guest for dinner at Dr. Shenneck's home. She found him and his wife very charming."

"This was a week before the migraine she had at the Harvard conference."

"Eight or nine days before the migraine."

"Her first and only migraine," Jane noted.

"I understand the need for a detective to question everything, but I can assure you Dr. Shenneck will lead you nowhere."

"On what grounds can you assure me of that, Sidney?"

"On the grounds of his accomplishments. He's a humanitarian. There's nothing nefarious about him. It's laughable to think so."

"You're probably right. Thank you for your time, Sidney. I can't imagine I'll be bothering you again."

"Oh, you've never been a bother. I understand your obsession, the grief that drives it. I hope you find acceptance and peace."

"You've been kind," she said. "And I'd enjoy talking with you again. But though it might be only my FBI way of thinking, I'd bet almost anything that there's a third ear on this call, in addition to yours and mine. Just one thing. In the last year, did you ever go to a conference with your wife and stay overnight?"

"No. In our personal lives, Eileen and I were as tight as two people ever were, but our professional lives were worlds apart."

"I'm relieved to know it. Relieved for you. Good-bye, Sidney."

After switching off the phone, she cruised a nearby residential area until she found a house under construction, a Dumpster standing at the curb. Although she had burned through only a fraction of the minutes that came with the phone, she chose not to risk its further use. From her open window, she tossed it into the open Dumpster and drove away.

She headed for Pierce College, which was only a few miles away and no doubt boasted a good library with Internet access.

19

AT PIERCE COLLEGE, SHE BOUGHT a parking pass from a dispenser. Numerous trees—oaks, conifers, ficuses—graced the lovely campus.

No demonstrations were under way in support of one utopian vision or another. Good. College and university libraries were problematic if she might be delayed by angry placard-bearing crowds and in danger of being captured on camera by the media that raced to cover such events regardless of their frequency.

With its dramatic clock tower and massive canti-levered roof over the main-entrance stairs, the li-brary was a bold and handsome structure. The computer lab lay in the northwest corner of the ground floor, at the moment deserted.

She sat in the back row of workstations, where no one could sit behind her.

Dr. Bertold Shenneck proved to be a big deal. His name came with so many links that she would need weeks to read everything that had been written about him.

She went to the Shenneck Technology website, a trove of data. There were numerous videos featur-ing Shenneck, crafted to explain aspects of his work and to elicit multimillion-dollar grants from govern-ment and industry.

In the most recent one, Shenneck was a youngish-looking fifty-year-old with a full head of dark hair, the face of a kindly uncle, and a smile as appealing as that of any of the more benign Muppets. If he was an intellectual giant, he was also a superb salesman whose enthusiasm for the potential of biotechnol-ogy would be contagious when he was pitching his plans to the captains of industry and to politicians who controlled the biggest purse strings.

The computer-lab door opened. A man entered.

Early thirties. Clean but tousled hair, a carefully crafted disarrangement. Tall. A tan so even it had to have come from a machine. One of those laser-bleached smiles.

He wore an upscale blue sport coat with a somewhat loose cut, leaving room for a weapon if he was licensed to carry. A chambray shirt with the tail out. Pale-gray chinos. Rubber-sole Rockports instead of loafers or other leather-sole shoes. Rockports provided excellent traction if you had to move fast and chase someone down. Jane usually wore Rockports. This guy had the right look for a certain kind of undercover assignment.

She did not return his smile. She focused again on the computer screen, but she remained aware of him with her peripheral vision.

He went to the workstation at the farther end of the row that she had chosen.

Reading descriptions of the other Shenneck videos, Jane settled on one that mentioned light-sensitive proteins, reading-out brain implants, and thought-translation software. It covered the same ground as the TV story she'd seen while waiting in bed for Nick, six days before his death. In fact, she suspected Bertold Shenneck had been one of several researchers who appeared in that news piece, for his face had looked vaguely familiar to her in the previous video.

The hope-filled story of brain implants that would one day allow mute patients to *think* what they wanted to say and have their thoughts become speech through a computer had remained with her the past four months. She'd thought it stuck in her memory because it was the last thing she'd seen on TV that night before Nick had come to bed, raised her hand to his lips, and said, *You rock me.*

At the farther end of the row, the newcomer hadn't yet powered up his computer.

He made a call on his smartphone. His voice was so low that Jane couldn't make out a word. The call was at most a minute long.

She was acutely conscious of time passing, but she did not believe she could already be in danger. The conspirators who seemed to be able to identify her explorations of sensitive websites, who seemed to be able to track-to-source the computer she was using, might be on to her right now if Shenneck was somehow related to the increase in suicides. But they couldn't possibly get here and take her down mere minutes after she logged on to Shenneck Technology.

Yesterday, she had told Gwyn Lambert that she was going to see someone in the San Diego area, so the hunters had been given a few hours to seed their people at key points in the metropolitan maze. She was not nearly as vulnerable today.

She quickly scanned the descriptions of Bertold Shenneck's many videos. When she saw the words NANO-MACHINE BRAIN IMPLANTS AND THE POTENTIAL TO CONTROL LIVESTOCK FOR MORE EFFICIENT HUSBANDRY, her interest was piqued, and she clicked on that selection.

At the end of the row, Rockport Man made another phone call.

The video that Jane selected began. With his usual avuncular charm, compelling presentation, and authoritative voice, Bertold Shenneck pitched a futuristic—though soon achievable—system for livestock monitoring and control. Nano-machines were constructed of a minimal number of molecules, invisible to the human eye. Programmed like computers, they could be injected in tiny units that self-assembled into a network once inside the animal. If they weren't self-replicating, only self-assembling, they wouldn't endanger the body by consuming its carbon to make more of themselves. They would be perpetually powered by tapping a host animal's own electrical activity. The nano-machines could monitor and transmit details of the animal's health, could even identify a communicable disease when it was still limited to a few individuals in the population. Through such technology, poultry flocks and cattle herds and other animals could be controlled to eliminate fighting as well as stampedes and other panic responses that led to stock deaths and damage.

"Excuse me," said the man at the other computer.

Jane turned her head, met his eyes.

"Are you a student here?"

"Yes," she lied.

"What's your major?"

"Child development. Excuse me, but I don't want

to miss anything in this video." She returned her attention to the screen.

Assume a third ear had been listening to her and Sidney Root.

Assume they figured she was still somewhere in California.

Assume Bertold Shenneck was up to his neck in this.

Assume that just fifteen minutes after she terminated the call to Sidney, her enemy's security software alerted them to a search of Shenneck Technology's website from a Pierce College workstation.

If those assumptions were correct, depending on the extent of their resources, especially if they were able to call on a spectrum of government agencies for manpower, they might reach her sooner than she, even in the worst throes of paranoia, thought possible.

She watched the screen with her head turned slightly to her right, keeping Rockport Man in sight just enough to know if he suddenly rose from his chair.

Still facing her, he had not yet turned on his computer.

Bertold Shenneck, using a pack of forty white mice with nano-machine brain implants, provided a vivid visualization of how a herd of larger animals might one day be managed more efficiently. Turned loose in a room, the mice raced helter-skelter. When a technician at a computer keyboard transmitted a command to the implants, the mice froze all in the same instant. As other commands were given, the forty rodents moved as one in the same direction, wall to wall and back again; formed into single file and circumnavigated the test room; came together into four groups of ten each and went to the corners and waited for whatever was required of them next.

The video ended a minute after the mice. She was grateful for that. She had seen enough to be iced to the bone, a chill so deep it couldn't be soothed by warm air, hot coffee, or anything but time.

When Jane logged off, Rockport Man said, "Friends call me Sonny. What's your name?"

"Melanie," she lied.

"You sure have a look, Melanie. Edgy but stylin'."

She had all but forgotten the purple wig and eye shadow and West Hollywood clothes.

"I like your look. You in your second year or first?" he asked.

Getting up from her computer, she said, "First."

He rose to his feet as well.

As the guy reached under his jacket with his right hand, Jane reached under her open biker's jacket to the Heckler & Koch.

Instead of a gun, he produced a long ID wallet of the kind that might have contained a badge. From it, he took a business card. "My people and I were meeting with the director of library services about using the library as a location. Film location." He held out the card.

Her clutched stomach relaxed. Acid eased back down her throat but left a bitter taste. She withdrew her hand from her jacket and picked up her purse.

When she showed no interest in the card, he approached, holding it out to her.

"I'm not into movies," she said.

"When opportunity knocks," he said, "it doesn't cost anything to listen." He had a killer smile—or thought he did. "Anyway, it doesn't have to be about business."

"I'm married."

As she turned away, he said, "Me, too. Second wife. Life is complicated, huh?"

She faced him again. His bleached teeth looked radioactive. "Yeah," she said. "Complicated. Damn complicated."

"Take the card. Look at the name. You'll know it. What've you got to lose? Make a new friend. Nothing more. A quiet dinner."

That damn bitter acid taste.

Purse slung over her left shoulder, she reached under her jacket with her right hand and drew the pistol and held it at arm's length, a foot from his face, as steady as if she were a statue carved in stone.

His chambray shirt had a gray warp and a green weft, and both colors seemed to flush his face under the machine-smooth tan. He was either unable to find words or unable to speak.

She couldn't believe what she was doing. She couldn't stop herself from doing it.

"For dinner," she said, "let's say we put an apple in your mouth, bury you in a pit of hot coals, and have a luau later."

He needed to make an effort to speak. "I . . . I have two children."

"Glad for you, sorry for them. Back up and sit down."

He backed into the chair at the computer that he had not used.

"You sit there five minutes, Sonny. Five full minutes. You come after me, I'll spare those two kids the ongoing misery of a rotten father. Are we clear?"

"Yes."

She holstered the pistol. She turned her back on him. It was a test, and he passed it, remaining in the chair.

At the door, as she went out of the room, she turned off the lights. Darkness was conducive to contemplation.

20

SHE DROVE FROM SUBURB TO suburb, the lowering sun orange behind her, the shadow-filled world tilting all its distorted silhouettes eastward.

More than once, when she stopped at a red traffic light, she adjusted the rearview mirror to look into the reflection of her eyes. She didn't see crazy yet, but she wondered if it was coming.

She had long thought of herself as a rock. But

rock, too, could fracture. Under enough pressure, even granite crumbled, decomposed.

Pulling her gun on that asshole Sonny had been stupid. He might have reacted recklessly. Someone might have walked into the room as she was drawing down on him.

She told herself that the problem arose from too little sleep. She needed a long night of rest. If there were bad dreams that woke her, well, she would have to roll over and give herself to them for whatever rest nightmares allowed.

She couldn't bear the thought of eating in a restaurant, of ordering from a waiter, of smiling at the busboy, of listening to the table talk of other customers.

Some days she grew sick of people, maybe because she had to interact with too many of the wrong kind. She recalled the mother and the asthmatic boy on the bus bench, a friendly salesclerk in West Hollywood, but they weren't enough to bring balance to the day.

She cruised in search of takeout for dinner and found a deli that wasn't a plastic-and-plain-bread franchise. A reuben sandwich that weighed nearly a pound. A dill pickle, huge and fragrant. A quarter pound of champagne cheese for dessert and two bottles of Diet Coke filled the bag.

At the motel, after she filled the ice bucket in the vending-machine alcove, she locked her door and closed the draperies.

She stripped off the leather jacket. Removed the

purple wig and brushed out her hair. Washed off the eye shadow and purple lipstick.

She looked tired. She did not look defeated.

There was a clock-radio on one nightstand. She couldn't locate a classical-music station and settled for one playing oldies. Taylor Dayne's "Love Will Lead You Back."

A small round table allowed dining for two. She sat across from the empty chair, put her pistol on the table, unpacked the deli bag.

In a motel glass, she mixed Coca-Cola and vodka over ice. The sandwich was delicious.

The deejay promised three hits by the Eagles, no commercial interruptions. The first was "Peaceful Easy Feeling."

Jane was overcome by a yearning as sharp as a razor's edge. At first she thought her longing was for Nick. But though she missed him every day, she was too practical to pine so intensely for what could never be. And though she longed for Travis, this wasn't about her boy, either. She yearned for home, a place of the heart where she belonged, which was almost as useless as wishing Nick's death could be undone, for she had no home anymore and no prospect of one.

21

SHE LEFT A WAKE-UP CALL FOR
6:30 and then sat in an armchair in the dark, the only
light a bone-white blade that stabbed out of the
bathroom through the gap between door and jamb.
Drinking vodka-and-Coke, listening to the radio,
she thought about Bertold Shenneck up there in
Menlo Park, south of San Francisco. On the edge of
Silicon Valley if not in it. The kingdom of tech miracles. She expected she would dream of regimented
mice, and most likely worse.

A busy day ahead. For starters, meeting Jimmy
Radburn in Palisades Park and getting out of there
alive with the information he brought her.

Not yet drunk, she dared not drink any more. She
undressed, went to the queen-size bed, and tucked
the pistol under the pillow that would have been
Nick's.

She lay listening to the radio, which had begun to
deliver a Bob Seger triple-play. "Still the Same" was
all right, but when the second number was "Tryin'
to Live My Life Without You," she had to turn off the
radio. These days, certain music, certain books, certain words had meanings for her that they'd never
had before.

Although she was troubled by strange dreams,
she seldom woke. When she did ascend briefly from
sleep, it was to the dire serenade of sirens waxing

and waning, more sirens than would have pierced the suburban peace only a decade or two earlier, as though some wicked master of a form of origami akin to quantum mechanics spent the night folding the evils of the world into places that had once been less afflicted by them.

22

JIMMY RADBURN IN THE HELL that is reality.

A warm day for March, sweat prickling the back of his neck and trickling out of his underarms. Sky clear blue, ocean a reflection of it, sun glare flashing off the water and between the trees and cutting at his eyes. Waves breaking softly and pushing onto shore the odor of decaying seaweed. None of it as vivid and enthralling and welcoming as any virtual-reality construct.

Under the trees, Palisades Park green and populated by fools on roller skates and idiot runners and girls dressed in Lululemon doing impromptu Pilates on the grass.

Damn seagulls shrieking. Crows perched on the backs of benches, on trash cans, on fence posts, crapping everywhere they sit. He hates birds. One day he is going to retire to a place that has no birds.

Once when Jimmy Radburn was nine years old,

a bird in flight dropped a shit bomb on his head. People laughed, he was humiliated, and he never forgot. Jimmy never forgets any offense, never, no matter how far in the past it lies or how minor its nature.

Jimmy Radburn has used that name only for five years. He lives so intensely in this identity, however, that he can rattle on for hours about Jimmy's childhood, every bit of it invented as he talks, and within a few days of having created a new piece of Jimmy's storied past—such as the bird disrespecting his head—he comes to believe it is true.

This ability to believe his own lies is of great value in his chosen work as a cracker and cyberspace pirate. In this brave new digital world, reality is plastic, and your identity is whatever you wish it to be. As is your future: Wish it, build it, live it.

He carries a packed briefcase in each hand, a metallic helium-filled balloon tied to his left wrist and floating six feet above his head. Because the balloon isn't for a special occasion such as a birthday, the sonofabitch florist gave him one that says in big red letters HAPPY HAPPY. Moronic. He is embarrassed by the balloon.

The purple-haired bitch, Ethan Hunt, whatever her real name is, comes into his life like a bad wind, blows it apart. She's right about the infinity transmitters sleeved on his phone lines. So if he's able to break down his operation and move it before the FBI realizes he's ghosting away from them, she will have saved him from prison. But he hates her none-theless, because she embarrassed him in front of his crew. Ever since that bird dropped a shit bomb on Jimmy Radburn's head twenty-one years earlier, anyone who embarrasses him earns his undying enmity, even though bird and bomb are imaginary.

Besides, because of her aversion to thumb drives, because she's "gone primitive," the heavy briefcases of printouts are killing him as he walks north on the park path from Broadway.

Some of the girls skating past or running past in shorts and halter tops are worthy of Jimmy's romantic interest, but none will give him a second look because now his face shines with perspiration and the sweat stains on his shirt are epic. It is simply a fact of Jimmy that he doesn't have the buffed look that can make sweat sexy.

He perseveres with a smile because he has a surprise for the bitch in the form of his partner in Vinyl, Kipp Garner, the money man who financed their enterprise.

She'd been right when she'd said Jimmy didn't have it in him to kill. He has a long list of bastards he would greatly *enjoy* killing, but he doesn't have the stomach for wet work.

On the other hand, Kipp Garner, a mountain of muscle, has a taste for violence. Maybe he was born twisted. Or maybe in order to pump ever greater amounts of iron, he mainlines so many steroids and testosterone supplements that sex alone can't tame the beast in him, so he needs the release of stomping someone now and then.

Even through the wireless receiver in Jimmy's right ear, Kipp's voice rumbles like distant thunder: *"You're almost to Santa Monica. You see her?"*

The tiny microphone that appears to be a collar button is wired under Jimmy's shirt to a battery-powered transmitter the size of a pack of gum in his right pants pocket. "She said somewhere between Broadway and California Avenue. The bitch will make me lug this shit all the way to California. And she won't have purple hair."

Kipp says, *"Of course she won't have purple hair."*

"I'm just sayin' I might not recognize her."

"You were hot for her, right?"

"Yeah."

"You were very hot for her."

"Yeah."

"Then you'll recognize her."

An old homeless guy like a shrunken and misplaced yeti, wearing a backpack, toting a trash bag bulging with belongings, shambles into Jimmy's path. "Give a dollar to a Vietnam vet?"

"You were never in Vietnam," Jimmy says. "Get away from me or I'll cut your tongue out and feed it to one of those stinking seagulls."

23

AT 11:55, STARTING AT CALIFOR-
nia Avenue, Kipp Garner swaggers slowly along the
fence that protects park visitors from tumbling
down the Palisades and onto Pacific Coast Highway.
To his right, the sea is shot with sunlight, like a sheet
of hammered steel, and to his left, beyond the narrow park, traffic surges on Ocean Avenue.

He wears black-and-white Louis Leeman sneakers, NFS ripped-and-repaired jeans, and an NFS
palm-print T-shirt that is almost tested to destruction by his shoulders, biceps, and pecs. Encircling a
wrist the size of some men's forearms, a Hublot
column-wheel watch in blue Texalium alloy, one of a
limited edition of five hundred, virtually shouts
power and money at any eye that beholds it.

Only on rare occasions does Kipp Garner carry a
handgun, and he isn't packing one now. His best
two weapons are his mind and body, though today,
tucked in one pocket, he also has a chloroform-
soaked rag in a Ziploc plastic bag to ensure the
woman doesn't struggle.

For the past hour and a half, spread across three
blocks from California Avenue to Santa Monica Boulevard, six of his people have occupied assigned positions in anticipation of a rendezvous between
Jimmy and the woman. Two appear to be college
kids with textbooks, studying while catching some

rays. One is on a woven-reed mat on the grass, practicing yoga. Another tries to flog Seventh-Day Adventist literature to passersby. Two in park-maintenance uniforms trim shrubbery as best they can. Four of them are men, two women, all carrying chloroform-soaked rags, and three are armed with pistols.

Parked at intervals along the west side of Ocean Avenue, next to the park, are six SUVs. Wherever the takedown occurs, one of those vehicles will be close enough to assure that they can convey the woman into it without too much of a scene.

On this first warm day of March, most people out and about are *not* in Kipp's crew. Dedicated runners are making time all the way from the Santa Monica Pier to the upper end of Will Rogers State Beach and back again, a six-mile round trip. People are walking dogs. Young lovers stroll hand in hand.

There is as well the usual human debris: two ragged alkies toting everything they own, destined to spend the night in a drunken sleep, hidden in nests of park shrubbery; a long-haired stripped-to-the-waist blue-jeaned pothead so anorexic and pale that he shouldn't take off his shirt even alone in the shower, sitting on a bench playing the guitar so indifferently that Kipp wants to take the instrument away from him and smash it. . . .

Jimmy, a born worrier and complainer, frets that a lot of people means too many witnesses. But as smart as he might be about computers, Jimmy is ignorant about the finer points of physical assault and kidnapping. The more people in the park, the more they will be distracted by one another, oblivious to what Kipp and his crew do to the woman. And when the action starts, more people means greater confusion, which assures fewer *reliable* witnesses.

Kipp carries with him a small pair of powerful binoculars. He uses them every couple minutes, sweeping the park to his left and ahead, what he can see of it among the trees, checking on his people and anticipating a first glimpse of Jimmy Radburn.

Through the receiver tucked in Kipp's right ear comes the voice of Zahid, one of the guys pretending to be a college student deep in his textbook. *"Jimmy's approaching me, a third of a block north of Santa Monica. Looks like he's wimping out."*

"Eat me," Jimmy says. *"Should've packed these freakin' bags with Styrofoam."*

Kipp says, "You wouldn't sweat, and the lack of weight would be obvious. Anyway, if this goes wrong, she gets the bags, nothing's in them—then she'd gas us with one phone call. Shut up and sweat."

He doesn't necessarily intend to kill the woman calling herself Ethan Hunt. He'll squeeze her, learn how the gutsy bitch got the information she needed to make them dance to her tune, understand why she's interested in all those autopsies and the dude named David James Michael. Then he'll either waste her or not. If not, he'll isolate her while they ease their operation out of the Vinyl space without alerting the FBI, then release her. If she's as hot as Jimmy says, he will give her a lot of Kipp Garner to remember before he lets her go.

Little more than halfway between Wilshire and Arizona, which both terminate in Ocean Avenue, Kipp turns from the Palisades railing, moving farther into the park, to be better able to see through the clusters of trees. He stops and glasses the way ahead.

Here comes Jimmy, lugging the stuffed briefcases, metallic balloon mirroring the sun and bobbing over his head. He's nearing Alika, where she's peddling religious tracts with few takers.

Kipp doesn't see any bitch, with or without purple hair, hot enough to match Jimmy's description. That doesn't mean she isn't here, because Jimmy is a horndog who will jump a goat if it happens to be the only female available when he needs one, a fantasizer who will, in the telling, turn the goat into first runner-up in the Miss Universe contest.

Then something unexpected happens.

24

THE RATHER PLAIN SEVEN-story hotel with some Art Deco details stood across from Palisades Park. The entrance gave it a needed element of style: Six steps flanked by stainless-steel railings coiled to form newel posts led to a portico

where marble columns supported a curved architrave under which stood a pair of polished-steel-
and-glass doors flanked by panels of art glass etched
with a scene of egretlike birds standing in the suggestion of water.

At the moment, the doors were closed, and Jane
stood behind one of them, watching the park on the
farther side of Ocean Avenue.

Outside, on the portico, stood a doorman-valet
dressed in black except for a white shirt, waiting for
the next arriving guest. He was also helping Jane by
keeping an eye on the park to the south, which was
out of her line of sight.

She had turned in her service pistol when she'd
gone on leave, and she'd been supposed to turn in
her FBI credentials, too. She intentionally kept them.
Her section chief, Nathan Silverman, didn't chase
her for them right away, maybe because she was one
of his most successful investigators and he expected
her to be tough enough to deal with her grief and
return in a few weeks, instead of months. Or maybe
he put a pin in it also because they had great mutual
respect and were friends to the extent that the difference in their ranks, ages, and genders allowed. By
the time he might have insisted on having her ID,
she'd been two months out of action, had sold her
house, filed a request for leave extension, and gone
underground.

She assumed that her current status with the Bureau was either problematic or nonexistent.

Nevertheless, because she had little choice, she

had presented her credentials to the hotel manager, a gracious woman named Paloma Wyndham, asking for cooperation in a minor sting operation. Paloma agreed to allow her to conduct surveillance of the park from the lobby, which was not busy because the hotel had only sixty luxury suites, no single or double rooms.

She had offered to have her section chief in Washington speak to the manager, which was where it could have fallen apart. But she knew that even in the current politically charged atmosphere, when people were encouraged to distrust or even openly disrespect law enforcement, the FBI was one of the few—perhaps the only—federal agencies for which most Americans still had respect. Because Jane was supposedly using the hotel only as a point from which to conduct surveillance for an hour, the manager merely Xeroxed the ID and asked her to check back when her work was concluded.

In fact, if Jimmy Radburn did not play according to the rules of their agreement, there might be more action within the hotel than Jane had led Paloma to believe. She had walked the premises earlier in the morning and knew how best to use the place.

From his post on the portico, the doorman-valet turned to Jane and gave her one thumb up, indicating that he had seen the man with the metallic balloon approaching from the southern end of the park, beyond her line of sight.

25

SWEATING, THIRSTY, WISHING
he'd remembered to coat his face with sunscreen because he burned easily, muttering to himself about
the weight of the briefcases, Jimmy arrives at a small
grove of huge trees that canopy the walkway. He
still doesn't see anyone who might be the slut who
turned his life upside down, and there are two long
blocks until he will reach California Avenue, by
which time he will probably be dehydrated and on
death's doorstep.

From nowhere, like a demon conjured, the rag-
and-bone creature that had claimed to be a Vietnam
veteran comes in a shrieking fury, having dropped
his trash bag of belongings and shed his backpack,
now assaulting Jimmy with bony fists like clenched
talons. "Cut out old Barney's tongue, feed it to a
seagull, will you? I'll stab out your eyes *and eat 'em
myself!*" He is all filthy crusted clothes and tangled
hair and bristling beard, wild-eyed and yellow-
toothed, spraying spittle with each threat, spittle
that no doubt carries with it diseases beyond counting.

Jimmy drops the briefcases to engage in self-
defense, slapping ineffectually at the old man, not
for the first time proving himself the furthest thing
from a gladiator. The walking scarecrow has too little substance to be a danger to a grown man, but he

rocks Jimmy on his heels before scrambling backward, spitting and cursing and stamping his feet like Rumpelstiltskin in the fairy tale that had made Jimmy, as a child, wet his bed when his mother read it to him.

The craziness seems to be over, but it isn't. Along the walkway comes a fiftyish, helmeted, roller-skating Amazon in black Spandex shorts and a canary-yellow sports bra. She spins into an abrupt halt and snatches up both briefcases.

She's tanned, solid, hard-muscled, grinning with disdain. He calls her what he thinks she is—"Gimme those, you freakin' dyke"—and he reaches to take back one of the briefcases. She executes a Roller-Derby maneuver, digs the rubber toe stop of one skate into the pavement, balancing on her left leg like a ballerina, and kicks him in the balls with her other skate.

Jimmy buckles at the hips, at the knees, and folds down to the ground, making a sound like a thin stream of air escaping a valve under extreme pressure. Although his eyes blur with tears, he sees Alika drop her Seventh-Day Adventist pamphlets and reach into the satchel at her feet, where she stowed a pistol. Gunfire will draw cops, but he wants Alika to shoot the dyke anyway.

What happens instead is that the Roller-Derby queen spins in a full circle, maybe twice, swinging one of the briefcases as if it's a discus and she's going to throw it, except that she slams it into Alika's head, knocking her to the ground, unconscious.

And the crazy bitch is off, from the park walkway across the grass, onto the public sidewalk along Ocean Avenue, to the corner and into the street at the crosswalk. She gets a horn blast from a Honda coming out of the side street and turning south on Ocean, but the light is with her as she skates away, carrying the briefcases.

26

JANE HAD HOPED THAT JIMMY would pull no tricks, that he would give the briefcases to Nona and walk away. But she had prepared for the likelihood that, after she had saved him from prison, he would prefer to pay her back with a kick in the head. These cyberspace cowboys thought of themselves as masters of the universe, and they resented being one-upped.

She had been in the park from eight o'clock till ten, studying the regulars, from the ragged panhandlers to the fitness fanatics. Her years of experience in the Critical Incident Response Group had given her the tools to analyze the candidates for an improvised crew of her own; and a ready supply of cash made it possible to induce them to help her.

She didn't like using people this way. They didn't mind being used, but their willingness didn't excuse her. Something could go wrong. Someone could be hurt, crippled, killed. But like everyone else, she had priorities. Her priority was her son. She would use anyone to keep him safe and to keep herself alive for him.

At 10:15, an hour and forty-five minutes before her rendezvous with Jimmy, she had been in her car at a meter on the farther side of Ocean Avenue from the park, scanning with binoculars for anything unusual, when the train of SUVs appeared northbound and curbed at intervals between Santa Monica Boulevard and California Avenue. Occupants of the vehicles convened briefly around a hulk who looked as if he had stepped out of a Marvel movie, and then they dispersed.

Maybe they weren't Jimmy Radburn's people, but they were of the type. If they were with Jimmy, Jane was not surprised that they would think being almost two hours early ensured they were in place before she showed up. Evil is unimaginative and lazy.

Now, after the dustup involving Jimmy and the pamphleteer, both briefcases in her possession, Nona skated into the street, and Jane winced when the Honda nearly clipped the woman. She flew across Ocean Avenue, glided up the curb cutout at the corner, climbed the six front steps by toe-walking in her skates, all so fast that Jane barely got the door open in time to admit her to the hotel lobby.

The doorman-valet on the portico looked astonished, and his astonishment increased when from a jacket pocket Jane withdrew a length of chain and a padlock that she bought earlier at a hardware store. She chained together the long vertical handles on the glass doors and padlocked them, so that the hotel could not be entered.

In Nona's wake, the traffic light had changed; and three guys were trying to cross Ocean—one of them the hulk—slowed by the need to dodge impatient motorists.

Brakes squealed and one of the three was knocked off his feet.

Nona had skated past Jane, across the terrazzo floor, past the entrance to the elegant Art Deco bar, into the elevator alcove. When Jane got there, the lift doors were gliding open.

They boarded the car and pushed the button marked GARAGE.

"That rocked," Nona declared.

"Sorry it got hairy."

"More hair, more fun."

"Was Barney hurt?"

"Nah. That old guy's tougher than he looks."

When the doors slid shut and the car started down, Jane thumbed the STOP button. They halted between floors.

She reached into an inner jacket pocket and withdrew a folded heavy-duty forty-five-gallon green-plastic trash bag and handed it to Nona.

As the skater shook open the bag, Jane checked the contents of the briefcases. Printouts packaged in clear, sealed plastic bags.

"I thought it might be money," Nona said as she sat on the floor of the car to pull off her skates.

The lining of the briefcases probably concealed sophisticated transponders, allowing them to be tracked. Dumping the contents into the trash bag, Jane said, "Sorry to disappoint. I never said money."

"Don't keep apologizing. It's been a boring week till now."

Jane jabbed the STOP button again. As the car continued to the garage, she knotted the trash bag with its Smart Tie closure.

Nona was first into the hotel garage, carrying her skates, the wheels clicking together, the bearings tick-tick-ticking.

Pausing only to push 7 on the floor-selection panel, lugging the trash bag, Jane hurried out of the elevator.

The valet-only garage smelled of automotive lubricants and the lime in the concrete and the lingering exhaust fumes of the most recent car to have been ferried in or out. Low ceiling. Inadequate lighting that allowed lurking shadows. Walls with water stains like huge distorted faces and twisted ghostly figures. She thought, *Tomb, catacombs.*

They had been moving fast. But maybe not fast enough.

27

CROSSING OCEAN AVENUE against the light, Zahid is knocked down but not run over by a blue Lexus. Sprawled on the pavement, he waves Kipp and Angelina on toward the hotel, saying, "Go, go, I'm okay."

Kipp doesn't need to be encouraged onward, doesn't care whether Zahid is okay or not, has no intention of stopping to administer first aid. The trap they intended to spring has instead been sprung on them, and a situation gone wrong needs to be made right. They are in a business where business always comes before personnel, with none of that romantic hokum from crime and mafia movies, none of that sentimental shit about family and honor among thieves. In this digital age, people are data troves; their primary value is whatever useful information they have that you need. At the moment, Zahid has no data they need; he has crashed.

When Kipp reaches the hotel, the doorman is standing in front of the entrance, peering into the lobby. Kipp shoves him aside and grabs a handle and discovers that the doors won't open.

For the most part, Kipp Garner is a practical entrepreneur with an orderly approach to life's problems. He isn't a screamer, nor is he given to violent outrage when he does not get his way. He enjoys occasionally beating someone into submission and leaving him with one kind of damage or another that will ensure the guy always fears him, but his targets are strangers met in bars or chanced upon in lonely circumstances. When responsible operation of one of his businesses requires him to kill someone he knows, he performs the task efficiently, with little emotion.

Kipp has engaged in much self-analysis during his thirty-six years, and he knows that his one weakness as a person, his one true fault, is that he cannot control his temper when a woman insults or in some way gets the better of him. Happily, most women sense this about him on first encounter and tread softly in his presence.

But this Ethan Hunt—he glimpsed her briefly and at a distance as she opened the hotel door for her roller-skating accomplice—has played him for a fool. His face burns with embarrassment. A woman has mortified him in front of his people. He feels that his entire crew is secretly laughing at him. Not just his crew. Everyone in the park, the motorists on Ocean Avenue, the scrawny doorman whom he has shoved aside—they are all laughing at him.

When this one fault, this singular weakness, manifests in Kipp Garner, he sometimes loses it and acts irrationally, never for long, for a minute, five minutes. This time, it's a minute or so during which he grips the stainless-steel handles and pulls-pushes, pulls-pushes the hotel doors, shakes them till it seems they will shatter, the padlock knocking against one of the interior handles, the chain rattling against the glass.

The red haze that clouds his thinking is finally penetrated by Angelina's voice. "Big guy! Hey, stud, Mr. Big, you'll want to see this." She is one of the pretend students from the park, the kind of girl who always knows her place. She came across the street with him and Zahid. She's waving her smartphone at him, because she's using an app, one of Jimmy's best, to track the briefcases. "They've gone vertical, big guy."

This app doesn't just map-point the transponder and track it horizontal in any direction. It also has something that Jimmy calls three-dimensional cubic-space signal-awareness processing capacity.

Kipp steps back from the doors and looks up at the hotel. "You mean they're going up?"

"Vertical, yeah," Angelina confirms.

"Up where?"

"Maybe they've got a room here. Otherwise, the roof."

"There's nowhere to go from the roof. They've got a room."

28

THE GARAGE HAD TWO ACCESS ramps, one for inbound vehicles, one for outbound. Jane carried the heavy-duty trash bag containing the research she'd ordered, and stocking-footed Nona carried her skates, and they sprinted up the outbound ramp and into the alley behind the hotel. Jane wouldn't have been surprised to run head-on into some of Jimmy Radburn's best buddies, but at the moment the backstreet was deserted.

The hotel stood at the north of the block, and midway down the alley, on the farther side, lay a large parking lot that served an office building fronting on 2nd Street. The alleyway provided access; ninety minutes earlier, Jane had moved her Ford Escape from a meter on Arizona Avenue to a visitor slot in the parking lot, the closest space to the hotel that she could find.

Racing along the alley with Nona, she expected to hear shouting behind them, but there was none. In the parking lot, she tossed the trash bag into the backseat of her car, and Nona got into the front passenger seat with her skates, and Jane got behind the wheel, and they were out of there, no pursuit visible in the rearview mirror.

29

KIPP APOLOGIZES TO THE DOOR-
man for shoving him aside a moment earlier, and he
folds a hundred-dollar bill into the man's hand.

He and Angelina retreat from the portico to the
sidewalk as Zahid arrives, limping from his encounter with the Lexus, insisting that he is not seriously
injured.

"Apparently they have a room in the hotel," Kipp
says. "They can't stay in there forever. We need to
keep a watch on the front entrance and the back.
Bring a car around to—"

"Big guy," Angelina says, focusing on her smartphone, "they're coming back down."

"What?"

"They were pretty high up, maybe one of the top
two floors. This app isn't perfect on the vertical.
Now they're coming down."

30

AT THE END OF THE ALLEYWAY, Jane turned left on Santa Monica and then right on 4th Street.

Nona Vincent, formerly a sergeant in the United States Army, now retired, on a weeklong vacation alone from South Carolina, said, "That was the most fun I've had in a while. But when I kicked Balloon Guy's *cojones* up to his Adam's apple, I hope I was giving some comeuppance to a bad guy, not a half-way good one."

"All the way bad," Jane assured her.

"I told him I can call myself anything I like, but he can't call me or anyone a dyke. I'm not sure he heard me, 'cause I said it after the kick, when he was off in a world of pain."

"I'm sure he got the message."

When Jane braked for a traffic light at the corner of 4th and Pico, Nona said, "So you're on suspension from the FBI?"

"Yeah," Jane lied. "Like I said before." She hadn't said she was on leave, because she didn't want to have to go into the whole story of Nick's suicide.

"Why did you say you were suspended?"

"I didn't say."

"You don't seem rogue to me."

"I'm not."

"Otherwise, I wouldn't be here now."

"I know. I'm grateful you helped."

The light changed. Jane drove, Pico to Ocean Boulevard.

"What I figure," said Nona, "is you were on some corruption case involving a politician, and the powers that be told you to drop it, and you didn't drop it, so they suspend you till you get your head on straight."

"You're psychic."

"And you're full of shit."

Jane laughed. "Totally."

"But I still think you're a good woman."

Nona was staying at Le Merigot, a Marriott hotel with an ocean view, south of the Santa Monica Pier and maybe half a dozen blocks from where she had roller-skated Jimmy Radburn's testicles. Jane didn't enter the hotel drive, but stopped at the curb, in the meager midday shade of palm trees.

Earlier, she had given Nona Vincent five hundred dollars with a promise of five hundred more. Now she offered the second payment.

"I shouldn't take it. You probably need it more than I do."

"I don't welch."

"I shouldn't take it, but I will." Nona tucked the five hundred into her yellow sports bra. "When I get back home and tell this story to friends, I can always say I refused to take it."

"But you'll tell the truth."

Nona regarded her with uncharacteristic solemnity. "You have a degree in psychology or something?"

"Something. Listen, those guys will probably split the area, but you shouldn't go out skating anymore today, 'cause they sure do hold a grudge."

"It's my last day, anyway. Hotel's got a spa. I'll stay in and allow myself to be pampered."

Jane held out her hand. "Pleasure to meet you."

As they shook hands, Nona said, "When the day comes you're out of whatever mess you're in, call that number I gave you. I'll want to hear the whole damn story."

"Truth is, I'll throw away the number. If the wrong people found it on me, that might not be good for you."

Nona peeled one of the hundred-dollar bills from the wad of five and dropped it in Jane's lap.

Picking up the money, Jane said, "What's this?"

"I'm paying you to memorize the number. If I never hear from you what this is all about, I'll die of curiosity."

Jane pocketed the hundred.

"I'm almost twice your age," Nona said. "When I was growing up back in the Jurassic, I never imagined the world would get so ugly."

Jane said, "I never imagined it ten years ago. Or one."

"Watch your back."

"Best I can."

Nona got out of the car. In her stocking feet, carrying her skates, she walked up the hotel drive.

31

KIPP AND ANGELINA STAND IN the hotel garage. By the elevator. They wait almost fifteen minutes. Neither of them speaks as they wait. Kipp isn't in the mood to talk. Angelina understands his state of mind. As always.

They are simpatico. He trusts her. She never wants to give him a reason not to trust her. He can have any kind of sex with her. Or with other girls. She isn't jealous. She just wants to be the one he trusts most. Not his only girl. His *best* girl. His best friend. If sometimes he needs to hurt her, he can hurt her. One day, she will learn where he keeps his biggest stash of cash, and she will be so trusted that when she shoots him in the back of the head, he will go to Hell thinking some hit man has wasted her along with him.

The hotel doorman has connected them to a bellman. The bell *captain*. Like he's military or something. The elevator pings. The bell captain appears out of it. He doesn't look like a bellman. He looks like a doctor. Wise, very serious. White hair. Wire-rimmed glasses. He says, "There were two empty briefcases in the elevator."

"Where are they?" Kipp asks.

"Ms. Wyndham, she's the general manager, she has them in her office. She says the FBI might want them."

Angelina *feels* Kipp's alarm. A sudden electricity in the air.

He says, "What's the FBI got to do with anything?"

"The lady who was with the roller-skater, she flashed an FBI badge or something at Ms. Wyndham. Ms. Wyndham thinks now it was phony ID, she needs to tell the FBI."

The situation is instantly clear to Angelina. The Ethan Hunt bitch is gone. Her dyke friend is gone. Time to forget them. Let them go. Get out of here.

To Kipp, she says only, "Better melt Vinyl faster than fast."

Kipp blinks at her. He nods. He's always like two seconds behind her.

He gives two C-notes to the bell captain.

The garage is quiet. Lonely.

"A little muscle, too," Angelina advises.

"Yeah," Kipp says, and he takes the bell captain by the throat. Rams him back against the wall. Gets in his face. "You never saw either of us. You never talked to either of us. You understand?"

The bell captain's voice is choked off. He can only nod.

"You say a word about us, I'll find you one night and cut your nose off and feed it to you. Same for the doorman. You tell him."

The red-faced bell captain nods. His eyes bulge. His mouth is an O as he sucks for breath. He doesn't look like a doctor now. He looks like a red-faced fish. He's nothing in his fancy uniform. He's a big zero. A feeb.

Kipp lets go of the feeb's throat. Throws a punch hard into his gut. The feeb goes to his knees.

Kipp lets the big zero keep the two hundred. It's a way of humbling him. Like saying he took the two hundred to allow Kipp to beat him.

Angelina and Kipp walk away.

Behind them, the feeb vomits on the garage floor.

Angelina will miss this when she kills Kipp. She will miss watching him show people how little they are, how nothing. And watching him hurt them.

32

AT TWO O'CLOCK, AS ARRANGED, Barney was waiting for Jane on Oceanfront Walk, sitting on the platformed steps that led up to the indoor amusement center associated with the Santa Monica Pier. This was where she had first seen him earlier in the day. He was hunched under the weight of his backpack, the trash bag of his worldly goods at his side, staring at the pavement between his feet as though the meaning of life must be written in the concrete shaded by his body.

That morning, by way of introducing herself, she had brought him a breakfast plate from a nearby café, which understandably would have been unwilling to serve him if he had entered in all his ragged splendor, for most of the other customers would have bailed upon his arrival.

He had wondered at her motives, but he'd eaten what she brought him. After fifteen minutes of conversation, she had made her motives clear when she counted five twenty-dollar bills into his hand and told him about a man who would, at noon, walk through Palisades Park with briefcases and with a metallic balloon tied to one wrist.

Barney was not as dirty as he appeared. His hands were careworn but reasonably clean, and in her company he had a few times lathered them with antibacterial gel. His hair and beard bristled as if with a dangerous electrical charge, but they were not matted with filth. She thought that he must shower at a shelter somewhere or else bathe in the sea at night.

His clothes were every bit as dirty as they appeared to be, however, and it was necessary to talk to him at a three-foot remove to avoid being withered and prematurely aged by his horrific breath.

Now she sat on the step he occupied, at the distance needed to avoid his halitosis. "You did a good job in the park."

He raised his bushy head and stared at her from under a tangled hedge of eyebrows, and for a moment it seemed that he did not know who she was. His watery eyes were a pale faded-denim blue, a shade she'd never seen before, and she wondered if too much alcohol and misfortune could have faded them from a darker hue.

Although his eyes didn't clear, awareness rose in them. "Most wouldn't come like they said, but I knew you would."

"Well, I owe you another hundred dollars."

"You don't owe me nothin' but what you want to owe."

"Nona said you scared the hell out of Jimmy."

"The baby-face balloon guy? He's an asshole. Pardon my French. He won't give even just a dollar to a Vietnam vet."

"Are you a Vietnam vet, Barney?"

"How old you think I look?"

She said, "How old do *you* think you look?"

"You're a regular damn diplomat. I think I look seventy-eight."

"I wouldn't argue with you about that."

"What I really am is fifty. Or maybe forty-nine. No older than fifty-one. I was a snot-nosed kid when Vietnam was hot."

From a coat pocket he fished out a bottle of Purell and began to sanitize his hands.

"You use a lot of that stuff," she said.

"I'd drink it by the quart if it did the job on my insides like it does my hands."

"Have you had lunch yet?"

"I don't eat three squares. Don't need 'em."

"Well, I can bring you some lunch from the café. You liked their food at breakfast."

When he squinched his hairy face, he seemed to be looking out at her from shrubbery.

"It won't come out of your hundred," she said, and she gave him five more twenties.

As he tucked the money away, he looked around suspiciously, as if countless thieves were gathered on the stairs behind him, waiting for the chance to turn him upside down and his pockets inside out.

"On the other hand," he said, "I can't abide offendin' a lady."

"What would you like?"

"They have a nice cheeseburger in there?"

"I believe they do. You want fries or something?"

"Just a nice cheeseburger and Seven Up."

She brought the cheeseburger in a take-out bag and a medium 7 Up in a paper cup. "I told them just a little ice."

He surreptitiously mixed part of a pint of whiskey with the soda. "You're a scary woman, the way you know a man's mind."

He didn't talk while he ate. She found it best not to watch.

High above, seagulls performed *ballets blancs*. They cried down the day, and though their voices would have been annoying if issued close at hand, they were otherworldly and haunting from a height.

When Barney finished eating, he said, "You don't have no damn reason to care, but you know what I like most about you?"

"What's that?"

"You give me money without naggin' about spendin' it on drink."

"It's your money now, not mine."

"Not many left who don't lecture about every damn thing."

After he threw away the burger bag and the paper cup, he picked up his trash bag of belongings. "You walk with me just up there past the pier? Till I'm sure no greedy pirate's followin' me?"

"Sure."

They had gone a little way when he said, "I made a whole lot of bad choices in my life, but you know what?"

"What?"

He chuckled. "Give me a chance, I'd make 'em all over again."

He was quiet for a few steps. Then: "It's a beautiful, terrible world, isn't it?"

She smiled and nodded.

"You know what I once was before I was this way? I once was a waiter in a fancy restaurant. Tips were big. Made good money. I once was like a youth counselor and lay minister in my church. I coached a Little League team. I knew baseball like nobody else." He had come to a stop. He regarded the gulls adance in the sun-shot air. "Funny, but most of the time, I can't remember how all that went away."

"It never went away," Jane said. "It's still part of who you are. It always will be."

His stare was clearer now than before. "That's a way of thinkin' about it. And maybe true." He looked back along the path they had followed. "Nobody's lurkin'. I'm safe enough now."

When he looked at her again, a memory from childhood for a moment carried her back twenty years. She had found a bird's nest that some predator must have cast down from tree to lawn. Three small eggs had been clawed and bitten open, their contents eaten. Barney's eyes were not faded-denim blue; they were precisely the pale robin's-egg blue of those sad and broken shells.

"What is it?" he asked.

"What is what?"

"What is it you want to ask?" When she didn't reply, he urged, "Go ahead, whatever it is. Nobody and nothin' offends me anymore."

After a hesitation, she said, "The other people who . . . who live the way you live. Do any of them ever commit suicide?"

"Suicide? Well, you got to set aside half of them, 'cause they're crazy as shithouse rats. Pardon my French. They don't know from suicide 'cause they aren't half sure whether they're alive or already dead. The rest of us? Suicide? Hell, we're clawin' at life every day just to hang on. Unless you mean slo-mo suicide like takes forty years of hooch and tick bites and rotten teeth and sleepin' out on cold nights 'cause I don't want any shelter nanny tellin' me what to do. But that's not suicide. It's more like early retirement and poor man's adventure. God wants to yank me out of here, He's gonna have to pull real hard, I got roots like an oak tree."

She said, "I'm glad to hear it."

Belated understanding softened his life-hardened face. "Who was it of yours who took their own life?"

She was surprised that she told him. "My husband."

For a moment, Barney seemed overwhelmed by this revelation. He opened his mouth but could think of nothing to say. He looked at the gulls far above and then at her again. Tears shimmered in his eyes.

"It's all right," she said. "I'm sorry. I didn't mean to upset you, Barney. I'm dealing with it. I'm okay."

He nodded, worked his mouth soundlessly, nodded again, said at last, "Whyever he might've did it, it never could've been you."

He turned from her and shuffled away, bent under his backpack, carrying his trash bag, hurrying as best he could, as if it must be this very kind of thing, the tragedies of the world, from which he had so long been running.

She called after him, "Roots like an oak tree, Barney."

He raised one arm to wave, indicating that he had heard her, but he never looked back.

33

FROM THE COAST, JANE DROVE Wilshire Boulevard east toward Westwood, the big risks of the day behind her, a smaller risk ahead.

The heavy traffic labored through the sunshine, the drivers aggressive, few conceding equality to others under the rules of the road, with the consequence of stop-and-go progress, much barking of brakes, much bleating of horns.

For some reason, she recalled Bertold Shenneck as he had been in his videos: the kindly face, the appealing smile. And she thought of the mice with brain implants, marching in organized phalanxes, as though to martial music on a parade ground. . . .

The one regret she had about the operation in Palisades Park was that she'd needed to use her FBI credentials to be allowed to scout the hotel thoroughly to determine the best way to use it and to conduct surveillance from inside its front doors.

Paloma Wyndham, the general manager, would perhaps feel that she had been played by an arrogant agent of the Bureau or she would figure that the ID had been forged. In either case, she was all but certain to call the Los Angeles field office to file a complaint or to do her citizenly duty and report an agent impersonator.

The last thing Jane needed was to have the Bureau diligently on her trail in addition to the still-nameless forces determined to put an end to her investigation into the plague of suicides.

Of all buildings opposite the park, the hotel had been by far the best facility to serve as a way station for the transfer of the files from the briefcases to the trash bag, though she'd considered using her Ford instead. She could have parked along Arizona Avenue, a few spaces off Ocean, could have been waiting behind the wheel with the engine running. Nona could have skated to the vehicle. But if Radburn's people were close behind her when she got to the Ford, there would have been no way to delay them—no equivalent of a chain and padlock—to keep them from dragging Nona down.

Besides, if she had used the car, Jimmy and his crew would have seen it and captured the license-plate number. If subsequently the conspirators behind the suicides tracked her to Vinyl and Jimmy, then *they* would know what she was driving, and she would have to abandon the Escape. She didn't have the federal government's deep pockets; she couldn't be tossing away cars every few days.

In Westwood, near UCLA, Jane cruised in search of a house where she had once attended a dinner party. She didn't recall the address; but she knew that she would recognize the place.

In ten minutes, she found it. Georgian architecture. Stately but not immense. A columned front porch without railing. Brick walls painted white.

She parked two blocks away on a parallel street and walked back to Dr. Moshe Steinitz's residence.

Moshe was a forensic psychiatrist, recently re-tired at eighty. He'd had his own psychiatric prac-tice in addition to being a valued professor at UCLA. He had lectured periodically at the FBI Academy in Virginia, and sometimes advised Behavioral Analy-sis Units 3 and 4 on difficult cases involving serial killers.

Three years earlier, Moshe half reasoned and half intuited the answer to why a killer operating in sub-urban Atlanta had cut out and taken away his vic-tims' eyes. That theory led to the capture of one twisted individual, Jay Jason Crutchfield, the very night that he would have murdered an eighth woman.

Jane doubted that a visit to Moshe Steinitz in-volved a large risk. He had stopped lecturing at the Bureau when he retired more than a year earlier. She and the psychiatrist weren't close friends. But he had advised on three of her cases; they liked each other.

She climbed the front steps, rang the bell.

He answered the door in a white shirt, blue bow tie, charcoal dress slacks, and pale-blue Skechers sport shoes with orange laces. He'd always worn Oxfords before. Skechers were retirement gear.

Scowling over reading glasses pulled halfway down his nose, he seemed to be expecting one an-noyance or another, but he smiled when he saw who had come calling. "What a world of wonders," he declared. "If it isn't the girl with eyes bluer than the sky."

"How are you, Dr. Steinitz?"

Taking her arm to escort her over the threshold, he said, "I am very well indeed, and I'm even better now that you have swept in like a fresh breeze."

"I'm sorry I didn't call ahead."

Closing the door behind them, Moshe said, "Then there would have been no surprise, and I enjoy surprises. But what happened to your long lovely golden hair?"

"Cut it, dyed it. Needed a change."

At five feet five, just an inch shorter than Jane but seeming shorter still, Moshe was slightly plump, with a warm smile and sad eyes. His face had been so gently folded by time and so respectfully drawn by gravity that advanced age was, in his case, a grace.

"I hope I'm not interrupting anything," she said.

He looked her over as if assaying a great-grandchild whom he had not seen in months and whose growth he found remarkable. "As you know, I'm retired for a second time, without a profession, with only leisure activities, so of course I'm *desperate* for interruptions."

"I'd be grateful for an hour of your time. I need your thoughts about something."

"Come on, come with, back to the kitchen."

She followed him past the archway to the living room, in which stood a Steinway. Arranged on the lid were silver-framed photographs of Moshe and his late wife, Hanna, with children and grandchildren.

Jane had not known Hanna, who had died nine

years earlier, but when she'd been here for dinner, she'd been cajoled into playing the piano for Moshe and his other guests. She performed two pieces of her choice: Beethoven's "Moonlight Sonata" and Cole Porter's "Anything Goes."

When there had been questions about her father, as there had been all her life, she explained that her mother was the one who encouraged her musicianship, and she turned the questions aside in such a way as to imply that she was most protective of her father's privacy. She'd been aware of Moshe watching her with keen interest during this, and she'd been certain he suspected the true reason for her discretion was darker than she suggested, though he had never broached the subject with her.

Now, a step or two past the living room archway, Moshe stopped and turned to her and put one hand to his mouth as if it had just occurred to him that he had committed a faux pas. "Before I retired, many of the students at the university took great offense if anyone used the word *girl* when referring to a female sixteen or older. I was advised that one must say 'woman.' I hope I didn't offend when I called you a girl there on the doorstep."

"I don't traffic in politically correct bushwah, Moshe. I like being the girl with eyes bluer than the sky."

"Good, good, I'm so glad. One reason I retired the second time is, these days, the more infantile the students, the more seriously they take themselves. They are generally a humorless lot."

In the kitchen, he drew out a chair for her at the dinette table.

"Coffee, tea, soft drink? Perhaps an aperitif? It *is* a quarter to five, only fifteen minutes short of a respectable cocktail hour."

She voted for the aperitif, and he poured two small glasses of Maculan Dindarello.

As he sat down to his drink, Moshe said, "I was shocked and dismayed to hear about Nick. A terrible loss. I'm so sorry, Jane."

Because he had been retired for a year and no longer consulting on Bureau cases, she had assumed that he didn't know Nick was gone.

Jane wondered if Moshe still had active ties with the FBI—and if she had made a grave mistake by coming here.

34

THE FIRST TIME MOSHE STEIN-itz retired, he was sixty-five. Hanna died five years later, and at seventy Moshe went back to work as a practicing psychiatrist, professor, and sometime Bureau consultant.

Upon his second retirement, at seventy-nine, he terminated all three jobs with no intention of returning to any. Or so he said.

He claimed that he knew about Nick only because Nathan Silverman, Jane's boss, emailed him the news when it was a week old.

"By then, I imagined you'd talked about it with so many people, the last thing you needed was to go over it again with me."

"I was grieving and furious at the same time, and didn't know who to be furious with. I wasn't fit to talk to anyone."

"Genuine as it might be," Moshe said, "too much sympathy can start to seem like pity, which only makes the grief more depressing. I asked Nathan to give you my sympathy, tell you to call me if ever you wanted. I'm sorry to hear he didn't pass the message along."

"He might have," Jane said. "There were some things I just wasn't hearing in the first couple weeks after it happened."

In her experience, Moshe was the furthest thing from a liar. She was impelled to trust him.

She sipped the Dindarello and said, "So how's retirement the second time around?"

"I read fiction, which I never had much time for when I worked. Take long walks. Garden, travel a little, poker with some friends who're old coots like me. I futz and fiddle and fart around."

By the time she got to the purpose of her visit and told him about the rising rate of suicides, he had poured a second serving of the aperitif. The sky beyond the window was a deeper shade of blue than before, gathering into it the first few sooty particles of dusk.

She took from her purse the spiral-bound notebook in which she entered coded names and facts pertinent to her investigation. There were also items written in plain English, including the contents of the final statements left by some who had killed themselves. She had collected information on twenty-two suicides, though there had been only ten notes among them.

"I've studied them until they've just become words," she said. "Maybe there's meaning in them I can't see. Maybe you'll see it."

Occasionally she shared the notes with those she interviewed, and a couple of Xeroxes were folded in the notebook.

When she gave a copy to Moshe, he put it facedown on the table. "Please read them to me first. Then I'll look at them. The spoken word and written word are weighted differently. There are nuances you get only by hearing, then seeing, then comparing impressions."

She started with the most personal of the ten. "This one is what Nick left. 'Something is wrong with me. I need. I very much need. I very much need to be dead.'"

Moshe sat in silence for a moment after Jane had read Nick's words. Then he said, "It's not a typical last testament. It doesn't explain his reasons or ask forgiveness. It doesn't say good-bye."

She said, "It's nothing like Nick. It's his handwriting, but otherwise I'd think someone else wrote it and put it with his body."

Closing his eyes and cocking his head as though hearing those eighteen words in memory, Moshe said, "He's saying he's compelled to kill himself, and he knows the compulsion is wrong. A significant percentage of suicides do not think they're doing the wrong thing. If they thought that, they wouldn't do it." He opened his eyes. "What was Nick's state of mind just before . . . ?"

"He was happy. Talking about the future. What he wanted to do when he retired from the Corps. I could read him like a newspaper, Moshe. He couldn't pretend happiness and fool me. Anyway, he was *never* depressed. I was making dinner. He set the table, opened a bottle of wine. Singing along with the music, a Dean Martin album. Nick was totally retro when it came to music. He said he was going to the john, he'd be right back."

"Read another."

She identified the second decedent as a thirty-four-year-old network television executive, highly paid and rapidly advancing in the company. He had left the note for his fiancée, an actress. " 'Do not cry for me. This will be a pleasant passage. I have been told. I am looking forward to the journey.' "

"A man passionate about his religion?" Moshe asked.

"No. As far as anyone knew, he wasn't a believer. He certainly wasn't a churchgoer."

" 'I have been told.' So if not God, if not a Bible or Quran or Torah, who or what told him the passage would be pleasant? The easy inference is that he must have been hearing voices."

"Schizophrenia?"

"Except there's no note of the paranoia, the sense of being oppressed, that characterizes schizophrenics so advanced in their delusions as to be contemplating such a radical solution to their suffering. Family, fiancée, fellow workers—did anyone witness him expressing false beliefs, obvious delusions?"

"No."

"He was in a job requiring communication skills. Did anyone see disorganized schizoid symptoms?"

"Which are what?"

"The most common would be speaking in an apparently normal manner, but his sentences would have no meaning."

"Nobody mentioned that. It's not something they'd forget."

"No, they wouldn't. It's an alarming symptom. How did he die?"

"He lived in Manhattan, on the twentieth floor. He jumped."

Moshe grimaced. "Read another."

The third decedent on her list had been the forty-year-old CEO of one of the largest real-estate development firms in the country. Married. Three children. " 'I'm not supposed to leave a note. But you must know I'm happy to be doing this. It'll be a pleasant journey.' "

"Shared words with the previous one," Moshe said, sitting up straighter in his chair. "*Pleasant.*

Journey. In both, it's implied they're following instructions, or at least some kind of guidance."

Jane quoted from the network executive: " 'I have
been told.' " Then from the real-estate developer:
" 'I'm not supposed to . . . ' "

"Exactly. Was the CEO in New York, maybe in the
same circles as the network executive?"

"No. Los Angeles."

"How did he kill himself?"

"In his garage. A vintage Mercedes. Carbon mon-
oxide poisoning. How likely is it the two notes
would be so similar?"

"Odds against are astronomical. Read another."

This note had been left by a twenty-six-year-old
woman, a gifted software writer who had graduated from a job at Microsoft to an entrepreneurial
partnership with the company. Unmarried. The sole
support of her disabled parents. " 'There is a spider
in my brain. It talks to me.' "

When she looked up from her notebook and met
Moshe's eyes across the table, Jane saw that he had
been as chilled by those words as she had been when
she'd first read them.

"Three out of four seem to hear voices," the psychiatrist said. "But in this fourth instance, as in the
others, the usual hallmarks of paranoid schizophrenia aren't as obvious as you might at first think. In a
classic case, the patient believes the menacing voices
come from outside, from powerful forces that wish
to persecute and deceive him. A spider in the
brain . . . that is new to me."

35

LATE SNOW FELL IN TELLURIDE, the Colorado night breathing softly, so that the storm had no bite, the flakes slanting at the slightest angle, an inch of ermine on the ground, Nature knitting lace on the rough bark of the conifers.

April Winchester shone the flashlight on the massive old hemlock, so tall that the beam could not travel to its uppermost reaches, which disappeared into the dark and snow. It was a tree taller than the night, reaching through the storm, all the way to the stars, a conceit that pleased her and made her smile.

When she brought the light down the trunk, she found their two names, where he had scaled away a section of bark and carved his declaration into the underlying wood. ED LOVES APRIL.

Edward, her Eddie, had always been a romantic. He had carved the same words into the trunk of a red maple in Vermont when they were both fourteen, almost sixteen years earlier.

This latest statement of profound affection had been scored into the hemlock only eleven months ago, when they bought their winter residence outside of Telluride. They were both avid skiers.

Out of season, they lived in Laguna Beach, California. Whether on the warm coast or in the San Juan Mountains, he wrote his novels, and she wrote songs, and the life they had imagined, as teenagers, unspooled with a grace exceeding their most extravagant dreams.

He'd written four novels, all memorable and significant bestsellers. She'd written more than fifty published songs, twenty-two of which, performed by various artists, had risen into the top forty, twelve into the top ten. Four had achieved the coveted number one.

She looked back at the house, a low-profile structure of native stone and reclaimed wood, its exquisite lines harmonizing with the landscape. The first-floor windows were full of warm light, but only Eddie's study was bright on the second floor.

He was powering through the end of a difficult scene and wanted to finish before they made dinner together.

She had been preparing something for him in the kitchen, just had to get away from it for a few minutes, so she'd come out to the hemlock on a whim. She was wearing high-top trainers, not boots, a pleated white silk skirt, and a thin over-the-hips sweater. This eclectic look delighted Eddie and would bring him to bed in full readiness after dinner, but it wasn't suitable to a winter storm.

When she had rushed out of the house, enchanted by the snow, she'd been oblivious of the cold. Now she began to shiver. When she acknowledged the chill, it took a firmer grip on her, and she began to shudder violently.

She hurried back to the house, where she pulled off the snow-caked high-tops and left them in the mudroom. In the kitchen, snow fell from her clothes and hair, melting on the reclaimed wide-plank chestnut floor. She felt that she should care about the melting snow, should wipe it up, but in fact she didn't care.

On the drainboard by the sink was the treat she had prepared for Eddie, to ease him through the final page of the troublesome scene in his novel. On a tray were a plate containing cubes of Havarti cheese and a measure of salted-and-peppered almonds, a wineglass, and a bottle of sauvignon blanc, from which she would pour him a serving after she put everything down on his desk.

Take it to him, take it to him, take it to him. . . .

She enjoyed doing special things like this for Eddie. He was always so appreciative.

Still casting off snow, hair dripping, she carried the tray to the back stairs. She was halfway to the second floor when she made the strangest discovery. She didn't have the tray. She was carrying a knife. A trimming knife.

She stared at it, bewildered. She had not been at the wine while she put together the treat for him. She did have a tendency now and then to be absentminded, but not to *this* extent.

No cheese, no nuts, no wine. Just a trimming knife. How silly. Where had her mind wandered? Well, this would not do, would not do at all.

She returned to the kitchen to get the tray.

36

BEYOND THE KITCHEN WIN-
dows, the sky over L.A. and environs was pure pea-
cockery, fanned with iridescent blues and greens
and smoky orange, a last bright challenge to the inevitable darkness coming.

The fifth decedent on Jane's list was an attorney,
thirty-six, recently appointed to a judgeship on the
Fifth Circuit Court of Appeals. Unmarried. His suicide note had been found in an envelope bearing
his parents' names. He had shot himself in the head.
" 'I love you. You have never failed me. Don't be sad.
I have done this a hundred times in my dreams. It
will not hurt.' "

"This is somewhat more in the tradition of such
notes," Moshe Steinitz said. "In particular, the as-
surances of love, the exemption from blame. But the
rest of it . . . I have never heard of anyone who had
repetitive dreams of suicide."

"Could dreams be programmed?" Jane asked.

"Programmed? What do you mean?"

"Say by a hypnotist, someone using drugs and
subliminal suggestion? Could programmed dreams
be used to somehow make the dreamer actually desire to kill himself?"

"In comic books, perhaps, or movies. Hypnotism
is a better stage act than it is a form of behavioral
modification or control."

The sixth example in Jane's notebook was the message left by Eileen Root, who, before she hanged herself, suggested that she was somehow fulfilling an obligation to an imaginary childhood friend. " 'Sweet Sayso says he's lonely all these years, why did Leenie stop needing him, he was always there for Leenie, now I need to be there for him.' "

"This is the fourth of six who hears voices," Moshe noted. "And there's a definite schizoid quality to an imaginary friend from her childhood resurfacing in the present. Did she mention this Sayso to her husband, to anyone, in the weeks before she killed herself?"

"Apparently not."

"How close were she and her husband?"

"Very close, I think."

"Did he see any signs of disassociation from reality?"

"No."

The seventh note had been written by the forty-year-old vice president of the mortgage division of one of the country's five largest banks. " 'I hear the call, it is ceaseless, waking and sleeping, the soft sweet whisper and the smell of roses.' "

37

APRIL IN THE MUDROOM, STAR-ing at the high-top trainers caked with melting snow . . .

She wanted desperately to return to the red maple and see the proclamation of love that Eddie had carved into it. But the maple was in Vermont, almost sixteen years in the past.

The hemlock, then. She needed to see the hemlock that stood little more than a hundred feet from the house, needed to see it with an urgency like none she had ever known before, as though her very life depended on putting her fingers to the trunk and tracing the letters that he had carved into the wood.

She found herself in the kitchen instead, standing at the sink, looking at the tray on the drainboard: Havarti, almonds, wine.

An unpleasant rhythmic electronic tone drew her attention to the wall-mounted telephone. The handset was lying on the counter.

How long had it been lying on the counter?

Had she called someone? Had she received a call?

She put down the trimming knife. She hung up the phone.

Take it to him, take it to him, take it to him. . . .

April picked up the tray and carried it to the back stairs.

Halfway to the second floor, she made the strangest discovery. She wasn't carrying the tray. In her right hand she gripped a chef's French knife, much larger than the trimming knife. And sharper.

38

IN THE DISTANCE, BLOOD pooled in the lower sky, red light as lustrous as the stuff of life, while here on the earth, darkness already pressed at the kitchen windows.

The eighth decedent, a thirty-five-year-old woman serving in the Florida State Senate, mother of four, in an apparent struggle with herself, had missed with the first two shots and had blown apart her neck with the third. Jane read, " 'Pick up the gun pick up the gun pick up the gun there is joy waiting in it.' "

Moshe was on his feet and pacing. "She's not writing the note to her family."

"No," Jane agreed.

"She's writing it to herself, arguing herself into doing this terrible thing."

"Or maybe . . ."

Moshe turned to her. "Maybe what?"

"Maybe she's writing down what she's hearing. The voice in her head. The spider in her brain that talks to her."

39

APRIL IN THE UPSTAIRS HALL, AT the threshold of the open door, her husband's study in the room beyond.

She entered quietly, bearing the tray.

He sat at his computer, his back to her. He was deep into the scene, backspacing to erase a phrase that didn't satisfy, rapidly typing a new line, scrolling backward to the previous page to review what he had written there. . . .

How deeply he fell away into his fiction when he was writing, much the way that the world around April faded when she was at the piano, working on a melody, seeking just the right third group of eight bars in a thirty-two-bar chorus.

His work was as lyrical as he was lovely, and as she watched him work, listening to him muttering critically to himself, she found herself weeping silently, moved by all that they had been through together, all they had experienced, the triumphs and the tragedies, their only child stillborn, their love enduring every loss and setback, as it would endure what came next.

Take it to him, take it to him, take it to him. . . .

Beyond the windows lay the mountains dark, fairies of snow dancing against the glass.

She put the tray on a worktable that was mostly covered with reference books. She picked up the bottle of sauvignon blanc and took it to him and swung it left to right, as if christening a ship, his head the bow. She swung it with such terrific force that the bottle burst, and he tipped over with his office chair, falling to the floor in a shower of fragrant wine.

April pushed the chair out of the way and looked down at Eddie and saw he was conscious but stunned, confused, uncomprehending. He spoke her name, but as if he wasn't sure that she was in fact April.

She had required both the bottle and the chef's French knife to do what needed to be done. To ensure it was done right. She took the blade from the tray and turned to Eddie.

"I love you so much," she said, "so much, so much," each word a sob, and she fell upon him with the knife.

40

THE NINTH HAD BEEN A THIRTY-seven-year-old university professor and acclaimed poet who had thrown himself into the path of a subway train.

Jane read, " 'The release from action and suffering, release from the inner and the outer compulsion.' "

Gazing at the night through the window above the sink, Moshe Steinitz said, "It sounds like poetry."

"It is, but not his own. I tracked it down. It's from 'Burnt Norton' by T. S. Eliot."

She had one more. The tenth decedent was by far the youngest, a twenty-year-old graduate student, so gifted that she entered college at fourteen, received her bachelor's degree at sixteen, her master's degree in astrophysics at eighteen, and was working on a doctorate in cosmology. She had set herself on fire.

Jane read, "'I need to go. I need to go. I'm not afraid. Am I not afraid? Someone help me.'"

41

WHEN EDDIE WAS WHERE HE needed to be, when he was with the dead, April would have carved a proclamation of her love into her flesh if she could have tolerated living long enough to finish the task, but with Eddie gone, she wanted no more of this dark world. She knelt beside him and held the French knife in both hands and pierced her abdomen with it, nearly to the hilt. Pain struck her like a lightning bolt and cast her into black silence. Not much later, she woke too weak to feel pain any longer and found herself lying on the floor beside him and fumbled for his hand and found it and held it and remembered long-ago Vermont and the red maples in bright autumn dress and young love, and in the last quick moment she thought, *What have I done?*

42

NOW THAT HE'D HEARD THE ten statements read aloud, Moshe sat at the kitchen table, reading them from the Xerox that Jane provided.

He had put on music that flooded the house through speakers in every room: Mozart's *K. 488*, an extraordinary concerto that, scored for clarinets, opened with a robust movement beyond the reach of any other composer, bringing even to this solemn moment in Jane's life a mood of soaring optimism that she wished she could catch and hold.

Sitting at the table, she listened with her eyes closed, one hand encircling the cordial glass of Dindarello.

In time, Moshe spoke as quietly as ever, but his voice carried through the music. "I am inclined to say that these people—or at least most of them—might have been in some altered state when they killed themselves. I get no sense of suicidal depression, nothing that convinces me the voices they

heard indicated schizophrenia, nothing that sug-
gests any classic forms of mental illness. There is
something here unique—and damn strange."

The concerto contained a sequence of a different
character from the music before and after it, an extraordinary slow movement of profound melancholy, which now came upon them. Jane did not
respond to Moshe, but kept her eyes closed and
traveled with Mozart where he conveyed her, into
the heart of deepest sorrow, and she thought of Nick
and of her long-lost mother. When that section concluded with a return to thrilling strains of dauntless
optimism, she found that she had been moved to the
depths of her soul and yet remained dry-eyed. The
lack of tears, the control her dry eyes confirmed, led
her to believe that she was ready for what might
come next, no matter how hard the way ahead might
prove to be.

43

THE PRIMARY RESIDENCE OF
Dr. Bertold Shenneck and his wife, Inga, is in Palo
Alto, an easy drive from his labs in Menlo Park.

They also own a getaway on seventy acres in
Napa Valley, in the foothills of the Coastal Ranges, a
property of woods and meadows rich with wildlife.

To some, the house seems misplaced in its rustic

setting, for it is an ultramodern structure of glass and steel and slabs of granite cladding. Bertold and Inga are both dominant personalities, however, and they appreciate the way that the bold house rises above the land and asserts superiority over Nature.

They sit on the back terrace, each with a glass of Caymus cabernet sauvignon, to watch the sunset and the coming of the wine-country night.

Inga, twenty-one years younger than Bertold, could pass for a lingerie model. Although she is a woman of strong appetites and complex desires, she is not the party girl that she appears to be. She has serious interests, ambition, and a will to power equal to that of her husband.

Most wives so much younger than their mates would resent him bringing his work with him to a getaway house. Inga encourages him to mix work and play.

In the chair beside hers, he sits with his laptop, entering commands that radiate from the microwave transmitter on the roof.

As dusk gives way to deeper night, the coyotes begin to arrive, slinking out of the tall grass and weeds beyond the mown lawn, eyes luminous with reflections of the low yard lights. They come within five feet of the terrace and sit at attention, one after the other, until a dozen are lined up side by side, as wild as any coyotes in appearance but at the moment as docile as family dogs.

"Make them lie down," Inga says.

Bertold's fingers fly across the keyboard.

Starting with the rangy specimen farthest to the left, the coyotes lie on the lawn, forepaws serving as chin rests, easing to the grass as though they are a series of slow-falling dominoes.

"Does anyone in the world have a more impressive security system?" Inga wonders as she considers these cousins of wolves.

The twelve predators watch the good doctor and his wife drink cabernet sauvignon and watch them eat roast-beef sandwiches and watch as well when Bertold and Inga share a single lounge chair for intimacies that both husband and wife find more thrilling because of the presence of an attentive audience.

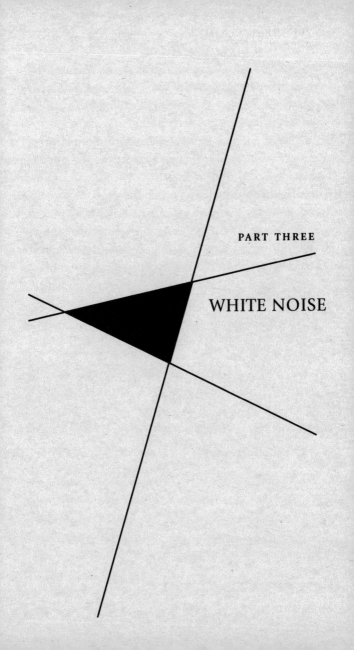

PART THREE

WHITE NOISE

1

MOSHE STEINITZ ASKED HER TO stay for dinner and said he was lonely. She accepted—and discovered that he had an ulterior motive.

Earlier in the day, he'd made a crab quiche, which now he heated. Jane mixed a salad. Moshe set the table, sliced a loaf of French bread, opened an icy bottle of pinot grigio.

She found it endearing that he put on a sport coat before sitting down to dinner at the kitchen table.

They talked about many things but didn't speak of suicide or of her investigation until, as they were enjoying a simple dessert of fresh strawberries and sliced kiwi, he asked how her son was coping.

She had come to him for his analysis and opinion of the notes, but she hadn't thought through what responsibility she would have to him once he had obliged her. She saw now that she owed him the truth to ensure that he would not endanger himself.

"This investigation of these suicides—it's not Bureau work."

"I didn't think it was."

"I'm on leave. And the last two months I've been off the grid to an extent that most end-times preppers only think they are."

She told him about Mr. Droog, who had sent Travis to her with messages about natsat and milk bars and a game called rape.

Pulsing candlelight reflected in his eyeglasses, obscuring his eyes, but she read the shock in his face, in the way he put down a berry that he was about to eat, as if he had no more appetite.

"My boy is safe. And I don't want to put *you* in danger, Moshe. Tell no one I've been here. I'm being hunted, and if they think I've shared too much with you, I don't know what they might do."

His solution was reasonable, but not feasible in this time of unreason: "Suicides are public record. If you get a few journalists interested in the story, and they break it open, then you're safe."

"If I knew a few journalists I trusted."

"There must be one."

"Maybe at one time. Young guys making their bones. But it so happens they're among the suicides that didn't leave a note behind."

He removed his glasses, as though he realized that she was straining to see his eyes through the candle glare.

"Don't use your computer to research any of this," she said. "Don't draw attention to yourself.

They cast a wide net, and it seems to be sized even to the littlest of fish."

"*They* with an uppercase *T*. Do you have some idea who *They* are?"

"They. Them. A nameless confederacy. I don't know where the center lies, though it might involve private-sector biotech."

"And government?"

"I think inevitably."

"The FBI?"

"Not the Bureau as a whole. But some people in it? Maybe. I can't take a chance turning there for help."

He sipped his wine, not so much as if he savored it, but as if he were delaying his response in order to think.

At last he said, "You're painting a picture of such isolation, I don't know how you can come out a winner."

"I don't, either. But I will. I have to."

"Have you considered . . . maybe you're too invested in this to be the best one to get at the truth?"

"Because of Nick, you mean. Yes, it's personal. But it's not vengeance, Moshe. It's about justice. And keeping Travis safe."

"There's more than Nick that drives you on this. And more than your boy. Is there not?"

She could see his eyes now. His gaze was direct and clear, and she was pretty sure she could read it. "You mean my mother."

"You've spoken of her in passing a few times

over the years that I've known you, but you never mention her suicide."

She recited the reputed facts without emotion. "She took an overdose of sleeping pills. To seal the deal, she sat in a hot bath and slashed her wrists. I was nine. I'm the one who found her."

"The first time I worked on a case with you," Moshe said, "I was impressed with your intelligence and dedication. I wanted to know more about you, and so I did background."

"Well, it is what it is. But this current situation doesn't have anything to do with my mother."

He offered her more wine. She shook her head.

He pushed aside the candles, so they would not reflect in the lenses, and he put on his glasses again, as if he wanted to see her clearly, to be aware of every nuance of expression.

"When Nick died, you were determined he couldn't have killed himself. You became obsessed with proving he didn't, which led you to the discovery of this increase in suicide rates, which then became your greater obsession."

"It's all real. And there *are* people trying to silence me any way they can. I'm not delusional, Moshe."

"I don't think you are. I believe everything you've said. My only point is that a person driven by obsession may not have the patience, the prudence, or even the fullest clarity of mind to investigate such a Byzantine conspiracy with any success."

"I know. I really do. But there's only me to do it."

"I might worry less if you were aware of the fullness of your obsession, the extent of its roots. Then you might be sensitive to how it could make you reckless, injudicious."

"Moshe, I can only assure you that I'm still the investigator I've always been. There's nothing more I can say."

For what seemed like a minute, he regarded her with his onion-peeling stare, which she met forthrightly. "Do you remember when you and Nathan and a few others came to dinner three years ago, the celebration after your capture of J. J. Crutchfield?"

"Of course I remember. It was a happy evening."

"You played the piano at my request. Played remarkably well."

She said nothing.

"Other guests had questions about your father, but you avoided the subject with practiced grace."

"When you have a famous parent, you learn early not to open the family to the world."

"Family secrets to protect?"

"Just a need for privacy."

"You praised your mother for encouraging your musicianship."

"She was a fine pianist herself."

"You rarely speak of her, but always with the highest regard. You speak even more rarely of your father—with cold indifference."

"We were never close. He was so often away on concert tours."

"Your coldness signifies more than dislike."

"Tell me, doctor, what else does it signify?" she

asked, and was dismayed to hear the dismissive note in her voice.

"Deep distrust," he said.

She broke their staring match, but then resumed it, lest he read some arcane meaning in her disengagement. "All children have issues with their parents."

"Dear, you must excuse me if I push some buttons."

"Isn't that what you've already been doing?"

"I can't play the piano as well as you, but I'm a reasonably competent button-pusher." He leaned back in his chair and folded his hands on the table. "It isn't sexual."

She frowned. "What isn't?"

"The problem with your father. You weren't molested. You have none of the issues of a sexually abused child."

"He's a creep, but he likes younger women, not children."

"He married a year after your mother's suicide."

"What could I do about it?"

"You wanted to do something."

"He dissed my mother's memory by marrying Eugenia."

"That isn't the issue, is it?"

"It's an issue with me."

"But not *the* issue."

"He was banging Eugenia's brains out when my mother was alive."

"Is that crude expression meant to stop me from going further?"

She shrugged. "Go where you want."

"Why do you believe your father killed your mother?"

Earlier, she had pushed aside her half-full wine-glass. Stunned by his insight, she picked up the glass and drank.

Moshe sampled a little of his wine, as if this drink they took together was some kind of communion that bonded them.

"There's always an autopsy after a suicide," he said.

"There's supposed to be, but there isn't always. Depending on the jurisdiction and the circumstances, the coroner has discretion."

He said, "So did you have evidence of any kind?"

"He'd flown out that morning. He was supposed to be in a hotel four hundred miles away. He had a concert in another city the next night. Yet when I woke, I heard them arguing."

"What did you do when you heard them?"

"Put the pillow over my head. And tried to go back to sleep."

"Did you go back to sleep?"

"For a while." She set her wineglass aside. "He was there that night. I heard him. I have another reason to be sure he was there. But no hard proof. And he's a master of intimidation, manipulation."

"You were afraid of him."

"Yes."

"You're still angry at yourself for having been afraid of him."

She said nothing.

"Do you blame yourself?"

"For what?"

"When you heard them arguing, you went back to sleep. If you'd gone to them instead, do you think your mother would now be alive?"

"No. I think . . . I'd be dead, too. He would have staged it to look like she killed me before killing herself."

Moshe's silences were as exquisitely placed and maintained as those in Mozart's *K. 488*, which had been playing earlier.

Jane said, "What I blame myself for is never speaking up later. For letting him intimidate me."

"You were only a child."

"Doesn't matter. In the crunch, you give it or you don't."

Moshe corked the wine bottle, which was almost half full.

He said, "This obsession doesn't begin with Nick's death. It has roots that go back nineteen years."

He ate the strawberry that earlier he had set aside.

He said, "You want vengeance for both Nick and your mother—but that isn't the primary thing you want."

She waited as he took off his glasses, plucked the display handkerchief from his breast pocket, and polished the lenses.

He said, "You want to break this conspiracy, imprison whoever's behind it, kill them if necessary, resolve the injustice, balance the scales, so there will be no danger that your boy might forever have the feeling that there's something he should have done or still could do to right the wrong. You can't spare him from grief, but you want to spare him from the guilt that has eaten at your heart all these years. Could that be the case?"

"It *is* the case. But there's so much more. I want for him a world where people mean more than ideas. No swastikas, no hammer-and-sickles, no bowing down to inhumane theories that result in tens of millions dead. I see the look you're giving me, Moshe. I know I can't change the world. I'm not suffering from Joan of Arc syndrome. Those things are what I want for him, but if all I can do is spare him from the guilt, I'll have done something worthwhile."

He put on his glasses. "If you realize precisely what powerful emotions drive your obsession, maybe you'll recognize when emotion begins to trump reason. If you can subdue the temerity that emotion fosters, rein in the recklessness, you might have a chance."

"The slimmest chance is all I need to keep going."

"Good. If your assessment of the situation is correct, the slimmest chance is probably all you have."

2

IN THE SAN FERNANDO VALLEY, in her motel room, Jane had neither the energy nor the clarity of mind to review the material that she had gotten from Jimmy Radburn. She put the heavy trash bag full of documents in the closet.

She didn't need vodka or music to sleep. She was in bed by nine o'clock and soon in dreams.

Near midnight, gunshots woke her. A racing car engine. In fact, two cars. Tires squealed. A man shouted, his words unclear. Three more shots in quick succession, perhaps return fire.

She drew the pistol from under the pillow where no head had rested. She sat up in the dark but didn't get out of bed.

A metallic shriek suggested one vehicle side-swiped another. Maybe one of the two in motion had skinned a parked car.

Then they were away. The Doppler shift of engine roar, fading to lower frequencies, receded in two directions, as if the drivers, following the exchange of gunfire, had fled from each other.

She remained sitting up for a while, but nothing more happened. No police siren in the night. No one had reported the gunfire.

She put the pistol under the pillow once more. After all, this wasn't the murder capital of the country. That honor belonged to Chicago, although other jurisdictions strove to be competitive.

As she was lying down again, she thought the incident had been only white noise, the continually simmering violence and chaos that was the backdrop of contemporary life. People became so accustomed to the white noise that episodes of violence with greater meaning, such as the rapid rise in suicides, escaped their notice.

She didn't lie awake. She thought of Travis safe with Gavin and Jessica, the German shepherds taking turns patrolling the house at night, and she slept.

3

JANE WOKE AT 4:04, SHOWERED, dressed, and sat at the small round dining table to pore through the medical-examiner reports on suicides in thirty-two jurisdictions. Four were from large cities, twelve from medium-size cities, eight from suburbs, and eight from areas of lower population, where one county coroner served all the surrounding little towns.

Each report came with photographs of the corpse in situ. She tried not to look at those. But the rebellious primitive that lived in the back of every human brain was drawn to what the forebrain deemed too dark for civilized consideration, and the eye sometimes turned traitor.

Although technically the law required an autopsy in the event of suicide, most jurisdictions allowed the medical examiner or the coroner, whichever title applied, some leeway in cases where he or she determined there was no doubt the deceased had self-destructed. Death by cop, which was a form of suicide, would always be followed by an autopsy as well as by a media frenzy and possibly a trial. By contrast, in the case of someone with a history of depression, who made previous attempts at suicide, blood tests would be conducted to detect drugs, and the corpse would be subjected to a thorough visual inspection for signs of violence unrelated to the cause of death; but in the absence of any indications of homicide, dissection and examination of internal organs wouldn't routinely occur.

When Jane sampled files from two large cities—New York and Los Angeles—she made three discoveries of interest.

First, the number of cases in which the suicide appeared to have been a well-adjusted member of the community, mentally stable, physically sound, with an intact family, prospering in his work, was higher even than the national statistics indicated. The phenomenon was so striking, medical examiners and deputy coroners who conducted basic or extensive autopsies often remarked on it in their reports.

Second, in New York, the state attorney general

in concert with the district attorney of New York City had approved new guidelines for medical examiners that not only allowed but encouraged a much higher percentage of suicide cases to be closed with only a visual examination of the body and the usual toxicology tests. They cited budgetary constraints and a lack of sufficient personnel. These new guidelines so disturbed some examiners that they made reference to them in their reports, in terms meant to insulate themselves from possible claims of dereliction in days to come.

Third, in California, some medical examiners were disturbed that the state attorney general had the previous year cited budget shortfalls and personnel shortages when issuing an advisory—not mere guidelines, as in New York—coupled with a warning of funding cuts to any city or county in which the coroner's office continued at its discretion to conduct full autopsies in "cases not involving clear evidence of or reasonable suspicion of murder, second-degree murder, or manslaughter." The reason given for curtailing autopsies in certain cases was the desire to focus in a more complete and timely manner on the rising number of homicides committed by drug-gang members and terrorists. Some coroners referenced the advisory in their reports or attached it complete, to protect themselves.

The growth in the number of government employees in recent years seemed to belie the claimed personnel shortages.

Any authority to whom Jane dared turn with this

suspicion would brand her with the word *paranoid* as surely as Hester Prynne, in Hawthorne's novel, had been made to wear the scarlet letter.

Yet she could not help but suspect that the attorneys general in the nation's two largest states were engaged in the suppression of evidence related to the surge in suicides among people who were unlikely candidates for self-destruction.

At whose direction were they so engaged? How much might they know about the reason for this recent plague?

If a private-sector biotech company and the government were involved in a project that sent suicide rates soaring, what might be their purpose?

Were the suicides an unexpected side effect . . . or perhaps an intended consequence of whatever they were doing?

The chill that stippled her skin with gooseflesh didn't pass, but worked its way deeper into her.

She went to the bathroom, where the motel provided a mug, foil packets of instant coffee, and a cheap appliance to boil water. She stirred up a full mug with two packets. She paced the room, drinking the brew as hot as she could tolerate, but the chill was stubborn.

4

JANE HAD NOT YET FOUND A brain dissection in the autopsy files. She was keen to discover a reference to some unnatural structure in the gray matter of a suicide.

When the coffee hardly warmed her, however, she decided to take a break from the medical-examiner reports and see what had been provided regarding the do-gooder, David James Michael. He sat on both the board of the Gernsback Institute, which produced the annual What If Conference, and the Seedling Fund, where he had served with a wealthy man, T. Quinn Eubanks, who was one of the suicides.

The report on David Michael appeared so complete that Jimmy Radburn would have deserved a prime position in the Hackers Hall of Fame if there had been one.

David Michael, forty-four, was the sole heir to a fortune made generations earlier in railroads, swelled by investments in oil, real estate, and everything else that provided a high return during the past century. Although he had inherited his wealth, he proved a first-rate steward of it, funding a venture-capital firm to back high-technology start-ups. His eye for new firms with big prospects was so sharp that eighty percent of the time he picked winners.

Three years earlier, he'd moved from Virginia hunt country to an estate in Palo Alto, to be near the many Silicon Valley companies in which he had an interest.

There were photographs of him. David might have come from starched and pinstriped stock, but he favored a free-spirit style. His blond hair appeared to have been shorn haphazardly and combed with nothing but his fingers, though Jane recognized the work of a five-hundred-dollar-per-cut hairdresser. He was known for attending important business meetings in sneakers and jeans, his shirttail untucked, but in several photos he wore different watches that were said to be from his collection of expensive timepieces that ranged in price from fifty thousand to eighty thousand dollars each.

In numerous publications, he had been cited for his generous philanthropy, his commitment to all kinds of public-spirited causes, from the San Francisco Symphony to wetland preservation, and he had made no secret of his progressive politics.

Jane knew his type. Everything he said and did for public consumption was carefully crafted. Everyone admired a young rebel billionaire who appeared distressed by his wealth and dispensed sums that seemed to risk impoverishing him. In fact, what he gave away amounted to one percent of his fortune. What parts of his public persona were genuine, if any, would be known only to him, his wife, and his image consultant—and possibly not to his wife.

Among the companies that thrived with his venture capital were Shenneck Technology and more recently, to a greater extent, Far Horizons. Shenneck and David Michael were partners in Far Horizons.

If she hadn't found the locus of the conspiracy, she had found one nexus: Bertold Shenneck, David James Michael, and Far Horizons.

The problem would be getting close enough to either man to get him in a nutcracker grip and encourage dialogue. The billionaire would have layers of security, bodyguards of the highest caliber.

And though Shenneck had far less wealth than his primary investor, if they were in fact involved in this conspiracy through Far Horizons, he possessed information that would severely damage or destroy both men. Therefore, he would be insulated from everything but the most considered and stealthy approach.

At the end of Jimmy's report, Jane discovered what might prove to be a back door to Shenneck. The last item consisted of only one sentence with inadequate details: *Bertold Shenneck appears to have a deeply concealed interest in a Dark Web operation that might or might not be a weird brothel.*

She knew what she needed to do next.

It would be dangerous.

As if that mattered. Everything was dangerous these days. Just driving to work in Philadelphia could be a death ticket.

5

SINCE EIGHT O'CLOCK, THE motel maids speaking softly in Spanish and the clink-and-clatter of their equipment carts had penetrated the room, growing louder as the morning matured. It was almost ten, and Jane didn't want to delay until eleven, when in spite of the DO NOT DISTURB sign, there might come a knock at the door and a polite inquiry about maid service. The less interaction she had with the staff, the less likely they were to remember her.

Besides, she had stayed there two nights, her maximum for any location. An object in motion tends to stay in motion, and an object too long at rest tends to have her throat slit.

She loaded her bags into the Ford and dropped the room key at the office, where she asked the address of the nearest library.

At a nearby McDonald's, she bought coffee and two breakfast sandwiches, threw away half the bread, and ate in the car. The food was better than it looked. The coffee was worse than it smelled. She fished a tiny pill from a bottle of acid-reduction medication.

At the library, she used a computer to search for the nearest stores selling art supplies, laboratory equipment, and janitorial supplies. None of that would bring her to the attention of the people who were looking for her.

By one o'clock, she'd acquired bottles of acetone, a container of bleaching powder, what minimal laboratory vessels she required, and a couple of items from a drugstore.

In Tarzana, she located an acceptable motel, where she chose to stay because she'd never before been in that town and would be a stranger to everyone.

She used a different forged ID from the one she had presented at the previous motel, and she paid cash in advance.

The king-size bed reflected in the mirrored rolling doors of the closet. She stowed the trash bag. Before putting the suitcases with it, she retrieved binoculars, a LockAid lock-release gun sold only to law-enforcement agencies but acquired illegally from the same people who had remade her Ford Escape, and finally a sound suppressor threaded to fit the barrel of her Heckler & Koch .45.

By five o'clock, working in the bathroom, wearing a surgical face mask and nitrile gloves, she derived a quantity of chloroform from the acetone by the reaction of chloride of lime, which was the bleaching powder. She filled a six-ounce spray bottle purchased at the beauty-supply store, set it aside, and cleaned up the mess.

When she stepped outside, the late-afternoon sun marinated the suburban sprawl in a sour light. The warm air smelled of vehicle exhaust that had been rinsed by catalytic converters into harmless compounds but nonetheless soiled the air with an unpleasant scent.

In a restaurant across the street from the motel, she enjoyed a dinner of filet mignon, more than once assuring herself that it was not her last meal in this world.

6

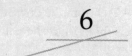

EARLIER IN THE DAY, SHORTLY before four o'clock Eastern time, Section Chief Nathan Silverman had been in his office at the Academy in Quantico when he received a heads-up call from the special agent in charge of the Los Angeles field office, informing him that the SAC would be sending him a report regarding an incident the previous day, in Santa Monica, involving either an imposter passing herself off as Special Agent Jane Hawk of the Critical Incident Response Group or Special Agent Hawk herself.

The incident was strange, the SAC said, but seemed to involve no crime other than the possible impersonation of a Bureau agent. As his field office was one of the busiest in the nation, he had little time to waste on something as seemingly small-potatoes as this. The five Behavioral Analysis Units had provided considerable assistance to the L.A. office in recent high-profile cases, however; and the

SAC respected Silverman and his people. The report would be finished and transmitted by nine o'clock East Coast time.

At 7:30 that evening, Silverman sat down to dinner with his wife of thirty years, Rishona, in their house on the outskirts of Alexandria, about twenty-five miles from Quantico. They sat catercorner to each other at the dining room table.

The children were through college and off on their own. He and Rishona could have eaten in the kitchen with much less fuss, but she insisted on the more elegant atmosphere of the dining room.

When she cooked, which was more nights than not, she made an event of dinner, with good china and sterling silver and crystal, damask napkins held in rings from her collection, and candlelight.

He thought himself among the luckiest of men, that his wife should be both lovely and his best friend, with whom he could share anything and trust in her discretion.

Over a Caesar salad with romaine of exceptional crispness, followed by thick fillets of braised swordfish, he spoke of his day.

Following the terrorist strike in Philadelphia on Monday, Investigations and Operations Support as well as Behavioral Analysis Units 1 and 5—all in the Critical Incident Response Group—had been overwhelmed with requests for assistance, and today, Thursday, was the first evening he'd gotten home before eight o'clock. He had much to tell her, but inevitably, Jane and the call from the Los Angeles field office featured prominently in their conversation.

With his finest people, Nathan Silverman managed to have both a disciplined professional relationship and a social one that was not common in the Bureau. Rishona knew Jane well and thought of her and Nick as extended family. She had grieved for Nick, no less for Jane, and regularly asked after her.

"I didn't chase her for the ID," Nathan said. "I thought I knew her well enough to be sure she'd be back to work in two months, even six weeks."

"She doesn't have a heart of stone," Rishona chided.

"No, but she's got the heart of a lion, that one. Nothing sets her back for long. Two months ago, when she surprised me by filing for a leave extension, you may remember she called."

"Yes, she was going to travel around the country with Travis. It might be good for the little guy. He so adored Nick."

"Well, she gave me a new phone number where I could reach her, but she hoped I would, as she put it, give her space. I had both her house and cell numbers, so I assumed this was just a new smartphone. Same area code."

He paused to savor the swordfish, but his wife, well aware of his subtle use of silences to add drama to his stories—it pleased him to make even the most mundane news entertaining for her—grew impatient after five seconds. "Don't make the scene Shakespearean, Nate. What about the phone?"

"Well, I've given her the space she wanted. But when this bit came in from L.A., I almost rang her up. I don't know why, I really don't, but instead I asked one of our younger computer whizzes to backdoor an address for the phone, just as a personal favor not as a Bureau matter. After all, no crime is involved. Turns out the number isn't a smartphone. It's just a cheap burner."

"Disposable?"

"Bought at Walmart in Alexandria and activated the day I last talked to her. None of the minutes on it have been used."

Announced by neither lightning nor thunder, a sudden hard rain roared down the night and drummed the roof, so that both he and Rishona looked at the ceiling in surprise.

She said, "We'll see now if that gutter repair works."

"And when it does, I will have saved us four hundred dollars."

"I sincerely hope so, dear. You can't know how I suffer for you when you're embarrassed by a do-it-yourself catastrophe."

"Isn't *catastrophe* a bit too strong a word?"

"I was thinking of the guest-bathroom toilet."

After a silence, he said, "Even then, the word *disaster* is more accurate."

"You're right. I exaggerate. It was merely a disaster. Now, why would Jane buy a disposable phone for you to call?"

"I don't know why, I really don't, but on the way

home, I took a side trip into Springfield to drive by her house. It's not there."

"What's not there?"

"Springfield's there, but not the house. It's been torn down. Attached to the construction fence is an architect's rendering of how the new place will look, and it's labeled THE CHEN RESIDENCE. No work has begun yet, no construction crew on site. They're no doubt still in the permitting stage. I'll talk to someone tomorrow."

Rishona was a portrait of skepticism. "Jane wouldn't sell, move, not give you a current address. It's a violation of rules."

The Silverman house was stoutly built, with snug masoncraft and tight joinery, but somehow the sudden storm pressed a vague draft through the dining room. In the crystal cups, the smooth and steady candle flames elongated and fluttered like serpent tongues.

Nathan said, "It would also be a violation of the rules if she changed her name to Chen and didn't tell us. And whatever's about to come in from Los Angeles . . . it's not going to be good, Rishona."

"Now, Nate, Jane is the last person I know who might break bad. Other than you."

"That's not what I mean," Nathan said as the hard rain fell even harder, as saving four hundred bucks with a do-it-yourself repair seemed less wise by the minute. "Although I'm probably wrong, I think she might be in some kind of trouble not of her making, so bad she can't bring it even to me."

7

SHERMAN OAKS HAD A HIGHER percentage of citizens over the age of sixty-five than most of the communities in Los Angeles County. The average household size—two—was among the lowest in Southern California. It was in general a quiet town, especially in the streets of pricy homes in the hills.

The stately house was brick with cast-work window surrounds and pediments. A pair of proud stone lions flanked the front steps, as if this were a library or courthouse, although the resident had no interest in libraries and imagined himself too clever ever to be standing before a judge in a courthouse.

Low pathway lanterns flanked the front walk. A carriage lamp by the door cast a welcoming glow across the porch. Light warmed the downstairs windows, but the upstairs was dark.

Two years earlier, at the age of fifty-four and fifty-three respectively, Richard and Berniece Branwick, who still owned the residence, had taken early retirement and moved to Scottsdale, Arizona. They had worked hard, but their extended time in the sun came courtesy of their only child, Robert, who was a great success in his chosen profession.

Jane parked across the street from the house and two doors uphill. She used the binoculars to pull the residence close, and for a while she studied the place.

No one would be stationed outside of the house. This wasn't an area where armed security was common. If neighbors were to see a man lurking in the shadows, they would call the police. The LAPD served Sherman Oaks out of the Van Nuys Station on Sylmar Avenue; they wouldn't be dismissive about such a report from this neighborhood.

Anyway, Robert Branwick didn't think he needed security here, except for the standard home-alarm system to foil burglars.

If he suspected she knew this address and name, he wouldn't be here. Not now. Not ever.

He might even be home alone, though probably not. Being alone usually made his type restless. Solitude risked self-reflection.

Two doors uphill, a house stood with no faintest glow at any window. Evidently the residents were away or out for the evening.

After putting on the black-and-silver gloves, Jane crossed the street and went to the back of the dark house, alert for a dog.

Beyond the patio lay a deep backyard. Privacy walls separated the flanking properties, but no fence defined the end of the lawn, where a woodlet rose at the brink of a shallow ravine.

The inky trees silvered with moonlight were like a forest dreamed into existence by an artist with etching needles, a black-wax ground board, and an eye for the eerie.

The property downhill of the first had a wall all the way around, concrete blocks clothed in stucco.

With a small flashlight, she found her way between the stucco and trees, past a plank gate, to the wall behind the Branwick house, where she switched it off.

Here no gate offered entrance, but the wall was only seven feet high, easily scaled. At the top, she sat on the cast-concrete cap for a minute, studying the night-veiled yard and the swimming pool where the flotsam of a broken moon floated on rippling black water.

She dropped to the lawn. Circled the pool.

Pale window light fanned onto the covered patio, and through those panes, Jane could see a kitchen and breakfast area at the west end of the house. No one in either space.

At the east end lay a family room. Beyond a pair of sliding glass doors, facing away from the patio, a couple sat in a large gray sectional, watching a car-chase scene on a wall-mounted flat-screen TV. The roar of supercharged engines and pounding music penetrated the windows.

Jane ventured to the kitchen door and tried it. Locked.

The movie boomed, but in the house's open floor plan, the kitchen lay too close to the people in the family room. If the car chase ended and a moment of silence followed just as she pulled the trigger of the LockAid, the snap of its spring and the click of the lock's pin tumblers might catch their attention.

She went to the west wide of the house. At the midpoint of that long wall, a single French door faced onto a pocket garden where two wrought-iron chairs flanked a basin-and-pedestal fountain that was currently not operating.

No lamp brightened the room beyond the door, but an interior door admitted some light from a hallway. The room appeared to be a study: the shadowy suggestion of a desk, bookshelves, an armchair.

Jane holstered the pistol. A quick flicker of flashlight revealed a mortise lock with a deadbolt cylinder in the escutcheon.

Earlier, she'd tethered the lock-release gun to her belt with a shoelace. Now she eased its thin pick into the keyway, under the pin tumblers. When she pulled the trigger, the flat spring snapped the pick upward, throwing some pins to the shear line, out of the way. She pulled the trigger four times before the lock was disengaged.

Drawing the pistol, she stepped inside. Closed the door behind her. A study. Computer on the desk. Instead of books on the shelves, there were high-end collectible *Star Wars* figures.

From the back of the house came the squeal of tires, racing engines, gunfire, music scored to insist on excitement even if the visuals and story didn't deliver any.

She eased into the brightly lighted hallway, hesitated, and moved toward the front of the house for a quick reconnoiter. From the foyer, she could see into the dining room on one side and the living room on the other, both lamplit and cozy and deserted.

Returning along the hall, she reached the kitchen

doorway just as a young blond woman appeared from the family room and opened the refrigerator, back to Jane, unaware of an intruder.

The girl was dressed to seduce in tight silky pants and a midriff-baring blouse with lacework.

Jane holstered the gun, took in hand the small spray bottle of chloroform, entered the big kitchen, and moved past the archway that provided a clear view of the family room, counting on the movie to keep the attention of the guy in there.

Fortune favors the bold, except when it doesn't.

She stepped behind the fridge browser, who was deciding which of five soft drinks to choose.

Before the blonde might have a can of soda in hand and drop it, Jane said softly, *"Pepsi."*

Startled, the browser turned into the first stream from the spray bottle. Sweet-tasting chloroform wet the girl's pink lipstick and the tip of her tongue, whispered up her nostrils. Her eyes went wide but rolled back in her head before she could cry out. Jane got one arm around her and held her against the refrigerator to prevent her from folding noisily to the floor, put the spray bottle on the counter, and lowered the unconscious girl to the ceramic tiles.

Chloroform was highly volatile. Already it had evaporated from the blonde's lips. Traces glistened only around the edges of her nostrils. What she'd inhaled would keep her out for several minutes. Maybe long enough, maybe not.

Jane tore two paper towels from a nearby dispenser. She folded them together, spritzed one side lightly with chloroform, and placed the barely damp-ened side over the girl's face. The makeshift mask fluttered slightly with each exhalation. Jane watched long enough to be sure there was no breathing prob-lem.

Then she put the spray bottle in an inner jacket pocket, drew her pistol, and returned to the arch-way between kitchen and family room. He was still sitting in the overstuffed gray sectional, feet up on a coffee table, enthralled. On the TV, one guy on a mo-torcycle chased another guy on a motorcycle along a highway, weaving among numerous other speeding vehicles, in a scene that required the brain of a tit-mouse to write and a demented genius to stage.

The cacophony masked what sounds she made as she circled behind him. When one of the motor-cycles went over a cliff and the other one shrieked to a halt at the brink, the bombastic music faded to a mere ghost of sound, to emphasize the long death drop.

Jane said, "Got any Oreos, Bobby?"

Surely her voice wasn't identical to that of the anesthetized blonde on the kitchen floor, yet he didn't react to her question except to gesture impa-tiently with one hand and say, "Yeah, yeah," as he watched the plummeting motorcyclist narrowly es-cape death when what had appeared to be a back-pack proved instead to be a parachute from which bloomed an acre of life-saving silk.

She rapped his head with the barrel of the .45, and he said, "What the hell," and turned and saw her and sprang off the sofa and nearly fell into the coffee table.

"You tried to nail me in the park. Then you stuck it in my eye with the last item about Shenneck. 'Weird brothel' and nothing more. I have questions. Lie or evade—you get a bullet in the head. Got it, Robert? Jimmy? Whoever you want to be?"

8

IN THE FAMILY ROOM, THE movie had gone from stunts to romance. The sex had fewer sound effects than the chase scene, softer music.

In the kitchen, the adult Kewpie doll, who had once been Jimmy Radburn and had always been Robert Branwick, sat in a dinette chair, his hairless and rubber-smooth android hands folded on the kitchen table. His baby-smooth face paled with fear, but his gray-eyed stare glinted like a pair of ice picks.

Jane had screwed the sound suppressor onto the pistol. As she intended, the silencer intimidated him no less than the gun itself did. He took it to mean she was serious.

On the table lay a notepad and pen that Jane had taken from the counter under the wall phone.

She stood between him and the blonde, who

breathed shallowly under her paper-towel mask. "Shenneck's brothel has a website?"

"It's Dark Web. Like the gig we just closed up. Except it's *so* dark it makes us look like we were Walmart. The Web address isn't officially registered, it's a blind pig."

"Which to you means what?"

"It piggybacks the domain system, dot org, but nobody managing the system sees it. The site name is a long series of random letters and numbers, so no search engine can take you there. Hundreds of millions of possible combinations. Typing such a long random address by chance is epsilon. You'd need centuries even with an automated search. In short, you can't get there unless you already have the address. Friends tell friends, I guess."

"How did you get there, Jimmy Bob?"

"Maybe one of my clients didn't adequately protect his address book."

"While you hacked someone for this guy, you hacked him, too."

"Win, win."

In her sleep, the blonde snorted, and paper towels fluttered over her face.

"You know the address?" Jane asked.

"It's forty-four random letters and numbers. It's bletcherous. I can't memorize something like that. Hardly anyone could."

"You've got it in your files from Vinyl."

"But they aren't accessible right now. We're down. Remember?"

"Have you been to this dark site?"

"Yeah."

"Tell me."

"You get a black screen. Then the name *Aspasia*."

"Write it down. And don't make me pull teeth."

Printing the name on the notepad, he said, "I looked it up. She was the mistress of the mayor of Athens or something, like in four hundred B.C. Then the screen gives you eight languages to choose from. A worldwide operation. In English you get three promises—'Beautiful girls. Totally submissive. No desire too extreme.'"

"Sounds like your dream bordello, Jimmy Bob."

"It says one more thing that's too creepy—'Girls incapable of disobedience. Permanent silence assured.'"

"What—you use her, then they kill her?"

"I *said* it was too creepy. I'm not the sleaze you think I am. Then there's the membership fee. A serious bignum. Like joining some ultraexclusive country club. Three hundred thousand bucks."

"Bullshit."

"They don't make it impossible to find the place just so they can pull a practical joke. The guy whose address book I raided could afford that a hundred times over."

"How do you know Bertold Shenneck's involved with it?"

"The guy who had the address is an investor in Shenneck Technology. He has office, home, cell, and all kinds of alternate phone numbers for Shenneck. He didn't list Aspasia under Aspasia. He listed it under 'Shenneck's playpen.' "

"Write the guy's name down."

"You're bustin' my balls here."

"Not yet. But I'd be happy to do the job. Write it down."

Scowling, he printed the name. "William Sterling Overton. He's a lawyer, a shakedown artist, wins huge settlements. Lives mostly in Beverly Hills. Married twice to hot actresses. Dates supermodels. If he also needs Aspasia, he must be so saturated with testosterone, you could wring it out of him like water from a sponge."

"You have millions, Jimmy Bob. You sure you didn't sign up?"

"I don't pay for sex."

"That can't be true."

"I don't. Not anymore. Anyway, I'm not in these guys' league."

"How does a new member pay the fee? Doesn't seem like something any rich freak would want linked to him by a paper trail."

"Screen said, 'Anonymity assured. Tracing payment impossible.' Plus people like Overton have foreign accounts, paper corporations."

"You didn't get payment details? Tell me true now."

Staring into the muzzle of the .45 instead of at Jane, he said, "Before they lay out the payment arrangements, they ask who you are, who referred you. I could've used Overton's name as my sponsor, but I figured they have the referral before you call. If you claim a referral they don't have, you're in deep shit with megabad people."

"You're a hacker genius," Jane said. "You go in anonymous."

"Maybe not with these people. Maybe you go that one last step, and they have a dragon with a long tongue, it licks all the way back to where you are and takes a taste. Because when I tried the site a day later, I didn't even get the name Aspasia. The first screen just said, 'Die,' went black, stayed black. I never went back again."

"So you don't have a physical address for this brothel."

"You'd have to be a member to know it."

Elsewhere in the house, a toilet flushed.

The sound was muffled but unmistakable, possibly originating from a downstairs powder room off the hallway to which the nearby kitchen door stood open. Someone had won a war with irregularity after a nice long sit-down with a magazine.

As Branwick flipped his pen in her face, he thrust to his feet, seizing the chair to swing it at her, thinking he could take her, shouting, "KIPP, SHE HAS A GUN! KILL THE BITCH!"

Killing another human being would have been impossible if she hadn't believed in the reality of evil, if she hadn't encountered it before, if she hadn't been trained to act reflexively in desperate circumstances. But she knew evil and reacted and shot him in the head point-blank.

His knees buckled, and as Jane rounded the end of the table to get a line of sight on the hallway, his corpse toppled backward into the life that had splashed out on the floor behind him.

9

JANE AT THE THRESHOLD, PIStol in a two-hand grip, eyes on the front sight and the hallway beyond. At the midpoint of that narrow passage, a door stood open that had not been open before. On the left. Across from the study where she had gained entrance to the house. The door to the half bath.

Kipp, whoever Kipp might be, could have crossed the hall into the study, could have gone forward to the living room or the dining room. Could still be in the half bath, playing her for stupid.

Hallways were shooting galleries almost as bad as staircases. And all those doorways to clear.

Better to leave by the patio door, split by the nearest exit. She had no further business here. No confrontation was necessary.

She backed off the hallway, glanced to the left, toward the gray sectional and the TV. If there was another route from the front of the house to the family room, he might come at her that way.

The thunder of running feet overhead. He had gone to the second floor. Now he was coming back. Coming with evident enthusiasm for a fight. A sudden change in the quality of the thunder, a hollow booming: He was bounding down the front stairs.

He must have gone up there for a weapon. He was returning with it, heedless of all risk. He could have fled the house; instead, he raced toward her as if he were a crazed bull and she caped in red.

She stepped to the dinette table, snatched the top page off the notepad, stuffed it into a pocket of her jeans.

The sound of him louder, in the ground-floor hallway now.

Jane turned toward the back door.

The shotgun blast rocked the house. A storm of pellets slashed into the kitchen, the spread constrained by the doorjamb, which spat off splinters. A sleet of lead shattered the glass panes in upper display cabinets, snapped against granite countertops, plinked off the stainless-steel hood above the cooktop.

She would never make it to the back door in time. He was *here*, she heard him cursing, he seemed insane with rage. He would enter the kitchen shooting.

She dropped to the floor, the table between her and the hallway door. The exit to her left and behind her. Dead man to her right, his remaining features distorted and seeming to be pulled by some black-hole gravity toward the wound where his nose had once been.

Peering under the table, between clusters of chair legs that allowed her no sure shot, she saw a pair of black-and-white man-size designer sneakers cross the threshold, and in the same instant the shotgun roared. The weapon was a pump-action because she heard him chamber the next shell, probably a short-barrel pistol-grip 12-gauge for home defense. The second blast was still echoing through the room, ringing in her ears when he squeezed off the third round, hosing the last section of the kitchen, intending to clear it of opposition, all three loads having cleaved the air at chest height, shattering or pitting everything that didn't repel the buckshot.

Temporarily half deaf, she saw his fashionably clad feet pivot toward the family room. When he didn't fire immediately, she knew—or thought she knew—the 12-gauge had a three-round magazine tube.

Jane got to her feet. The guy was a mountain. Had to be the one she'd seen chasing across Ocean Avenue after roller-skating Nona. He stood with his broad back toward her, calculating what family-room furniture someone might be hiding behind, thinking he had cleared the kitchen, not a guy trained at Quantico, his gun savvy learned from bad movies. He was digging spare shells from a pocket of his denim jacket.

From behind, she could have shot him through

the heart, if that had been who she was. Instead she backed toward the exit, and though she trod on buckshot and other debris, the giant's hearing was for the moment compromised, like hers, and loud music issued from the TV again.

He fumbled a shell, and instead of loading the other one in his hand, he stooped to snatch the dropped round from the floor, maybe because he was slow-witted, maybe because he was so big that no one had ever given him a reason to suspect that he was as vulnerable as any child born of a woman.

Jane labored under no illusion that he would fail to be aware of her opening the back door. Her hearing was fast returning, and so was his.

He rose with the dropped shell, and she squeezed off two shots into the ceiling over his head, popping a recessed lighting fixture. Glass and sparks from a shorting wire fell on him, but he also heard the shots, because no silencer fully lived up to its name.

The hulk ducked and half turned and saw her, his eyes lanterns of demented rage. In the heat of the moment, he didn't compute why she hadn't shot him instead of the ceiling. He didn't have a round in the shotgun yet, and he believed himself to be her target, and he scrambled into the family room, putting a section of lower kitchen cabinets between her and him.

Jane fired twice again, into those cabinets, the .45s splitting the wood as if it were balsa, clattering pans and pots inside.

Then she was out, on the patio, gasping lungfuls

of cool air, blowing them out hot, running for the west side of the house, into the cover of darkness, such as it was.

If he thought to load only one shell and came fast after her, he wouldn't have any qualms about shooting *her* in the back. And if the first blast didn't kill her, it would take her down and bleed her out, giving him time to load another shell and finish her.

As she passed the two chairs and fountain, and the French door where she had entered the house through the study, halfway along the side of the residence, she thought she felt something on the back of her neck. As if the red dot of a laser-sighting module guaranteed a bullet's track to sever her spine and lacerate her brainstem. But of course the guy had a shotgun, which didn't need a laser sight, and anyway you could not feel a laser dot when it marked you. All the training anyone could receive, at Quantico or anywhere else, couldn't tame the imagination in a crisis.

She reached the front of the house. Fumbled for a breathless moment with the gravity latch on a wrought-iron gate. Shouldered open the gate. Glanced back, saw no one. Glanced toward the front door. He wasn't there.

Shotgun fire, even contained within the house, would have been loud enough to stir the neighbors from their TVs and computers. If anyone happened to be at a window, Jane shouldn't be seen running now that she emerged onto the front lawn where pathway lamps and nearby streetlamps cast enough light for a witness to observe some details of a suspect's appearance. She detached the silencer, pocketed it, holstered the pistol. At a measured pace, she crossed the lawn and followed the sidewalk uphill under trees that whispered above her and trembled leaf shadows across the lamplit sidewalk.

She crossed the street to her Ford Escape and got behind the wheel and closed the door and picked up the binoculars with which she had been studying the house earlier.

If the hulk hadn't seen Robert Branwick lying dead beyond the kitchen table when he first charged into the kitchen, he had found him by now. Unless he was stupid, he'd realize that the shotgun assault had been impetuous, to say the least, and that he needed to be gone from the premises at something like the speed of light.

Sure enough, the garage door on the east end of the house rolled up, and a black Cadillac Escalade cruised out.

Jane glassed the Caddy as it arrived at the foot of the sloped driveway, where a streetlamp revealed the shotgun cowboy behind the wheel. She expected him to turn downhill, toward the flats. He might have been worried about encountering police answering a report of gunfire, because he turned uphill.

She put aside the binoculars and slid low, until her eyes were just above the sill of the side window. When the Escalade passed, the blonde in the passenger seat was blowing her nose in a Kleenex, probably groggy and dealing with the effects of chloroform. Most likely she entirely escaped the shotgun blasts, which had been aimed high while she was flat on the floor.

Jane waited until the Caddy was out of sight before she started the Ford and switched on the head-lights and drove uphill. She heard distant sirens, but in the rearview mirror, she didn't see any rotating beacons scattering cherry light into the night below.

10

NATHAN SILVERMAN WAS AT the computer in his home office when the report came in from Los Angeles at 9:10.

A career in law enforcement ensured an appreciation for the strangeness of life and for the unpredictability of human beings. The majority of criminals were as predictable as the sunrise, in part due to their lack of imagination. But often enough, the most innocent-seeming, gentle people were capable of stunning outrages that no one could have seen coming.

Likewise, in moments of crisis, average men and women, though not conditioned for combat, displayed courage equal to the legendary acts of valor on all the battlefields of history. This better aspect of humanity kept Silverman from sliding into an incurable cynicism.

He *expected* Jane to be valiant, to act always with courage and honor. As yet, he had no evidence that she had done otherwise. But the events at the Santa Monica hotel were beyond merely troublesome. Why had she claimed to be conducting surveillance in a Bureau sting when she was on leave? Who was the woman on roller skates, and what had been in those two briefcases?

Accompanying the brief report were photos, stop-motion video images from the hotel-lobby security cameras. The quality wasn't great—but good enough for him to identify Jane Hawk, even though she had cut and dyed her hair.

Mystified, Silverman emailed the SAC in the Los Angeles field office, requesting any pertinent video from other hotel cameras. In addition, if the park across the street was equipped with security video or if there were traffic cams in the area, he needed to know if they had captured the activity that had led to the skater fleeing across Ocean Avenue, as described by the doorman-valet.

The downpour that had begun at dinner continued unrelenting, although it was less threatening now than solemn, like the massed drums and the horses' hooves of a funeral cortege.

Silverman called up the clearest photo of Jane. He framed her face and enlarged it to full screen. Clarity diminished, but he used a program that repeatedly doubled the pixels until her face resolved in detail. You could read determination in the set of her mouth, her clenched jaw. You might read anxiety as well. Maybe the third thing that he saw was imagined, inspired by the affection and admiration he felt for her, but he thought he saw desperation, the haunted look of someone who was hunted and heard the baying hounds drawing near.

11

DRIVING FROM SHERMAN OAKS to the motel in Tarzana, Jane went over every move she'd made at the Branwick house.

She had worn gloves. No prints.

There had been an alarm system, a keypad by the door. But no obvious security cameras. Just the basic door and window alerts.

The five rounds she had fired would be recovered by the CSI team. As soon as convenient, she would need to break down the pistol and dispose of the pieces, but not until she obtained a replacement.

At the Tarzana motel again, she got ice and a can of Coke from the vending-machine alcove.

In her room, the door locked for the night, she retrieved a maintenance kit from a suitcase and addressed the .45. Considering how few rounds she fired in the past three days, the weapon didn't require cleaning, but considering what one bullet had done to the son of Richard and Berniece Branwick, Jane felt a need to clean it.

While she worked on the Heckler & Koch, she allowed herself to think about Jimmy Bob, how it went down with him, the inevitability of it once he'd thrown his pen in her face and lifted the chair to swing it and called out to the hulk to kill her.

During her career, she'd participated in ten investigations of mass and serial murders. Eight resolutions. Five cases wrapped with arrests involving no violence. In the sixth, another agent on the team took down a guy who killed little boys. The seventh was J. J. Crutchfield, collector of eyes, whom Jane shot in the leg. In the eighth case, she'd been in a tight place on a lonely farm—another agent dead—stalked by two sociopathic rapists and kill buddies; she killed both. No regrets. No guilt. Yet she couldn't repress memories of how even evil men cried out to God or their mothers and wept like children when hollow-point rounds gouged away chunks of them.

Robert Branwick was her third kill, a creep, a criminal driven by greed and a taste for power. Yet he was also a human being with a past, raised by loving parents who regarded him with affection, grateful for the gift of their early retirement, because they had no clue how he really made his money. If he was physically repulsive, he couldn't help that, and if he compensated with the ludicrous pretension of being a well-laid Casanova, he was not the only man to have an exaggerated sense of his appeal to women. Killing in self-defense wasn't murder.

Jane had no remorse about dropping the hacker, but to hold fast to her humanity, she must recognize his.

Investigative police work and soldiering were different worlds. In war, you often killed at such a distance that you never saw the faces of those who wished you dead and your country in ruins, and if in close combat you glimpsed their faces, you knew nothing of them.

To investigate a man, study him, and then be able to kill him, even to save the lives of innocents or in self-defense, required a stalwart sense of duty ... and ensured moments of doubt. She didn't doubt the rightness of what she'd done, but she sometimes doubted that she fully understood why she had the capacity to do it.

Robert Branwick had been raised by law-abiding people. Jane's father was a wife murderer. Did nature or nurture matter more?

Whenever she allowed herself to brood about it, she believed there were two reasons that she had forsaken a career in music for one in law enforcement: as a rejection of her famous father and as atonement for her childhood cowardice in the weeks and months after her mother's murder had been passed off as a suicide.

But if by nature she was more an heir of Cain than of Abel, it was also necessary to consider that she might have chosen her career as a way of legitimizing the violence of which she was capable.

The few times she raised this subject with Nick, he had said, *Yeah, life is complicated, but if it wasn't complicated, it would be a roller coaster on a flat track. Wouldn't be a ride worth taking. And, yeah, we never fully know ourselves, but that means we're mysterious enough to interest one another. And if we fully knew ourselves in this world, what reason would we have to still be here?*

Finished cleaning the pistol, she put away the maintenance kit. She took five cartridges from her stash of ammunition and pressed them into the half-empty magazine.

She mixed Coke and vodka over ice.

She sat in bed. Switched on the TV.

Breaking news. Two crazies in a Miami restaurant had chopped people with a machete and stabbed with knives. Wounded five, killed three. They would have killed more if they hadn't been dropped hard by a diner who was an armed off-duty policeman.

Jane surfed the channels, searching for an old black-and-white movie made in an age of innocence. Preferably a musical with a corny love story and a touch of comedy, not in the least ironic or hip. She couldn't find one.

Off with the TV, on with the bedside clock-radio.

She located a station risking oldies from the '50s, though few people alive remembered that decade anymore. It was something called "The Presley and Platters Hour." The Platters were just rolling into the opening bars of "Twilight Time," which was all right with her.

She put a pillow on her lap. She smoothed out the

crumpled page from the notepad on which Jimmy Bob had written at her direction, and she placed it on the pillow.

As she sipped the Coke and vodka, Jane studied the names on the paper. Aspasia, a brothel named after the mistress of a statesman of ancient Athens. William Sterling Overton, kick-ass tort attorney.

She wondered about beautiful girls who were totally submissive, who were incapable of disobedience, who would satisfy even the most extreme desires, whose permanent silence was assured. She remembered the video of laboratory mice moving in regimented cadres.

Her thoughts were colder than the ice in her drink glass.

David James Michael, the billionaire, would be hard to get at.

Bertold Shenneck might be more vulnerable but still difficult.

In the morning, she would research William Sterling Overton. At the moment, he seemed to be an easier target.

She hoped the attorney could be persuaded to reveal to her the location of Shenneck's playpen, Aspasia. She hoped he wouldn't do something stupid and leave her no choice but to kill him.

Although she had not yet researched him and though he was no less a human being than she was, Jane suspected that, if she were forced to kill him, she would have no reason for remorse.

12

AT NINE O'CLOCK FRIDAY MORN-
ing, in her office in Springfield Town Center, Gladys
Chang used a booster pillow on her chair, to bring
her into a correct relationship with her desk.

Nathan Silverman sat in one of the two client
chairs, smiling too much for an FBI agent making
serious inquiries. He *knew* he was smiling exces-
sively, but he couldn't maintain a solemn expression
because he delighted in looking at the woman and
listening to her.

Mrs. Chang, thirtysomething, a second-generation
Chinese American, was a stylish dresser and a petite
dynamo—maybe all of five feet if she were to take
off her high-heel shoes—with delicate features and
jet-black hair and a musical voice. She insisted on
being called Glad. Silverman was greatly charmed
by her, and though his appreciation didn't have an
erotic edge—well, not much—he felt vaguely guilty
because he was in fact a happily married man.

"Oh," Mrs. Chang said, "Mrs. Hawk's house, a
whirlwind sale, zip-zoom-zap, listed and sold the
same day to a developer who builds on spec. Very
sad deal. I took longer to decide which hummingbird feeder to buy for my patio. Do you like hum-
mingbirds, Nathan?"

"Yes," he said. "They're quite pretty, aren't they?"

"Wonderful! Those iridescent feathers! And so industrious. Of the many species, in Virginia we see mostly the ruby-throated. Did you know the ruby-throated migrates from South America and flies nonstop for five hundred miles across the Gulf of Mexico?"

"Five hundred miles nonstop. That's remarkable."

"They build nests from plant down and spiderwebs. Spiderwebs!" She put one hand to her breast, as if the thought of building with something as delicate as spiderwebs took her breath away. "And they decorate the nests with lichen. Decorate! How sweet is that?"

"That's delightful. Mrs. Chang—" She held up a hand to correct him. "I'm sorry," he said. "Glad. A moment ago, Glad, you said . . . 'very sad deal.' If Jane's house sold so quickly, isn't that good?"

"Not at her price. Crazy low. It pained me. She didn't care as much about price as about how quick I could move it, and the poor girl wouldn't listen to reason."

"Maybe she couldn't bear living there . . . after what happened to her husband."

Mrs. Chang made a fist of her right hand and rapped it three times over her heart. "How terrible. I knew him a little. I sold the house to them. He was such a nice man. I knew about the suicide, of course. I know everything in neighborhoods where I sell houses. But she lived there two months after it happened, before she came to me. May I tell you something, Nathan, and you won't think I'm bragging? I am very good at reading people. I'm not gifted with many talents, but I have that one. And I am sincerely sure it wasn't grief that made her sell the house fast. It was fear."

"Jane isn't someone who scares," he said. "Not easily, anyway."

"Fraidy-cats don't become FBI. Of course. But she wasn't afraid for herself. She was scared for her sweet hummingbird, her little boy. What a darling little boy! She kept him close, didn't want to let him out of her sight."

"She told you she was afraid for him?"

"No. She didn't have to. It was as plain as the print on a billboard. Anybody she didn't know approached the boy, Mrs. Hawk tensed up. Once or twice, I thought she might draw her gun."

Nathan leaned forward in his chair. "You think she had a concealed weapon?"

"She's FBI. Why wouldn't she have a gun? I got a glimpse of it once. She was leaning over the desk. Her blazer was unbuttoned and it hung open, and I just happened to see the holster, the handle of the gun along her left side."

Less to Mrs. Chang than to himself, Silverman said, "But who would want to harm Travis?"

The Realtor leaned over her desk and pointed at him, jabbed her forefinger at him. "There is the question for your FBI, Nathan. Your FBI should investigate just that very thing. What horrible kind of person would want to hurt that beautiful little hummingbird? You go find out. You go find that horrible person and lock him up."

13

FRIDAY MORNING, IN HER MO-
tel room, Jane spent two hours with more autopsy
reports. She found three cases in which the forensic
pathologists trephined decedents' skulls and examined their brains.

One of the three was in Chicago. The part of the
report dealing with the dead man's gray matter was
heavily redacted. Fully half the words had been
electronically blacked out.

Autopsy reports were public records. These electronic files were the original documents. If a court
ordered files released to a petitioner, authorities
could attempt redaction of *copies* within the limits of
the law. But it wasn't legal to tamper with originals.

In the second case, involving the autopsy of a
woman in Dallas, examination of the brain was one
of the numbered items on the table of contents. But
that section of the report had gone missing.

The third decedent, Benedetta Jane Ashcroft, had
died by her own hand in a hotel in Century City. The
L.A. medical examiner's attending forensic pathologist, Dr. Emily Jo Rossman, examined the brain and
made extensive observations, some of which were
reported in language too technical for Jane to fully
understand.

Photos of the brain were referenced in the report.
The file contained no such photos.

14

AT 9:15, ON HER WAY OUT FOR the day, Jane stopped in the motel office to pay cash for another night.

The clerk was a girl, nineteen or twenty. Chopped everywhichway black hair. Dangling silver-spider earrings. A badge pinned to her shirt identified her as CHLOE. Engrossed in something that she was doing on her smartphone, Chloe put it aside reluctantly.

On the screen, Jane saw a photo of the actor Trai Byers.

After paying, she said, "Do you have one of those celebrity-tracking apps? Star Spotter or Just Spotted, anything like that?"

"Cooler than that. There's always something way cooler like about every six months."

"Could you do me a favor? This famous guy I'm interested in—is he in L.A. right now or where?"

"Sure. Gimme his name."

"William Sterling Overton." She spelled the surname.

"What's he star in?"

"He's an attorney. But he's been married to actresses and he dates supermodels, so I think he'll be in the celebrity pool."

After maybe ten seconds, Chloe said, "Yeah, he's cute. But I gotta say, he's kind of old for you."

Chloe shared the screen, and Jane saw a man who resembled the actor Rob Lowe with a rougher edge.

Working the phone again, Chloe said, "He's forty-four."

"Ancient," Jane said. "But cute. And rich."

"Rich is best," Chloe said. "Rich is forever young, huh? Yeah, he's in town. He's got a one o'clock lunch reservation at Alla Moda. That is a super-expensive joint." She looked at Jane's outfit. "You maybe want to change if you're gonna try to slide up to him there."

"I will," Jane said. "You're totally right."

"More style, more hot," Chloe advised.

15

ON HER WAY TO A LIBRARY IN Woodland Hills, Jane passed a high school where six or eight police cars had gathered. Uniformed cops were arrayed on the public sidewalk, mostly in pairs, as if they expected something worse to happen than what had already occurred.

Scores of students milled about at the top of the school steps, watching the police.

Two handcuffed teenagers sat at the bottom of the steps, talking to each other, at the moment laughing.

Forty feet from the comedians, a dead man lay on

the sidewalk. The scene was so fresh, no one had covered the body, although an officer was taking a blanket from the trunk of a patrol car.

The victim had gray hair. Maybe a teacher. Or just someone passing by at the wrong time.

Not long ago, ninety percent of homicides were committed by people who knew their victims. Now as many as thirty percent involved people who didn't know each other. Once a crime of intimacy, homicide was becoming as random as death by lightning.

She arrived at the library in Woodland Hills without another disturbing incident. She was grateful for uneventful moments.

At a workstation in the computer alcove, she googled William Sterling Overton. She took her time. The people looking for her would not have included the lawyer on a red-flag list of names, words, phrases, and websites that might identify her use of library Internet access. She had first learned of his creepy connection to "Shenneck's playpen"— therefore to Shenneck—because Jimmy Bob had used his criminal expertise *against* his clients as well as for them, but those in conspiracy with Shenneck would be unaware of that.

Within half an hour, she had all she needed. In fifteen minutes, she also got the basics on Dr. Emily Rossman, the L.A. forensic pathologist whose autopsy report she had found pertinent.

Last of all, she googled Dougal Trahern, a name she had finally remembered this morning, after it had teased at the back of her mind since Monday in San Diego. Interesting.

During her time in the library, a change had come over the morning. The ocean, far off and unseen in the south, had spawned a towering fog, which now was driven inland by an onshore flow. The sky beyond the Santa Monica Mountains loomed white. The distant heights of rock-shot earth and chaparral were dissolving from view as if the mist were a universal solvent. Easing through those mountain passes, the fog might never reach here, but it pushed before it a cooling breeze that had a faint metallic scent she couldn't identify.

For no reason she could define, as she breathed in that thin astringent odor and stared south at the dead-white sky, she wondered if things were all right at Gavin and Jessica's place, if the German shepherds remained alert to trouble, if Travis was still safe.

16

ACCORDING TO HIGHLY LAU-datory magazine profiles in *Vanity Fair* and *GQ,* the house in Beverly Hills was only one of five residences owned by William Overton. The attorney had a Manhattan apartment, another in Dallas. A golf-course home in Rancho Mirage. A penthouse in a glittering San Francisco high-rise.

The Beverly Hills home was his primary residence. Jane could have used the city directory to get an address; but a photo of the house in a newspaper article had revealed the street number.

Google Earth had provided a satellite look at the property. Street View gave her a 360-degree scan of the entire block.

She arrived at 2:30 in the afternoon with a plan.

After learning about Overton from Chloe, Jane had read a magazine piece in which it was said that a Friday lunch at Alla Moda—Italian for *fashionable*—was sacred to him, his favorite meal of the week, that he ate with the chef, who was his co-owner, and that the two-hour lunch marked the start of his weekend.

She was banking on him holding to his habits.

The Moderne-style two-story house with stepback details at the front door and roofline had been featured in a *Los Angeles Times* piece. This bachelor's pad was "only" seven thousand square feet in an area where houses were often fifteen thousand or even larger.

Given the size of the house and Overton's reputation as a Don Juan, she doubted he needed or wanted live-in help. A full-time maid could keep the place clean. In all likelihood, she was expected to be gone for the week when the master of the house came home from his sacred lunch, which might be between three-thirty and five o'clock.

After parking around the corner, Jane walked back to the place, carrying a large purse. She followed a walkway of limestone pavers and rang the bell. When no one answered, she rang again, and again.

Staked in a nearby flowerbed, a foot-square sign with red-and-black lettering announced:

PROTECTED BY

VIGILANT EAGLE, INC.

IMMEDIATE ARMED RESPONSE.

Most home-security companies used the same central station, to which all breaches of premises were first reported. Depending on its protocols, the central station summoned the police if it deemed the signal not to be a false alarm.

A company that dispatched its own licensed-to-carry officers, who were likely to be there well before the cops, was an expensive alternative and daunting to would-be burglars.

As Google had revealed, Overton's house was screened from the adjacent properties by privacy walls against which had been planted a series of *Ficus nitida*—trees with dense foliage, trained into tall hedges. The neighbors could not see Jane at the front door. Nor could they see her as she walked around the side of the house to the big backyard, which was screened from view on all three sides.

Lined with blue-glass tiles, the sparkling lap pool was about a hundred feet long. The nearer end shaped into a spa to sit eight.

An enormous patio paved with limestone. An outdoor kitchen at one end. Enough teak chairs and lounges, fitted with blue cushions, to seat at least twenty people. A second-story deck with more teak furniture shaded half the lower space.

The house was a miniature resort. Manicured shrubs and flowers. Ultramodern statuary that resembled nothing, just shapes. Sleek and tasteful. The Beautiful People would feel at home here when invited, and a few might even be beautiful on the inside, too.

According to gossip sites, Overton was currently between main squeezes. If the gossipers could be believed, no heiress, model, supermodel, or actress lived with him.

Because Jane had no way to get inside until Overton arrived and deactivated the alarm, she settled into a chair toward the corner of the house that adjoined the garage.

Earlier, at the library, using a police passcode to the DMV records in Sacramento, she learned that two vehicles were registered to Overton at the Beverly Hills address—a white Bentley, a red Ferrari—and one to his law firm, a black Tesla. If he was driving the electric vehicle, she might not be alerted to his arrival until the garage door began to rumble upward.

The coastal fog hadn't reached Beverly Hills. The day remained warm. The light, refreshing breeze came scented with jasmine.

Jane waited. Waiting could be more stressful than

action, even when the action involved a pumped and pitiless giant with a shotgun.

At 3:30, from her large handbag she extracted the LockAid lock-release gun and put it on her lap.

She slipped her hands into the black-silk gloves with the decorative silver stitching.

Twenty minutes later, the quiet of discreet wealth gave way to the growl of money loudly celebrated in the twelve-stroke engine of an Italian racing legend. Out toward the front of the house, tires lipped a thin squeal off blacktop as the Ferrari executed a turn too sharp, too fast from the street into the driveway.

Lock-release gun in one hand, purse in the other, Jane sprang off the patio chair. She stepped to the kitchen door, put the purse down, and inserted the LockAid's thin pick into the keyway. She wanted to get the noise of the automatic pick out of the way before Overton entered the house.

As the garage door rumbled up, a shrill continuous warning tone sounded throughout the residence. Depending on how the alarm system might be programmed, Overton had one minute—at most two—to enter a disarming code in the keypad mounted on the wall beside the interior door that connected the garage and the house. If he didn't enter the code, or if he entered a second disarming code that signified he was under duress, Vigilant Eagle would have armed guards and maybe a dog en route, with the local police in their wake.

By the time the Ferrari drove into the garage and

the throaty engine choked off, all the pin tumblers in the lock were cleared, and the knob turned freely.

Jane picked up her handbag, dropped the Lock-Aid into it, and stepped into the house. With the alarm shrilling throughout the residence, she closed and locked the door.

The muffled clatter of guide wheels following their tracks issued from the adjacent garage as the sectional door descended.

She hurried across the spacious kitchen, through a swinging door, into the ground-floor hallway. Doors to the left and right.

Dining room on the left. No.

On the right, a home gym full of circuit-training machines. Three walls featured floor-to-ceiling mirrors. Nowhere to hide that he wouldn't see her reflection the moment he opened the door. No.

Above the alarm came the digital tones of the disarming code as Overton entered numbers in the garage keypad.

A half bath. No. It might be his first stop.

A soft *ka-chunk*. The door closing between the garage and house.

A step-in closet. Housekeeping supplies, a vacuum cleaner. Yes. She eased the door shut, put down the handbag, drew her pistol, and waited in darkness.

17

IN COURT, HE IS MR. OVERTON, and elsewhere he is usually Bill or William, but among his closest friends—and in his own mind—he is Sterling.

This week has brought him a legal triumph: the settlement of a class-action case that will further enrich him, make the law firm that bears his name more greatly feared than it already is, and even to some extent benefit his clients. His leisurely lunch with Andre has been as usual satisfying both as to the cuisine and the company. For a culinary master who insists on the purity of all ingredients, Andre has a deliciously impure sense of humor.

In the kitchen, Sterling goes to the Crestron panel by the back door, which controls all the house systems. He calls up the security screen. He doesn't intend to spend part of the afternoon outside, so he presses the key labeled H, which activates the perimeter sensors at doors and windows, but not the interior motion detectors.

The recorded voice of the system robotically declares, *"Armed to home."*

Sterling is in a festive mood. He calls up the through-house music system and from his playlist selects SALSA. The irresistible beat reverberates through the house, and Sterling moves with the music as he goes to the refrigerator and gets a bottle of Perrier.

He prefers instrumentals to other forms of music, because no matter how good the songwriter, half the lyrics will inevitably be sentimental bullshit that annoys him. He does, however, include tunes that are sung in languages he doesn't speak, because he can't be irritated by words he doesn't understand.

Carrying the Perrier, he pushes through the swinging door and sings a duet with the Spanish-language vocalist as he makes his way along the downstairs hall. He has learned the lyrics phonetically and mimics them with no idea of what he's saying.

Climbing the stairs with something like a samba step, Sterling is amused to think that the judges before whom he has appeared would be amazed to see this playful side of him, as would the defendants' attorneys he has eviscerated with trial strategies as razor-edged as filleting knives. He is a merciless tiger in the courtroom, as he is also with the women who submit to him, the only difference being that the women like his toughness and the defense attorneys do not.

His fourteen-hundred-square-foot bedroom suite is a Moderne masterpiece, inspired by the residence once owned by the Mexican actress Dolores del Río, a classic built in 1929 and still standing at the end of a Santa Monica Canyon cul-de-sac. Since childhood, he has been fascinated by Hollywood. He would have been an actor, a leading man, if he hadn't been drawn to the law. He is enchanted by the power of the law and by the infinite ways that the system can be manipulated to achieve any desired end.

In his large walk-in closet, he changes into a red-accented blue polo shirt by Gucci and blue pants by Officine Générale, barefoot in his private world. Later, he will shower and spend a long, intense evening at Aspasia, doing what he does best.

As he steps out of the closet, softly singing salsa, it seems that Aspasia has come to him. He is face-to-face with the most remarkable-looking girl, hair aniline black and eyes so hot-blue they look as if they could boil water as efficiently as gas flames.

She is holding a spray bottle, as though she wishes him to sample a new men's fragrance from Armani or Givenchy.

He is for an instant frozen by surprise. Then he startles backward a step, and he is surprised again when she sprays his lower face. Something sweet-tasting but with a faintly bleachy odor wraps him in sudden darkness.

18

STERLING DREAMS OF DROWN-ing, and at first he is relieved to wake up.

Salsa enlivens the moment, though he never goes to bed with such festive music playing. His vision is blurred, and a chemical taste makes him grimace, and for a moment he can't determine whether he is standing or sitting, or lying down.

He blinks, blinks, and as his vision clears, some of the mist lifts from his mind as well, but only some of it. He is lying on his back on the bathroom floor, of all places, alongside his prized Deco-period antique bathtub.

When he attempts to move, he realizes that he is restrained. His wrists are bound one to the other with a heavy-duty plastic cable tie. A second tie loops from the first to a third, and the third is secured to one foot of the tub, which stands on balls gripped in the wicked claws of stylized lion paws.

His ankles are likewise shackled to each other and then, with more looped cable ties, to the stainless-steel drainpipe of the bathroom sink.

The basin of the sink is carved from exotic amber quartz and appears to be floating, although it is actually supported by inch-thick, cunningly hidden steel rods that fasten it to a red-steel beam inside the wall. The drainpipe and two stainless-steel water lines exquisitely describe parallel arcs from the bottom of the quartz bowl and disappear into the granite-clad wall. He has long been proud of the sink's elegant, unconventional design.

As his mind clears a little further, he discovers that he is lying on his clothes but is not wearing them. His Gucci polo shirt has been cut off him. Likewise, his wonderfully comfortable Officine Générale pants have been scissored up each leg and through the waistband, the material splayed to each side of him; and the crotch panel has been cut away entirely.

That is twelve hundred and fifty dollars' worth of top-of-the-line wardrobe. He would be incensed, except that in his current semidreamy state of mind, he takes satisfaction in knowing that he looks good in his Dolce & Gabbana gray briefs with black waistband, his package nicely displayed in the snug pouch.

Someone switches off the salsa music.

Sterling begins to come further to his senses when the girl enters from the bedroom. Her face is as lacking in expression as it is beautiful. She towers over him like some goddess. She drops to her knees at his side and places her left hand, in a kinky black glove, on his muscular chest. Slowly she slides her hand down to his abdomen. In spite of his restraints, he doesn't feel imperiled. But then she displays the scissors in her left hand, works the blades—open, closed—still as blank-faced as a mannequin, her eyes such a bright blue, they seem illuminated from within. In a voice as flat as her expression, she says, "What else might be fun to cut off?"

Sterling is now wide awake.

19

OVERTON'S EYES WERE hemlock-green with the faintest purple striations. Jane had never seen a more poisonous stare.

The venom in his eyes was spiced with fear, however, and that was good. Narcissists were usually spineless cowards, but some of them were so extravagant in their self-regard that they believed themselves untouchable. Even in such a dire situation as this, the crazier ones could be incapable of imagining themselves dead.

She needed this attorney to imagine himself dead.

Which he might be.

Overton summoned his boldest courtroom bravado. "You've made a big mistake, and there's damn little time to set things right."

"Have I got the wrong man?" she asked.

"There are a thousand ways you've gotten the wrong man, girl."

"Isn't your name William Overton?"

"You know it is, and you know that's not what I mean."

"The William Overton whose closest friends call him Sterling?"

His eyes grew wide. "Who do you know that knows me?"

That fact had been disclosed in a magazine profile. How odd that those who loved the limelight could reveal personal details to curry favor with an interviewer and later forget what they had said.

"You hired a Dark Web hacking service. Maybe to steal some corporation's trade secrets so you could threaten to blow up the business, get a pretrial settlement. Something like that, huh?"

He said nothing.

"You never met the hacker, never saw the sleaze you hired. He used the name Jimmy."

"You're talking nonsense. You're operating on bad information."

"While Jimmy hacked for you, he also hacked into you, taking one of your best-guarded secrets."

In the courtroom, with his clothes on, not shackled, he would have maintained a deadpan stare. Under these circumstances, he found it rather more difficult to remain poker-faced.

All his secrets schooled like sharks through his mind, and there were no doubt so many that he had no hope of guessing which one had motivated her to violate the sanctity of his home.

"You want hush money? Is that all this is?"

"*Hush money* is such an ugly term. It implies extortion."

"If you really have something on me, and you don't, but if you did really have something, going at it this way is bug-shit crazy."

She would not mention his close friend Bertold Shenneck or nano-machine brain implants. *That* secret was so big and dark, he would know he had no future anymore if it were exposed. He must continue to believe that he had hope, however thin it might be.

"Jimmy says you belong to some totally hot club."

"Club? A few country clubs. It's just smart business, making contacts. *Hot* isn't the word for any of them. Unless you think golf and golf talk and white-jacketed waiters are *totally* the thing."

"This club is some sick damn rich-guy whore-house."

"Whores? You think I need to pay *whores*? Screw you. Screw Jimmy. I don't know any Jimmy."

"But Jimmy knows this thing about you. Three hundred thousand bucks to join. You move in exclusive circles."

"This is a stupid fantasy your Jimmy cooked up. There's no such place as far as I know."

"What's three hundred thousand buy, and what are the ongoing charges? You're a guy who gets value for his money. What do you get in the club? Beautiful, submissive girls? No desire too extreme? Just how extreme are your desires, Sterling?"

She had noticed a poker tell: When she told him a truth about himself that he wished she didn't know, his right eye blinked, only the right.

"They call the place Aspasia," she said. "Your type probably think that, naming it after the mistress of an ancient Greek statesman like Pericles, you've made it a classy establishment." She raised the scissors and worked them. "Snip-snip. Keep lying to me, Sterling, damn if I won't tailor you a little."

He ignored the scissors and met her eyes, but this long and considered stare was not an adolescent challenge. He was taking her measure, as perhaps he took the measure of jurors in a courtroom.

When he spoke, he clearly had determined that continuing to play innocent was the most dangerous path he could take. But he still didn't give her the satisfaction of acknowledging the fear that he repressed. He shook his head, smiled, and pretended the admiration of one predator for another. "You are something else."

"Yeah? What am I, Sterling?"

"Damn if I know. Look, no more bullshit. Yeah, Aspasia's real. It's not a whorehouse the way you mean. It's something new."

"New in what way?"

"You don't need to know. I'm not selling information here. I'm just buying my ass out of a sling. You could publicly embarrass me. Damage my business. Blackmail. You came here for money."

"Is that really what you think this is about?" she asked.

"It's always what everything's about. You came here for money, I have it, so let's do the deal."

"I can't walk into a bank with a blackmail check, Sterling. I don't have accounts in the Cayman Islands that you can wire it to."

"I'm talking cash. I said no more bullshit. From either of us, okay? You know I'm talking cash."

"How much?"

"How much do you want?"

"You're talking a home safe, right here?"

"Yes."

"Is there at least a hundred thousand in it?"

"Yes."

"Then I'll take everything in it. What's the combination?"

"Isn't one. The key to the lock is a biological identifier."

"What—your thumbprint?"

"So you cut off my thumb and hold it to the reader? Nothing that easy. You need me. Alive. When I'm dead, it's locked for good."

"All right. Anyway, it's not my intention to kill you unless you give me no other choice."

He rattled the plastic cable ties that cuffed him to the bathtub. "Let's do it, then. Let's get it done."

"Not now," Jane said. "After I've been there and come back."

Overton looked baffled. "Been where?"

"Aspasia."

Alarmed and unable to conceal it, he said, "You can't go there. You can't get in. Only members can get in to any of them."

"Any of them? How many clubs does Aspasia run?"

He looked abashed that he had given up a bit of essential data. Too late. "Four. Los Angeles, San Francisco, New York, Washington."

Jane seemed to have opened something that was

both Pandora's box and the figurative can of worms. "Jimmy says when you get to that Dark Web site, it offers to deal with you in any of eight languages. So there's members all over the world, huh? Oligarchs with extreme desires."

Instead of responding to her supposition, he repeated, "Only members can get in."

"You're a member. Tell me how it works. What's the security?"

"That's not the point. There is no security. Not the way you mean it. But you're not me."

"Aspasia uses facial-recognition software?" she asked.

"Yes."

"You said no more bullshit."

"It's true."

"Famous guys, überrich guys put their faces on file at a place like that? Don't jerk me around, Sterling. I'm getting sick of it. I said I'd kill you only if you gave me no choice. What do you think you're doing? Giving me no choice is what you're doing. The only way Aspasia works is no cameras, no names asked or given. No way for anyone to prove you ever went there."

Overton shook his head, thought of another lie, decided not to risk putting it into words.

"You and people like you must have developed these places. You must believe you can come and go from them as anonymous as ghosts."

He wanted to argue, persuade, litigate, but no jury waited to be convinced, no judge to rule in his favor. There was just Jane, who had no courtroom role. She was only, possibly, his executioner.

His frustration was so great that his fists were clenched within the cable ties, his neck muscles taut, his rapid pulse visible in his temples, his face flushed less with fear than with fury. "Damn it, you stubborn, stupid bitch, you can't go there, you can't get in. The money you want is all here and more where that came from. *There's nothing for you at Aspasia!*"

Leaning over him, she lied in a whisper: "There's my sister."

He knew at once what she meant, and he was stunned. His anger evaporated. "I have nothing to do with that."

"With what?"

"Procuring the girls."

"The beautiful, submissive girls?" she asked.

"I have nothing to do with that."

"But perhaps you used her. Maybe you were cruel to her?"

"No. That's not me. That's not the way I am. And whatever I might have done—*I didn't know you then.*"

The absurdity of his defense elicited a sour laugh from Jane. She pinched his cheek, as a grandmother might pinch that of a little boy who charmed her. "Aren't you precious, Sterling? You didn't know me then. And now that we're friends, of course, you would treat my little sister like a princess."

At last he could no longer conceal his fear, which swelled quickly into a barely contained terror. His tanned and toned body prickled with gooseflesh, and not because the bathroom had grown chilly. "She might not even be at the L.A. facility."

"Facility? How respectable a word for a place of such hideous corruption. I'm going there, Sterling. You're going to tell me how to get in, everything I need to know. Then I'll come back here with my sister, and we'll open the safe, and we'll leave you in one piece to think about how fragile life is."

"You don't understand."

"What don't I understand?"

He shuddered violently and said only, "My God."

"What God is that, Sterling?"

She slipped one blade of the scissors between his bare thigh and the fabric of his underwear. She began to cut the cloth.

"All right, wait, stop. You can get in and out of the place."

She ceased cutting. "How?"

"No cameras. No alarms. The only security is two men."

"Armed?"

"Yes. But you'll enter my password at the gate and at the front door, and because it's a member's password, they won't see you."

"Won't see me? Am I invisible?"

"Essentially, yes." He took a deep breath, blew it out, met her eyes to make a claim of sincerity. "They don't see members."

"Am I to believe these armed thugs are blind?"

"No. Not blind." He was pale, both chilled and

sweating, lying there like an overgrown baby in his soft, gray designer diaper, the waistband announcing DOLCE & GABBANA across his flat stomach. "But they don't see members because . . . because they're . . . If I explain, if I say more than another word, you might as well kill me now. If you don't, others will."

She parsed what he had said. "'More than another word,'" she quoted. "So there's one more word that you can say and maybe not be killed by your own kind?"

He closed his eyes. After a silence, he nodded.

Jane quoted him once more. "'They don't see members because they're'—what?"

"Programmed," he said, without opening his eyes.

20

"PROGRAMMED," STERLING SAYS, and dares not look at her hovering over him, because she will call his answer bullshit or she will want to know more. Who wouldn't want to know more? But it really means his certain death if he betrays Bertold Shenneck and David James Michael and the others. Not just his death. His ruination *and* his death. There is no hope of turning state's evidence and bargaining to rat them out in return for being allowed to go on living in style, not after what they have all done. This has been an all-or-nothing enterprise from the start. He bought in knowing the stakes.

After the bitch is silent for a while, Sterling opens his eyes and finds her waiting to meet his stare. He wonders how a face can be so contorted with contempt and yet remain so beautiful, how such dazzling blue and inviting eyes can look so pitiless.

Closing the blades of the scissors, she says, "I won't carve more revelations out of you. I think only torture would get more, and I don't have the stomach to touch you, which is the only way to get it done. So here's what's going to happen. You'll give me the address of Aspasia and your membership password. I'll drive your Bentley there. When I come back, we'll open the safe, and I'll take what I want."

"And me?"

"That'll be up to you."

"What if something happens? What if you don't come back?"

"When you miss appointments on Monday, someone will come looking. You probably won't die of thirst by then."

She gets to her feet and plucks a washcloth from a nearby towel rack. With the scissors, she cuts off a third of the cloth, throws aside the scrap, and rolls the larger piece into a tight ball.

For Sterling, she has become something more than a woman, has ascended to the status of mystery, holding over him the power of life and death as no one has before, a creature of flesh and blood yet mystical and fearsome and unknowable. He watches her with dread, her every action now enigmatic and potentially a preparation for a mortal blow.

Holding forth the rolled-up portion of the washcloth, she says, "I'm going to stuff this in your mouth, then duct-tape it in place. You try to bite me, I'll bust out all your teeth and *then* stuff it in your mouth. Believe me?"

"Yes."

"First, tell me where to find the keys to the Bentley and the house. Also the address of Aspasia and what I do when I get there."

He tells her without hesitation.

"Now the code to disarm the house alarm."

"Nine, six, nine, four, asterisk."

"If that's the crisis code that disarms the alarm but also alerts them that you're under duress, if it summons help, here's what'll happen. Once I switch off the perimeter alarm you set when you came home, I won't just drive away and let them come to free you. I'll stand here for five minutes, ten, to see if there's going to be an armed response from Vigilant Eagle or the cops. And if there is, I'll shoot you in the face. Now . . . do you want to give me another disarming code?"

He hardly recognizes his own voice when he says, "Nine, six, nine, five, asterisk."

"One digit different. Nine, six, nine, five—not four. Is that it now?"

"Yes."

She kneels beside him again, and he opens his mouth, and she shoves the rolled cloth in there. From her big purse, she takes a roll of wide duct tape. It's not a handbag; it's the sack of a damn witch. With the scissors, she cuts a piece of tape and seals the gag in his mouth. She winds a longer length of tape twice around his head to hold the shorter piece in place.

She goes away to the Crestron panel in the bedroom. Tones sound as she enters the code, and the recorded voice says, *"Control is disarmed."*

When she returns, she draws a pistol from under her sport coat. She stands over him, the weapon at arm's length, the muzzle no more than a foot from his face.

He has given her the safe code. He knows that no armed response will be coming. Nevertheless, whether five or ten minutes, that wait is the longest hour of his life.

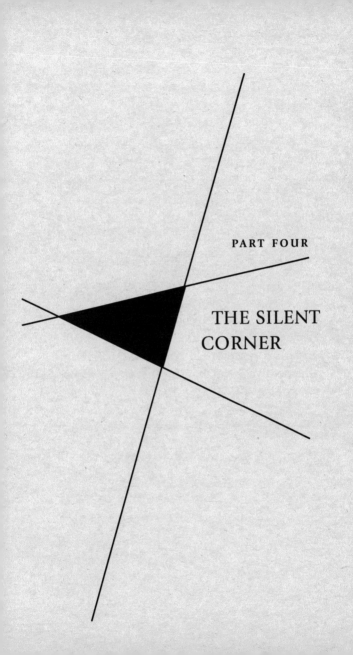

PART FOUR

THE SILENT
CORNER

1

IN VIRGINIA, NATHAN SILVER-
man stayed an hour later than usual in his office so
that he could review again the edited and compiled
video from Palisades Park in Santa Monica and from
the hotel, which had come in from L.A. late in the
afternoon.

The hotel cameras were confined to a limited
number of interior public spaces, but the video was
high definition.

*Here is Jane at the lobby entrance, back to the camera.
She opens the door. The Amazon skates inside carrying
two briefcases and makes her way directly to the elevator
alcove. Jane chains and padlocks the front doors. Here is
Jane joining the skater at the elevators. Into the cab. The
garage as they step out of the cab. The skater carries her
skates. Jane carries a trash bag. The two women racing
up the ramp.*

They must have had a car in the alleyway or

somewhere nearby. Sensitive about being accused of violating the privacy of the public, the hotel had not mounted a camera in the alley. The city had no coverage there, either. Where Jane and the skater had gone from that point was unknowable.

The park video and traffic-cam footage came from cheaper, older cameras with dust-filmed lenses. The quality of the images was poor. The video would have to undergo considerable, patient enhancement if there was to be any chance of identifying the various players.

One thing, however, was clear beyond dispute: Jane had set up a swap of some kind in the park, and she had feared a trap. Judging by the number of people associated with the man bearing the briefcases and the metallic balloon—HAPPY, HAPPY—she was right to expect a double cross.

Silverman had not yet assigned these inquiries a case number. Initially, he, himself, would be the special agent in charge.

Neither had he alerted the director to the possibility of an agent having gone rogue. Nothing was worse. The Bureau had to come down hard on any individual who would wear its name but break the laws that she was sworn to uphold. If the charge was lodged but then proved false, Jane would nevertheless be stained forever by the mere accusation, and her life, already fractured by the loss of Nick, would be shattered.

In his mind's ear, he heard the voice of Gladys

Chang: *She wasn't afraid for herself. She was scared for her sweet hummingbird, her little boy.*

This was Friday. Investigations of crimes continued 24/7, but in cases where no lives hung in the balance and national security was not an issue, the Bureau cranked down the intensity of its work on Saturday and Sunday. Nathan could justify putting a pin in the matter of Jane Hawk until Monday.

What he did during the next seventy-two hours, however, might seal his own fate even as he worried about hers. He and Rishona had reservations for dinner at a favorite restaurant in Falls Church. He would share with her all his thoughts about what steps to take next in this matter. After all, if he walked a long way out on a limb, he was taking Rishona with him. If at the moment there wasn't anyone with an intention to saw that particular limb off behind him, there would most likely be one by sometime next week. When you acted on principle tempered by compassion, there was sooner or later always someone with a saw.

He drove home through lighter traffic than expected.

The weather had taken a turn toward an early spring.

Twilight was a magical Maxfield Parrish shade of blue.

The stars seemed to be born moment by moment as they appeared sequentially in the darkling heavens.

And just the previous night, the rain gutter that he repaired had not collapsed in the storm.

Perhaps fate was at the moment on his side to such an extent that taking a long walk on a limb would be worth the risk.

2

ALTHOUGH MONEY COULDN'T buy happiness, driving a Bentley calmed an agitated mind. The rush hour in greater L.A. was at least four hours long, and this state that built the greatest highways in the nation now rated last in the quality of its roads. In Overton's Bentley, the rudeness of ill-maintained pavement was rendered almost mythical by a suspension system that smoothed away all shocks.

And there, Jane thought, was the problem with a man like Overton. Wealth had not corrupted him. What he'd *chosen to do* with his wealth corrupted him. First he insulated himself from ordinary human experience, and then deemed himself superior to the masses, excused himself from all constraints not only of morality but also of tradition, and subsequently felt justified in casting off his conscience as a worthless artifact of primitive and superstitious minds. He had made of himself a malignancy in the human community.

Although the smooth ride in the Bentley planed away the rough edges of her agitation, it did not diminish her indignation, which seemed to be condensing into cold, hard wrath.

The local Aspasia was located in an area of unincorporated county land adjacent to San Marino, a lovely community of grand old homes and estates next door to Pasadena. The Bentley's GPS talked Jane there in the same uninflected tones with which it would help her find her way to a bookstore or a church.

According to Overton, the *facility*—how deeply she despised the evasion represented by that word—occupied a reconstructed mansion on three acres. The voice of the GPS advised her to turn left off a quiet suburban street, and she braked to a halt in a driveway, the headlight beams splashing upon a pair of ten-foot-high iron gates heavy with decorative radials and scroll work. Nothing of the house or grounds could be seen from beyond the property. The gates stood between sections of a ten-foot stacked-stone estate wall graced with ivy and crowned with spear-point iron staves.

The mailbox offered no name, only the street number.

When Jane powered down the window to look at the call box, she could see no watchful lens. Apparently, as Overton had promised, no camera was associated with the gates, either.

Using the oversized keyboard on the call box, she entered the four digits of Overton's membership number followed by his password—VIDAR—which was the name of the Norse god who survived Ragnarok, the war to end all things and all other gods. As the immense gates began to swing inward, she wondered if all these power-mad fools gave themselves the names of pagan gods.

She drew the Heckler & Koch, screwed the sound suppressor to it, and put the weapon on the passenger seat, within easy reach.

Considering Overton's circumstances when she had grilled him, and the suffering he would endure if she didn't return, Jane doubted that he had deceived her. Security guards *programmed* not to see members would at one time have struck her as an absurd lie, purest fantasy, but she remembered the regimented mice in Shenneck's video.

Before her waited not just a property to reconnoiter, not just an investigation to be conducted. Before her lay something new and terrible and still unknown in spite of all that she had learned.

Apprehension gripped her, and she hesitated to proceed.

But there was nowhere else to go. To anyone who didn't know her well, her story would be taken for the ravings of a paranoid. And friends who might believe her, even if they were in a position to provide help, might pay with their lives for doing so.

Overton knew more than he'd told her, but he wouldn't willingly tell her more. She did not have it in her to torture him, to twist more out of him with pliers, carve it out of him with blades.

She reached into a pocket of her sport coat and brought out the silver oval in which was embedded a carved-soapstone profile of a woman. Half of a broken cameo locket.

In memory she heard Travis's voice. *I knew right away it was good luck.*

She smoothed her thumb across the soapstone portrait, palmed the charm, and held it tight in her fist.

After a moment, she pocketed the cameo and drove through the gates with the expectation that she would have to fight her way out.

3

BORISOVICH HAS A THREE-room suite with a private bathroom on the ground floor of the mansion. It is very comfortable. He is given everything he needs. He is happy. His life is without stress.

Volodin has a ground-floor suite of his own. Volodin, too, is given everything he needs. He is happy. His life, too, is without stress.

Borisovich and Volodin are playing cards at the dinette table in Borisovich's rooms. They are competitive players, though they do not play for money. They have no need of money.

Much of their time is spent in games. All kinds of

card games. And backgammon. Chess. Mah-jongg. So many games.

In the communal game room, they often play billiards or darts, or shuffleboard. And there is a bowling alley with an automatic pin-setter.

Members of Aspasia never use the game room. It is provided for Borisovich and Volodin and the girls.

Their employers are thoughtful and generous. Borisovich feels fortunate to have been hired for this job. He knows that Volodin likewise feels most fortunate. And grateful. Their employers are thoughtful. And generous.

In the morning, between nine o'clock and eleven o'clock, when members are not welcome, Borisovich and Volodin will each choose a girl to service him. There are currently eight girls in residence. They are very beautiful girls. They are submissive.

Borisovich and Volodin may do anything with the girls—except hurt them. Borisovich and Volodin are not members.

On this occasion, they are playing gin rummy.

Each of them has a glass of Coca-Cola.

They were once heavy drinkers. Neither man indulges in alcohol anymore. They do not need it.

That sad life is far behind them. They do not dwell on it. They hardly remember.

They are happy now.

Borisovich does not talk much as they play. Neither does Volodin. When they do speak, their conversation is mostly about the game or the girls, or what they had for dinner.

For many people, conversation is mostly complaint and worry. Borisovich and Volodin have nothing to complain or worry about.

They do not leave the property. The travails of life in the world beyond these walls no longer affect them.

Within reach of each man is a Wilson Combat Tactical Elite .45 fitted with a sound suppressor. In the ten months that this facility has been in operation, they have needed to kill and dispose of only two intruders who entered the grounds together on the same night.

It felt good to kill them. A change of pace.

As Volodin lays down a full set of matched cards, earning bonus points, Borisovich hears the pleasant female voice of the official enunciator: *A member has been admitted at the gate.*

The enunciator is not a person. It is a mechanized monitoring system of important developments at Aspasia.

Volodin also receives the message. He stiffens, and he cocks his head as if the words come to him by virtue of his ears, which they do not.

There is nothing for the two men to do. They have no authority over—or interest in—the members.

Volodin records the score.

Borisovich shuffles the cards.

4

BEYOND THE GATES, THE LONG driveway passed between colonnades of up-lighted phoenix palms, their massive cascading crowns forming a roof over two lanes of paving stones. This spectacular approach raised in Jane the expectation of the grandest of grand hotels at the farther end or perhaps an ornate palace.

In fact, something rather like a palace appeared: an enormous Spanish-themed villa. Under the barrel-tile roof, the textured stucco walls were either a pale gold or the exquisitely staged landscape lighting painted them that shade. An imposing balustrade outlined the generous terrace in front of the Roman-arched entry.

Overton had told her to drive past the house to a secondary but imposing structure with ten garage stalls. One of the doors opened automatically to receive the Bentley.

Jane was reluctant to park in the stall, for fear that once the door closed, she would not be able to get it open and retrieve the car in an emergency. But supposing this adventure turned sour, the front gate would be a greater problem than the garage; she could never drive *through* that barrier. If her luck went bad, she would most likely have to escape on foot, over the high estate wall.

Overton had said that in foul weather or fair, a

club member could use an underground passage-way between garage and house. In Jane's circumstances, such a route sounded like a death trap.

When she stepped out of the garage stall, the segmented door descended behind her.

She carried the pistol openly, though she held it down at her side, the silencer-elongated barrel reaching to mid-calf.

Here in the gentler precincts of the valley, the quiet of the night was almost deep enough to suggest that the metropolitan hive lying to every point of the compass had been largely depopulated.

The moon seemed to smoke like a chalice of volatile venom.

She climbed three steps from the driveway, between sections of the balustrade, onto the front terrace.

The solid-wood door was contained within the Roman arch, which was flanked by columns. Above the arch and the spandrel, capitals supported an architrave, above the architrave a fluted frieze, and above the frieze a cornice on which stood two carved-stone life-size conquistadors, each holding a shield and a lance.

Across the façade of the house, light warmed the bronze-framed windows and made jewels of the beveled panes between the muntins.

The great house had a fairy-tale quality as it stood among the palm trees, but in spite of its beauty and its magical aura, Jane thought of Poe's "The Haunted Palace" and its hideous throng.

No camera focused on the threshold, but beside the door was a keypad like the one that had gained her entrance at the main gate. Again she entered Overton's membership number and the name Vidar.

The bolts in an electronic lock retracted, and the door swung open to reveal a deep foyer with an elegant parquetry floor in two marbles—black veined with gold, white veined with black.

Pistol at her side, Jane stepped inside.

The automatic door swung shut behind her, and the lock bolts shot home.

5

IN A VOICE NO EAR CAN DEtect, the enunciator declares, *A member has been admitted to the house.*

Borisovich deals the cards.

"Will there be another disposal?" Volodin wonders.

"There will or there won't," says Borisovich.

"Never before twice in one day. Or at least not that I recall."

"Never twice in one month. Disposals are rare."

"They *are* rare," Volodin agrees.

"They are very rare."

Volodin reviews his cards. "Do you really want to play more gin rummy?"

"I'm all right with it."

"We could bring out the chess set."

"I'm all right with either."

"Me, too," Volodin says.

"Stay with the gin rummy?" Borisovich asks.

Volodin nods. "For a little while. Why not?"

"Why not?" Borisovich agrees.

6

BEYOND THE FOYER, THE MAIN hall soared twenty feet to a coffered ceiling, and the floor featured French-limestone tiles. The house was constructed in a U, embracing three sides of a court-yard that could be seen between limestone columns, through floor-to-ceiling bronze-framed windows. The outdoor space was softly lighted by antique lampposts, and in the center of it, a swimming pool the size of a lake glowed as blue and sparkling as an immense sapphire, from which undulant currents of steam rose like yearning spirits.

The house stood in preternatural silence, a more profound quiet than Jane had ever heard before.

Along the hallway significant bronze statues stood on plinths and elegant sideboards held matched pairs of large Satsuma vases.

If Aspasia was what it claimed to be, every cliché of bordello décor had been avoided. An atmosphere of refined taste and high style allowed the members to satisfy extreme desires while imagining themselves to be superior to the hoi polloi who lived in flyover country or went to the wrong universities or to none at all.

From Overton, she knew that the ground floor had apartments for the security men, common rooms, a kitchen, and other spaces. But the truth of the place would be found on the second floor, where each girl had a suite of her own.

Two grand staircases lay beyond the foyer, one to the right ascending to the east wing, one to the left ascending to the west wing. Limestone treads and risers. Intricate bronze balustrades. The marble-clad walls of each staircase featured niches in which stood larger-than-life-size figures of the goddesses of ancient Greece and Rome: Venus, Aphrodite, Proserpina, Ceres. . . .

Jane stood in the silence at the bottom of the stairs, gazing up into the higher silence, and felt that this elaborate brothel was in fact a mausoleum, where dreams and hopes came to be entombed. She didn't want to go farther. She thought of the lab mice parading in lockstep, and she wondered if, by learning more about Shenneck and his conspirators, she would discover something so monstrous that it would be difficult to see the future past it.

There had been corruption in every civilization since time immemorial. If the corruption was of the heart, the culture could think its way to health with great effort. If the corruption was of the mind, it was more difficult to *feel* a way toward recovery, for the heart was a deceiver. If both mind and heart were riddled with malignancies—what then?

In the end, she had no choice.

Jane climbed the stairs.

The second-floor hallway was at least twelve feet wide and no less sumptuously finished than the spaces downstairs.

According to Overton, there were ten suites on the second floor—five in the east wing, five here in the west. Beside each door, in an ornate gold-leafed frame, hung a portrait of the girl who occupied the suite beyond. The portrait was a photo processed by computer to look like a high-quality oil painting, and the space within the frame was a large flat-screen display, not a canvas.

In the event that the girl was currently with another club member or otherwise indisposed, the screen would be blank, as though some art thief had cut the canvas out of the frame. In this wing of the house, two frames lacked portraits.

If extreme desires were at the moment being satisfied, no sound of pleasure or pain escaped from any suite into the hallway.

She stopped before a portrait of a stunning Eurasian beauty posed in a Chinese side chair with an elaborately carved rosewood back depicting dragons in conflict. The girl wore red-silk pajamas with a white-carnation motif along one side. Over her left breast, the flower bloomed in a state of early dissolution, spilling snowy petals down the side of the blouse and along one silken pant leg.

Jane turned the knob, and the door proved to be automated, swinging open of its own power. No less than four inches thick. Its weight must have been formidable, making its automation necessary.

She stepped into a foyer decorated in tasteful Shanghai Deco, paneled in honey-colored wood with ebony accents, and otherwise restricted to a color palette of silver and sapphire-blue.

When the door closed softly behind her, a brief sucking sound issued from it, as if it seated in an airtight seal.

Jane felt not as if she had moved from a hallway to a room, but as if she had stepped into a vessel from another world and was about to have an encounter with something so alien that she would never be the same.

7

BEYOND THE FOYER LAY A LIV-ing room in which sat the girl in the portrait, wearing the red pajamas with a deflowering chrysanthemum, posed in the dragon chair.

Jane had thought the computer must have idealized the woman's beauty as it also restyled the photograph into a faux oil painting. But she proved no less beautiful and perhaps even more stunning than the picture could convey, in her early to mid-twenties.

She smiled and rose from the chair and stood not in the boldly seductive pose of a prostitute, not even with the cultured and genteel knowing air of a courtesan, but with her arms at her sides and her head ever-so-slightly bowed, wings of shoulder-length ink-black hair framing her delicate face, almost as a well-mannered child would stand in hope of a parent's praise. Her dark-eyed stare was direct yet somehow shy, and when she spoke, her voice seemed ten years younger than she and sincere rather than practiced.

"Good evening. I'm so happy you could visit me."

The girl had seen the pistol that Jane held at her side, but she exhibited no alarm or even the slightest interest, as if it was not for her to judge or even wonder about what a visitor brought into this suite.

"May I bring you a cocktail? Perhaps tea or coffee?"

"No," Jane said. And then, "No, thank you. What is your name?"

The girl tilted her head, and her smile sweetened. "What would you like my name to be?"

"Whatever it really is."

Their voices were subdued not only because they spoke softly but also because the walls seemed to absorb sound, as if lined with soundproofing akin to that in radio-station broadcast booths.

The girl nodded. "You may call me LuLing." Whatever her name might be, it was not LuLing. "And what may I call you?"

"What would you like my name to be?"

"May I call you Phoebe?"

"Why Phoebe?" Jane wondered.

"In Greek it means *bright and shining*," said LuLing, and ducked her head shyly. "Would you enjoy music, Phoebe?"

Moving past her toward the nearest window, Jane said, "Not just yet. Could we first . . . talk for a little while?"

"That would be lovely," said LuLing.

Jane rapped a knuckle against a pane of glass. The window seemed to be exceptionally deep, triple-pane at least.

"Will you join me on the sofa?" asked LuLing.

The girl sat with her legs drawn up under her, one arm extended gracefully along the back of the sofa.

Jane sat a few feet from LuLing and put the pistol on the cushion at her side, not between them.

"It is a special pleasure when a lady visits me," said LuLing.

Jane had wondered if the club restricted membership to men, but evidently that wasn't the case. "I suppose it doesn't happen often."

"Not often enough. Girl fun is special fun. You are quite lovely, Phoebe."

"I'm not in your league."

"You are as modest as you are lovely."

"How long have you . . . been here, LuLing?"

The girl's smile didn't freeze exactly, but it was tempered with puzzlement. "There is no time here. We have no clocks. We have stepped out of the world, out of time. It is sweet here."

"But you must know how long it's been. A month? Three months?"

"We must not talk time. Time is the enemy of all good things."

"Do you ever think about leaving this place?" Jane asked.

LuLing raised her eyebrows. "Why ever would I want to leave? What is out there other than ugliness and loneliness and horror?"

The woman's conversation did not quite seem canned, but there was a quality of conditioning in her every gesture and response. As genuine as she sounded with her adolescent voice, as sincere as her every expression seemed to be, there was something about her so unreal as to be almost extraterrestrial.

8

AS BORISOVICH PUTS DOWN A hand of cards totaling less than ten, thus ending the game, the enunciator reports on an inappropriate question that a member has put to one of the girls. The enunciator isn't privy to the conversations in the upstairs suites, but it receives from the girls those questions and phrases that have been deemed to be potential breaches of protocol. In this case: *Do you ever think about leaving this place?*

Having received the same report from the enunciator, Volodin looks up from the cards and meets Borisovich's eyes.

Borisovich shrugs. From time to time, members say things that are problematic, although none has ever caused a serious incident.

The most annoying thing that ever happens is when, on rare occasion, a disposal is required. Otherwise, they have it easy. He and Volodin are given everything they need. They are happy. Their employers are thoughtful and generous. The sad life is far behind them. They do not dwell on it. They hardly remember. They do not wish to remember, and therefore they do not.

Volodin shuffles the cards.

9

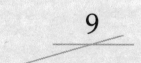

IN SPITE OF LULING'S EXCEPtional beauty and her apparent self-possession, her sense of vulnerability had become nearly as visible to Jane as were the red silk pajamas. This girl was lost and alone, and in denial of both truths.

Or maybe her mental condition might be more

terrible than mere denial. Perhaps she was profoundly delusional, unable to recognize her condition and express her true feelings.

"LuLing, how do you pass the time when visitors aren't here with you?"

"I am responsible for keeping my suite clean, but that is not difficult. I am given every convenience. My employers are generous."

"Then you are paid?"

LuLing nodded, smiling. "I am paid with kindness, with anything I need, with escape from the ugliness of the world."

"There is no ugliness here in Aspasia."

"None," LuLing agreed. "None at all. It is the most beautiful place."

"And when you're not cleaning?"

"I prepare my own meals, which I greatly enjoy. Greatly. I am given every convenience, and I know a thousand and one recipes." She suddenly brightened and clapped her hands as though delighted by the prospect of cooking for her visitor. "May I make for you a wonderful dinner, Phoebe?"

"Maybe later."

"Oh, good. Good, good. You will like my cooking."

"You clean and cook. What else—when there's no visitor?"

"I exercise. I love to exercise. There is a fully equipped gym downstairs. I have a precise exercise routine. A different one for each day of the week. I must maintain my good health and appearance. I have a precise exercise routine and a precise diet, and I follow them precisely. I do not stray. I am very good about this."

Jane closed her eyes and took slow, deep breaths. She had interrogated serial killers regarding their cruelest desires and their methods of murder, but this conversation was taking a toll from her that she'd never paid before.

She could not stop picturing the regimented mice in the video. She could not ban from her mind the image of Nick bathed in blood drawn by his own Ka-Bar knife. The fates of Nick and the mice and this girl were determined by the sinister application of a powerful technology about which she could theorize in only the vaguest terms; and though the people behind this scheme, this conspiracy, this new cartography of Hell, had purposes she understood too well, they also had intentions—why the suicides?—that she could not understand at all.

"Would you enjoy a cocktail now?" LuLing asked.

Jane opened her eyes, shook her head. "What about the other girls here. Do you know them?"

"Oh, yes, they are my friends. They are wonderful friends. We exercise together. Sometimes we entertain a visitor together."

"What are their names?"

"The girls?"

"Yes. What are their names?"

"What would you like their names to be?" asked LuLing.

"You don't know their names," Jane said. "You don't know who they are or where they came from, do you?"

"Of course I know them. They are my friends. Good friends. They are wonderful friends. We exercise together."

"Do you laugh together, LuLing?"

Lines formed in that previously smooth and flawless face, but they were like ripples on a pond made by a tossed stone, formed and fading even as they formed, gone by the time that she had spoken. "I do not know what you mean, Phoebe."

"Do you cry together?"

A knowing look came over the girl. Red silk whispered against the upholstery of the sofa as she slid closer to Jane. She put one hand on her visitor's thigh. "Would you be pleased to make me weep, Phoebe? There is beauty in pain, even greater beauty in humiliation. There is nothing but beauty in Aspasia, nothing ugly, and I am yours completely. You own me."

Here was abomination in this dark palace of beauty, and Jane rose from the sofa with a shudder of abhorrence, nauseated. "I don't own you. No one owns you."

10

THE ENUNCIATOR RECEIVES from the girl a problematic statement by the visiting member and conveys it to Borisovich and Volodin: *I don't own you. No one owns you.*

The men put aside their cards. They consider the Wilson Combat .45s lying on the table, but they do not pick them up.

"It is only a member," Volodin says.

"No breach of the premises has occurred," says Borisovich, for there has been no alarm.

Violence is never used against a member.

Rarely, a member becomes so enamored of a particular girl that the desire is to have her exclusively at his or her side, beyond the walls of Aspasia. This cannot be permitted. The member must be dissuaded from doing anything rash. Two other members, whoever is available, must come to confer with him or her and effect a change of mind.

As yet this member does not seem to have said or done enough to reach the threshold at which an intervention is required. The enunciator will make that decision according to its program.

11

AS JANE THRUST UP FROM THE sofa, LuLing rose as well and put a hand on her shoulder as if to comfort. "Phoebe, nothing that happens here is wrong. You have your desires, and I have mine—that is all."

The girl's eyes were disturbing, though not because she met Jane's gaze so boldly, nor because her stare was fixed and shallow like that of a glass-eyed doll, which it was not. LuLing's eyes were lustrous pools of darkness, her stare as bottomless as that of every mystery that is a human being. But there was a difference to that depth, for it seemed not to teem with life as did other eyes, not to harbor countless hopes and ambitions and fears all schooling like fish. Instead, for all their depth, they were vacant eyes, offering a view into an oceanic abyss where the pressure was oppressive and life was sparse and the silence of drowned things seldom disturbed.

Jane said, "Do you have desires, LuLing? Do you?"

A childlike shyness overcame the girl again. Her soft voice became still softer. "Yes, I have desires. Mine are yours. To be useful and be used—that is what fulfills me."

Stepping out from under the hand on her shoulder, Jane picked up the pistol that lay on the sofa.

As before, the girl showed no concern about the

weapon. Perhaps she would even take a bullet with a smile. Nothing that happened in Aspasia could be ugly, after all, and every wrong that a member committed was instead a right.

"I need to go now," Jane said, and she moved toward the door.

"Have I disappointed?"

Jane stopped, turned, regarded LuLing with a sadness unlike any she had known until now, sadness woven through with frustration and anger and dread and disbelief and belief. This was not merely a girl who had been brainwashed by a cult that deprived her of her freedom; this was more than mere washing; this was scrubbing away the mind until only broken threads remained, and then knitting those threads into someone new. Jane didn't know to whom—to what—she spoke, whether in part to some filament of the girl who had once been fully alive or only to the body of that girl now operated by some alien software.

"No, LuLing. You haven't disappointed. You couldn't possibly disappoint a member of the club."

The flawless and radiant face brightened with a smile. "Oh, good. Good, good. I hope you will come back. I could cook a perfect dinner for you. I know a thousand and one recipes. I would like nothing more than to make you happy."

If far down inside this girl there had seemed to be some small imprisoned consciousness issuing a scream that couldn't be heard here far above the bottom of the abyss, Jane would have taken her out of

Aspasia. But to whom, what, where? To have her identified by fingerprints or otherwise, to return her to some family that she no longer knew and who would not know this new girl woven from the fragile threads remaining of who she had been? No counseling would restore her. If a surgeon trephined her skull and found a nanotech web woven across her brain, he would not know how to remove it, and she most likely would not live through its removal.

"I would like nothing more than to make you happy," LuLing repeated. She sat on the sofa once more. Smiling, she used one hand to smooth the fabric where her visitor had been sitting. She smoothed and smoothed the fabric.

Jane wondered . . . When the girl was not cleaning her suite, which wouldn't take much time, and when she was not making her meals, and when she was not exercising, and when she was not being owned by some visitor, how often did she sit staring into space, alone and silent and still, as if she were a doll abandoned by a child who had moved on from childish things and no longer loved her?

The doorknob felt like ice in Jane's hand. Responding to her touch, the door eased open of its own accord, and she stepped into the hallway, and the door closed behind her.

The hall seemed colder than it had been earlier, and she was shaking, and her legs felt unsteady. She leaned against the wall and took slow, deep breaths. The pistol was terribly heavy in her hand.

12

THE ENUNCIATOR REPORTS NO new transgression on the part of the member with Girl Number Six.

Borisovich and Volodin wait for developments, for the moment having lost interest in card games.

When there are no immediate developments, Volodin says, "It has gotten dark. We can go ahead with the disposal now."

"We might as well," Borisovich agrees. He rises from the table and picks up his pistol and holsters it in his shoulder rig.

Volodin does the same.

Neither man is wearing a jacket, their weapons revealed. They do not expect to encounter a member where they are going.

They leave Borisovich's suite together.

13

JANE CONSIDERED CHOOSING another portrait, opening another door, talking to another girl. But she would learn nothing more than the bleak truth that she already knew. The conversation would be as disturbing and depressing as that between her and LuLing.

Sex was a truth of Aspasia, but it was not *the* truth. The larger truth was raw power, domination, humiliation, and cruelty. These sexual encounters involved no love, no slightest affection, and certainly no procreation. The girls were uncommonly beautiful, as was the house, so that these visitors who had descended into depravity could pretend to themselves and to one another that there was beauty as well in their pitiless barbarity, that their absolute power made *them* beautiful, too, rather than base and demonic.

Only once before in her life had Jane been this afraid and felt this powerless—and that had been a long time ago.

If talking to other girls reduced to LuLing's condition would lead her nowhere, something useful might be learned on the ground floor. The back stairs were nearby. They were enclosed on both sides, unlike the grand main stairs, the ultimate vertical shooting gallery, but she went to them and descended as fast as she dared.

Stairs were one of the challenges she had been taught to meet at the Academy, in Hogan's Alley, a little town of brick and wood buildings, with its courthouse and bank and drugstore and movie theater and Pastime Bar and motel and used-car lot and more, the most well-conceived and authentically constructed reality-training center in the world. No one really lived in Hogan's Alley. All its criminals were actors provided by an agency.

As she descended the back stairs, Jane felt almost as if her training in the faux town of Hogan's Alley had been expressly to prepare her for Aspasia, which was in its way also a stage setting, where the girls and the security men resided but where no one really *lived*.

During her sixteen weeks at Quantico, she'd now and then passed through Hogan's Alley when no scenario was being played out, when no one else walked the streets. Although she was not given to easy superstition, the place had sometimes seemed to be haunted and had sometimes given her the feeling that she was at the end of the world when all human habitations were abandoned and hers was the last heart beating on the planet.

By the time she reached the bottom of the back stairs, she had been overtaken by that end-of-the-world feeling once more, and this time for a better reason. In Aspasia, the darkest desire of humankind—to hold absolute power, to control, to command obedience, to eliminate all voices of disagreement and dissent—had found its full expression. The technology that made LuLing happy to be used, happy to sit and wait to be hurt and humiliated, was the technology of hive masters who would order the world into their idea of utopia, and in so ordering would destroy it.

The west wing on the ground floor remained deserted, the long hallway dwindling toward the front stairs and the foyer, telescoping out before her, as if it would grow longer with every step she took.

She opened one of a pair of doors on the left, found the light switch, and saw a gym with weight-training machines, treadmills, Exercycles. . . .

She thought that the first door on the right might lead to the kitchen, but instead she found a strange windowless room where the overhead fluorescent lights had been left on. White ceramic-tile floor. White walls. In the center of the space stood a table with a pedestal base tiled to match the floor and a stainless-steel top. It seemed like a chamber in a starship in some science-fiction film.

Lying on the table was a naked girl.

14

FROM A DISTANCE, THE GIRL on the table appeared to be sleeping, but that illusion passed when Jane stepped farther into the room. The corpse's hyacinth-blue eyes were open wide as though she had been shocked by the last thing that she'd seen. Ligature marks around her graceful throat were proof of a violent strangulation, though the necktie or scarf or length of rope with which the deed had been done was nowhere in evidence. Blood on her chin had issued from her tongue, which she had bitten in her death throes and which remained trapped between her teeth.

In life, this blonde had been as beautiful as LuLing, her face perfection, her body sculpted by Eros himself. As with LuLing, as far as looks went, Jane would not have been in the same league with this girl.

And yet she thought, *This could be me, this is me. This is me tomorrow or next week or a month from now, because there's no way to beat people with this power.*

Another room connected to this one. The door between the two stood half open.

If she had been a person who ran from trouble instead of into it, she might have fled. But to flee would be to dishonor herself and to further fail her mother, whom she had failed nineteen years earlier. This was a world that didn't reward flight. Whenever you fled from anything, you inevitably fled into its equivalent.

She went to the half-open door. Pushed it wider. Crossed the threshold.

Before her stood a super-efficient gas furnace that had no role in heating the grand house. The manufacturer had labeled it POWER-PAK III CREMATION SYSTEM. It was usually found only in mortuaries.

In memory she heard LuLing's voice: *Would you be pleased to make me weep, Phoebe? There is beauty in pain.*

Jane had known this must happen sometimes in a place that catered to the exercise of absolute power and to all the depravities attending it. She had known, but she had repressed the knowledge. When you were David against Goliath, you didn't want to dwell too much on your adversary's size or his capacity for violence, or his taste for cruelty.

Murder in the act of sex couldn't happen too often, because they would have to be continuously scouting for girls, snatching them or otherwise procuring them, *programming* them. But if it didn't happen often, they had anticipated that it *would* happen from time to time, and they had prepared to deal with the occasional inconvenient corpse, apparently with no quiver of conscience greater than what had troubled the Nazis or Stalin when murdering millions.

She felt small standing in front of the cremation system. She felt as small as a child.

Inside the Power-Pak III, the gas was escaping

under pressure; and the flames roared with the burning of it. The cremation system was being pre-heated for the job ahead.

With that realization, Jane retreated to the first room and started for the door. Two men entered from the hallway.

15

BIG MEN, BRUTISH IN APPEAR-ance, they wore shoulder rigs adapted to accept—and quickly release—pistols fitted with silencers.

Jane was carrying her Heckler & Koch. She didn't need to draw it. Without making a conscious effort to bring it up from her side, she found that she had it in a two-hand grip, arms extended.

Neither of the men reacted to her. She might as well have been made of clearest glass.

As they approached the dead girl, who was lying like a figment of a nightmare on the steel slab, the bigger of the two said, "It has to be dark for this."

"It has been dark awhile," said the other. "For two hours."

"It has to be dark because of the smoke."

"No one will see any smoke. This system hardly produces any smoke to see."

The presence of the corpse, the *fact* of it, seemed not in the least to affect them.

"This is a good system. I like this system. But it produces some smoke."

"This is a very good system. Anyway, the night is here."

For a moment Jane thought they were playing a mind game with her, that they would suddenly draw their guns and pivot toward her. But then she remembered Overton's words: *They don't see members because they're . . . programmed.*

Believing what William Overton had told her, she had dared to come here. Until she experienced this form of passive invisibility, however, she hadn't been able to imagine how it might work.

Their eyes were not blind to her. The image of the room transmitted along their optic nerves to their brains included Jane as surely as it did the dead girl on the table. But some filtering program erased her from the brain's interpretation of the image. She had used Overton's member number and password at the gate and again at the front door, and because no alarm had sounded to announce that the perimeter of the house had been violated, these guards believed that the only people in the house were the girls and members who had come here to use them. The read-in from their eyes was the truth, but the readout from their brains was a lie.

Because the members of Aspasia didn't want their faces on file anywhere in association with this enterprise, a fault existed in the security program, and that fault spared Jane's life.

It was technology, but its effect was magic, a dark damn magic that she didn't trust. While keeping the pistol trained on the men, she had eased backward, away from them, convinced that to move boldly past them in the direction of the hallway door would break the spell that they were under. She had retreated into a corner.

The taller man, six-four if he was an inch, went through the door into the crematorium.

The other one remained at the steel table, staring at the naked dead girl. If he raised his head, he would be looking directly at the corner where Jane stood.

And then he frowned. Until he frowned, his features were so placid that Jane wondered if any thought at all traveled through the landscape of his mind. Frowning, he looked up and turned his head side to side, scanning the room.

Perhaps it was imagination, but she thought his gaze paused for just an instant on the very space she occupied.

Still frowning, he cocked his head.

Jane held her breath. If his program did not allow him to see her, it would not allow him to hear her, either. Nevertheless, for that moment, she did not breathe.

The bones of his face were heavy, as if he had been crudely forged rather than born of man and woman, his brow a ledge from under which his eyes regarded the world with suspicion.

Finally, he looked down again at the dead girl,

though with no greater emotion than if he had been staring at an empty table.

Rolling a stainless-steel gurney in front of him, the first man returned from the crematorium. As he positioned the gurney beside the table, he considered the naked blonde and said, "Number Four."

"Number Four," the shorter man agreed.

"We need to clean the room."

"Make it ready for the new Number Four," the shorter man confirmed.

Among computer gurus, there was a word for people who thought they were off the grid but weren't. The word was *fools*. Only the tiniest fraction of those who believed they were off the grid—including dedicated end-of-the-world preppers—were in fact off it. Those who were truly untrackable, like Jane, and yet remained able by various means to use the Internet undetected were said to be "in the silent corner."

She had been in the silent corner for two months, and right now, she was in the silent corner twice over, untrackable by all modern technology as well as by the five senses of these security men, and able to move about freely.

"Let's burn it," said the taller one.

"Burn it," the shorter man agreed.

They moved the blonde from the table to the gurney as if they were handling bags of garbage, as if she was nothing and never had been anything.

This was one barbarity too many, an inexcusable indignity, and Jane could have shot them dead for their thoughtless treatment of the girl. But in their way, they were victims, too, and if they had been crude and vicious men before they had been subjected to brain implants, there was no way to prove it, no evidence sufficient to condemn them to death now. Anyway, they were already something akin to the walking dead.

As the two men maneuvered the gurney through the open door to feed the corpse into the Power-Pak III Cremation System, Jane backed away from them and out of the room. In the ground-floor hallway once more, she walked briskly toward the front door.

As she passed the stairs, she glanced up at the niches in which stood Venus and Aphrodite, white marble and larger than life-size.

Maybe it was the way they were uplighted or maybe Jane's black mood affected her perception, but they no longer looked like pagan goddesses, not both glorious and terrible as before, but now only terrible, like beings that might preside over an Aztec altar upon which hearts were torn from living children.

At the front door, to be granted exit, she entered Overton's membership number and password in another keypad. There was a delay of mere seconds that nonetheless she found nearly intolerable.

There could be no menace in the moon, and yet it hung over the night as if it were a dragon's egg from which some world-ending beast would hatch.

At the garage stall, another keypad required another entry, but against her expectations, the segmented door rolled up to reveal the Bentley.

The phoenix palms canopied the driveway, and in that tunnel of boles and fronds, headlights approached her on the inbound lane. She was prepared to accelerate and slam through it if the vehicle swung across both lanes to block her, but a Maserati with tinted windows cruised past her without incident.

No keypad waited on this side of the gate. The two great panels of ironwork swung inward automatically as she approached, and she was granted exit.

She piloted the Bentley into a world that was immeasurably more precious to her than it had been when she had driven to Aspasia, a world imperiled under a vault of blind bright stars.

16

SHE SHOULD HAVE PARKED THE Bentley in another block and walked past William Overton's house from the farther side of the street, should have reconnoitered before entering the place, just in case he had gotten loose or gotten help. Instead, she drove directly into the center stall of three, parking between the red Ferrari and the black Tesla, and remoted the garage roll-up to roll down behind her. At the connecting door between the garage and the house, she entered the disarming code in the keypad and used the attorney's house key and went inside, pistol in her right hand.

She had been cold to the bone since Aspasia, and the car heater had not warmed her. As chilled as she was, she remained nonetheless at a boil emotionally. Indignation, which is always controlled, had given way to a rage that threatened to drive her beyond the bounds of prudence and discretion. She wanted the guilty to pay. She wanted them to pay with everything they possessed, every dollar and drop of blood, wanted to strip from them their overweening pride and smug superiority. Her fear was twined now with horror, and she was afraid not just for Travis and herself, but for everyone and everything she loved, for her friends and her country, for the future of freedom and the dignity of the human heart.

Overton was lying in the master bathroom, where she had left him, still shackled to the sink drain and cuffed to the leg of the antique bathtub. For at least part of the time that she'd been away, he had struggled to free himself. His badly abraded ankles oozed a bloody serum, because he had tried either to snap the heavy-duty cable tie or strip the one-way plastic zipper that could draw the tie tighter but never let it loosen. Or in his total ignorance of construction and plumbing techniques, maybe he thought it possible to pull the steel drain pipe out of the wall, though all he had succeeded in doing was cracking the marble cladding. He must have tried mightily to wedge his right shoulder and right knee under the bathtub and lever it off the floor enough to slip free the cable tie looped around one of its sturdy legs. But the large cast-iron tub with its baked-enamel finish weighed at least half a ton, probably two or three hundred pounds more than that; anyway, its water lines and drain line further secured it to wall and floor. He succeeded only in skinning his knee and bruising his shoulder. Hair lank and wet, body glistening with perspiration head to foot, Dolce & Gabbana underwear dark with sweat and perhaps with something else, he had proved to be a failure as an escape artist.

When Jane stepped into the bathroom doorway, Overton startled, turning upon her an expression of such abject fear that the woman she had been four months earlier might have had pity for him. But she wasn't that woman; she might never be that woman again. Besides, his face was wrenched no less by purest hatred than by fear.

He flinched when she approached him with the scissors. She cut through the duct tape that wound about his head and did not care if it pulled his hair painfully. She made him use his tongue to press the partial washcloth from his mouth. He gagged and choked but at last expelled it.

She had said that she needed to liberate her younger sister from Aspasia, and Overton had known in what condition her sister would be found, forever altered and beyond any hope of liberation.

He must think that he was now as good as dead and that his death would not be easy.

Looking down at him, she said, "Fancy place."

"What?"

"Fancy place, that Aspasia."

He said nothing.

"Don't you think it's a fancy place?"

When he still said nothing, she prodded him with the toe of her shoe. He said, "I guess so."

"You guess what?"

"It's a fancy place."

"It's a very fancy place, Sterling. Wow. I mean, no expense spared to make it feel respectable."

Again, he said nothing.

"You were right about the guards. They pretended not to see me. How does that work, Sterling? How do they pretend so well?"

"I've told you all I know."

"You've told me all you dare. That's different."

He turned his face away from her.

She did not goad him this time. She waited.

The silence grew intolerable for him. Still averting his face, he said, "Did you find her?"

"Did I find who?"

"You know who."

"I don't seem to know."

"Why are you doing this to me?"

"Did I find who?"

"You're trying to make me say it so you can shoot me."

"What a strange notion."

"It's what you're doing," he insisted.

"I don't need an excuse to shoot you, Sterling. I already have a lot of good reasons to shoot you."

"I didn't have anything to do with Aspasia."

"You're a member—Vidar, god of gods, survivor of Ragnarok."

"That's all I am. A member. I didn't build the place."

"Ah, the old I-didn't-build-Auschwitz-I-only-operated-the-gas-chamber defense."

"Go to Hell."

"I'm sure you can give me good directions."

"You're a gold-plated bitch."

"If you stop being stupid, you can survive this. Is stupidity such a part of your character that maybe you can't save yourself?"

"You want me dead. Just get it over with."

"Speaking of dead people, I found a dead girl at Aspasia."

Lying there in his sweat and blood, he shuddered.

She said, "A lovely blond girl naked on a stainless-steel table. She'd been strangled, perhaps at the very moment one of your fellow club members achieved his peak of pleasure."

"Oh, shit," he said, his voice breaking. "Shit, shit, shit."

"I watched them getting ready to shove her poor body in a cremator and burn her all up."

He was crying now, crying for himself. "Just do it to me."

She gave him another long silence before she

said, "She wasn't my sister. I don't have a sister. That was a lie."

Jane could almost hear him reaching down into some internal darkness to dredge up a near-extinguished hope.

"Liars," she said, "are always the first to fall for the lies of others."

He turned his head to look up at her. His eyes were full of tears. His mouth was as soft as an infant's.

Jane said, "I needed to understand Aspasia before I could go after Shenneck."

His tears made his eyes harder to read, and perhaps he realized as much, because he said, "Shenneck? What's Shenneck?"

"Maybe you are terminally stupid. Did you think the only thing Jimmy hacked from you was the Dark Web address for Aspasia? You're a friend of Bertold Shenneck. Is *friend* the right word? Are people like you and Shenneck capable of friendship?"

"We . . . we have similar interests."

"Yes, that's probably closer to the truth. It's something like the instinctive loyalty predators have for one another. And you're an investor in Far Horizons."

He closed his eyes. He was calculating whether the immediate threat she posed or Shenneck might be the more certain door to death.

"Did you pee yourself?" she asked.

Without opening his eyes, he said, "No."

"I smell pee, and it's not mine."

Eyes still closed, he said, "What do you want to do with him, with Shenneck?"

"Expose what he's doing. Bring him down. Stop him. Kill him."

"Just you? Against *him*? You and who else?"

"Never mind who else. I'm the interrogator. Not you."

He opened his eyes. "I don't know as much as you probably think I do."

"Let's find out."

She went into the bedroom, and he nervously asked where she was going, and she returned with a straight-backed chair.

She sat on the chair, looked him over, shook her head. "Yeah, you peed yourself. So tell me, the nanotech brain implants that control those girls . . . how are they installed? Not with surgery."

He hesitated but gave it up. "Injection. The control mechanism is made up of thousands of parts, each just a few molecules. They migrate to the brain and self-assemble into a complex structure."

"And the blood-brain barrier doesn't screen them out?"

"No. I don't know why. I'm no scientist. It's just part of Shenneck's . . . genius."

The blood-brain barrier was a complex biological mechanism that permitted vital substances in the blood to penetrate the walls of the brain's capillaries and enter the brain tissue, while keeping out harmful substances.

"How do all these tiny parts, all these machines

made of a handful of molecules, know how to self-assemble when they get into the brain?"

"They're sort of programmed. But not exactly by Shenneck. It's all about precise design. If all the parts are perfectly designed to fit together like a long series of puzzle pieces, like locks and keys, *and if each piece has only one place it will fit in the larger structure*, then Brownian movement makes it inevitable that they'll link up properly."

"Progress by random motion," she said. "A drunkard's walk."

"Yeah. Shenneck says it happens in nature all the time."

"Ribosomes," she said, remembering that example from Shenneck's video about the mice.

Ribosomes were mitten-shaped organelles that existed in great numbers in the cytoplasm of every human cell. They were the sites where proteins were manufactured. Each ribosome had more than fifty different components. If you broke down a slew of them into their separate parts and thoroughly mixed them up in a suspending fluid, then Brownian movement—caused by encounters with molecules of the suspending medium—kept knocking them against one another until the fifty-some parts assembled into whole ribosomes.

If the thousands of parts in Shenneck's control mechanism were each perfectly designed to fit only one place in a larger structure, the forces of nature would ensure they linked up in the brain. At every level from the subatomic to the formation of galaxies, nature routinely created complex structures because the perfection of its operative designs made its various constructions inevitable.

"Once a control mechanism is in place in the brain of one of these poor girls," Jane said, "is there any way to undo it, any way she can ever be again who she once was?"

Her question clearly stressed Overton, and he read in it a judgment of himself that unnerved him. "Shenneck built it this way. I didn't have anything to do with how he designed it."

"Good for you."

"There should have been . . . I don't know, it's not the right word, but there should have been an antidote."

As if a sleeker design would have made Frankenstein's monster less of a monster and his maker a hero.

"So there's no way to undo it?" she asked.

"No. The controller breaks down the existing personality and deletes the memories that helped to form it. The result is a new level of . . . call it consciousness. Shenneck has been adamant about . . ."

Unthinkingly, he chewed his lower lip, breaking the fragile clot that had begun to heal the split, bringing forth fresh blood.

"Keep going, Sterling. It's show-and-tell day. You remember show-and-tell from elementary school? Earn your gold star, your works-well-with-others checkmark on your next report card. Tell me what Bertold Shenneck has been adamant about."

"He's adamant that the design can allow no possible pathway for rebellion."

"So once they're enslaved, it's forever."

Overton clearly didn't like the word *enslaved*, as though there could be any other, but after a hesitation, he said, "Yes. But they don't see their condition the way you do. They're content. More than content. They're happy."

Jane worked her tongue around her mouth and nodded sagely, as if considering his argument, when in fact she was suppressing the urge to pistol-whip him. "I found your smartphone in the closet. You must have Shenneck's numbers on speed dial. Give me your password, tell me how I get everything you've got."

Alarmed, he said, "You can't call him."

"Sure I can. I know how to use a phone."

"He'll know it's me you got the numbers from."

"As if that's your biggest worry."

"You're a real piece of shit."

"You like having two eyes, Billy?"

"You couldn't torture anybody."

"That's what I said before I saw Aspasia. I have a new appreciation for extreme measures. Which eye don't you need?"

He gave her the password.

She went into the bedroom, worked with the phone, got his address book, scrolled through it. Good enough. She switched the phone off.

In the bathroom again, she said, "Okay. I understand Aspasia. Some sick, twisted people are self-absorbed adolescents all their lives. Other people aren't fully real to them. Know what I mean? Of course you do. But why this other project of Shenneck's?"

Overton pretended ignorance. "What other project?"

"What's the intention of engineering thousands of more suicides every year? Why program people to kill themselves, sometimes to kill others and then themselves? Why did Dr. Shenneck inject his self-assembling control mechanism into my husband and direct him to kill himself?"

17

PERHAPS A NATURAL TAN WOULD have sustained better, but William Overton's machine tan seemed to react chemically with his sweat and with the pheromones of terror that his body expressed in abundance. His beach-guy glow acquired a gray patina, the way copper will in time develop one that's green.

Overton had thought he would be killed because of a sister, and when the sister turned out not to exist, he had thought there might be hope of a reprieve. But now his captor had a husband. And the husband was dead.

"Billy?" she said.

His dread was palpable. He closed his eyes again, as if the sight of himself in his current condition could not be borne. "How do you know about this?"

"The engineered suicides? It doesn't matter how I know, Billy. All that matters is I know, and I need answers."

"For God's sake, who *are* you?"

She considered his question and decided to answer it. "Let's talk movies. You want to talk movies?"

"Something's wrong with you. What's wrong with you?"

"Just humor me, Billy. It's always wise to humor me. You've probably seen that old movie *Butch Cassidy and the Sundance Kid*."

"Newman and Redford."

"That's right. They're being chased by this posse that just won't quit. At one point they look back across a vast landscape and they're still being pursued, and they can't believe the doggedness of that posse. Butch says to Sundance—or Sundance says to Butch, I don't remember which—he says, 'Who *are* those guys?' He says it like maybe they're supernatural or they're fate personified. See, Billy, all you need to know is—I'm those guys."

When Overton opened his eyes and shifted uncomfortably in his plastic shackles, he appeared to be resigned, at last, to complete cooperation. "It's not Shenneck's intention or mine, or anyone's, that ninety percent of the population will end up programmed like those girls at Aspasia. Or even fifty percent. That's not a world anyone would want to live in."

"So even Shenneck has moral limits? Or is it merely a matter of practicality? Might be impossible to produce the billions of injections that would enslave all but the elite."

He soldiered on. "There are people in all professions who have greater influence on society than they should."

"What people would they be?"

"Those who push the culture in the wrong direction."

"What direction would that be, Billy?"

"Anyone who knows history well enough can see what the wrong directions are. It's plain as anything." In touch now with his inner fanatic, he found himself capable of a defiant tone even as he lay there in squalor. "Identify those who have the potential to press civilization to the brink, diminish their influence—"

"By killing them," she said.

He ignored the interruption. "—and it won't be necessary to use Bertold's technology on the masses. There will be *less* death, not more, less poverty, less anxiety, if we restrain those who are most likely to screw up the country with bad policies."

He could not entirely conceal his enthusiasm. He might be an investor in Far Horizons for profit, but he had drunk the Kool-Aid.

"Nick," she said, "that was my husband's name. You don't care what his name was, but I care. Nick was in the Marine Corps. A full colonel at thirty-two. He was awarded the Navy Cross. You wouldn't know what that is, but it's really something. He was a good man, a caring husband, a damn fine father."

"Wait, wait, wait," Overton said. He was capable of a self-righteous reaction. He amazed her. "Don't lay this on me. You have no right to lay it on me. I don't decide who's put on the list."

"What list?"

"The Hamlet list. Like the play. If someone had killed Hamlet in the first act, a lot more people would've been alive at the end."

"Seriously, is that how you read it, you're a Shakespeare scholar now?"

In frustration he rattled the series of looped cable ties that secured his wrists to the bathtub. "I haven't *read* the damn thing. Shenneck calls it the Hamlet list. I don't have anything to do with it. *I told you,* I don't decide who's on the list."

"Who does decide?"

"No one. The computer decides. The computer model."

She could feel her pulse beating in her temples. "Who wrote the computer model? You design a model to get what you want to get. And the model has to be given names of candidates to choose from. What sonofabitch inputs the names?"

"I don't know."

"You're an investor."

"But I don't work in the freakin' damn lab!"

She drew a deep breath. Her forefinger had

slipped onto the trigger of the Heckler & Koch. She moved it back to the trigger guard. "One of the people on your Hamlet list was Eileen Root in Chicago. She worked in a nonprofit, helping people with severe disabilities. What do you think she might have done to become a danger to civilization?"

"I don't know. How would I know? *I don't choose the names for the list.*"

"One of them was a poet. He threw himself in front of a subway train. One was a prodigy, a twenty-year-old graduate student, she was working on a doctorate in cosmology. *Cosmology!* What could either of them have done to be a threat to civilization?"

"You aren't listening to me."

"I'm listening. I'm all ears, Billy. What could they have done?"

"I don't know. The computer model knows."

She got up from her chair, thrust it backward into the bedroom, loomed over him. "This Hamlet list. How many are on it?"

"I tell you, and you won't like it."

"Try me. How many have to be killed?"

"You're not in control of yourself. You're overwrought."

"Try me!"

"All right, okay. Anyway, Shenneck says they aren't being killed. They're being culled. No herd remains healthy if its weakest individuals aren't culled from time to time."

"I don't want to kill you," Jane said, by which she meant that she didn't want to kill him just yet. "How many are on the list?"

He closed his eyes against the sight of the muzzle. "The computer model says, in a country the size of ours, two hundred and ten thousand culled in each generation will ensure stability."

She had to swallow a reflux of acid before she could say, "How do you define a generation?"

"I don't define anything. The computer model defines it as twenty-five years."

"So eight thousand four hundred a year."

"Something like that."

She kicked him in the hip. She kicked him in the ribs. She could have kept on kicking him until she was exhausted, but she turned away from him and went into the bedroom and kicked the straight-backed chair, which slammed into the dresser.

18

JANE TOOK THE SCISSORS OUT of her handbag and returned to the bathroom with them and the pistol.

Overton turned on his side as best he could, trying to shield his pathetic package from her. "What now, what are you gonna do?"

She had convinced him that she was capable of

committing the most cruel and gruesome offenses. Maybe she had convinced herself, too. "Another thing I need to know."

"What?"

"No more of your stupidity. All I have time for is straight-up answers."

"So ask."

"How hard will it be to get at Shenneck?"

"What does *get at* mean?"

"Get him in a situation like this, make him talk."

"About impossible."

"Nothing's impossible. Look where you are."

"I'm a few steps down the food chain from Shenneck. I was easy. He won't be. I ever get out of this, I won't be, either."

She worked the scissors. The sound of the blades sharpened his anxiety. "Shenneck Technology in Menlo Park?"

"The labs have layers of electronic security. Fingerprint readers. Retinal readers. Armed guards. Cameras everywhere."

"What about his house in Palo Alto?"

"You ever seen it?"

"Maybe I have. But you tell me."

He answered every question she asked about the house, and if he wasn't lying, the place had forbidding security.

She said, "I read he has a getaway place in Napa Valley."

"Yeah. He calls it Gee Zee Ranch. Gee Zee for Ground Zero."

"What a self-important ass."

"He likes his little jokes, that's all," said Overton, taking mild offense on Shenneck's behalf. "He spends like two weeks there every month. He's there now. He can work from there as easy as if he's in the labs. The lab computers are accessible to him there."

"Is he more vulnerable there?"

Overton's laugh was sour, bleak. "If you can get through all the coyotes and rayshaws, he's vulnerable. But you can't get through them. If you'd gone there first, you'd be dead, and I wouldn't be where I am."

"So tell me about the coyotes and the whatevers."

"The rayshaws." He took dark delight in describing the difficulty of an assault on Gee Zee Ranch, as if he had embraced the idea of his own death and could find pleasure only in the certainty that she would soon meet hers.

When she understood the setup at the ranch and felt Overton had not withheld anything, she said, "So I'm going to cut the tie between your ankles. You try to kick me, I'll shoot your balls off. Got that?"

Pretending indifference, he said, "You'll do what you'll do."

"That's right."

With the scissors, she cut through the plastic zip tie.

"Same rules apply," she said. She cut the tie connecting him to the leg of the bathtub, though she left his wrists bound together.

She backed out of the bathroom, put aside the scissors, and stood just beyond the doorway, watching him try to get onto his hands and knees and then try to rise.

His muscles had cramped, and he had further tortured them by his efforts to free himself. He needed a minute to crawl to the fancy amber-quartz sink and grip it and struggle to his feet. The visible spasms in his calf and thigh muscles couldn't be faked. He didn't exaggerate the agony by crying out, but instead clenched his jaws and stifled his groans, breathing as hard as a well-run horse, as if to exhale the pain, still possessed of enough macho self-image to want to conceal from her how weak the ordeal had left him.

He came around the room rather than directly across it, legs still shaky, supporting himself with the sink, then with the bar handle on the walk-in shower, then with a towel rack, then with the door handle.

Jane backed farther into the living room. She didn't have the pistol in a two-hand grip, because she didn't find him threatening and she wanted him to know that she didn't. His mind was a field of ashes, most of his hope gone. But there were hot coals of anger under the ashfield, and any indication that she still respected him as an adversary would feed his ego and fan flames from those coals.

When he had cleared the doorway, he declared,

"I need to sit down a minute," and he wobbled toward the bed.

She said, "If why you want to sit there is the Smith & Wesson in the nightstand drawer, it isn't there anymore." She indicated the straight-backed chair she had kicked into the dresser and that now stood in the middle of the room. "You could sit there till you feel better."

"Bite me, bitch."

"Is that right?"

"Bite me."

"Such adolescent shit. You should hear yourself."

"I hear myself just fine."

"You don't really. You probably never have."

"You're a gash with a gun, that's all you are."

"And what are you?"

"I don't need to sit anywhere."

"So show me the safe, tough guy."

"It's in the closet."

She said, "Behind the mirror, most likely."

"You know everything, huh?"

"Not everything."

The walk-in closet was big, maybe fifteen feet wide and twenty deep. The hanging clothes were hidden behind doors, everything else in drawers of various sizes. In the center of the room stood an upholstered bench where he could sit to put on socks and shoes. At the back wall, a full-length mirror was inlaid between cabinets.

She let him get nearly to the mirror before she stepped into the closet behind him.

He was watching her in the looking glass and saw her take the pistol in a two-hand grip. "Gonna shoot me in the back?"

"It's an option."

"Just like a woman."

"Is that supposed to rile me?"

"If I'm dead, you're dead."

"So this is where you say you've got friends who'll never stop till they find me and cut off my head?"

"Wait and see."

"None of your friends are your friends, Billy."

"Mirror, mirror on the wall."

The mirror slid aside, disappeared behind adjacent cabinetry, evidently responding to those five words and perhaps to the specific timbre of his voice.

He now stood before a brushed stainless-steel panel. He leaned forward, putting his right eye to a round glass lens embedded in the steel. The pattern of each person's retina was as unique as any of his fingerprints.

Jane heard a series of lock bolts retracting, and the steel panel whisked up into the ceiling with a pneumatic sound.

"Here's your money, more money than you've ever seen."

His body blocked her view of the contents of the safe.

"Five hundred thousand bucks."

He reached into the safe, perhaps to pick up a bundle of cash.

"Don't," she said.

He started to turn to his left, bringing his zip-tied hands cross-body. He thought he was fast. He assumed she would be thinking about half a million dollars.

She said don't, but he did, and he was so much slower than he thought he would be that when her first round took him high in the left side, just under the arm, he fired reflexively into a cabinet door less than halfway through the 180-degree arc that he imagined completing. During firearms instruction at the Academy, having worked diligently for weeks to improve her hand strength, Jane had been able to pull the trigger ninety-six times in one minute with her right hand, using a practice revolver, which surpassed the standard required by the instructor. In pitched combat, a weak hand could quickly be a dead hand. Her be-sure shot, less than a second after the first, changed the shape of Overton's head, instantly stopped his incessant scheming, and dropped him to the floor.

19

THE WEAPON OVERTON HAD used was a customized Sig Sauer P226 X-Six with a nineteen-shot magazine. It had boomed in the confines of the closet. Even with a sound suppressor, Jane's pistol had a voice, louder than it would have been in a larger space or outdoors. But she was confident that none of the three shots would have attracted attention beyond the walls of this well-built house.

Considering how many enemies he'd made and further considering the nature of his associates, the attorney had most likely stashed handguns throughout the residence, so that he would always be within easy reach of a weapon. The safe was a miniature armory, holding a 12-gauge pistol-grip shotgun, two revolvers, and another pistol in addition to the one with which he had hoped to kill her.

The pistol he had chosen not to use was a Colt .45 ACP. The engraved name of one of the finest custom shops in the country at once intrigued her. The gun had evidently been completely rebuilt and among the improvements were Heinie night sights. There was also a silencer for it.

If the pistol had been used in a crime, Overton would have disposed of it. She might have found the replacement for her Heckler & Koch, which was now tied to two killings. They were killings in self-defense, therefore neither of them a murder, but even if all this turned out better than she hoped, she wasn't going to spend ten percent of the rest of her life in a courtroom, explaining herself.

Among Overton's collection of expensive luggage, she found a leather tote bag with a zippered closure. She put the Colt and the silencer in it. She added two boxes of ammo. And his smartphone.

Overton had lied about the half million. The safe contained a hundred and twenty thousand. Twelve banded packets of ten thousand each. She put the money in the tote bag.

She had noted earlier that the only security cameras in the house were in the ground-floor and upstairs hallways. Each was ceiling mounted behind a plastic bubble. Night-vision capability.

She had thought the recorder might be in the safe. It was not. Nor was it anywhere in the master closet.

After a fifteen-minute search of likely places, using Overton's house keys, she opened a locked door in the garage, found a storage room, and located the recorder in a cabinet. From the machine, she ejected a disc that saved images for thirty days before recording over them. She put it in the tote with the money and the gun.

Before she had entered the house the first time, earlier in the day, she had put on the black gloves with silver stitching. Never having taken them off, she could have left no fingerprints.

She had not taken a drink from any glass, had not

shed a drop of blood, leaving nothing that would give them an easy DNA match.

Inevitably, she had lost a few hairs in the house. But CSI had to find them, which wasn't as easy as it was portrayed on TV.

She almost went back through the house to turn off the lights, so they would not burn all weekend and perhaps make someone curious, suspicious. She could not do it. She surprised herself that she could not do it. Dead men do not get up and walk again. She did not believe in ghosts. But she could not do it. Let the lights burn.

She left by the back door and locked it with Overton's keys. She dropped the keys in the tote bag and zippered the bag shut.

Walking residential streets at night in Beverly Hills was viewed by the local police as an all-but-certain sign of criminal activity, especially if the suspect in question was carrying a bag larger than a clutch purse. She had to walk to the end of the block and around the corner, where she had left the Ford Escape. If she happened to come to the attention of the city's finest, she was screwed, because she would not shoot a cop.

As Jane stepped off Overton's driveway and onto the public sidewalk, the moon watched blinkless, a milky and accusing eye.

She reached the Ford without incident. She drove back to the San Fernando Valley, where she would spend a second night in her most recent motel room and move on in the morning.

Tomorrow, she would start with Dr. Emily Jo Rossman, the L.A. forensic pathologist who examined the brain of Benedetta Ashcroft, the woman who had committed suicide in a Century City hotel. The autopsy report, provided by Robert Branwick, alias Jimmy Radburn, referenced photographs, but the photos were not in the file.

Jane didn't know where she would go after Dr. Rossman. Sooner than later, she had to make a move on Bertold Shenneck. But getting at him on his seventy-acre property in Napa Valley looked like a job for a Navy SEAL team, not for a lone woman.

She had half an idea, a crazy and reckless idea, based on a wild guess. But she had come to a crisis point in the investigation. There was no way back, and she was at a brink. If Overton's body was discovered on Monday, his associates in Far Horizons might assume that he'd earned his death by some bit of shady business unconnected to them, but they were more likely to raise their guard even higher than it already was. With a cliff ahead and no way back, crazy and reckless ideas had an appeal if they were the only ideas you had.

20

NOW THE SAN FERNANDO VAL-
ley. The monocular moon in the black cowl of the
sky. Friday-night traffic, drivers jostling for every
advantage. The attack in Philadelphia, not yet five
days in the past, had been consigned to a memory
hole as everybody hurried to one weekend pleasure
or another before there might be no pleasures anymore.

Jane stopped at Pizza & More to get takeout. Two
submarine sandwiches and an order of pepper slaw.

At the door to her motel room in Tarzana, she put
down the tote bag with its incriminating treasures
and the bag of takeout. She fished the key from a
pocket of her sport coat and suddenly thought, *He's
in there waiting for me.*

The *he* in this flash of fantasy was the hulk from
Palisades Park, the same who had come blasting a
shotgun into the kitchen at the Branwick house the
previous night.

He could not possibly have tracked her to this
place. Her alarm had no origin in intuition or even
in cruder instinct. The events of the evening had
pulled her nerves as taut as bowstrings.

She considered drawing her pistol, but she did
not, could not. If she started doing firearm protocol
because of an obviously bogus threat, there would
be no end to the bogeymen springing from her

imagination. The edge she needed would be worn away until she would one day mistake a real threat for just another phantom.

She unlocked the door. Reached inside. Flipped the wall switch.

No one waited for her in the bedroom.

She picked up the tote bag and the takeout and went inside and pressed the door shut with her hip. She set down the tote bag and engaged the deadbolt.

After putting the takeout on the small table, she went to the bathroom, pushed open the door, turned on the light. No one.

She returned to the bedroom with a drinking glass and put it on the table, and then she slid open the closet door. The only things in there were suitcases and the trash bag full of autopsy reports.

"Better have a peek under the bed," she said sourly as she took off her gloves, but she didn't allow herself to look.

She went outside to the nearby vending-machine alcove to fill the ice bucket and get a couple of Cokes.

When she returned to her room, she did not check the bathroom and closet again.

Coke and vodka over ice. She took a drink. Added some Coke.

She went into the bathroom and washed her hands and dried them and stared at herself in the mirror and thought she looked different in some fundamental way, though she couldn't name the difference.

In the bedroom, sitting at the table, for a while she held in her hand the half of the locket, the silver oval with the soapstone cameo. Then she put it on the table beside her drink.

She tore open the takeout bag and used it as a placemat. She took the meat and cheese and other filling from one sub and stuffed it into the other sandwich, and discarded the empty bun. There was a plastic fork for the container of coleslaw.

She didn't turn on any music. At the moment, it seemed that music might mask some other sound she would need to hear.

Later, lying on her back in bed, the Heckler & Koch under the neighboring pillow, she thought about how she had killed two perps in almost seven years as an FBI special agent, about how she had killed two more in just the past two days, and she wondered who she would be a year from now, or tomorrow.

She thought of LuLing, those dark eyes of oceanic depths in which little or nothing swam.

When she slept, she dreamed that she was naked, lying on a slab of stainless steel, alive but unable to move. The two men whom she had most recently killed now appeared as they had been in life. With great solemnity, they rolled the steel slab toward the flame-filled maw of a cremator. Although paralyzed, she was able to speak, and in the voice of LuLing, she said, "I would like nothing more than to make you happy." The two men gazed down at her and opened their mouths to speak, but instead of words, from them issued white mice swarming as if they were bees.

21

AT TEN O'CLOCK FRIDAY EVE-
ning, Bertold Shenneck rolls a kitchen cart onto the
terrace of his house in Napa Valley.

The clarity of the cool air is such that the sky is
replete with stars uncountable that are rarely if ever
seen above cities.

The moon rides high. Its secondhand sunlight
haunts the dark valley and paints an ectoplasmic
glow along the crests of the mountains to the west.

On the two shelves of the kitchen cart are dish-
pans containing raw chickens that one of the rayshaws purchased at the supermarket in town that
afternoon.

Shenneck carries a dishpan into the yard. He
places the poultry at intervals across the grass. The
pale flesh glisters in moonlight.

The coyotes are not at the moment present. These
are their hunting hours. They prowl the meadows
and the woods singly and in small packs, chasing
down rodents and rabbits and other prey.

From the second dishpan, Shenneck plucks the
denuded birds and distributes them as he did the
first group.

There is some evidence, far from definitive, that
the coyotes he controls are proving to be less successful hunters than they were prior to their brain
implants. Until he can study the matter further and

gather more data, he finds it advisable to augment their diet in this manner.

In the past month, there have been two incidents that Shenneck doesn't want to see repeated. The coyote, *Canis latrans*, is a fierce predator, but it is not among the very few species that will eat its own kind. Yet twice in this very yard, during the night when Inga and Bertold have been asleep, one coyote has attacked another and killed it and partly eaten it.

He would have thought a mountain lion had done the deed, but the security camera had revealed the disturbing truth.

Shenneck assumes that a diminishment in the coyotes' ability to track and seize their usual prey has left some of them hungry enough to turn on others of their kind. He is, however, considering other curious aspects of these incidents that may give rise to another theory.

Because he can electronically track every individual that has been injected with a self-assembling nano-implant, he knows that the other twelve are still mobile and alive. The only two that have fallen victim to other coyotes are the two killed on this lawn.

Why here rather than in the wild?

It almost seems to the good doctor that these two killings have a ritualistic quality, as if they were meant to make a statement of some kind. This is not possible, of course, because beasts of such low intelligence have neither the capacity to formulate rituals nor the desire to make a statement. And yet . . .

Shenneck rolls the cart into the kitchen and switches off the backyard lights. He leaves the dish-pans for one of the rayshaws to clean and put away in the morning, and he goes upstairs to bed.

He sleeps well and deeply, but he does not dream.

His considered belief is that men dream primarily for two reasons. First, in life they are routinely frustrated and tormented, with the consequence that all their angers and anxieties are shaped into nightmares while they are unconscious. Second, if their dreams are pleasant, it is obviously because they yearn for a perfection of experience that they cannot hope to find in life, and so they dream of it.

Shenneck rarely dreams, because he has full command of his world and is never frustrated or tormented. And as for a perfection of experience, he intends to fashion the utopia that humankind has long pursued and failed to establish, and to live in the perfection that he has created.

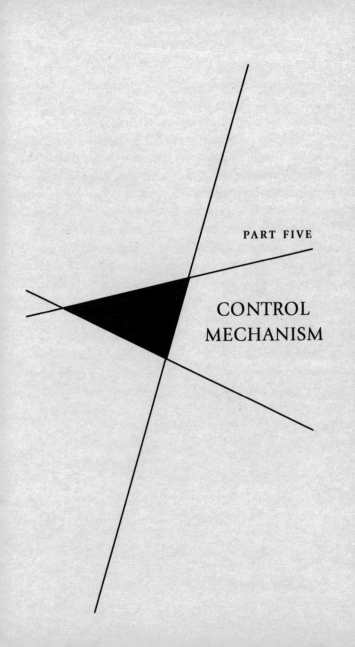

PART FIVE

CONTROL
MECHANISM

1

DR. EMILY JO ROSSMAN, FORmerly a forensic pathologist, worked now as a veterinary technician in her sister's animal hospital.

Jane was waiting as employees came to work at seven o'clock Saturday morning. She recognized Dr. Rossman from her Facebook photo: freckled face; bobbed auburn hair; bangs almost to her eyes.

The woman appeared younger than thirty-eight and had a tomboy air. Her hazel eyes were so lively, her smile so quick, it was difficult to believe that she had ever wanted a career in a morgue.

When shown Jane's FBI credentials, Emily responded as if it were still the age of Norman Rockwell, when trust in government had been well deserved. "My sister's off today. We can use her office."

The office walls were hung not with the expected portraits of animals, but with prints of the fashion—rather than fine—art of Kandinsky, elaborately decorated amoeba forms. Jane suspected that she would not have found much common ground with the absent sister.

Instead of sitting behind the desk, Emily took one of the two client chairs and angled it toward the one in which Jane sat. "I hope I know what this is about, I really hope I do."

"What do you think it's about?"

"Benedetta Ashcroft."

Jane said, "Killed herself in a hotel suite, last July."

Thumping the side of her fist twice into the arm of her chair, Emily said, "*Yes*. About time somebody took this seriously. It damn well wasn't what it seemed."

"But didn't your autopsy report confirm suicide?"

"A massive overdose of a tricyclic antidepressant—desipramine. With vodka. A lethal combination. She'd swallowed more than forty one-hundred-milligram capsules. That takes determination. And another thirty-six capsules were on the nightstand."

"That's more than one prescription. So she was saving them up?"

"No. No way." Emily pushed her thick bangs off her forehead, and they at once fell back into place. "No prescription. The pills weren't in pharmacy bottles. Just a Ziploc bag on the nightstand."

Jane said, "Street purchase."

Emily shook her head adamantly. "Benedetta wouldn't have known how to make a street purchase. She was a Mormon. She didn't drink. Didn't do drugs. Twenty-seven years old, with a devoted husband. Two children. She was a counselor for kids with severe disabilities, and she loved her work."

Jane thought of Eileen Root in Chicago, who'd been an advocate for people with disabilities. In Shenneck's new world, designed by a computer model, there evidently would be no place for paraplegics, quadriplegics, the blind, the deaf, the infirm of any kind.

"Dr. Rossman, is it fair to say that in the absence of severe trauma to the skull, if an obvious other cause of death is present, the coroner's office would not conduct an examination of the brain?"

Emily leaned forward and spoke more quickly, as if defending her autopsy procedures. "I had a case where a young man fell off a ladder, twenty-two feet to the ground. Dead at the scene. No cranial fracture, no contusion, no laceration of the scalp. But examination of the brain revealed diffuse axonal injury. Small perivascular hemorrhages in the brain stem. Death was caused by the sudden acceleration-deceleration of the head, not by an impact fracture."

"All right. But in that case, no anatomic injuries supported the determination of accidental blunt-force trauma. So you *had* to look at the brain. But with Benedetta Ashcroft, the cause of death was obvious. And the security cameras in the hotel corridors proved no one entered her room until the maid found her body the next day."

Emily's mouth set in a tight grim line, and then she

said, "The family couldn't believe she killed herself. Simply couldn't believe it. They wondered—could her suicide be explained by a brain tumor?"

"Does the coroner's office conduct more extensive autopsies than its protocols require if the family insists?"

"There was a time it did. No more." She hesitated, holding her hands above her lap, frowning at them as if she didn't recognize them as her own. "The public story is I grew tired of forensic pathology and quit. But if I hadn't quit, I'd have been fired."

"On what grounds?"

"I'm Benedetta Ashcroft's aunt. I should have recused myself from performing the autopsy. Instead, I aggressively maneuvered to have it assigned to me, and I didn't reveal my relationship to her."

"A misdemeanor. Or at least a reason for justified dismissal."

Emily's stare was direct and unwavering as a laser beam. "The family was in shock. They needed to know. This lovely woman, always so happy, this devoted mother, checking into a hotel suite to kill herself ... A brain tumor would have explained everything."

"The family could have paid for a private autopsy when the coroner's office was finished with the body."

Emily nodded, but did not look away from Jane. "That would take time—days, a week, or longer.

Her husband, her sister, her mom and dad were in such grief, such anguish. I did what I did, and I'd do it again . . . but, God, I wish I hadn't."

Here it was. If there could be any doubt that something new and terrible had entered the world, what Dr. Rossman saw when she opened her niece's skull was about to banish any remaining skepticism.

"I didn't fully understand this part of your autopsy report," Jane said. "Anyway, phrases and even sentences were redacted."

The pathologist took a deep breath. "When I looked down on the forebrain, the two hemispheres of the cerebrum, for just a moment, I thought I was looking at gliomatosis cerebri, a particularly vicious cancer that doesn't produce a localized tumor. It spreads like a spiderweb across all four lobes of the cerebrum."

"But it wasn't gliomatosis cerebri."

Jane's sustained eye contact clearly suggested to Emily that they already shared the knowledge that she was about to reveal. "My God, you know. You know . . . what I found."

"Maybe. Tell me."

"It wasn't organic. Not the chaos of cancer. I was looking at geometric, intricately designed circuits . . . a system, apparatus. I don't know what to call it. It netted all four lobes, disappearing into various sulci, those fissures in the gray matter between the folded forms, between the gyri. It didn't have a lot of mass, almost a fairylike structure, though there was a heavy concentration on the corpus callosum. Looking at it, I felt . . . I *knew* I'd never seen anything so *evil*. What was it? What was that thing?"

"You could call it a control mechanism," Jane said.

Emily broke eye contact, looked at her hands, which tightened into fists. She shivered. "Who? Why? For God's sake, *how*?"

Instead of answering those questions, Jane said, "You had a camera running throughout the autopsy."

"Yes. But it didn't capture that damn thing to the extent I would have liked. Shortly after I opened the skull, maybe as a reaction to contact with the air, I don't know, this thing—this control mechanism, as you call it—began to come apart."

"Come apart how?"

Emily looked up from her hands, having paled so that her freckles appeared brighter than before. "It seemed to evaporate, dissolve. No. It was more like . . . the way certain salts absorb moisture from the air and just *deliquesce*."

This was nothing that Jane had expected, and she felt again that she was dealing with forces so cunning and powerful that they might as well have been supernatural. "There was a residue?"

"Yes. Thin, almost clear. I sent a sample to the lab. If they ever analyzed it, I was never told."

"You filed your report that same day."

"Yes."

"You weren't alone during the autopsy."

"There was an assistant pathologist. Charlie

Weems. He was terrified. He's a fan of sci-fi. He thought what we saw meant an alien invasion. Hell, so did I."

"He confirmed your report?"

"At first. But I'd told him Benedetta was my niece. And pretty soon . . . within hours, he wasn't backing me up anymore."

"You were forced out—when?"

"The next day. Leave with severance pay or be fired. Not much of a choice, really."

"And where is Charlie Weems right now?"

"He's been promoted. He has my job. And welcome to it." She worked her hands as if her fists had been clenched so tight that her fingers were numb. "So the FBI is on this now, huh? Really on this?"

"On it but not announced. A quiet investigation. I have to ask you to keep our discussion to yourself. You can understand why."

"People would panic, everyone would think they're controlled, whether they are or not."

"Exactly. You told Benedetta's sister, husband, mom, dad?"

Emily shook her head. "No. It was too insane, too . . . awful. At first I said tests were under way. Then I said a brain tumor."

"Did they wonder why you left your job?"

"I told them I'd spent too much time with the dead. It's a job no one understands why you took, and everyone gets why you'd quit."

"And what about you? Eight months you've lived with this."

"I never used to stress about anything. Now I stress about everything. But I don't dream about it as much as I first did." She looked at the Kandinsky prints—the brightly colored, energetic, and meaningless forms. "So many things happen anymore, the world going so fast, you find yourself accepting things that once would have broken your heart or driven you crazy. It's like life used to be a carrousel, now a high-speed roller coaster." She turned her eyes on Jane again. "I live with knowing what I saw. What else is there to do? But deep down, I'm terrified."

"I am, too. We all are," Jane said, implying that scores of agents were seeking the truth, a lie that was the only comfort she could give.

2

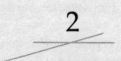

IN SPITE OF THE TIME-ZONE change, it was still mid-morning when Nathan Silverman landed at Austin International, received his rental car, and left the city on U.S. 290. As the highway ascended the Edwards Plateau, there was far more sky than land, so that the Texas plains falling to every side were vast yet felt insubstantial.

He had worked many weekends during his career in the Bureau. Never before, however, had he devoted a Saturday to an investigation that did not yet have a case number or an open file.

This would also be the first time he paid out of pocket for airline fares and other expenses with little hope of reimbursement.

He had not even bothered to learn whether one of the Bureau's Gulfstream V jets might be scheduled for a flight to Texas, with an empty seat available. The Gulfstreams were primarily for counterterrorism and weapons-of-mass-destruction operations. They might be needed for travel related to the Philadelphia investigation. Anyway, the attorney general had authority over the FBI, and the most recent three often commandeered the Gulfstreams for their personal travel, whether that was entirely ethical or not.

By one route and another, trusting to the soft voice of the GPS, he came to a private lane. Low stone posts supported an iron framework that arced overhead and incorporated letters that spelled HAWK. From there on, the GPS had no more advice for him.

Flanked by ranch fencing, overhung here and there by an oak, the blacktop had been poured on bare earth and rolled out hard and patched as weather potholed it and furnished with new borders when time crumbled it at the edges.

Rich green grasslands lay all around. On the left, brown-and-white cattle grazed. On the right were sheep.

The two-story white-clapboard residence, shaded by ancient oaks, stood well separate from the immense barn to the south and the tree-shaded stables

to the north. In a graveled parking area were a
Ford 550 truck and a paneled van. He left the rental
beside them and climbed the front porch steps and
rang the bell.

The day was warm but not hot, still but with a
feeling that the stillness might be precarious.

He had met Clare and Ancel Hawk, Nicholas's
parents, when Nick and Jane were married in Virginia, almost seven years earlier. He doubted that
either of them would remember him.

She answered the door, fifty-something, tall and
trim and lovely, graying hair cropped short, wearing boots and jeans and a white blouse. "Mr. Silverman. You're a long way from Quantico."

"Mrs. Hawk, I'm surprised you recognize me."

"We thought you'd call or someone would come
around. But here you fetch up at our door yourself.
I'm more surprised than you."

"I'm so sorry about Nick. You have my
sympathy—"

She held up one hand to stop him. "I don't talk
much about that. Maybe I never will. Anyway, you
haven't traveled halfway to nowhere just to share
the grief. Come on in."

She led him through the shadowed, quiet house
to the kitchen, where ledgers and receipts covered
most of the dinette table.

"I'm doing the accounts, work I dearly hate. If I
don't get it done today, I'll scream. You'll want to
talk to Ancel, but he's at the stables with the vet. A
favorite horse has come up lame."

"Actually, Mrs. Hawk, I'd like to speak with both of you."

She smiled. "With all these numbers fighting in my head, I'm no good for conversation. If you'll kindly wait for Ancel on the back porch, he won't be long. Can I get you a drink—soda, water, tea?"

Gracious though she might be, she was also wary of him.

Silverman said, "I'll have tea if it's not too much trouble."

She gave him a bottle from the fridge, led him onto the porch, and left him in a rocking chair with his tea and his suspicions.

Ten minutes later, Ancel Hawk stepped out of the kitchen, onto the porch, and Silverman got up, wondering why it surprised him that the rancher was wearing a cowboy hat.

They shook hands, and Silverman asked, "How's the horse?"

As they sat down, Ancel said, "Synovitis of the coffin joint, left front foot. Caught in time, no degeneration. Donner is a good old horse. We've been through some times together."

The rancher was a big man with strong work-worn hands. Sun and wind had cured his face.

"Sweet place you have here," Silverman said.

"Sweet it is," Ancel agreed, "and all ours. But you didn't come here to talk real estate."

"I'm not here officially, either. Though it could come to that, depending. I'm concerned about Jane and wondering what she's up to."

Staring out at the yard and the fields beyond, giving Silverman only his profile, Ancel said, "Whatever she's up to, it's the right thing, and she'll get it done. You know how she is."

After a silence, Silverman said, "Did she leave the boy here?"

"No, sir, she did not. You'll just have to believe me about that, but it's true."

"I've been given to understand that she's afraid for him."

"If she is, she's probably right to be."

"Why would the boy be in danger? From whom?"

"We're all in danger in this world, Mr. Silverman. It's mostly not a peaceable place."

"I can't cover for her if she's breaking the law, Mr. Hawk."

"She wouldn't want you to."

Silverman set his half-finished bottle of tea on the porch floor beside his chair. "I'm her friend, not her enemy."

"That well may be. I'm not in a position to know."

"I can't help her if I don't know what help she needs."

"I'm sure if she thought you could help, she'd be in touch."

"There was an incident in California. She's deep in something."

"I don't know what's what in California. You're ahead of me there, Mr. Silverman. Should be me tryin' to pick *your* brain."

"Texans," Silverman said with frustration.

"You've had some experience of us, have you?"

"On a few occasions."

"Then you've been seasoned for some disappointment here."

Silverman got up from the chair. He went to the porch railing and stared past the yard, across the great flatness of grassland, toward a horizon as far away as if he had been at sea. He was city-born and city-raised, and these great open spaces made him uneasy. It seemed as if gravity wasn't at full strength here, as if he and the house and anything not rooted in the earth might float up and away into the immense all-encompassing sky.

His back to Ancel Hawk, he said, "Her mother's dead. She's estranged from her dad. If she won't turn to you, she has no one."

"You better believe that troubles me and Clare. We love the girl like she was our own daughter," the rancher said.

"Well, then?"

"She won't come to us because she feels she'd be puttin' us in harm's way. That maybe isn't the same reason she won't come to you."

Silverman turned his back to the daunting vista and faced his host. "Do you mean she doesn't trust the Bureau?"

Ancel Hawk's eyes were the clear gray of rain on weathered cedar. "Sit down a bit, why don't you."

Silverman returned to the rocking chair. Neither man rocked. Crickets sang in the stillness, but there was little else.

After a while, Silverman said, "You thinking about cooperating with me or what?"

"I'm thinkin', Mr. Silverman, so let me think. Jane respects you. That's the only reason you're still here."

With agitated cries, a flock of nuthatches burst out of the clear air as though flung into this world from another, swooped past the porch, and disappeared into nests and cavities in the big oak tree at the northwest corner of the house, as though taking refuge from some pending change in the weather.

Finally the rancher said, "Nick's suicide wasn't suicide."

"But Jane found him, and the medical examiner—"

The rancher interrupted. "Suicide rate started climbin' last year, now it's up more'n twenty percent."

"It fluctuates, like the murder rate."

"No fluctuation. No down. Just higher every month. And these are people like our Nick, with no reason to kill themselves."

Frowning, Silverman said, "A suicide is a suicide."

"Not if people are somehow made to do it. Jane started lookin' into it, diggin' deep like she does. So they come into her home, and they promise to rape and kill Travis if she doesn't drop it."

Stunned to hear this paranoid conspiracy theory coming from the no-nonsense rancher, Silverman said, "They? They who?"

"Wouldn't that be what she needs to find out?"

"Forgive me, but if I'm not suicidal, no one can make me—"

"Jane doesn't lie except to other liars, of which I'm not one."

"I'm not questioning your truthfulness."

"No offense, Mr. Silverman, but I don't care what you think of me." The rancher got to his feet. "I've told you what little I can. You either look into it or you don't."

Getting up, Silverman said, "If you know how to reach Jane—"

"We don't. Blunt fact is, she doesn't trust everyone in your Bureau. Maybe you shouldn't, either. If you folks come after me and Clare with your agents and lawyers and all the angels in Hell, it doesn't matter. There's no more you'll get here. Now, I'd be obliged if you'd leave by walkin' around the house instead of through it."

Ancel Hawk closed the kitchen door behind him.

Going down the porch steps and rounding the house, Silverman tried to pinpoint where he'd gone wrong and lost the rancher, whose Texas grace and natural demeanor ordinarily made him polite almost to a fault. He decided that what offended Ancel Hawk was not that his own veracity had been challenged but that Silverman had seemed to question his daughter-in-law's story. *Doubt me and we can still talk,* the rancher was saying, *but doubt Jane and I'm done with you.*

As he reached the front of the house, out of a sky

as blue as moonflowers, sudden hard gusts of warm wind seemed to blow the very sunlight past him and across the pastures in bright shudders. The illusion was born of flickering shadows from the thrashing oaks and, far above, from a scrim of cirrus clouds that, lashed by higher currents, gave off a stroboscopic pulse.

Looking out across the vast land, Silverman wished that he were not in this lonely, alien place but back in Alexandria with Rishona, cities crowding all around them.

3

JANE IN A SOUTHBOUND HURRY on Interstate 405, grateful for the light traffic, had nothing now except the half of an idea that had come to her the previous night, the crazy and reckless idea based on a wild guess. She tried to put this half-assed plan in a better light by telling herself that she wasn't really operating on a wild guess, that it was keen intuition inspired by her bear-trap memory, which didn't let go of even the most esoteric facts once it sank its teeth into them. But she was no good at self-delusion. She couldn't deny that she hustled now toward San Diego out of sheer desperation.

Of the things she had learned from Dr. Emily Jo

Rossman, the revelation that most disturbed her was not the image of the control web across Benedetta Ashcroft's brain, but was instead the image of it deliquescing in mere moments, leaving little evidence that it had existed, except for whatever an autopsy camera might have captured.

These days, however, when digital photographs could be easily manipulated, few people gave any credence to that old maxim *Words may deceive, but photos never lie.* Every form of evidence, except perhaps DNA, was now within the domain of liars. To arouse the public, an entire world of doubters would have to be present at an autopsy when the top of the skull came off and, for a minute or so, the truth of Shenneck's implant lay revealed.

And this happened to be a bizarre age, a strange time when great numbers of people believed every manipulative junk-science claim, dreading armageddons of infinite variety, yet denied the most common-sense truths that lay luminous before them. Even if millions could be shown the control mechanism that guided Benedetta Ashcroft to kill herself, perhaps most of them would turn their faces from the truth and prefer the more comforting fear that civilization would be destroyed by an imminent invasion of extraterrestrials.

Jane had been an optimist all of her life. But after the events of the past twenty-four hours, she worried that she might be racing toward oblivion, that the only thing waiting for her in San Diego was disappointment, a blank wall into which she would take a header at high speed.

In San Juan Capistrano, before transitioning to Interstate 5, she found a Mailbox Plus store at which she purchased two large padded envelopes, a roll of tape, and a black Sharpie.

In a deserted corner of the parking lot, she slipped thirty thousand of William Overton's cash—three bundles of hundred-dollar bills—into the first envelope and thirty thousand into the second. The envelopes were self-sealing, but she further secured the flaps with tape. With the Sharpie, she printed DORIS MCCLANE on the first envelope, then the address. Doris was Clare's married sister, Nick's aunt, and lived sixteen miles from the Hawks' ranch. Jane addressed the second envelope to Gavin and Jessica Washington; if she could trust them with her child, she could trust them with mere money.

When she had taken a considerable sum from some bad guys in New Mexico, she had sent Doris and the Washingtons a previous package of cash to stash against her future need of it. Then as now, she didn't include a note of explanation. They would identify the sender by the fact that the return address in each case was the same as that of the recipient, and the sender's name above it was in both instances simply Scooter, the name of a beloved dog from which Nick had been inseparable during eleven years of his childhood.

Jane returned to the mailbox store and paid to send both envelopes priority.

She had kept sixty thousand of Overton's money for operating expenses. She hoped to God she would have some use for it.

When she had chosen to stop in San Juan Capistrano instead of in any other town, she had intended to send only one envelope, that to Doris McClane, and to hand-deliver the other thirty thousand to Gavin and Jessie, who were only an hour inland from there.

But in her current state of mind, she dared not go there. Optimist though she long had been, she was more than half convinced that this would be the last chance she would ever have to see her child, to tell him that she loved him. The urge to go to him was overwhelming. But Travis was a sensitive boy, as intuitive in his way as she was in hers. He would read her fear and know why she had come, and she would leave him more unsettled than before her visit.

She sat in her car, in the parking lot, gripping the soapstone cameo, working her thumb over the carved profile, as Travis must have done, thinking of her as she now thought about him. She didn't cry easily, but for a while the world blurred away.

When she was dry-eyed, she pocketed the cameo and started the engine and followed the directions to the library that she'd gotten from the clerk in the mailbox store. At a computer, armed with the address she had pried from William Overton, she used Google Earth to make a quick study of Shenneck's ranch in Napa Valley, especially the gatehouse at the entry and the area around the main house.

From the library, she drove south on Interstate 5, determined to be in San Diego before noon. There might be nothing there for her, but she had nowhere else to go.

4

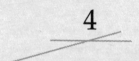

HAVING COME A LONG WAY FOR a short interview, Nathan Silverman was back in Austin International hours before his flight to D.C. Claiming a seat near the gate by which he would later be boarding, he returned to his copy of Erik Larson's *In the Garden of Beasts*, the true story of an American family in Berlin during Hitler's rise to power. Soon he was enthralled by it again.

At first he didn't realize he was being spoken to. "Is that you? Good heavens, it is." He assumed someone seated nearby was the target of the query. "Nathan? Nathan Silverman?"

For an instant, the face looming over him seemed to be that of a stranger. Then he recognized Booth Hendrickson. Booth had been a special agent with the Bureau for more than a decade, during which he had earned a law degree, after which he had transitioned out of the FBI into the Department of Justice proper, three or four years earlier.

"No, no, don't bother getting up," Booth said, taking the seat beside Silverman. "Austin isn't at the end of nowhere, far from it, but it's rather a small world when two old Quantico dogs find themselves knocked together in the capital of the Lone Star State."

Booth Hendrickson had the diligently practiced grace of a bad but earnest dancer, the air of a patrician New Englander who in fact had been born and raised in Florida, and the face of a hawk, though he was barbered to suggest a lion. As an agent, he had worn custom-tailored suits and shoes that cost as much as a mortgage payment, and he currently dressed in that same fashion.

Although they had crossed paths many times, they had not often worked the same case. Now Silverman remembered that he didn't much like the man. "Looking well, Booth. Justice must agree with you."

"The place is a maelstrom of ambition—or instead of maelstrom, should I say cesspool? In either case, I swim in it well enough." He laughed softly at this self-deprecation. "Some good gets done, of course. It always does no matter what."

"What brings you here?" Nathan wondered.

"I was on the flight that just landed, saw you as I came off the air bridge. I've got to get my luggage if it isn't still stuck somewhere on the East Coast. I'm on vacation. First here and then San Antonio. How's Rishona? Well and good, I trust."

"Very well, thank you. And your missus?" Silverman asked, unable to recall her name.

"Divorced. No, don't commiserate. I'm the one who filed for it. Thank God, we never had children. How are your kids, Nathan? How are Jareb and Lisbeth and Chaya?"

Silverman was only mildly surprised that Booth remembered their names. The man assiduously memorized such things to later flatter valuable contacts, like Silverman, with the implication that he actually found them interesting and memorable.

"All done with college. Lisbeth graduated last year."

"All safe and healthy and taking on the world?"

"Safe, healthy, and best of all employed."

Booth laughed more than the line deserved. "You're a lucky man, Nathan."

"As I tell myself every night and first thing every morning."

Booth tapped the Erik Larson volume that Silverman held. "Terrific book. Read it a couple years ago. Makes you think."

"Yes, it does."

"Makes you think," Booth repeated. He glanced at his watch, shot to his feet. "Got to run. A week of leisure calls."

He thrust out his right hand, and they shook, and Booth held it a beat or two longer than he should have.

"Lucky man," he repeated, and then he was off.

Silverman watched Booth Hendrickson blend in with travelers on the concourse and dwindle away through the terminal.

He didn't at once return to the Larson book.

Did even a man like Booth Hendrickson go on vacation in a three-piece suit and tie?

He hadn't seen Booth in maybe three years. He wasn't sure he would have recognized him from a distance, as Booth had spotted him.

Unless the man had the memory of an array of supercomputers, which he didn't, it was remarkable that he recalled the names of the kids. Rishona, yes. Booth had met her once or twice. But he'd never met the children. *Jareb and Lisbeth and Chaya.* The names had come off his tongue as if he'd heard them only an hour earlier.

And now it seemed to Silverman that when Booth had spoken their names, his stare had sharpened and a different tone had come into his voice. A subtle solemnity.

Perhaps Silverman's many years with the Bureau had steeped him too long in suspicion. Or maybe Ancel Hawk's tight-lipped paranoia was a bit infectious.

All safe and healthy and taking on the world?

Most people would ask if your kids were healthy and happy. How odd for anyone to ask if they were *safe.*

In memory, he heard Booth's voice: *Makes you think. Makes you think.*

Silverman looked at the book in his hands.

He had asked Booth what brought him to Austin, but Booth had not returned the question. As if he already knew what Silverman was doing there.

5

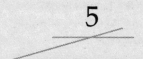

THE FREE KITCHEN THAT HE had mentioned, to which he intended to contribute the forty dollars that Jane had given him, turned out to be only a block from the branch library in San Diego where she had first seen him five days earlier. The librarian gave her directions.

The operation was housed in what had once been a building owned by a fraternal club. The letters of the club's name had been removed from the limestone façade, but the ghost of them remained lighter against the time-darkened stone.

A new and simple sign identified the place as RED, WHITE, BLUE, AND DINNER. Lest anyone misunderstand that only dinner would be served, an explanatory line promised three square meals a day.

The interior layout seemed unchanged from the days when a fraternal order ran the place. The bar was still there, though it no longer operated. The dining room was paved with terrazzo. A long-unused wood dance floor lay in front of a raised bandstand.

In the past, no doubt round tables had been encircled by elegant, upholstered dining chairs. Now there were folding chairs and rectangular tables without cloths.

Lunch service began at 11:30. Now at 11:50, already thirty or forty people were eating or in the cafeteria line. The majority were men, most gray-faced and trembling alkies burned out on booze. Eight women sat alone or in pairs, and though a few might have known a bottle or two, the others appeared just sad, weary, and worn out.

The lunch theme was Mexican. Aromas of onions and peppers and cilantro and limes and warm corn tortillas threaded the air.

Jane stepped to the end of the cafeteria line but didn't pick up a tray. When she got to the first server—CHARLENE, according to the name tag—she said, "There's a man comes here to eat. I wonder if he's been here lately." She had in hand the old newspaper photo that she'd printed out in the Woodland Hills library Friday morning. "His name's Dougal Trahern. He doesn't look much like this anymore."

Charlene declared, "Lordy, but he looks no way the same these days. The man has thrown himself off some high cliffs in his time, and it shows." She called the attention of the next server to the photo that Jane held up. "Rosa, give this a look."

Rosa shook her head in what might have been a mix of dismay and wonderment. "If the fella in that picture had made TV commercials, he could've sold a girl anything from perfume to fish sticks. How many buses have to run a man down to change him so?"

"You have business with Dougal?" Charlene asked.

"Yes. If you can give me any lead on him, I'd be grateful."

"Is he expectin' you?"

"We met once, briefly. But, no, he's not expecting me."

"Good. If he was expectin' you, he'd duck out the back door just when you were supposed to arrive." Charlene put down the soup ladle. "Come with me, dear. I'll take you to him."

"He's here?"

"He better be if we are."

Jane followed Charlene into the busy restaurant kitchen and from there into what seemed to be a kitchen manager's office with a desk and computer and shelves of cookbooks. For some reason, the two windows were painted black, giving the room a subterranean feel.

Behind the desk sat the bearish man from the library, his hair a wilder mass than she remembered, his dark bristling beard shot through with a bride-of-Frankenstein bolt of white. When Jane and Charlene entered the room, Trahern looked up from his work, his face as menacing as a thunderhead just before a storm broke.

"This fine young lady," Charlene said, "has business with you."

"Get her out of here," Trahern growled, as if his hibernation had been interrupted midwinter.

Charlene took offense or pretended to take it. "I'm a cook, not a porter who hauls whatever you need hauled anywhere you say to haul it. I'm already cookin' *and* workin' the line. You want her out of here, you pick her up and throw her out your own self."

As she left the room, Charlene winked at Jane.

Trahern aimed the full force of his glower on his one remaining annoyance. "You come here to get your forty dollars back?"

"What? No. Of course not."

"What is it, then? There's a long way to Thanksgiving."

Uncomprehending, she said, "Thanksgiving?"

"Every damn politician and celebrity wants to work the line on Thanksgiving, when the news people come take pictures."

"I'm not a politician or a celebrity."

"Then why the hell do you look like a celebrity?"

"I wasn't aware that I did." Frustrated by the man's needless hostility, Jane put the photo of a beardless, barbered Trahern on the desk. "What happened to this guy?"

Trahern turned the photo so that his younger self was looking not at him, but at Jane. "He got wise."

"So now he does what—menu planning for a soup kitchen?"

"And *you* do what—rescue babies from burning buildings?"

"DDT—the tattoo. It's your initials and your nickname, because you took out bad guys the way DDT took out mosquitoes. I read about you years ago. It took me a while to remember."

His impatience was colored now by alarm. He

glanced at the open door between the office and the kitchen.

She said, "You were awarded the Distinguished Service Cross, just below the Medal of Honor. At great jeopardy, you rescued—"

"Keep it down," he grumbled. "What's wrong with you, barging in here and talking about stuff like this?"

Jane went to the door, closed it. No ready chair was provided for a visitor, but a folding version leaned against one wall. She unfolded it, said, "Don't mind if I do," and sat down. "You regret those things you did? Are you embarrassed about them?"

He looked like the wrathful Old Testament God getting ready to throw down some well-deserved punishment on the earth. "This might be hard to understand, lady. But in war, you do the right thing, whatever it takes, and if you come out alive, you know how easy you could have screwed up, so bragging on it is dead-solid *wrong*. Only assholes do that. I don't Facebook. Don't tweet. Don't Instagram. I don't talk about the past, and it pisses me off that you remembered that old DDT thing and were able to find that newspaper photo."

For a long silence, she met Trahern's fierce stare, and then with relief, she said, "Maybe you're not a shithead, after all."

"Is your opinion supposed to matter to me? I don't even know your name. You have a name, or are you just some anonymous gremlin who spins into people's lives and wrecks their mood?"

She rummaged in her handbag, pulled a rubber band off a bundle of five forged driver's licenses, and spread them out on his desk. "I've got a lot of names, but none of those are true. My real name is Jane Hawk. I'm FBI on leave, although they might have suspended or dismissed me by now." She threw her Bureau ID on the desk. "My husband, Nick, was a decorated Marine, received some big medals, including the Navy Cross. Full colonel at thirty-two. They killed him, tried to make it look like suicide. They threatened to rape and kill my five-year-old boy if I didn't fade. I've hidden him. They'll kill me if they find me. I've killed one of them. I know where to find the guy who is the biggest sonofabitch behind it all, but I can't get at him alone, and I can't turn to anyone I know because they'll be waiting for that. I need someone with your exact skills, if you still have any. Skills, that is."

He watched her as she picked up the forged licenses and the FBI credentials, and as she returned them to her handbag. Then he said, "Why should I care? I wasn't Marines, I was Army."

She stared at him, speechless.

He said, "Relax. It's a joke."

"I didn't know you were capable of making a joke."

"That's the first in a while." He looked at one of the blacked-out windows, as if he could see through the opaque pane to a view that troubled him. "You're desperate or delusional, coming to me."

"I confess to desperation."

"Nothing I can do for you."

"There is if you want to do it."

"My wars were a long time ago."

"All wars are one war. And it never ends."

"I'm not the man I was then."

"Any man who earned the Distinguished Service Cross is always going to be that man, somewhere in himself."

He met her stare. "That's just rah-rah bullshit."

"Maybe to an Army prick, but not to a Marine's widow."

After a silence, he said, "Are you always this way?"

"What other way is there to be?"

6

THE BLACKEST, RICHEST COFFEE that she had ever tasted got Jane through the next hour and a half. Dougal Derwent Trahern was only slightly less of a bee-stung bear than he had been when she first entered his shabby office. Blunt, gruff, often rude, grumbling when he wasn't growling, his stare like surgical steel, he had a drill-into-it interrogation technique straight out of Quantico. He made notes, looped back to issues she had already discussed, to see if she contradicted herself, and sweated her through her story as if he must be convinced she was a serial killer rather than a hunter of them. He read Emily Rossman's autopsy report and listened to Jane's account of what the pathologist had told her at the animal hospital.

She watched over Trahern's shoulder as he used Overton's smartphone—and the forty-four-character Web address Jane had found on it—to plunge into the Dark Web and review the messages that Aspasia presented to a visitor. She had not seen this before, and she was chilled when Jimmy Radburn's description of the experience proved to be spot-on. After getting to the screen that promised beautiful girls who were incapable of disobedience and whose permanent silence was assured, Trahern issued a colorful curse.

"The world is zombified," he said. "They're just sleazeballs and freaks instead of the walking dead, but more of them than us."

Jane returned to her folding chair. "What now?"

Trahern switched off Overton's smartphone. "Why don't you go out to the dining room for a while. I need to talk to some people."

"What people?"

"You've made a convincing case. I'm not going to rat you out."

"What people?" she repeated. "You make a mistake, talk to the wrong one, I'm finished. I'm dust. And my boy."

"I may look deranged, but I'm not. You either trust me or you don't. If you don't, just leave and we'll forget each other."

She stared at him. He returned the stare.

After a silence, she said, "You're one hard-nosed bastard."

"What do you want—someone who breaks the grindstone or someone who's broken by it?"

She got to her feet but didn't move toward the door. "One big question. On Monday, at the library, you were looking at porno."

"Not for pleasure. As a citizen activist."

"That sounds real to you?"

"Look, I work with various concerned groups in the city. We try to set things right where we can. It took a while to get libraries to block the nasty websites so kids couldn't get on them. Now and then a librarian or somebody decides it's a free-speech issue and opens the lid on the sewer. I was told that branch was backsliding. I had to see for myself. Today, the lid's back on, kids are safe."

She remembered how he had considered the pornography on the computer screen with a combination of boredom and puzzlement, not with lascivious interest. And he had soon switched to dog videos.

"Good," she said. "I'm glad I asked."

"You want to ask if I bathed this morning?"

"I know you did. When I was looking over your shoulder, I could smell your shampoo."

7

DURING THE HOUR AND A HALF she had spent in Trahern's office, the lunch rush had subsided. Two men, five women, and three children were finishing their meals at the long tables. For just a moment, when the kids looked at Jane, they all seemed to have Travis's face.

Charlene, Rosa, and two other women were cleaning the serving side of the cafeteria line. As Jane approached them, Charlene said, "Goodness be, look at this, Rosa. Her eyebrows aren't even singed."

"Seems to still have all her teeth, too," Rosa said.

Jane said, "He's all growl, no bite. How long's he been here?"

"Since he bought the building. What is it, Rosa? Five years?"

"Closer six."

Since he bought the building. Those five words revised Jane's understanding of the situation.

"A girl like you," Charlene said, "can't be lookin' for a job in this place. Are you wantin' to volunteer?"

"Never enough volunteers," Rosa said.

"Actually," Jane said, "I'm trying to persuade *him* to volunteer for something."

"He'll do it, whatever it is," Charlene assured her. "Our Mr. Bigfoot doesn't know how to say no. He has a finger in everything from veterans' needs to no-kill animal shelters to Toys for Tots."

"After-school programs for kids, scholarships," Rosa added.

"He spends so much time spreadin' his money around," Charlene said, "I don't know when he has the time to make more of it."

"Just the one thing," Rosa said, and gave her co-worker a meaningful look.

Charlene said, "If sometime he goes pale and breaks into a sweat and seems not himself for just a minute, pay him no mind."

"Is he ill?" Jane asked.

"No, no, no. It's just a bad memory, maybe from one of his wars. He works his way through it quick. It doesn't mean nothin', child." Charlene and Rosa returned to their work, subject closed.

8

WHEN JANE RETURNED FROM the women's lavatory, Charlene waved her over to the cafeteria counter. "The boss said, 'Send that young lady back in here.' If he forgot your name, child, don't take offense. He's got a lot on his mind, and he remembers everybody's name after a while. By the way, what *is* your name?"

"Alice Liddell," Jane said.

"I hope we'll be seein' a lot more of you, Alice. Now, do you remember how to get to his office?"

"I do. Thank you."

In Trahern's office, Jane closed the door and regarded the man hulking over his desk, wearing his homeless-guy clothes, behind his lightning-shot beard. Her respect for what he had done in the past was corroded by suspicion, by the apprehension that the country was afflicted by a pandemic of corruption. She thought about David James Michael, who was widely viewed as a generous do-gooder, cover that allowed him to back Shenneck and use the girls at Aspasia. Suddenly it was possible to see Trahern's clothes as a *costume*, his unruly hair and Moses beard as part of a crafted image.

She said, "So you're rich, huh?"

He raised his untrimmed eyebrows, which were as lush as a pair of mustaches. "Is being rich a strike against me?"

"Depends on how you made it. You spent twelve years in the Army, which isn't known for big salaries."

Trahern watched steam wisp from his coffee. He picked up the mug and blew on the coffee and cautiously took a sip. He might have been striving to control his temper, which he had indulged before. Or maybe he was buying time to spin a convincing lie.

"When I left the service," he said, "I had an inheritance waiting from my father, who died the year before."

"How did *he* earn it?"

Trahern's face knotted like a gnarled scrub oak.

"Someone in as much trouble as you are shouldn't ask for help and then throw stones with both hands."

Self-righteous indignation was not an answer.

"In case you've forgotten," she said, "I've recently had my life knocked out from under me by some rich people who think they can own anyone they want and kill anyone they don't own."

"Painting all rich people as villains is purest bigotry."

She was keenly aware that a charge of bigotry was a popular technique used to shut up an adversary who was no more a bigot than she was a blue giraffe, to make her doubt herself and misdirect her, while implying the moral superiority of the accuser.

Whatever Trahern's motivation, benign or sinister, she wouldn't be manipulated. "Do you hang out with a bunch of rich people? Seems to me like they hang out with each other and no one else."

Rising from his chair, standing perhaps six feet four, chest describing an arc like that of a fifty-gallon wine barrel, face now red with displeasure, he said, "I hang out with millionaires and paupers and near saints and certain sinners and anyone I damn well want to hang out with. Now, why don't you sit down?"

"I'm waiting for the answer."

"What answer?"

"How did your father earn the fortune he left to you?"

Trahern made a wordless sound not unlike a dog shaking a garden snake to death. Then he said, "Dad was an investment advisor, and a good one. It wasn't a massive fortune. A few hundred thousand when the estate was settled. I'd just gotten out of the Army, back in 2000, at the turn of the millennium, when you were a snot-nosed kid in pigtails. There were opportunities. I took the three hundred grand and proved to be a much better investor than my father."

She remained standing. "Yeah? What did you invest in?"

He waved his big hands in the air and rolled his eyes. "Drugs! Guns! Huge scary knives! A company that made Nazi uniforms!" He took another deep breath and snorted it out as before. Still displeased but in as normal a voice as he could muster, he said, "On 9/11, when those creeps took down the World Trade Center, everyone bailed out of stocks in a panic. I bought into the market with everything I had. In 2008, 2009, when the bottom fell out of the economy, I bought stocks and real-estate big-time. See the pattern? It's always smart to bet on America."

"You got rich by betting on America?"

"And it still works for me."

She went to the folding chair and sat down, not entirely at ease with him, but convinced that his indignation was real, not contrived. "I pushed your buttons pretty hard there, but I won't apologize for asking. It's my life, my boy's life. I need to know that you are who you seem to be. It's a rare thing these days."

He sat behind the desk once more. "I guess it works both ways. I called someone who might have known your husband. Relax already. Will you relax? Give me a chance here? All right. So this is a guy, if he was starving on a desert island with nothing but a dog, he'd eat his own arm before he'd take a bite out of the mutt. Turns out he *did* know your Nick, and he talked about him kind of like the Pope might talk about the baby Jesus. This guy never met you, but he was in action with Nick, and he says there's no way Nick would have married a nutcase or an airhead, no matter how good she looked."

9

FROM GOOGLE EARTH, DOU-gal Trahern had printed satellite views of a few key areas of Shenneck's seventy-acre Napa Valley ranch at different magnifications. The stack of pages was more than half an inch thick, held together by a binder clip.

Jane was sitting at Trahern's desk, studying the photos, when the big man returned with a fully loaded duffel bag, which he put on the floor beside the office door.

"You're right," she said. "My way in won't work."

"But my way will."

"What's your way?"

"To save time, I'll tell you when we're on the road."

"Where are we going?"

"Los Angeles. To see a guy."

"What guy?"

"You trust me or you don't."

"I do and I don't. These days, there's only eight people in the whole world I trust completely—which is why I'm not dead already."

"Do and don't. Maybe that's good enough for now. But soon you'll have to make up your mind. Are you carrying?"

She pulled aside her sport coat to reveal the rig and pistol. "Not licensed when on leave from the Bureau. But if I'm going to Hell, it won't be because I broke the concealed-carry laws."

Trahern had put on the voluminous black quilted-nylon garment that he had been wearing when she'd first seen him in the library. The zipper was not engaged, and he spread both panels of the jacket, revealing a dual rig with pistols snugged against his left and right sides. "Have good connections and a reputation for philanthropy, you can be licensed to double carry."

"You really need those at Toys for Tots meetings?"

"I mostly carry just one. I know ministers, teachers, little-old-lady retirees who pack everywhere they go."

As he spoke, he looked toward the blacked-out windows, first one and then the other.

"Why'd you paint the glass?" Jane asked.

"I don't like having a window at my back where anyone could be looking in at me."

"Blinds wouldn't work? Draperies?"

"Not good enough. Paint it black. That's the only sure thing." He picked up the duffel bag. "Better be going."

As she watched Trahern open the door and leave his office, Jane wondered if, by turning to this man, she had improved her chances of getting to Shenneck or instead had guaranteed failure.

10

AS JANE STARTED THE ENGINE, Trahern dropped his duffel bag in the back of the Ford Escape. He got in the front passenger seat and closed the door, holding the satellite photos on his lap.

In the confines of the car, he seemed not merely bigger than before but also stranger, sitting there in his lace-up boots and camouflage pants and black T-shirt and shiny black nylon jacket. He was forty-eight years old, yet in spite of his size and his age, at times he had a childlike quality. Sometimes when she looked at him, when he didn't realize that he was being observed, he appeared lost.

"What're you looking at?" he grumbled.

"Are you sure you know what you're maybe getting into?"

"Trespass, breaking and entering, false imprisonment, assault, kidnapping, homicide."

"And you met me just a couple of hours ago."

"You're convincing. I saw the Aspasia website. I trust you."

She didn't put the car in gear. "That's really all it takes to plunge like this—that you trust me?"

"It's more than that. It's like I've been waiting most of my life for this. I've got my reasons. And don't ask what they are, 'cause they're *my* reasons. You can't do this alone, you've got nowhere else to go, and you're damn lucky I said yes. Hit the road."

11

SINCE MID-MORNING, CLOUDS had been sailing in from the north, an armada of gray galleons that raised their sails to screen out the high blue vault with which the day had begun. Now, at 2:30, the low lead-colored overcast suggested the possibility of rain but didn't promise it. The wind that drove the clouds was at high altitude, while here at ground level, the city stood in stillness, its many trees untroubled, its flags and pennants and banners and awnings limp, motionless. This seemed to be a city waiting for something, and not for anything good, poised in tense expectation.

On the freeway, heading north toward Interstate 5, Trahern said, "I'm talked out. Let's be quiet awhile."

"All right."

"I need quiet. To think."

Jane said nothing.

He closed his eyes and sat there, big and strangely costumed and bristling and perhaps unknowable. As she drove, Jane glanced at him from time to time, and she vacillated between being comforted by his presence and being disturbed by him.

In mutual silence, with only the drumming of the engine and the drone of the tires, they had gone maybe twenty-five miles on I-5 and were passing Oceanside when, eyes still closed, Trahern said with bearish gruffness, "I have absolutely no romantic interest in you."

"Likewise," she replied, amazed that he felt it necessary to broach the subject.

He wanted to be sure his point had been taken. "I'm old enough to be your father. And for another thing, I'm beyond all that."

"I was only recently widowed," she reminded him. "For the foreseeable future, I'm beyond all that, too."

"Not that you aren't attractive. You're quite attractive."

"I understand."

"Good. I'm glad we've got that straight. Now let's can the chatter for a while."

In spite of the gray sky and the gray sea to the west and the dismal scrub-covered hills to the east and the potential bleakness of events to come, a small smile settled on Jane. She didn't hold it for long. Somehow, a smile seemed dangerous just now, a challenge to Fate that Fate would not ignore.

12

AFTER CANCELING HIS RETURN flight to Reagan International in Washington, Nathan Silverman booked passage on a direct flight out of Austin to San Francisco and from there a one-hour shuttle to Los Angeles. If Booth Hendrickson, on behalf of the attorney general or anyone else in the Department of Justice, had indeed been conveying a message to cease and desist, the effect on Silverman was the opposite of what had been intended.

At 2:50 Saturday afternoon, in San Francisco International, as he sat near the appropriate gate, awaiting a boarding call for the commuter flight, he received an email from the L.A. field office. Enhancement of the park video and facial-recognition processing had determined that the man carrying the two briefcases, with a metallic balloon tied to one wrist, was Robert Frances Branwick, alias Jimmy

Radburn, who operated a collectible-record store called Vinyl, which was a front for a cybercrime operation. The FBI had been conducting electronic surveillance on Radburn's business, gathering data about his client list in preparation for a sweeping series of arrests.

The musclebound specimen who had been foiled at the hotel entrance by the chain and padlock was Norman "Kipp" Garner. He was of interest to various police agencies because they believed that he was a conduit for dark money coming out of certain totalitarian regimes for investment in criminal enterprises in the United States, though insufficient evidence existed to press charges against him.

As the boarding call came and Silverman got to his feet, he was unable to imagine anything in those briefcases, given their source, that wouldn't incriminate Jane. Depending on what evolved in Los Angeles, he might not be able to delay much longer before reporting her to the director and opening an official investigation.

He refrained from doing so now only because of his faith in her and because, according to her father-in-law, unnamed players had threatened to kill her child. Ancel Hawk's claim that young Travis was a target had become more credible following Silverman's encounter with Booth Hendrickson.

13

ON INTERSTATE 405, BY THE
time Jane was drawing near to Long Beach, one
thrombosis after another began to form in the traffic.
Even the carpool lane was stop-and-go. She resorted
to the kind of driving that annoyed her when others
did it, frequently changing lanes to get around a clot
of vehicles, weaving in and out to take advantage of
a length of open pavement that might gain her only
a hundred yards.

She was propelled by the thought of Overton's
corpse lying in his big walk-in closet since the previous night. Initially she had told herself that he
wouldn't be found until Monday. Now she could
imagine a variety of scenarios in which a missed
weekend engagement might motivate a friend to become concerned enough to pay a visit to the house.
News of the attorney's death would not necessarily
be at once conveyed to other members of his vicious
confederacy, but if it was, Shenneck would be even
more security conscious.

In the passenger seat, for the past hour, Dougal
Trahern had been studying satellite photos of Gee
Zee Ranch. Occasionally he muttered to himself, but
he didn't speak to Jane until they were passing Ingle-
wood. "Take the ten west to PCH and then north."

A short while later, Jane turned onto the Pacific
Coast Highway. She again passed Palisades Park,

where roller-skating Nona had drop-kicked Jimmy Radburn and snatched the two briefcases on Wednesday, though this time she was on the ocean side of the park, the Palisades rising on her right.

"Now where?" she asked.

Trahern recited an address in Malibu, and at last he gave her a shorthand version of how to get past security at Gee Zee Ranch.

Although he didn't plan to fly the bird, she expected the part with the helicopter. He'd been a Special Forces helo pilot, which was one reason she had gone to him.

The other component, however, seemed over-the-top. She didn't say as much right away. She owed him thoughtful consideration. But she began to worry that in spite of his military heroism and his genius as an investor and his management skills evident in the free kitchen that he had established, his psychological problems made him a less-than-ideal strategist.

14

NATHAN SILVERMAN PARKED the airport rental car a block from Vinyl, stiffed the parking meter, and walked to the record store.

Sunset was almost an hour away, but the gunmetal sky plated over the sun so effectively that the

San Fernando Valley huddled under a premature dusk.

An agent at the front door of Vinyl checked Silverman's ID before letting him inside. "Sir, the action's on the second floor."

The framed vintage posters on the walls and the bins of collectible records remained as they had been. The back room contained even more of that inventory.

He heard voices on the second floor. When he got upstairs, he found a forest of abandoned furniture and a table heaped with snack foods. But there wasn't a single computer or scanner or other piece of equipment used in the Dark Web business that had been conducted there, not even so much as one extension cord or cable tie.

Present were John Harrow, SAC of the L.A. office, whom he knew, and two other agents who were unknown to him.

Harrow, with his gray crew cut and shoulders-back posture and sharply pressed suit and alert demeanor, was as clearly ex-military as a man could be. As the section chief of the Critical Incident Response Group, Silverman oversaw among other things the five Behavioral Analysis Units. Unit 2, which dealt with cybercrime and related issues, had been advising Harrow in the matter of Robert Branwick, alias Jimmy Radburn, for the better part of a year.

"There's a bogus traffic cam," Harrow said, "watching the front entrance. Phone and off-phone conversations are on auto-record for delayed review. With everything else going down these days, we don't have personnel for twenty-four/seven surveillance, but we do regular drive-bys. Never seemed they'd bail from here without discussing it, which we'd have caught in plenty of time with the delayed review."

A dreary mood had overtaken Silverman. "So they vacated quickly but discreetly."

"Yeah. As if they discovered we had them boxed and ready to put away." He waited a beat, then said, "Do you have a rogue, Nathan?"

Silverman didn't miss the calculation in Harrow's use of the word *you* instead of *we*. These days, the Bureau was, as it had always been, a loyal brotherhood—except when it wasn't.

Instead of answering, he said, "Branwick's ego weighs as much as his brain. He's convinced he's been clever about his identity, that no one but Kipp Garner knows his real name isn't Radburn."

"Yes. Unless . . . someone told him different."

"Have you grabbed him?"

"Not yet. An hour ago we put surveillance on the Sherman Oaks house. We're going after all the rats before they scatter, and at the same time, so they can't warn one another."

"Are you going with SWAT at the Branwick house?"

"Yeah. That's where the big prize is, and where we're likely to get a hard pushback. All those guys in the hacking crew that worked here—they're gutless wonders. The moment they see a badge, they'll be outbidding one another to sell each other out." He looked at his watch. "It goes down after dark. We're on our way over there now."

"I'll be there," Silverman said.

"If Branwick knows we have his real name, if he's skipped, you have a rogue."

"It's not that simple, John," Silverman said, and hoped that he would not have to eat his words, at least not just a few hours after speaking them.

15

THE MALIBU MANSION MIGHT have stood on one acre or three, but it was nobody's idea of a tract home. Jane found it hard to size it from outside the stacked-stone estate wall.

The guard at the gatehouse wore gray slacks and a white shirt and a maroon blazer. The cut of his coat allowed a concealed weapon. Mr. Trahern and guest were expected. In their wake, the solid green-patinaed copper-clad gate swung shut across the quartzite driveway.

The grounds were expansive and tropical, graced with phoenix palms and royal palms and palms she couldn't name, with all manner of ferns. Flowers everywhere. Lawns as smooth as putting greens.

The house was a marvel of white stucco and glass

and teak, curved at every corner, with dramatically cantilevered decks.

She parked in the circular drive and said, "Here we go again."

"You've been here before?" Trahern asked.

"No. Here we go again with rich people. Is there no limit to the number of them?"

"You'll like this one. He's a San Diego boy. Donates big-time to every good cause I bring him—"

"Half the do-gooders in the world are bad-doers pulling a con."

"Donates big-time to every good cause I bring him," Trahern repeated, "and never uses it for publicity."

She walked with him to the front door. It was opened by a man dressed in white shoes, white slacks, and a tasteful white Hawaiian shirt with no decoration except the outlines of palm trees stitched in the palest of blue thread.

Jane mistook him for the owner, but he was a casually dressed butler. "The mister is waiting in the garage. I'll take you to him."

"That's all right, Henry," Trahern said. "I know the way."

In those expansive rooms of sleek modern furniture accessorized with Asian antiques and art, the lumbering Dougal Trahern looked even more out of place than did the humble Ford Escape parked in the grand driveway. But he seemed to feel at home.

They passed a wall of glass beyond which lay a breathtaking view of the sea, gray under the ashen sky, phalanxes of whitecaps marching toward the shore.

An elevator took them down to a subterranean garage paved in limestone and containing a collection of maybe two dozen cars.

The owner was there, too, a surprise to Jane. One of the most famous movie stars of his time. Tall and handsome and black. His killer smile had melted hearts worldwide.

He and Trahern hugged, and upon being introduced, the actor took both of Jane's hands in his. "Any friend of Dougal's is—highly suspect! But not in your case. What agency represents you?"

Trahern was quick to translate, "He means talent agency." To the actor, he said, "Jane isn't in the business. You might say right now she's something of a private investigator."

"I've played a P.I. more than once," the star said, "and I've had to hire a few, but none of them with your impact, Miss Hawk."

The Gurkha RPV Civilian Edition was parked in the center of the garage, under pin spots. It appeared as formidable as the tactical armored vehicles, armored SUVs, and special-purpose law-enforcement vehicles that Terradyne, its Canadian manufacturer, sold around the world. Over eight feet high, more than twenty feet long, with maybe a 140-inch wheelbase. The Gurkha stood on large run-flat tires. The only obvious difference between it and the military version was the lack of gun ports.

It looked as if it were a Transformer just starting to change from an ordinary vehicle into a robot colossus.

The actor beamed with the affection of a passionate collector as he said, "Six-point-seven-liter V8 turbo diesel. Three hundred horsepower. Gross weight of this baby with all the options and both forty-gallon fuel tanks filled is like seventeen thousand pounds, but it handles sweet, gives you all the speed you need, and while you're in it, you're safe unless you plan to go up against a tank."

Trahern handed an envelope to the star. "A check for four hundred and fifty thousand dollars. I'll need the pink slip signed."

Bemused, the actor said, "Dougal, I still don't get this."

"What's to get?" Trahern harrumphed. "I can't wait months and months for Terradyne to deliver one. And you'll be gone for months on location for those two movies . . . which, by the way, don't have a snowball's chance in Hell of winning you another Oscar. You can order a new Gurkha and have it when you get home."

"But you can *borrow* this for nothing."

"No good," Trahern said and glowered and shook his massively haired and bearded head. "I could get myself in trouble with this, so it's better for you to have sold it than loaned it to me."

Not with concern, but with the interest of a born adventurer, the actor said, "Trouble? What kind of trouble?"

"Every kind," Trahern replied, his expression dour and his brow beetled as if he were a gifted fore-teller who could see no possible futures except dark ones. "And that's all I'll say. You need to have plausible deniability. Unless you want to change your mind, not do this at all, leave your old friend with his bare ass hanging out."

The actor fashioned his face into a God-forbid expression. "I'd be blinded by the blight. Keep it under wraps, Captain."

Trahern said, "If we do what we need to do and bring the Gurkha back, you can buy it from me minus the cost of any repairs, if you want, or I just keep it, whatever. But now we've got a long night's drive ahead of us. As much as I'd be enchanted to hear you tell some of your interminable Hollywood stories, I need that damn pink slip."

The actor grinned at Jane. "Isn't he something?"

"He's something," she agreed.

"I guess you know what you're getting into with him."

"I guess I do."

16

WHEN THE LONG, SLOPED street was clear from intersection to intersection, Bureau cars pulled across two lanes, barring traffic from entering either end of the block in which stood the Branwick residence.

The neighbors in the house downhill from Branwick's were not home. The neighbors on the other side had been quietly shepherded out of their place under the cover of night and escorted a safe distance from any potential action.

Uphill and across the street from the target house, Silverman and Special Agent Harrow stood watching from the darkness under the street trees and from behind a Roto-Rooter van that was in fact an undercover vehicle on loan from the Drug Enforcement Agency. In the back of the van waited the six members of the SWAT team, who were suited in hard high-impact armor, waiting for the order to go.

The night had been still. Now a light breeze came out of the west, stirring the trees into a whispering conspiracy.

In the target residence, lights glowed through most if not all of the ground-floor rooms, but only in part of the second story. Draperies hung open, the rooms beyond apparently vacant.

Initially, two agents approached the Branwick place dressed in street clothes with light-ballistic

Kevlar vests under their shirts. No head protection. Their appearance did not scream *police*.

One of them climbed the four steps between the stone lions and moved to a section of wall between the front door and a window. The second man went to the east side of the house, let himself through an iron gate, and moved out of sight to the back of the residence.

The agent at the front, standing beside the window, pressed to the glass a two-inch-diameter suction cup at the center of which was a highly sensitive condenser microphone with a wide pick-up pattern. Clipped to his belt, an analytic audio processor the size of a pack of cigarettes was programmed to identify and screen out the rhythmic noise of bathroom-vent fans, refrigerator motors, and appliances, in order that voices and the irregular sounds of human activity would be more easily discerned. He wore an earpiece, so that he could hear what the processor deemed relevant.

The listening device also transmitted to a remote receiver, which in this case was Silverman's smartphone.

He and Harrow listened for perhaps two minutes. The quiet was so unrelieved that if there were people inside the house, they must have been in cryogenic suspension.

The agent who had disappeared along the east side of the house reappeared through the iron gate. He crouched beside a hedge, all but invisible in his dark clothes.

A moment later Harrow's phone vibrated. He listened, gave the order to fade back, and terminated the call. To Silverman, he said, "Through a window, he saw a dead body on the kitchen floor."

Harrow stepped to the back of the van and gave the go order to the SWAT team to take the Branwick house and clear its rooms.

This was a day of revelations, each with greater import than the one before it, and the weight of them seemed to be compounding into a prophecy that Nathan Silverman didn't want to believe. Even if Jane was in the jaws of a vise through no fault of her own, her son at risk, even though her motives might be pure, she was tangled in a very dark web. In desperation, people did things that the law could not forgive regardless of the circumstances. He liked her, he understood her, he trusted her . . . and yet his image of her had begun ever so slightly to fray around the edges.

17

JANE BEHIND THE WHEEL OF the Gurkha RPV, racing north on I-5, the six-speed automatic transmission smooth, road noise less than she expected because of the insulating armor. Las Padres National Forest to her left, Angeles National Forest to her right, she piloted the Gurkha high into the Tehachapi Mountains, with only flyspeck towns immediately ahead—a couple thousand souls here, a few hundred there—otherwise a vast darkness under a shrouded sky in which the moon and stars were buried.

Her Ford Escape waited back in Malibu, parked in the actor's garage, from which she would one day retrieve it if she lived.

Trahern in the passenger seat, seeming smaller than he did in the Ford. Looking less comical, more menacing, by association with this military-style vehicle. Looking in fact like a dangerous revolutionary bent on blowing up banks and stock exchanges. Although mumbling to himself from time to time, he invited no conversation.

They were a few miles from the Tejon Pass when Jane said, "So he takes your check and gives you the pink slip and doesn't even want to know what you might do that could maybe link him to one kind of mess or another, screw up his reputation?"

"Yes, I remember."

"That was a question."

"To what point?"

"Why would he do that?"

"We go way back."

"Well, that explains everything."

"Good."

"I was being sarcastic."

He took a handkerchief from a pocket, hocked up phlegm, spat it in the hankie, and tucked it away.

She said, "I go back and forth about you."

"Everybody does."

"So why would he do that, no questions asked?"

"You won't let this go, will you?"

"I need to understand you."

"Nobody can understand anybody," he groused. "In a nutshell, the man lied about his age to join the Army at sixteen. Served four years, three in Special Forces. We went through some shit together."

"War?"

"It was like a war. They didn't call it that."

"What was the shit you went through together? Specifically."

"You never heard this."

"Never heard what?"

"He thinks I saved his life."

"Why does he think that?"

"I killed a bunch of people who were trying to kill him and a few other spec ops guys."

"How many are a bunch?"

"Twelve, maybe fourteen."

"And you got the Distinguished Service Cross."

"No. That was for another thing. Now will you just shut up for a while?"

"Shutting up," she said.

They crossed the Tejon Pass at four thousand one hundred feet and began the descent into the San Joaquin Valley, thousands of square miles that had once been the most productive farmland in the world.

On both sides of the highway, boundless reaches of flat land darkled away to distant mountains that stood moon-abandoned and only half real, like faintly limned mystical peaks in a vision. Here and there in that immensity glimmered the lonely lights of isolated farmhouses, as well as twinkling clusters that marked small towns with names like Pumpkin Center and Dustin Acres and Buttonwillow.

Jane wondered if in this bucolic realm there might be people who lived with a sense of peace and belonging, untouched by the stresses and anxieties borne elsewhere in the modern world. And if there were such people ... how numbered were their days?

18

IN SPITE OF THE GRIEVOUS FACE wound and the early effects of decomposition, the dead man on the floor was recognizably Robert Branwick, also known as Jimmy Radburn. In his wallet, teased out of his hip pocket without disturbing the position of the corpse, a driver's license confirmed the visual ID.

The kitchen cabinets had been significantly damaged by shotgun blasts. Having ricocheted off hard surfaces, spent buckshot littered the floor.

"Branwick doesn't have a weapon," John Harrow said.

"Maybe he did and his killer took it," Silverman suggested.

"Doesn't feel that way."

Silverman had to agree that it didn't.

"If Branwick had a shotgun and was up against someone with a pistol, he'd still be alive, and there'd be a different stiff on the floor."

Three bits of video ran through Silverman's memory: this dead man when alive, carrying two briefcases through the park . . . the roller-skating woman taking the two bags from him . . . the skater and Jane fleeing the hotel garage after emptying the briefcases into a large trash bag.

Perhaps Harrow was remembering the same video when he said, "Shot point-blank in the face, no apparent weapon on him. If his hands test positive for gunpowder residue, I'll concede he had a weapon. If they don't test positive, he was essentially executed."

"Not necessarily. But let's wait for the lab report."

The SWAT team had gone. Another agent leaned in from the hallway. "L.A. police and CSI van are five minutes out."

When the agent retreated, Harrow said to Silverman, "Hawk's husband killed himself."

"That's right."

"She's on leave."

"She was."

"But she's not now? If she was working on something in my jurisdiction, why wasn't I given a heads-up?"

"Cut me some slack, John. I'll do whatever needs

to be done tomorrow. There are pieces of this you don't have, and I'm still trying to put them together."

"What I *do* have is the whole Vinyl operation evaporated under my watch, and one stone-dead guy who was the heart of it."

"I understand. But you've got the list of Vinyl's clients you've been gathering for months. Now we can start moving against the worst of them."

"Without Branwick to testify."

"You'll have some of the other rats to testify."

"I'm just saying, there are consequences to delay."

"There are consequences to delay," Silverman agreed, "and there are consequences to hasty action, always consequences."

He consulted his wristwatch, which read 11:05 P.M. because it was still counting by East Coast time. His eyes were grainy. He was running on fumes. Nothing more for him here. He needed to check in to his hotel, grab something to eat, and consider the events of the day to determine if, in retrospect, they had the same dark implications that they had seemed to have as he'd experienced them.

19

JANE WANTED TO DRIVE FASTER, but she feared being pulled over by the highway patrol. The armored vehicle was an eye-catcher that would tend to interest cops. Trahern—like some huge Bolshevik bomb-thrower displaced in time— did not remotely resemble a man who could pay nearly half a million for a set of wheels. If a patrolman asked them to step out of the car, he was likely to discover that they were packing concealed weapons. If Jane was taken into custody, she would have nothing to do but wait for her enemies to find her.

This particular Gurkha offered all the amenities of a luxury sedan, including a first-class music system. But Jane deferred to Trahern's preference for brooding silence.

More than two hundred miles into what the GPS said would be a nearly five-hundred-mile trip, they left the interstate for a truck stop. With Trahern's credit card, they filled up the nearly empty primary fuel tank. Jane bought four turkey-and-bacon sandwiches and two twenty-ounce bottles of Coke.

Trahern took the wheel, eating and driving at the same time. When they were finished, he pulled off the pavement, so that she could drive again. She thought he intended to nap in the passenger seat. Instead, he remained awake, staring at the highway, although his stare was fixed, like that of a man self-tranced.

Jane was weary. Aching back. Sore butt. In one interminable day, she'd driven from L.A. to San Diego and then from San Diego all this way, almost ten hours on the road since the morning. She wasn't sleepy yet, but mental fatigue accompanied her physical weariness. Lively conversation would have helped her remain alert, but Trahern was not a raconteur with a trove of sparkling anecdotes.

Seventy miles north of the truck stop, the night loosed a hard rain. The torrents washing across the road tugged at the tires. Jane didn't know if four-wheel drive would help if they hydroplaned, but she shifted into that mode on the fly.

In Trahern's company, every mile of this journey had been strange. Now it became stranger, eerie. Gusts of conflicting winds shaped the falling water into pale-winged phantoms that billowed across the highway, and the world beyond this hurtling mass of armor seemed to melt away, until there was only the dark and nothing in it but a short length of pavement that might feather away into a void.

Trahern broke his long silence to say, "You probably think it was war that made me the way I am, but it wasn't."

She decided that if he needed to say something, he would more surely say it if she didn't speak. He was less in conversation with her than in communion with himself, gazing at the windshield, where the wipers swept away the blur but could not sweep back into sight the washed-away world beyond the shoulders of the highway.

"In fact," Trahern said, "the Army was the best thing ever happened to me. It made me feel I had value and could do something worthwhile. I'd felt useless for a long time."

The taillights of an eighteen-wheeler loomed closer, and Jane followed the trucker's lead by slowing from seventy to fifty.

Trahern said, "When I was ten years old, I had to listen to my sister being murdered."

20

SEARCHING AHEAD FOR A ROOM at the last minute, before he had flown out of Austin earlier in the day, Nathan Silverman had been given few choices. Most hotels around LAX and on the west side of Los Angeles were booked full. With only a few higher-end options to consider, he had splurged on a small suite—sitting room, bedroom, richly marbled bathroom—in a Beverly Hills establishment.

Now, after checking in and being shown to his suite at nine o'clock—midnight his time—the quiet and comfort and pampering touches, like a plate of fresh fruit, seemed worth every penny.

Although he had intended to be home in Virginia for the night, years in the Bureau had taught him to travel with toiletries and a change of clothes, just in case.

The room-service menu was large, and as always when traveling, he preferred a meal in his suite to dining alone in a restaurant.

By the time he showered, wrapped himself in the complimentary bathrobe, and opened a beer from the honor bar, his dinner arrived.

Evidently new to his job, the young waiter ineptly dressed the round game table for dinner with a white tablecloth, a small vase of flowers, flatware, and napkins. With some clumsiness, he transferred dinner from the room-service cart. He was polite and well-meaning, apologizing for his errors, and Silverman tipped him too generously, as a way of saying, *Don't worry, everyone's a beginner at your age.*

The filet mignon and side dishes were perfect. Strawberries and blueberries in cream. Excellent coffee in an insulated pot that kept it hot.

He had arisen at four o'clock that morning, and it had been a long, stressful day. As tired as he was, however, he doubted that he would sleep well. Too many worries. Too many unanswered questions.

After pouring a second cup from the insulated pot, but before taking a sip, he woke and realized he'd fallen asleep in the chair.

Silverman's weariness was profound, bone-deep. Getting to his feet required a conscious effort. The floor tilted, as if the hotel were a ship at sea. The bedroom eluded him. But then he found it. And the bed. The expectation of insomnia proved unfounded.

He dreamed of an immense and silent Texas

plain, flat to every distant horizon, the wild grass halfway to his knees and dead still except where he stirred it as he ran. The fierce sun was enthroned directly overhead, unmoving, so that he sprinted miles and miles, yet never cast a shadow. Although no pursuer was visible either at his heels or at the farthest limits of vision, he felt pursued. He feared the vastness of the cloudless sky and thought that something beyond all human experience would swoop down to seize, emasculate, and disembowel him. A door closed, an unmistakable sound. Silverman stopped, turned in place, 360 degrees, but no structure existed at any point on that eternal plain, no place with doors. A man spoke his name—*Nathan? Can you hear me, Nathan?*—but he remained alone, utterly alone. The sun. The sky. The grass. He ran.

21

RAIN RATTLED LIKE VOLLEYS OF buckshot against the bullet-resistant windshield.

"Her name was Justine Carter," Dougal Trahern said, "because her father was my mother's first husband. Justine. My half sister. Four years old when I was born. I knew her all my life until . . ."

For a minute, he fell silent, as if he had decided not to share his torment, after all.

Jane suspected that he had not spoken of this for many years, perhaps not since it happened. A murdered sister was not part of what could be learned about him from the Internet, no doubt because his sister's surname did not easily link her to him and because he was only ten when it happened, back in a day when children were rigorously protected by law from the curiosity of the media.

"Justine," Trahern continued, "was brilliant and kind and so funny. In spite of the four-year age difference, we were close, always close from as early as I can remember. Twins couldn't have been closer."

A new quality had come into his voice. Gruffness had given way to tenderness, but a tenderness haunted by sorrow.

When Jane glanced at him, she saw that his face glowed as pale as the streak of white that blazed through his beard. Fine drops of sweat beaded his brow. His eyes remained fixed on the highway, which at the moment led him not to the future but far into the past.

"I was ten. She was fourteen. A Saturday. Our father . . . my father, her stepfather . . . away on business. Our mother was out, visiting a sick friend. Me and Justine at home. The doorbell rang. This normal-looking guy. I saw him through the sidelight, a man delivering flowers. Roses. A normal-looking guy with roses. We knew not to open the door for a stranger. We knew. I knew. I opened the door. He said, 'Hey, kiddo, I got these here for some girl named Justine.' He holds the roses out to me. I take them, and he punches past the roses, hits me in the face. He's inside then. Pushes the door shut. I'm on the floor, roses scattered. He drops down, punches my face again. I don't even have a chance to warn Justine. I'm out. For . . . for a while, I'm out."

After their visit to the actor's Malibu house, Jane had told Trahern that she needed to understand him. He had said that no one could understand anyone. Maybe there were times when it was better not to understand.

"When I come around," Trahern continued, his voice growing softer, "I'm trussed up with duct tape. Can't move at all. In pain. Face swollen. Teeth missing. Blood in my mouth. I hear voices. They don't make sense at first. My vision's blurred. I blink it clear."

Rivulets of sweat trickled down Trahern's chalk-white face, perhaps blended with tears. On his thighs, his hands clenched into fists, opened, clenched, opened, as though he was grasping for something to which he could hold tight and steady himself.

"I'm on the floor in her . . . in Justine's bedroom. After he subdued her, he carried me there. To her bedroom. Now he . . . he's doing things to her." The horror that contorted his face belied the quiet equanimity of his voice. "She begs him to stop. He won't. She's crying. Begging him. But he won't stop. He sees I'm awake. Tells me to watch. No. I won't. My eyes tight shut. Can't move to help her. Duct tape. Can't move. Hands numb. Feet numb. The duct tape. I can't move, but I can't stop hearing. Can't make myself deaf. It goes on . . . for an hour. Longer. I'm sick with fear and rage . . . and self-hatred." He whispered now. "I want to die."

Jane could not bear even to glance at him anymore, to see the depth of his suffering, for which the passage of time and all of his achievements could provide no balm. She focused on the highway, on the cataracts of rain and the slick pavement. The greasy highway and the rain were things with which she could deal.

"I want to die. He kills her instead. He's done with her. So he just . . . just throws her away. He does it . . . does it . . . with a knife." The big man's voice had grown small, from a whisper to a murmur, yet each word was too clear. "It takes a while. And then he says, 'Hey, kiddo, look at this.' No. I won't look. He says, 'You're next. Look and see.'"

Jane couldn't deal with the rain and highway, after all. She had to pull to the shoulder of the road and stop. She leaned back in her seat, eyes closed, listening to the madness and the rain.

Trahern continued in a voice louder than a whisper. "I never hear our mother come home. Neither does he. My dad keeps a gun in his study downstairs. My mother comes into the room. Shoots the killer. Once. Shoots him once. She picks up a paperweight from Justine's desk. Throws it through a window. She screams. My mother screams. Keeps the gun on him and screams. Not just for help. She screams because she can't not scream. She screams until her voice is raw, until the police come, and still she screams. She doesn't shoot him twice. She doesn't kill him. I don't know why she doesn't. I don't know why she *couldn't*."

Trahern opened the passenger door and got out into the night. He stood in the rain, staring out into the dark valley.

Jane waited. There was nothing to do but wait.

In time, he returned, pulled shut the door, sat sodden and dripping.

She would have expressed her sympathy; but all the words that she could think to say were not merely inadequate but also offensive in their inadequacy.

He said, "Our mother was a gentle person, not tough at all. She was never the same after that. Broken. Empty. Five years later, she died at forty-one. A blood clot broke loose from somewhere and went to her brain. I think she must have wished it on herself. I believe that's possible. The killer was Emory Wayne Udell. He'd seen Justine walking home from school one day. He stalked her for a week, watched the house, waiting. He's still alive. In prison for life, but alive, which isn't right. Me, too. I'm still alive."

Jane said, "I'm glad you are."

He wasn't angling for her endorsement. He sat in silence until she put the Gurkha in gear and returned to the highway. Then: "Why do some people—so many—need to control others, tell them what to do, use them if they can, destroy those who won't be used?"

She sensed that the question wasn't rhetorical, that he cared what she would say. "Why Hitler, why Stalin, why Emory Wayne Udell? I don't know. Demonic influence or just miswired brains? In the end, does it matter which? Maybe what matters is that some of us *aren't* broken by it all, that we can take it to the Emory Udells and the William Overtons and the Bertold Shennecks, take it to them and stop them before they can do everything they dream about."

North of Stockton, the rain diminished. Two miles later, it stopped falling altogether.

Although an hour of silence had passed since either had spoken, Dougal said, "If I'd had the gun, I would have shot him twice. I would have emptied the magazine into him. I would have killed him."

Jane said, "So would I."

In Sacramento, they transitioned from Interstate 5 to westbound I-80. An hour later, they arrived on the outskirts of Napa at 1:40 A.M., Sunday.

A sprawling motor inn displayed a neon sign that promised VACANCY.

To avoid the Gurkha being captured by the motel's security cameras, Jane parked a block away. Because the sight of Dougal was more likely to alarm the night clerk, he remained with the vehicle while Jane walked back to the office. Using cash and a forged driver's license, she signed the register as Rachel Harrington, booking two rooms for her, an imaginary husband, and two imaginary children. On the registration form, she identified her vehicle as a Ford Explorer and made up a license-plate number.

The night clerk had a monk's fringe of white hair. "Any pets?"

"No. None."

"We allow pets in the north wing."

"We had a dog, but he passed away not long ago."

"I'm sorry to hear that. Losing one is always hard on kids."

"Hard on their dad and me, too," she said.

"What was it—the dog?"

"A golden retriever. We called him Scootie."

"Wonderful dogs, golden retrievers."

"They are," she agreed. "They're the best."

They left the Gurkha a block away and walked to the motel with their luggage. Dougal carried his duffel bag to his door and one suitcase to hers. She carried the second suitcase and the leather tote that held sixty thousand dollars.

He said, "All that back there on the road . . ."

"Stays back there on the road," she assured him.

"Good." He started toward his room, then turned to her again. "I'm going to say something, and you're going to say nothing."

"All right."

"Somebody's blessed to have you for a daughter."

He went into his room, and she went into hers.

Later, lying in bed in the dark, with the pistol

under the pillow next to hers, she thought about her father and about how he had made her who she was, though not by his example.

For a few hours, she slept deeply, but hers was not the sleep of angels sublime in their innocence.

22

NATHAN SILVERMAN WOKE WITH a headache and with a bitterness in his mouth, a taste like vinegar and ashes. For a moment, he didn't know where he was. Then he remembered Austin, San Francisco, Los Angeles, Robert Branwick shot in the head, the hotel.

A brief dizziness overcame him as he sat up and swung his legs off the bed. He wore an undershirt and boxer shorts. A luxurious complimentary robe lay in a heap on the floor, and he sat frowning at it, unable to remember taking it off.

Nathan? Can you hear me, Nathan?

Startled, he surveyed the room, but the voice was internal, remembered from . . . somewhere.

The night maid had turned down the bed before Silverman had checked in, but he had fallen asleep on the blanket and top sheet rather than slipping under them.

The bedside clock read 8:16 A.M. Morning light at the windows. He must have gone to bed around

10:30 in the evening, after dinner. Nine and a half hours? His best nights of sleep were seven hours, and his norm was six.

The room lights glowed. He'd left them on throughout the night.

He felt dissipated, unclean, as if he had drunk too much, which he rarely did, or had been with a prostitute, which he never was.

In the living room of the suite, he saw the empty bottle that had held the one beer he'd drunk. The empty dinner plate. A full cup of cold coffee. He had dropped his napkin on the floor.

At the door to the hallway, he found the deadbolt as it should be. He wondered why he'd thought it might have been unlocked. The security chain hung loose; but he never engaged them because they were flimsy and easily defeated, supplied by hotels largely for psychological purposes, to assure guests that they were doubly safe.

He took a short bottle of Pepsi from the honor-bar fridge and twisted off the cap and washed the bitter taste from his mouth.

In the bathroom, standing at the toilet, he was surprised to see that his urine was unusually dark. He wondered what he might have eaten to have such an effect.

At the sink, washing his hands, he saw the small red bruise in the crook of his right arm. At the center of it was a darker spot, like a pin prick. Directly over the vein. As if a phlebotomist had recently drawn his blood, though none had. He supposed it might be an insect bite coincidentally on the vein. He examined himself for other bites, but there were none.

He always had aspirin in his kit of toiletries. With the Pepsi, he took two, and hoped this wasn't a sinus headache, which aspirin never much relieved.

After a long, hot shower, he felt better, more himself.

Drying off, pulling on a fresh pair of boxers, he began to think about booking a flight back to Virginia.

The telephone rang. Each room had a phone, and the one in the bathroom was wall-mounted. "Hello?"

Booth Hendrickson said, "Good morning, Nathan. I wish you had reacted differently to what I told you in the Austin airport."

"Booth? How did you know where I was staying?"

Booth Hendrickson made an unusual suggestion.

"Yes, all right," Silverman replied, and he stood listening for a few minutes. He hung up.

He felt weak. Shaken by what he had been told, he sat on the bathroom floor, his back to the wall. Shock soon gave way to sorrow threaded through with dismay that Jane could have so profoundly betrayed his confidence in her. He was mortified that his assessment of her, both as an agent and as a person, had been so wrong.

Eventually he got to his feet. As he was combing his damp hair in front of the bathroom mirror, he saw the phone reflected from the opposite wall, beside the towel rack.

He turned to stare at it, puzzled. He had the strangest feeling that the phone was going to ring and that it would be Randolph Kohl, director of Homeland Security, calling again.

He waited, but of course it didn't ring. He had never in his life had a premonition that came true; and neither did this one.

Kohl had called minutes earlier, as Silverman had been pulling on a fresh pair of boxer shorts and thinking about booking a flight back to Virginia. Considering the devastating news about Jane that the director of Homeland Security had delivered, there could surely be nothing more to add to her list of crimes.

Finished combing his hair, he switched on his electric razor and began to shave, meeting his eyes in the mirror. Gradually, his sorrow became twined with anger, with resentment that Jane had for seven years played him for a fool.

Although it was Sunday, Silverman had work that must not be postponed. He needed to do something about Jane Hawk. She had gone to the dark side. Hell, she had *plunged* into the dark side. A stain on the Bureau. He needed to stop her.

When he had dressed but before putting on his sport coat, he took his shoulder rig from the nightstand drawer and shrugged into it, adjusted it, and slipped the snub-nosed Smith & Wesson into the holster.

The drawer contained a second gun. He had not put it there. He had never seen it before. It was stowed in a Blackhawk reverse-carry holster with adjustable belt clips.

Mystified, he took the holster out of the drawer and the gun out of the holster. A .45 ACP Kimber Raptor II. Three-inch barrel. Eight-shot magazine. Hardly more than a pound and a half, it was made for easy concealed carry.

As strange as the existence of the gun might be, stranger still was the fact that he quickly accepted the necessity of it, fixed the holster to his belt, and inserted the pistol.

A thought kept circling through his mind: *Randolph Kohl wants me to have the second weapon.* Kohl wasn't with the Bureau, had no authority over Silverman, and carrying a gun that wasn't a properly registered duty piece violated FBI rules, but for some reason none of that mattered. Within a minute of finding the pistol, Silverman was fine with it and no longer either concerned or curious.

He put on his sport coat, looked at himself in the full-length mirror on the back of the closet door, and decided the weapon was all but undetectable.

PART SIX

THE LAST
GOOD DAY

1

HAVING FALLEN ASLEEP SHORTLY
before 2:00 A.M., Jane broke out of a nightmare, fully
awake, at 6:10. She hadn't gotten enough sleep to be
refreshed for what lay ahead, but she wasn't going
to get a minute more just then.

She showered, dressed, and sat in an armchair
with a pen and a notepad and William Overton's
smartphone. After leaving the attorney dead in his
closet on Friday night, she'd been too emotionally
and physically wrung out to deal fully with the
phone when she got back to her motel in Tarzana,
and since getting up Saturday morning, she'd been
on the run. Now, using the password Overton had
given her, she accessed his address book and scrolled
through it, writing down names and phone numbers.

She recognized some of the names, power players in the legal system, as well as in politics, news
media, finance, entertainment, the arts, sports, and

fashion. Not all of them were likely to be members of Aspasia, but surely at least several were. David James Michael, the Silicon Valley billionaire, was among them, and Bertold Shenneck, of course. The collection of names and numbers was too small for a man whose life had been as complex as Overton's, which probably meant that these were those he deemed most important and that he kept another digital Rolodex elsewhere.

Under the listing labeled SHENNECK'S PLAYPEN, in addition to the forty-four-character Web address that she had previously recovered, there were also four street addresses in Washington, New York, San Francisco, and Los Angeles. The L.A. address was the one for the Aspasia that she had visited.

When she had completed transcribing the contents of his address book, she consulted the numbers she had for Bertold Shenneck. There were two listings for the scientist's residence in Palo Alto: the main line and one labeled CLIVE CARSTAIRS, HOUSE MANAGER. She called the second.

The man who answered had a British accent. Informed by the caller-ID window on his phone, he said, "Good morning, Mr. Overton."

"Mr. Carstairs?" she asked.

"Speaking."

"Oh, Mr. Carstairs, this is Leslie Granger, Mr. Overton's personal assistant. We haven't spoken before."

"Good morning, Ms. Granger. Pleased to make

your acquaintance. I trust that nothing untoward has happened to Miss Nolan."

At the top of Overton's address book, programmed for speed dial, had been the name Connie Nolan.

"Oh, goodness, no. Connie's just fine. I'm junior in the job, the assistant to the personal assistant. If Mr. Overton gets any busier, I'll probably have an assistant of my own before too long. The thing is, Mr. Overton wants me to messenger a package to Dr. Shenneck. He thinks the doctor is there in Palo Alto, but he wanted me to confirm as much."

"Good that you did," Carstairs said. "Dr. and Mrs. Shenneck will be at the ranch in Napa Valley through Thursday."

"Ah! Then I'll see that it goes directly there."

Overton might have lied. Confirmation of Shenneck's whereabouts meant that she and Dougal would make a run at him later in the day.

Carstairs asked, "Should I alert Dr. Shenneck to be expecting a package?"

"Oh, gee. I don't know. My boss is incommunicado right now. Let me think. Hmmm. You know what? This is quite a special gift for Dr. and Mrs. Shenneck. I know Mr. Overton spent a small fortune on it. I suspect he'd rather surprise them."

"Then I shall remain mum."

"Thank you, Mr. Carstairs. You've been most helpful."

After she turned off the phone, Jane took it into

the bathroom, put it on the tile floor, and cracked it underfoot.

At 8:20, dead phone in hand, she stepped out into a cool, overcast morning. In the leafy branches of the red-bark arbutuses that softened the architecture of the motel, unseen birds with unpleasant voices sounded angry with the way the day had thus far unfolded.

In front of the diner associated with the motel, she dropped Overton's phone into a trash can with a domed top and a hinged lid. She went into the restaurant, bought a cruller and a large coffee and a copy of *The New York Times*. In her room once more, she ate the pastry and drank the coffee and paged through the *Times* to see how much further the world had descended into chaos since she had last read a newspaper one week earlier.

2

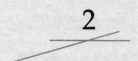

ANGER WAS A VIOLENT AND vindictive emotion. Nathan Silverman's character was such that he could sustain anger only for a short while. In this case, it quickly settled into righteous indignation and piercing disappointment.

After dressing, he used the hotel-bedroom phone to call the 24/7 cell number of John Harrow, the special agent in charge of the Los Angeles field office.

When Harrow answered, Silverman said, "John, I'm alerting the director, we have a rogue agent from my section, evidently on your turf. It's Jane Hawk."

"Sorry to hear it, but I think you're being prudent. We need to meet, work out how to proceed."

"We have to move faster than that. She's my responsibility, so I hope you'll work with me to jump-start this."

"Of course, Nathan."

"Get her Bureau ID photo, when she had long blond hair. Pair it with one from Santa Monica, showing her with shorter, dark hair. Get them to every field office with the proper wanted-person wording."

"Wanted for what?"

"Illegal use of FBI ID, impersonating an agent, racketeering, destruction of aircraft, assaulting a federal officer, and murder."

"Holy shit, Nathan, what information did you get between last evening and now?"

"Randolph Kohl called me. He has the goods on her."

"Kohl from Homeland Security? Tell me those glory seekers won't be tramping on our heels every step of the way."

"I've been assured they're giving us the professional courtesy of allowing us to rope our own stray calf."

"What's this all about?" Harrow asked. "What's she up to that involves national security?"

"For now, that's classified. I'll . . . I'll . . ." A tremor

of doubt and confusion quivered through Silverman, but passed quickly. "I'll lay it out for you in
detail as soon as Booth tells me I can."

"Booth? Who's Booth?"

Silverman frowned. "I meant Kohl. As soon as
Randolph Kohl tells me I can share it, I will."

"Usually, we'd handle something like this quietly
in family as long as possible."

"This is an extraordinary matter. Also get her on
the NCIC."

The National Crime Information Center would
put her name and face in front of the entire criminal-
justice community, from big-city to small-town police agencies.

"You mean on the outstanding-warrants list?"
Harrow asked.

"Yes."

"Do we have a warrant?"

"A judge will be issuing one momentarily."

3

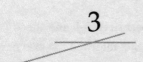

DOUGAL TRAHERN WAITED UN-
til ten o'clock to phone Jane's motel room. After
seeking her permission, he came to her room to dis-
cuss something with her.

"I could die today," he said.

"We both could."

"I don't want to die this way."

Wondering if he meant to back out after coming this far, she said, "What way?"

He pointed to his mountain-man reflection in the mirrored closet door. "That way." He handed her a shopping list and his credit card. "Could you get these things for me?"

Reading the list, she said, "Why don't you come with me?"

"I don't know. I just woke up feeling . . ."

"Feeling what?"

He scowled. "Self-conscious. All right, already?"

"Self-conscious about what?"

He pointed at his reflection again. "Do you mind getting those things, or are you gonna grill me like you would a suspect?"

"Relax, Mr. Bigfoot."

"Damn it, you got that from Charlene."

"Good woman. Give me an hour. But are you sure about this?"

"Hell, yes. I'm done being this. I'll wait in my room."

"Leave the do-not-disturb sign on your door so you don't terrify the maid." She returned his credit card. "I've got cash."

He looked distressed. "You shouldn't have to pay for my stuff."

"*You* paid nearly half a million for wheels to get us here."

When she returned from shopping, they started with his hair. She had bought a painter's drop cloth, which she spread on the floor of his room. He put a chair on the cloth, sat down, and used two bath towels to form a makeshift barber's smock over his clothing.

She had also bought a pair of barbering scissors and a steel-toothed comb. "This will be way less than a professional cut."

"Every pioneer woman cut her family's hair, and they lived through it. Just start choppin'."

She began by determining which knots couldn't be combed out. She ruthlessly scissored them away.

Using the facts about Gee Zee Ranch that Jane squeezed out of William Overton and the satellite photos that Dougal printed, they knew how they planned to get onto the ranch, into the house, and out again alive. But they had not yet discussed other important issues.

As she clipped his hair, he said, "What is it you could pry out of Shenneck that would make this raid a success?"

"We can't get into his Menlo Park labs directly. But when he's working from the ranch, he has computer access to his research and other files in Menlo Park. I want him to download the specs for the nano-implants, every iteration of the design from day one to the point when they could be injected and would reliably self-assemble."

"Will that be enough to bring him down?"

"Maybe. But I want more. Overton said Shenneck captures and converts coyotes on the ranch, like I told you, so he must have vials of the injectable solution at the house. The thousands of infinitesimal parts of a control mechanism are kept floating in a chilled liquid. They're designed so they can't self-assemble till they're in an environment where the temperature is at least ninety-six degrees Fahrenheit, sustained for at least an hour."

Dougal said, "Inside a living mammal."

As a greater volume of shorn hair began to fall from Dougal's head, Jane said, "The nano-parts of the control mechanism are brain-tropic, specifically to concentrations of hormones produced in the hypothalamus. By the time they pass through the capillary walls into the brain tissue, they've been in a warm environment long enough to start assembling. I'll take as many vials as I can find. Preferably some of each kind—those that reduce the girls of Aspasia to a lower level of consciousness, those that program people for suicide and homicide, as many kinds as there are. We need to have them analyzed by authorities . . . if I ever find an authority I trust."

"How long will it take to get all this?"

"Not long once he starts cooperating."

"What if he doesn't? How do you make him?"

"Scare the shit out of him," she said.

"If that doesn't work?"

"Depends on how much pain he can tolerate."

"Are we talking torture?"

She realized that he was watching her in the mirrored closet doors. "Are we talking the future of freedom?" she countered. "Do we want to stop the enslavement of millions of people, the deaths of millions more? Shenneck is Emory Wayne Udell writ large."

The name of his sister's murderer clearly stung Dougal. "I'm not saying torture is never justifiable. I'm just wondering . . . are you sure you're capable of that?"

Meeting the stare of his reflection, she said, "There was a time I wouldn't have been capable. But then I went to Aspasia. To put a stop to that horror . . . I can do just about anything."

4

FROM THE PHONE IN THE LIVing room of his suite, Silverman called the front desk and secured his accommodations for another night, this time using his Bureau credit card. His intuition told him that whatever those two briefcases had contained, whatever Jane's reasons for engaging with Vinyl and Robert Branwick, her business hadn't concluded when Branwick lay dead on his kitchen floor. More likely than not, she was still in the San Fernando Valley or at least somewhere in greater Los Angeles. Silverman wanted to be here when the quarry surfaced.

As he was about to go out for a late breakfast or early lunch, his smartphone rang.

It was John Harrow. "You remember last night,

Sherman Oaks, in that kitchen, a pen on the floor, notepad on the table?"

"I saw the notepad, not the pen."

"The lab found indented writing—actually printing—on the top page of the pad. Odds are, it was Branwick doing the printing. He pressed hard with the pen, the way a man will if he's under duress."

"With a gun to his head."

"Yeah. The actual page he printed on can't be found, so it was probably taken away by whoever he printed it for."

The lab would have employed oblique lighting to visualize the indented words on the notepad, would have photographed them and subjected the photographic image to enhancement.

"First," Harrow said, "there's a word or name— Aspasia." He spelled it. "Under that, there's a name—William Sterling Overton."

"Why does that sound familiar?"

"He's a hotshot lawyer, a shakedown artist, master-of-the-universe type. Turns out, he's on our list of people doing business with Branwick when Branwick was Jimmy Radburn. We'd been building a case against him before this blow-up. We've got enough to get a search warrant, which we're doing now that the Vinyl situation has gone critical. Get this, the judge giving it to us is signing it in church. Sure, it's Sunday, but did you know judges went to church?"

"I'd heard it rumored about a few."

"Overton lives in Beverly Hills. You're already there, and I'm on my way. Pick you up at your hotel?"

"I'll be waiting out front," Silverman said.

5

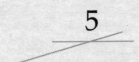

WHEN JANE HAD DONE AS much damage as she could to Dougal's hair, she retreated to her room while he dispensed with his beard using the electric razor that she had bought.

As she waited for him, she studied the Google Earth photos of Gee Zee Ranch, looking for an error in their plan.

After a while, Dougal called ahead to say that he would be knocking at her door and preferred not to be shot.

When he entered the room, his hair was an acceptable version of the everywhichway cut that the motel clerk, Chloe, had sported when, on Friday morning, Jane had asked her to check Star Spotter or Just Spotted to see if William Overton was in town. No one would ask Dougal for the name of his barber, but in this age when imaginative hairstyles of all kinds were in vogue, he wouldn't draw attention.

Gone were the camouflage pants. He had gotten a pair of jeans from his duffel bag. Instead of a checkered-flannel shirt, he wore a blue crewneck sweater. He still stood in lace-up butt-kicker boots, and he wore the shiny-black quilted-nylon jacket to conceal the two-holster shoulder rig, but he no longer had a freak-of-the-day look that would cause people to take phone video for sharing on YouTube.

"Handsome," she said. "Kind of a punky John Wayne."

In truth, without the beard, he looked at least a decade older than forty-eight, and he had a doleful quality. He smiled at her compliment, but his face was not enlivened, and in fact the smile itself was sad. Almost forty years of grief and settled sorrow had worked upon the flesh and bone, and a single smile—perhaps even ten thousand of them—could not erase the engraved melancholy.

"Don't blow smoke at me," Dougal said. "I look like I was sewn together in a lab, brought to life by lightning. Let's check out of here and get lunch. Then we'll see a man about a helicopter."

6

STANDING IN FRONT OF THE hotel, waiting for Harrow, Nathan Silverman didn't understand himself.

He kept thinking about what Ancel Hawk had told him in Texas: *So they come into her home, and they*

promise to rape and kill Travis if she doesn't drop it.
That confirmed Gladys Chang's contention that Jane
wanted to sell the house fast, below value, because
she was afraid for her son. Then there was the implied threat in Booth Hendrickson's chatter at the
Austin airport. Until a short while ago, Silverman
had remained convinced that whatever her situation, Jane must be a victim, not a victimizer.

How had one phone call from Randolph Kohl of
Homeland Security caused him to accept that Jane
was guilty of a series of crimes? Yes, Kohl had a
good reputation. But Silverman didn't change his
opinion of *anyone* based on unverified secondhand
information.

Yet he had at once called John Harrow and put
the relentless machinery of the Bureau into gear
against Jane. Why?

There was also the disturbing fact that he couldn't
recall with what detail Kohl had supported the
charges against the woman.

As the traffic rushed past him on Wilshire Boulevard, Silverman was overcome by nausea. He was
disoriented, as if he had stepped out of the hotel expecting another city a thousand miles from Beverly
Hills. He put one hand against a nearby lamppost to
steady himself.

He had felt something akin to this in Texas, standing on the porch of the Hawk house, looking out at
an enormous flatness of wild grass under a sky so
big it seemed that up and down were about to re-

verse, that he would fall away from the earth into the heavens.

In that instance, there had been a reason for what he felt: the unfamiliar vista so vast that it fostered in him a recognition of how small he was in the scheme of things. But in this case, he was in his element, city all around him, traffic humming. There seemed to be no external cause for his distress.

The nausea and disorientation passed quickly. He lowered his hand from the lamppost.

Perhaps he should not have put so much credence in Gladys Chang's claim that Jane feared for her son. After all, the Realtor was a stranger to him. He had been charmed by her; but he had no reason to believe that she was a keen observer of people.

And Ancel Hawk was not merely a stranger to Silverman but almost an alien, hailing as he did from the plains, a world far different from Washington and Alexandria and Quantico. Besides, Ancel only knew what Jane told him. He could not verify her story. She had lied to the hotel manager in Santa Monica, claiming to be an agent on a case, and surely she had lied to Branwick and his crew, because lies and deception were their coin and currency. So if she was lying to some, there was no reason to think she wouldn't lie to all, to her father-in-law and to Silverman as easily as to a hotel manager.

The indignation he'd felt earlier, the piercing disappointment in Jane, welled in him once more, sharper and more acidic, corroding his mood, shading his every memory of her with darker colors.

John Harrow pulled to the curb in a Bureau sedan. Silverman got in the passenger seat and shut the door.

"Ramos and Hubbert will meet us at the house with the warrant."

Silverman knew Ramos and Hubbert. "Good. If she forced Branwick to give her Overton's name at gunpoint, we better expect the worst."

Harrow seemed surprised. "You've made the leap that it was her at Branwick's house?"

"I hope I'm wrong," Silverman said. "But I doubt it."

7

SILVERMAN HAD BEEN IN THIS neighborhood before, more than once, but it felt different this time.

Big houses, deep lawns. Huge trees overhanging the street. In some yards, jacarandas were in early bloom, blue blossoms cascading through the branches like fireworks frozen in mid spectacle. If the day had been sunny, the effect would have been dazzling.

In the somber light of a gray overcast, however, the beautiful street had a funereal quality, as if all of this—including the culture that produced it—was in its twilight, as if something new and disturbing might be rising to take its place, so that one day, even when the sun shone, the scene would be ashen and bleak.

They parked in front of Overton's house. Within minutes, Ramos and Hubbert arrived with a warrant specifying that the search was essential to preserve the lives of innocents under imminent threat.

There was no reason to suppose a citizen of Overton's stature might be a serious physical danger to the warrant-serving officers, regardless of what illegal and ugly business he might have been doing with Robert Branwick. He was a winning attorney whose weapon was the system, which he used *against* the system, and he didn't need to turn to violence. A SWAT team was not deemed necessary.

After Harrow rang the doorbell repeatedly and no one responded, Ramos and Hubbert went around the house, looking for evidence that someone might be in residence, but found none.

With a lock-release gun, the front-door deadbolts were disengaged. When Harrow opened the door, the house alarm did not sound, suggesting that someone must be home.

Harrow loudly announced that they were FBI, acting with an emergency search warrant. No one responded.

Lights glowed throughout the house. The gray day wanted lamps, but this was lighting suitable only to a house at night.

The silence seemed to be more a substance than a condition, so heavy that it repressed the sounds the agents made as they cleared the ground floor, being careful to touch nothing. Ramos remained at the foot of the stairs, while the other three ascended.

By the time Silverman followed Harrow and Hubbert to the second floor, the silence thickened. Experience and intuition—and perhaps the unconscious awareness of a subtle malodor—told him this must be the silence of death, coiling through the fashionable house from the slack-jawed mouth of a screamer no longer capable of screaming.

When they entered the master bedroom, the bad odor was not subtle anymore.

Cut-away clothes, linked cable ties, and a few drops and smears of blood on the limestone floor of the adjoining bathroom did not bode well for William Overton.

In the walk-in closet warmed by overhead lights that had been burning a long time, the bad odor became a stench. Leaking onto a carpet that must have cost upward of two hundred dollars a square yard, the corpse might have been Overton's; but identity would have to be determined by the medical examiner. Judging by the progress of putrefaction—a greenish discoloration of the lower abdomen, lesser discoloration of the head and neck and shoulders, swelling of the face, and marbling—the victim, dressed only in briefs, had been dead longer than thirty-six hours.

If Robert Branwick had been killed Thursday evening, as the condition of *his* corpse had suggested, Overton had been killed about twenty-four hours thereafter.

They retreated to the upstairs hall, where Harrow called the Beverly Hills Police to report a homicide.

Silverman said, "Security cameras in the hallways."

"Yeah. We need to find the recorder."

"Then we'll know she did it," Silverman said, and he wondered that he had not said, *Then we'll know* if *she did it*.

His certainty could have been intuition, although it felt like something far more intense. It felt like an article of faith, as if Jane's villainy were the central dogma of a new religion that had come to him fully formed by divine revelation. Once he'd thought of her with admiration and affection. But now in his mind's eye, she had a dark aura, and there was a wickedness in her face that he had not recognized before. A voice spoke to him, an interior voice but not his own, and the voice named her for him: *Mother of Lies.*

8

VALLEY AIR SOLD, LEASED, RE-paired, and garaged helicopters, serving corporations and well-to-do individuals. The company also maintained a helo air ambulance under contract to several hospitals in Napa and Sonoma Counties, and operated a crop-dusting service.

The co-owner of Valley Air, Ronnie Fuentes, was waiting for them in the front office, though this was a Sunday. In his late twenties, he had the self-possession of an older man and the manners of an earlier century.

"Sergeant," Fuentes exclaimed at first sight of Dougal, "you've been groomed and broomed! Are you planning to re-enlist, sir?"

"Hell, kid, I'll *always* be too uncouth for today's Army."

When Dougal introduced Jane as his friend and associate, Fuentes bowed slightly from the shoulders and offered her his hand. "Friendship is as sacred to Sergeant Trahern as God is to a good priest. So it's a real honor to meet you."

Instead of decorating the walls with pictures of the aircraft in which the company dealt, management had chosen to hang large works of colorful military art—helicopter gunships and troop carriers and medevac units—portrayed under fire in chaotic and stirring circumstances.

"So your dad and mom are on a Caribbean cruise?" Dougal said.

"Yes, sir. For their thirty-fifth anniversary. Did you hear, Mom talked him into a year of dancing lessons before the trip?"

"Quito Fuentes on a dance floor. These must be the Last Days."

"It's the only time he ever used a pity defense," Ronnie said. "Claimed it was cruel to tell a one-armed man he could dance."

"Break dance, maybe."

"They got darn good, sir. You should see them waltz, cha-cha, fox-trot." He grinned at Jane. "Though Dad will never let his old sergeant here see him doing what he calls 'fancy-boy steps.'"

Minutes later, when they got down to business, Dougal said, "You say no to what I want, nothing changes between us. Understand?"

"Valley Air always fulfills its slogan." Ronnie Fuentes sang a variation of the lyrics from an old Joe Cocker song, "We lift you up where you belong," as Dougal pretended to be pained.

Fuentes refused Dougal nothing, though they haggled over the price, Fuentes insisting there would be no charge, Dougal insisting the charge would be enormous.

9

IN THE OVERTON RESIDENCE, the FBI agents advised and watched over the Beverly Hills police, and the cops quietly asserted their authority. The exaggerated consideration that each of them gave the others could not disguise the frustration that stiffened every neck in the house.

Jurisdiction was clouded. Overton had been a target of an FBI probe, but no charges had been filed. From the perspective of the BHPD, this was the murder of a citizen—nothing less, nothing more. And the Bureau did not get involved in murder cases unless a perp operated across state lines or killed a federal officer.

Silverman felt it was best to allow the locals to proceed with quiet Bureau oversight, in the interest of expediting the search for evidence and perhaps for a clue as to where Jane had gone from here.

Although he was convinced she had whacked Branwick and Overton, he as yet had little admissible evidence to support his conviction. Likewise, he lacked a theory of her motive and future intentions.

Silverman kept thinking about Randolph Kohl's phone call, after which he had officially labeled Jane a rogue and worse. He had told John Harrow that a warrant for her arrest would be issued by a judge at the request of Homeland Security, related to matters of national security. But when he tried to recall what else Kohl told him, his memory, previously a palace of brightly lighted chambers, seemed to have collapsed into a small and shadowy apartment.

Because of his murky memory and an unusual free-floating anxiety, Silverman thought that something must be wrong with him. Each time he began to doubt himself, however, he was propelled forward by a surge of self-confidence so powerful that it seemed chemically induced. These sharp swings in mood also disturbed him.

It was Ramos who realized that no cell phone had yet been found. Given the nature of William Overton's professional and personal lives, the attorney would have been tethered to his phone almost as intimately as an unborn baby to its mother.

The initial areas of interest to investigators had been the closet where the dead man lay, the bath where the victim had been restrained for a time, and the bedroom. All drawers had been carefully opened, contents inspected visually but left undisturbed, lest evidence be compromised before the CSI unit arrived. No phone.

"If he entered the house through the connecting door to the garage," Ramos said, "he might have left the phone in the kitchen."

"Or forgot it in the car," Harrow suggested.

Leaving Hubbert in the master suite, Silverman accompanied Harrow and Ramos to the ground floor, where a search for Overton's phone proved fruitless.

The three ended up on the back patio, overlooking the spa and the immense pool, checking the chairs and tables, in case Overton had spent a little time out there when he'd come home. No phone.

"She took it," Harrow guessed. "There was something on it she wanted."

"If she's had it since Friday night," Silverman said, "she got what she needed and ditched the phone by now."

"Maybe not," Ramos said. "Maybe she figured nobody would find Overton sooner than Monday, so she had time."

"We can hope," Harrow agreed. "And the case file we've been building on Branwick includes the names and phone numbers of his clients, including Overton. If Homeland Security's seeking a warrant for her arrest, maybe with some help we can get a current location on Overton's phone. If she's still got it, we'll get her."

Earlier, they had found the security-camera recorder tucked away in a garage cabinet. Jane had removed the disc and with it the evidence of her presence in the house. Silverman expected her to have been no less careful with the dead man's phone, but it was worth an interagency request for urgent cooperation in the matter.

THE SILENT CORNER   469

10

HAVING CHECKED OUT OF THE motel before coming to Valley Air, Jane now left her suitcases and the bag of autopsy reports with Ronnie Fuentes. She also left the tote containing sixty thousand dollars. Where they were going, they could not be encumbered, and the money would be a particular distraction.

Dougal entrusted his duffel bag to Fuentes, after taking from it a pistol-grip short-barrel pump-action twelve-gauge Mossberg shotgun plus two boxes of shells. He put the weapon and ammunition in the back of the Gurkha.

As she drove away from Valley Air, Jane said, "Ronnie's dad, Quito—he served under you in Special Forces?"

"No. I served under him. He was my lieutenant for a while."

"And you saved his life."

"Forget about all that. None of it matters."

"Well, but you did."

"Don't hose me with hero," he grumbled. "Quito saved my life twice before that. I still owe him one."

11

SILVERMAN MADE THE PHONE call to the National Security Agency while walking beside Overton's hundred-foot-long swimming pool. The wind had scattered scarlet bougainvillea petals on the lizard-skin-gray water, where his distorted reflection ghosted his every step.

Non-military organizations dealing with terrorism and national security—the CIA, the NSA, Homeland Security, and the FBI—had long been jealous of their turf and cautious of too much cooperation with one another lest they cede some of their authority.

The horrific terrorist attacks in Europe and South America the previous year, combined with four hundred deaths in Seattle, led to a greater willingness of various agencies to work with one another.

As section chief of the Critical Incident Response Group within the FBI, Silverman phoned his counterpart in the National Security Agency, Maurice Moomaw, to request an urgent determination of the location of William Overton's smartphone, for which he was able to provide the number.

"No problem," Moomaw said. "In payment, you need only transfer to me your best Human Resources person and sixty million bucks."

Pretending to be amused by bureaucratic humor, Silverman said, "We're phasing out humans from the FBI, and anyway I only have three dollars left in my budget for the year."

"Then I'll settle for undying gratitude," Moomaw said. "Back to you soon, Nate."

At the end of the swimming pool, Silverman stopped and looked toward the house. Harrow and Ramos sat on patio chairs. In spite of the overcast, Harrow wore sunglasses. Ramos smoked a cigarette.

Something about the scene struck Silverman as deeply sinister, though he could not explain why. His inexplicable anxiety, unrelated to Jane, intensified. The skin prickled on the nape of his neck.

Maurice Moomaw would at the moment be in contact with someone at the Utah Data Center, built by the National Security Agency and completed in 2014, a facility with more than a million square feet under its roof. Among other things, the Data Center was tasked with snatching from the air every telephone call and text message, as well as other digital transmissions, and storing them for metadata analysis. The NSA did not listen to the calls and read the text messages, but had the capacity to scan the exabytes of data for key words likely to indicate terrorist activity and to analyze signals of foreign origin to deduce the intentions of the nation's enemies.

Like every car with a GPS, every smartphone contained a locater that issued a unique identifier, which could be satellite-tracked as easily as the phone could send and receive calls, whether it was on or off. Even if Jane had taken what she wanted from Overton's phone and had thrown it away, there would be some value in knowing where she had been when she disposed of it.

Eleven minutes after Maurice Moomaw disconnected, he called. "The phone is on the grounds of a motel on the outskirts of Napa, California." He gave Silverman the precise address.

12

TOWARD SHENNECK'S RANCH. The madding crowd of Los Angeles far behind, the elegant rusticness of Napa swiftly receding, Jane felt as though she were also driving out of reality—or out of reality as she'd known it—into a fantasy, into a kingdom where the acolytes of darkness ruled, unspeakable spells were cast, and the living dead served their living masters.

The two-lane county road rose through the foothills, with the fabled valley of vineyards on the left. To the right were open woods of live oaks and cork oaks and plums underlaid with golden sedge.

As they approached a single-lane dirt fire road angling off the blacktop, Dougal said, "Turn left here."

"You're sure?"

He rattled the sheaf of satellite photos in his lap.

"I've got these memorized. That's the road, all right."

She turned onto the narrow lane. The deep tread of the Gurkha's tires clawed up pebbles and rattled them against the undercarriage.

"It's called the Singularity," Dougal said.

"What is?"

"The point where human and computer intelligences will merge with the help of nanotechnology, when humans and machines combine in the next evolutionary step. There've been a lot of books about it."

"Singularity. Sounds sweet."

"They say it'll be Utopia. They say human intelligence assisted by machine intelligence will make us a thousand times smarter. They say with nanomachines living by the thousands inside us, constantly cleaning the plaque out of our arteries and monitoring organ health and repairing damage, we'll live for centuries, maybe forever."

"Who are *they*?"

"A lot of very smart people."

"Uh-huh."

"Smarter than me. They've identified like fifteen objections to proceeding with nanotech and refuted each one. Some critics think it's not possible, a waste of resources. Others say it's dangerous, like if the nano-machines start replicating and consume the entire biomass of the planet in a few weeks."

She said, "The video by Shenneck, the one with the mice, talks about *non*-replicating nano-machines."

"The smart people have convincing answers to their critics."

Jane wondered, "Those fifteen objections . . . does one of them say there's a tendency to evil in human beings? Do they explain how to guarantee such powerful technology won't be used for evil?"

"No, it's not one of the fifteen."

"Uh-huh."

"They seem to think the more intelligent people are, the less evil they do."

"Uh-huh."

For a while, the woods became less open, trees crowding closer to one another. The overcast robbed the day of sunshine, and trees crowning the fire road wove a gloom without benefit of shadows.

Deer roamed these foothills, and she slowed down in regard for them. If an ordinary vehicle impacted a buck or even a doe at high speed, it could be totaled, but the armored Gurkha would probably plow forward, straight over the animal, with no significant damage.

Concern for the Gurkha wasn't why she reduced speed. There were already two people dead, even if they had been venomous reptiles in human form, and surely more deaths to come, perhaps including her own. She didn't want to have to get out of the vehicle to administer a mercy shot to a crippled deer. She had the curious conviction that such a moment would undo her emotionally as nothing else could.

Dougal said, "Another mile or so, the woods start

to give way to open land, rolling hills. A mile after that, you'll turn west."

She glanced at him. He looked older than he was and battered and haunted, yet tough and ready and serene. She sensed in him no fear, but instead a pleasant anticipation that caused a humorless half smile, a wolfish smile, to come and go across his face.

"You really have been waiting for something like this."

He gave her that pellucid gray call-of-the-wild stare, and she imagined that in battle he'd be brutal without being cruel, dealing swift death without hesitation, for he knew there was a profound difference between killing and murder.

"The free kitchen, after-school programs, keeping porn out of libraries—all that needs done, but it's dealing with the aftermath, not with the causes. I'm in the mood to deal with a cause."

13

UPON LEARNING FROM MAUrice Moomaw that Overton's stolen phone was on the grounds of a motel in Napa, Silverman had called to hire a private jet from a charter company operating out of Van Nuys Airport, which he'd used in another matter a year earlier. He might face ques-

tions about the expenditure, especially because
there would be a surcharge for the last-minute booking, but if he nailed a rogue agent, cost would cease
to be an issue.

Using a window-hook suction-cup beacon on the
unmarked sedan and sounding the siren all but continuously, John Harrow had driven Silverman and
Ramos from Beverly Hills to Van Nuys, via Santa
Monica Boulevard and the Hollywood Freeway, approximately twenty-four miles through gruesome
Sunday afternoon traffic, in thirty-one minutes, in
spite of encountering a backup related to a three-
vehicle accident.

The Citation Excel, a midsize eight-seat jet, was
readied just as the three arrived, but though the co-
pilot was aboard, they had to wait fourteen minutes
for an on-call pilot to get there.

They were in the air just under an hour after receiving word from the NSA regarding the location
of Overton's phone.

Already, four agents out of the FBI's Sacramento
field office would be closing in on the motel to put it
under surveillance.

Silverman's job involved more management
meetings and boring bureaucratic politics than street
time. He was usually energized and buoyed by
being out of the office and in the thick of things.

As the suburban sprawl of the San Fernando Valley fell away beneath them, however, his anxiety
grew worse. Although every action he had taken
thus far was what he ought to do, what he needed to

do, he felt . . . felt as if he were not fully in control of himself, as if he must be sliding ever faster down a slippery slope. In Texas the previous day, the vastness spawned in him a sense that he might float into the all-encompassing sky. That feeling returned as the jet gained altitude. He seemed to be getting lighter by the minute. He waited for gravity to let go of him, for the jet to pierce Earth's atmosphere and drift toward eternity, its engines no longer functioning in the vacuum of space.

"Are you all right?" John Harrow asked from his seat across the aisle.

"What? Oh. Yes. I'm fine. I just realized I forgot to call my wife this morning. And last night."

"Better spend the flight time composing an apology," Harrow advised. "And don't go home without something expensive."

"Oh, Rishona's not like that. She's as understanding as the day is long."

"You're a lucky man, Nathan."

"As I tell myself every night and first thing every morning," Silverman said, though his words rang hollow to his ear. He had begun to feel like a roulette player who never got the color right, whether he bet the red or the black.

14

THE FIRE ROAD ENDED, AND the woods opened out to meadowed hills, as Dougal had promised. In four-wheel drive, the Gurkha tamed the territory, and a mile farther, they came to a stream, which had also been visible on the Google Earth photos. Much of the year it might be dry, but at the moment water flowed over a course of time-smoothed stones. Here, Jane turned west and drove until Dougal told her to stop halfway up a long slope.

Together, they got out of the Gurkha and ascended on foot through a meadow carpeted with a variety of grasses and decorated with formations of chaparral lily in early bloom. Rabbits dining on sweet grass hopped away from them or sat up on their hindquarters to watch them pass. Cicadas sang, and orange butterflies with narrow dark margins on their wings took flight.

Near the top, Jane and Dougal proceeded in a crouch rather than walk erect, and then crawled onto the crest. A hundred yards below them lay the main house at Gee Zee Ranch, large and low-slung, a sweeping ultramodern structure of glass and steel, with dark-gray granite support walls polished in some places, textured in others.

Half concealed by wild grass and made small by distance, Jane and Dougal each had a pair of binoculars with nonreflective lenses that wouldn't betray them. She surveyed the house, which she'd seen before only as roofs and extended decks on the Google Earth photos.

A long blacktop driveway led southwest from the main house to the distant county road. At the end of the private drive stood the gatehouse, the original residence before the Shennecks had bought the land: a two-story Victorian with minimal decorative millwork.

According to Overton, six rayshaws lived in the gatehouse. They did the cleaning and maintenance on the entire property, but their primary function was security. They were men who, like the girls at Aspasia, had been reduced to a lower level of consciousness, their sense of self greatly diminished, unfailingly obedient to their masters, Bertold Shenneck and his wife. Programmed.

This wasn't a working ranch. It housed no animals; therefore, it had never been fenced. Combination heat-and-motion detectors were installed throughout the seventy acres, arrayed to sound the alarm only when an intruder was more than three feet tall and produced a body-heat signature suggesting a gross weight of a hundred pounds or more. This prevented false positives by coyotes and other creatures outside the intruder profile, though now and then deer triggered an alert that brought the heavily armed rayshaws to investigate.

Lying beside Jane on the crest, glassing the property below, Dougal said, "So the character in the novel was named Raymond Shaw."

"In *The Manchurian Candidate*. Yeah. The book and the movie."

"Haven't read it, didn't see it."

"Shaw's a prisoner of war in Korea. Brainwashed by communists, sent back to the U.S. to assassinate political figures. He doesn't know what's been done to him. When he's activated, he kills—and forgets the killing."

"So the control mechanism wires into one of these guys, strips away most memories, most of his personality, programs him to kill, and Shenneck calls him a rayshaw. What a twisted sonofabitch. He's not just vicious and evil. He's also an asshole."

Remembering Overton's defense of Shenneck for naming the ranch Gee Zee, Ground Zero, Jane said, " 'He likes his little jokes.' And according to Overton, that's Shenneck's favorite book and movie since he was fourteen. He didn't identify with either the hero or with Raymond Shaw. But the brainwashers really inspired him."

15

AFTER AN HOUR IN THE AIR, the Citation Excel descended through the overcast to the Napa County Airport runway.

Silverman enjoyed no sense of relief that he was on land again. Completing the task ahead was likely to leave him feeling as empty as the pale high-altitude sky through which they had come north.

As the trail grew hot and the quarry seemed within reach, he should have felt a simmering sense of gratification, a building excitement, but he did not. He needed to find Jane Hawk, and he would. But he wouldn't take pleasure in arresting her. Considering that the charges against her would include murder, she might resist. Once, he would have thought it impossible that she would turn a gun on him, but now he believed she might do anything. He dreaded that she might create a situation in which he would have to use violence against her, would have to shoot her, this girl who, under other circumstances, he could have loved as if she were his own daughter.

As he deplaned and walked across the tarmac with Harrow and Ramos, toward the waiting car and driver from the Sacramento field office, a cold resolve came over Silverman, a resolution that at first surprised him and that he resisted. But by the time they were in the car and being driven to the motel where Overton's phone had been found, he resigned himself to the necessity of answering Jane's resistance with lethal force if it came to that. She had betrayed him, after all. She had betrayed the Bureau. She had betrayed her country. If, in the penultimate moment, she chose to commit suicide by cop, he would oblige her and not be troubled by remorse. She was no longer the person he had known. She had become a stranger, a danger to society, a threat to the innocent. If it fell to him to pull the trigger and put her down, he'd do it without hesitation. This was his job. And the job had never been easy.

16

IF THE PLANET MIGHT BE ALIVE, as some believed, and if Earth might be the mother of humanity, it was a mother with a heart of ice, for the ground was cold under Jane as she lay in the grass at the crest of the hill, its glacial soil leeching the warmth from her flesh and bones. The day lay mild upon the land, winter fading into spring, yet the slaty zinc-gray clouds chilled her spirits, so that the binocular image of Shenneck's house shivered like a mirage as tremors passed through her.

"See anything?" Dougal asked.

"No."

Before they launched an assault, they needed to be sure that Bertold and Inga Shenneck were in the house.

Nothing moved across those seventy acres except the grass and the trees as they were stirred by a faint breeze. For long minutes, the scene might have been laid past the end of civilization, when some of humanity's structures remained, but not humanity.

Then . . . a figure beyond a wall of glass. At first without convincing substance, like a shadowy shade spooking through a house forsaken by the living. Then she passed closer to the windows, in what might have been a family room, a woman in white slacks, white blouse, tall and lithe, with the in-motion posture of a model on a fashion-show runway.

"First floor, on the left," Jane said.

"I see her," Dougal said. "Where's he?"

The woman disappeared behind granite . . . and reappeared in the kitchen.

"If she's there," Jane said, "maybe we assume he is, too."

"What if we go roaring down there, and he's *not*. We'll never get a second chance."

"I have a burner phone. I know the number at the house. If he answers, I hang up and we go in fast."

"If she answers?"

"Then I'm Leslie Granger again, assistant to Mr. Overton's personal assistant, Connie, and I have a question for Mr. Shenneck."

"Either way, if they're suspicious, it could give them a one-minute warning," Dougal worried.

17

THE MOTEL OFFICE FEATURED racks of pamphlets enticing Napa Valley tourists to numerous attractions, most of them wineries. It looked clean and smelled clean and was well lighted, a simple but cheerful space.

Tio Barrera, the general manager, was also the front-desk clerk this shift. The sight of FBI credentials furrowed his young brow and brought forth a visible pulse in his right temple.

He provided Silverman with the motel registry, which indicated that only one guest in the past twenty-four hours had paid cash for a room. Her name was Rachel Harrington. She supposedly lived in Fort Wayne, Indiana. She had provided an Indiana driver's license for ID, and the night clerk had confirmed the license number as well as the address on it. She had taken two rooms.

"Two?" John Harrow said. "Someone was traveling with her?"

"Is she still in residence?" Silverman asked, though she had paid for only one night.

Barrera checked his key drawer. "No. I've got two keys here for each of those rooms."

"Someone was traveling with her?" Harrow repeated.

Barrera didn't know. Phil Olney, the clerk on the

graveyard shift, lived nearby. The manager summoned him with a phone call.

Olney, a retired hospital orderly who was supplementing his pension with the motel job, arrived in less than five minutes. His fringe of white hair bristled around his head as if Barrera's phone call had given him an electric shock.

When Silverman produced a photo of Jane with shorter dark hair, Olney said, "Yeah, that's her. Lovely lady."

"Why two rooms?" Silverman asked.

"For her husband and the kids."

Harrow said, "You saw the husband, the kids?"

"No. They were in the car."

Consulting the register, Silverman said, "A Ford Explorer."

"That's right."

Silverman read aloud the license-plate number she had provided. Although it was no doubt as phony as her address in Fort Wayne, Special Agent Ramos made note of it in the pocket-size spiral-bound notebook he carried.

"You see the Explorer?" Harrow asked Phil Olney.

"No, sir. But she was a nice lady, she wouldn't lie. You could hear her choke up a little when she talked about her golden."

"Her what?"

"Her golden retriever. Scootie. He passed away not long ago."

Silverman asked Barrera, "Have those rooms been cleaned?"

"Yes, of course. Hours ago."

"Did the maid find a cell phone, a smartphone, in either room?"

Barrera looked surprised. "No. But it's funny . . . another maid found an iPhone in the trash can at the diner next door."

"Where is it?"

"The phone? It was broken."

"But where is it, Mr. Barrera?"

"I think she still has it. The maid."

18

SEEN THROUGH THE WIDE WIN-dow above the sink, in radiant white arrayed, pale-blond hair piled up and pinned, Inga Shenneck looked too celestial for kitchen work. Even with the powerful magnification that the binoculars provided, Jane couldn't tell what the woman was doing. Maybe washing vegetables or fruit.

"Ground floor, left," Dougal said.

Jane followed his advice. She saw another figure passing the wall of glass doors between the back terrace and the family room. Almost certainly a man. But he was too far from the glass to be identified.

Shenneck or one of the rayshaws?

He disappeared behind granite, but then reap-peared in the kitchen. He embraced Inga from behind, cupped her breasts in his hands, and buried his face in her neck.

She tipped her head back to allow him more of her throat.

After nuzzling her, he raised his head. Bertold Shenneck.

19

PILAR VEGA, MAYBE THIRTY years old, pretty and self-possessed, was not humbled by her job or by her maid's uniform, or by being a person of interest to the FBI. She assumed that they had come upon her while she was cleaning Room 36, after a late checkout, because they had mistaken her for an illegal alien.

"I've always been a legal resident," she said proudly. "For a year now, I've been a *citizen*."

"We aren't interested in your immigration status, Ms. Vega," Silverman said.

"I have the same rights as you. They can't be taken from me."

If her boss, Tio Barrera, had not been present to reassure the woman, Silverman and Harrow might have needed even longer to allay her doubts about their motive.

"What we're interested in is the phone you found in the trash can this morning," Silverman said.

"I didn't steal it," Pilar Vega said, taking offense at the imagined accusation, raising her head defiantly, chin up, eyes glittering with challenge. "I never steal."

Frustrated but well aware that patience would be rewarded more quickly than intimidation, Silverman said, "I have no doubt of your honesty, Ms. Vega. Not any doubt at all."

Tio Barrera took longer to smooth the woman's feathers this time. At last she seemed to believe they saw her as a source of important information, not as a target.

"I came to work early. I was sitting in my car outside the diner. I was drinking coffee. This woman dropped something in the trash can. It looked like a cell phone. She went into the diner."

Silverman showed her the photograph.

"Yes, that's her. She came out with a large coffee and a bag of something. After she was gone, I looked in the trash can. It was a phone she threw away."

"I understand you may still have the phone," Silverman said.

"It's broken."

"Yes, but do you have it?"

"She threw it away. Now it's mine."

"But if it's broken—"

"Maybe it can be fixed. I know someone who can fix phones."

"Ms. Vega," Harrow said, "that phone was involved in a crime."

"What crime?"

"Murder."

"Who was murdered?"

"We're not at liberty to say. But we must have the phone."

"The woman who threw it away doesn't look like a murderer."

"No," Silverman agreed, "she doesn't. The phone is evidence, Ms. Vega."

Reluctantly, Pilar Vega took the phone from a skirt pocket of her uniform and surrendered it.

The casing was dented and slightly torqued, but the screen appeared not to have been damaged. When he tried to turn it on, a pulse of pale gray light washed from the top to the bottom of the screen, just once, but no display appeared.

"Battery's got juice," Harrow said.

"No use as a phone," Silverman said, "but obviously the locater still transmits."

Just then his own phone rang. He handed Overton's iPhone to Harrow and took the call. "Silverman."

"Play Manchurian with me, Nathan."

"Yes, all right."

"This is Randolph Kohl from Homeland Security. Are you alone that we might speak?"

The voice was that of Booth Hendrickson, of the Department of Justice, and though Silverman *knew* it was Booth's voice, not that of Kohl, he heard himself say, as though from a distance, "Give me just a moment." To Harrow, he said, "It's Homeland. I need to take this in private." He went into the bathroom and closed the door and turned on the water in the sink to mask his voice from those in the adjoining motel room. He said, "Yes, Mr. Kohl," confused about why he should be playing along with Booth in this manner.

"Update me, Nathan. Have you gotten a lead on Jane Hawk?"

"We're closing on her. She killed a man named William Overton in Beverly Hills, in his home, evidently on Friday night."

"Overton? Sterling Overton, the attorney?"

"Yes. William Sterling Overton."

"Bloody hell. How did the stupid bitch finger Overton?"

"Through Robert Branwick, alias Jimmy Radburn."

"I don't know who that is," Booth Hendrickson said. "Why don't I know who that is?"

"He was a Dark Web entrepreneur. We had him on the hook, but he didn't know it. We were letting him run to see what other fish he'd lead us to. Overton hired him to hack someone, and Branwick hacked Overton, too. Is this really Mr. Kohl or is this you, Booth?"

After a silence, Booth said, "Play Manchurian with me, Nathan."

"Yes, all right."

Randolph Kohl said, "Who am I, Nathan?"

"Who are you?" Nathan said, perplexed that the head of Homeland Security should ask such a thing. "You're Randolph Kohl."

"You said you're closing in on her. How so?"

"We found the motel where she stayed last night. We're here now. She brought Overton's phone, got from it whatever she wanted, dropped it in the trash."

Kohl said, "You think he gave her his password?"

"The condition he was in, yes. She put him through a wringer."

"Where is this motel?"

"Just outside Napa."

"*Holy shit!* She's going after Shenneck."

"Who?"

Kohl gave him a rural-route address. "That's where she's going. Be there *now,* Nathan. Kill her. *Kill* her. I've got to make a call."

Booth hung up. Kohl. Kohl hung up.

A rushing sound. Like something coming fast at Silverman. No. Just the water in the sink. He cranked off the spigot.

He still *felt* something coming fast at him.

20

AS BERTOLD POURS TWO glasses of pinot grigio and brings them to the cutting board beside the kitchen sink, the nearby wall-mounted phone rings. It had also rung a few minutes earlier; but he is in a mood that doesn't welcome an interruption. As before, he lets it go to voice mail.

Inga glances at her wine and smiles, but she continues to scrub the potatoes.

With his glass of wine, Bertold stands watching her. There is something erotic about the way her elegant hands fondle the tubers.

Usually one of the rayshaws, programmed with a thousand and one recipes, prepares lunch and dinner for the Shennecks when they are in residence at the ranch. During this visit, however, Inga has become convinced that the rayshaws aren't maintaining their personal hygiene to the standard required of them, that in particular the one who cooks isn't washing his hands as frequently as he should and that he may be touching himself in unclean ways during his culinary duties. As a consequence, she insists on making their meals until Bertold can study the problem and find a fix for it.

Bertold is not convinced that the rayshaws are, in Inga's words, "on their way to becoming dirty little animals." She has observed two or three small aberrations in their behavior, from which she has elaborated an imagined catastrophe impending.

Her insistence on the rightness of her conclusion and her nagging about the matter are annoying.

The nearby wall phone rings yet again. Even though the number is unlisted, they have been plagued recently by robocalls placed by marketers of everything from time-share condos to organic steaks. Again, he lets it go to voice mail.

As a student of history, he has long believed that

a man who seeks to reach the heights of power is most likely to fulfill his ambitions if at his side is an equally ambitious and ruthless wife. No matter how brilliant the man, the mate who is twined with him in the pursuit of dominion brings to the enterprise a female insight and cunning that must not be under-valued.

And what a bonus it is that Inga, in addition to her unslakable thirst for ever more wealth and ever more power, is so exquisitely and entirely *hot*.

The drawback to such a wife, of course, is that she is intent on having her own pleasures and satis-factions, which requires of him both time and energy—and not least of all the sharing of the power that they have acquired. There are times when he thinks an Aspasia girl could be programmed to be tireless and ruthless in helping her husband to reach Olympus and yet remain sublimely submissive to him, so that he would not have to humor her about such fanciful concerns as that the rayshaws are not washing their hands often enough.

As he watches her begin to peel the potatoes, which for some reason is less erotic than watching her wash them, he hears a harsh noise and looks at the sky beyond the window. At first it sounds like one of the low-flying executive helicopters that ferry other émigrés from Silicon Valley to their getaway homes in this land of wine and roses.

The wall-mounted phone rings, rings. Bertold impatiently plucks the handset from its cradle. "This better not be phone sales."

"She's coming for you," says Booth Hendrickson, their good friend in the Department of Justice.

Those words are at first mystifying, but they begin to take on meaning as Bertold realizes that the racket outside doesn't have the air-chopping rhythm of a rotary wing.

"The Hawk bitch," Booth elaborates. "She's coming *now.*"

"What the hell is that?" Inga asks.

Bertold's attention is drawn from sky to land, to movement on the long, sloped meadow behind the house. Racing toward them through wild mustard and grass and exploding flocks of butterflies is some damn thing that seems to be half SUV and half tank.

He drops the phone as Inga drops potato and peeler, for it seems as if the armored car might crash through window and wall, shoving the sink and the cabinets into them and crushing them into the center island. The Shennecks are strangers to fair combat, and for a crucial moment their reason is plucked from them by the claws of panic. He steps right as she steps left, knocking against each other, unbalancing each other, for it seems that whichever way they run, they will pitch into the impending destruction instead of escaping it. The weirdness and suddenness of the assault paralyze them, the hurtling mass less like a vehicle than like an instrument of divine wrath thrown out of the sky, its judgment inescapable.

An instant later, the machine veers away from the kitchen, jumps the few low steps between lawn and terrace, crashes through the view wall, quaking the entire house, breaking upon the family room in a glittering surf-spray of shattering glass, like some Leviathan of the deep beaching itself in sparkling foam, though it does not lie helpless. The armored behemoth might have collapsed the floor into the basement if there had been a basement, but the house was built upon a slab. Instead, it plows forward, shoving aside what furniture does not splinter apart under its hardened tires, turning toward the breakfast area and kitchen, and the open floor plan is nearly as accommodating as a carpool lane.

The house includes a safe room, with secret doors and walls of steel plate, with its own air and power supply, where Bertold and Inga could safely wait out a home invasion, but there are just two entrances, the first in the living room, the second in the master suite. They can reach neither as the massive vehicle roars into the breakfast area, scattering into splinters a pair of Palecek chairs, and halts, engine idling with a sound like the panting of a panther god out of some Congolese myth.

The front passenger door is thrown open, and out steps a tall man with a pistol-grip shotgun. He has a face for noir films, made hard by dark experience, and his gray eyes cut at the Shennecks, so that they hold fast to each other in a way that they have never done before.

But it is the woman stepping out of the driver's door who for the first time in Bertold's memory gives him cause to take seriously his mortality. For a moment, he thinks that she must be a girl from Aspasia, her intellect and personality restored by some failure of her control mechanism, for she turns on him a blue-eyed stare as bright with the memory of suffering as with the fire of vengeance. But then he recalls Booth's words, which in the midst of chaos did not fully register—*The Hawk bitch, she's coming now*—and he knows that before him stands the relentless force that has for two months evaded steadily growing legions of searchers, she whose husband might have had a post-military career in politics if the computer model had not identified him as a problematic individual, she who has successfully hidden her child from those same legions. She holds a pistol in a two-hand grip, arms straight out before her as she approaches him, and it seems that he will die here before the rayshaws can arrive from the gatehouse.

She says, "If you didn't put me on your Hamlet list, you should have. Because you're sure as hell on mine."

21

UNDER A SKY DARK AND SWOLlen, two sedans raced east on the county road, into territory where neighbors were few and far between. They slid in hard turns onto the private drive and braked abruptly before a ranch-style gate that was fashioned from three-inch-diameter pipes. Silverman, Harrow, and Ramos got out of the first car, leaving their driver, a Sacramento agent, behind the wheel. In the second sedan were three more men out of the Sacramento field office.

Far back on the property and uphill, under thunderheads that seemed to be avalanching toward it, a large ultramodern house with cantilevered view decks overlooked the valley, as if it were a fantastic glass ship washed up there by a flood.

Near the gate stood a modest Victorian home.

Before Silverman could push the button on the call box, the front door of the nearer house opened, and two men stepped onto the porch. They were of a type: tall, solid, clean-shaven, their faces expressionless, their eyes as watchful as those of Dobermans trained to protect and defend, kin to the wrong kind of hired muscle that you sometimes saw around certain entertainment-world celebrities unhinged by their sudden wealth and fame.

One of the men came along the walk to the gate, while the other remained on the porch.

Silverman flashed his FBI badge. "We need to see Dr. Shenneck right away."

"You're not on the admissions list."

"Who are you?" Harrow asked.

Instead of offering a name, the man said, "Security."

The guard's stare was direct, even bold, yet Silverman saw no discernible emotion in it, just as there was none in his face, not the suspicion that his job required, not the latent hostility that motivated some men to take a job that might now and then provide an excuse for violence.

"Call your boss," Harrow said. "We need to see him right away, it's a matter of life and death. *His* life and death."

From somewhere beyond the main house rose the racket of a racing engine. Both the guard who had spoken to Silverman and the one on the porch looked toward the noise.

A thunderclap and its echoes masked the engine, but then the thunder faded and the growling of the unseen vehicle could be heard again.

In addition to their size and demeanor, some elusive quality about these guards riveted Silverman's attention. Their formidable appearance and direct manner seemed like a mask, their status as security personnel more of a role than a truth.

From a distance, the growl of the engine rose to a roar, and a third man, alike to the first two, came out of the open front door, onto the porch. He looked uphill toward the main house, and then at Harrow, and then at Silverman, his comportment machine-like.

Abruptly Silverman intuited that each man's mask was less veil than gloss, that behind the mask was not a different man but instead an emptiness. He knew this because he saw himself in them, himself as he had been a few times during this strange day, as he had been at the Beverly Hills hotel when he had awakened in confusion, as he had been when he'd found the second gun—the .45 Kimber Raptor II—in his nightstand drawer, as he had been when he'd experienced nausea and disorientation while he stood in front of the hotel to wait for John Harrow, as he had been when an interior voice renamed Jane the Mother of Lies, as he had been when the jet lifted off from Van Nuys Airport and gravity seemed to be deserting him. At times today, he had felt lost, and these security guards looked as he had felt, lost beneath their gloss of dutiful concern and competence. He thought of the puncture mark on the vein in the crook of his arm, which he'd dismissed as an insect bite, of Randolph Kohl speaking with the voice of Booth Hendrickson, of how he twice forgot to call Rishona, whose heart and his were synchronized. A flash of insight told him that, impossibly but certainly, these three guards were hollow men, *shape without form, shade without color,* and that to some degree he was becoming like them. If he could be hollowed out, if he could become someone he had never been before, then *anything* could happen. In fact the impossible *would* happen here, now and going forward. In recognition of whatever horror was unfolding, he backed away from the ranch gate and from the guards.

Ramos said, "What's wrong?"

"Nathan?" John Harrow said.

As Silverman backed between the sedan and the gate, the engine roar from the vicinity of the main house terminated in a colossal crash, the unmistakable ringing as huge sheets of glass dissolved.

As lightning pulsed behind the clouds like the lamps of some enormous vessel passing in the shroud, John Harrow stepped onto the low gate and swung over it and shouted at the nearest of Shenneck's security guards to admit the cars. But as hard thunder chased the lightning, as Harrow sprinted up the driveway toward the main house, the two men on the porch drew pistols from under their jackets and shot him in the back.

22

JANE WITH DOUGAL, PERHAPS fleeing the past, perhaps hoping to redeem it, venturing into a future darker than the darkest days of history, heard the knocking of her heart and ignored it, tasted the acid of fear and swallowed it.

Across a brittleness of broken wall glass and a hard clatter of splintered chair wood, harried at gunpoint to the stairs and to the second floor, Bertold Shenneck progressed weak-limbed and shuddering, as might a dung beetle stripped of its exoskeleton. Having set out to change the world and rule it through mass murder and slavery, he had seemed to act with courage when, at enormous personal risk, he broke laws and trashed two thousand years of philosophical consensus as to the equal value of each human life. But what might have looked like courage proved to be a deficit of common sense and an excess of self-importance, too strong a faith in his genius and superiority—not courage at all, but the rash actions of an ordinary narcissist incapable of imagining that he might fail. The invasion of his house and an up-close view of a gun muzzle had been all that was required to reduce him from king lion to a quivering peasant mouse.

On the other hand, treading on glass and climbing stairs, not in the least concerned about being shot in the back, Inga Shenneck seemed unfazed by this turn of events, her faith in herself only enhanced by any setback. "You don't know who you're dealing with, what hell you're bringing down on yourselves. If you take this one step farther, you're going to end up in a deep room, in a world of pain, taken apart piece by piece. This is stupid, this is idiocy, you will pay for this, you'll beg for death. History will roll over pieces of shit like you. *We* are the future, *we* will rewrite history, and you will never have existed, useless human debris, both of you."

On the second floor, Dougal dragged a hallway sideboard away from the wall, blocked the head of the stairs with it, and took up a position behind the furniture. The rayshaws should already have been there.

At gunpoint, Jane hurried the Shennecks onward to Bertold's home office. There, she instructed him to sit at his desk and fire up his computer.

She pointed to a side chair and said to Inga, "Take

it to the corner over there. Sit in it, face the wall, your back to the room."

The woman's mouth twisted in a sneer of dismissal and purest hatred that belied the impression of angelic radiance encouraged by her all-white ensemble. She gripped the chair by its head rail, her intent as evident as if she had announced it.

"You have to swing the chair to throw it," Jane warned, "so you'll be in Hell before it leaves your hands."

"When you're dead," Inga promised, "I'll take a long piss on your corpse."

Jane gave her only amused contempt. "What a potty mouth. Get in the corner, Bad Barbie."

As Inga settled in the chair, her back to the room, thunder rocked the sky once more, and peppered through the rolling sound of a storm impending, there also came a barrage of gunfire rattling in the distance. The rayshaws shooting at—whom?

23

HARROW FALLING FORWARD into a blood spray from the exit wounds in his chest, a colony of crows exploding from nearby trees with a raucous denunciation of those who would disturb their peace, black wings sculling the gray sky, Ramos and the nearest security guard drawing their weapons simultaneously, Ramos the quicker and better shot, putting a round in the mannequin face of the emotionless assassin, surviving a death-reflex near miss in return.

With the first Bureau sedan now between him and the house, Silverman saw Harrow's killers leap from the porch and head uphill toward the main residence, as two other guards appeared around the side of the Victorian, one of them with a shotgun, the other with an Uzi machine gun.

Silverman dropped to the ground, sheltering behind the car, just as the driver, recognizing his profound vulnerability, shifted the sedan into reverse, either forgetting about the vehicle behind him or assuming the other driver would also at once speed backward out of an untenable situation. Bumpers clashed, taillights and headlights shattered. Silverman lay flat on the ground behind the first sedan as the Uzi and the shotgun opened fire. Car windows dissolved. Sheet metal shrieked as bullets tore it. Fiberglass cracked. Tires popped. Men screamed in pain but only briefly.

He found himself under the sedan without memory of having taken shelter there, his face turned toward the house. Ramos dropped into sight, part of his head gone, peering into Silverman's refuge with rolled-back and sunken-away eyes entirely white and ghostly in their sockets, like the spirits of ancient primitives lingering in caves where they once lived in centuries past.

Although a part of the man whom he had been
remained somewhere deep within him, Silverman
did not join the firefight. His once-keen sense of
honor no longer insisted that he act with moral authority, and his formerly acute awareness of where
his loyalty should lie was now at best confused. He
had seen himself in the hollow men guarding the
ranch. Their hollowness was at first terrifying but
then seemed darkly attractive, a spiritual abyss but
also a relief from making choices and striving to do
what was right. As the gunfire volleyed insanely
and then diminished, he remained under the sedan.
Within him, a still, small voice whispered that there
was really only one thing he needed to do, that he
needed only to deal with she who betrayed her
country, betrayed the Bureau, betrayed him. No
moral ambiguity. No complex reasoning required to
assess the situation. Complete just one task, and
then rest free of doubt, free of that lifelong fear that
is called misgiving, free of remorse. One task. *Kill
her. Kill her. Kill her.*

The soft *drip-drip-drip* and the smell of gasoline
brought him out from under the sedan before a fire
erupted. The silence in the bloody aftermath remained so complete that the ranch might have been
a diorama mocked up and sealed in a glass box. If
there had been a breeze, the crows had winged it
away with them.

Then a sledgehammer of thunder walloped the
day and broke the rain out of the clouds.

The driver of the front car slumped dead behind the wheel, as did the driver of the second. The two other Sacramento agents in the rear sedan had gotten out of the car alive and fast enough to take a toll on Shenneck's security team even as they, too, were cut down. The hollow men whom Silverman had seen with a shotgun and an Uzi were now carrion waiting for the return of the birds, as was the one whom Ramos had shot. Of the six agents who arrived at Gee Zee Ranch, only Silverman survived.

The slaughter neither angered nor moved him, as once it would have. It was just a thing that happened. There could be no value in brooding about it.

He stood in the rain, waiting to know what to do next.

Fifty or sixty yards beyond the ranch gate, another security guard, on foot, hurried up the long driveway toward the main house, unaware that anyone lived in his wake. He carried what appeared to be another Uzi.

As Silverman watched the guard move out of sight into the silver sheets of rain, his phone rang. He took the call, listened, and said, "Yes, all right."

24

A PORTION OF THE UPPER HALL was a gallery open to the living room and foyer below. Connecting the two levels, floating treads curved down with railings on both sides, allowing Dougal Trahern a clear line of sight on every approach to the stairs.

Behind the sideboard that blockaded the head of the staircase, Dougal had two pistols and one shotgun with a three-round magazine. He thought he was well positioned and well armed, but the gunfire that had clattered up from the direction of the gatehouse concerned him. Now the rush of rain built to a vehement sibilation, as of a crowd of thousands chanting in a stage whisper, which denied him the sounds that the rayshaws might make in their approach.

Even on a gloomy afternoon, adequate light had found its way into this many-windowed residence, and there had been no lamps lit on the ground floor, other than in the kitchen. Now the storm draped the world with layers of beaded curtains, and a lurid half light seeped through the open rooms, not only obscuring things but also distorting them. Below him, for just a moment, a bell-shaded floor lamp behind a chair in the living room appeared to be a helmeted man. As corners darkled, it was easy to believe that menacing forms crouched within them, waiting to charge the stairs in force.

In fact, the rayshaws didn't need overwhelming numbers to mount an effective assault, because they were no more fearful than would have been a regiment of deathless machines incapable of feeling pain. He didn't yet understand that they would sacrifice themselves in a kind of samurai suicide.

It began when sheet lightning traveled the brainlike folds of the curdled clouds and pulsed through the rooms below and also down through the skylight above the stairs. Out of those pale luminous throbbings, a rayshaw appeared in the foyer as though materializing in a pentagram, a tall man with a gun. He gazed up at Dougal, who rose above the sideboard only enough to monitor activity below. The gunman moved openly toward the foot of the stairs, as if inviting a bullet, a boldness that caused Dougal to hesitate, lest the purpose might be to encourage him to rise farther and make a better target of himself for a second gunman.

25

BERTOLD SHENNECK DERAILED from the path to power, switched to a siding, his utopia having hurtled away from him on diverging tracks, lives in a moment now when genius doesn't matter, when neither money nor connections count for anything, when science cannot save him, when

he can no longer afford pride. The gun is two feet
from his head. Her finger is on the trigger. She has
said that if she can't ruin him and subject him to a
public shaming and imprisonment, she will kill him
in such a way as to maximize his suffering. He does
not doubt her sincerity. This woman is beyond his
experience, as unknowable to him as would be a
creature from another galaxy, but one thing he fully
gets about her is that she possesses the awful power
of death and is ready to use it without hesitation.

The terror that fills him now is new to him, a
fright that reduces him to the condition of an animal
driven by one thing—the survival instinct. As she
tells him what she expects him to retrieve from his
project files and copy onto the flash drives that she
has brought, when with dread he considers how
much time this will take, time during which the gun
will be aimed at his head, he dares not conceal from
her that what she wants is already available on
backup files copied to flash drives and stored in a
home safe. At any moment, the rayshaws will arrive, and when she realizes they will prevent her
from getting what she wants, she'll surely kill Bertold.

"It's my life's work," he explains in a voice that
seems too thin and shaky to be his, "so I have backup
files not just here but in other secure locations."

As he makes this revelation, Inga tries to silence
him from her corner-facing chair, calling him a fool
and worse.

When Inga is incensed about anything, no one

exists who can produce a greater torrent of words with more passion.

But her vitriolic insistence only annoys the widow Hawk, who says, "*Shut up, bitch!* I don't need you like I need him. I'd as soon blow your brains out as listen to another word."

On occasion, Bertold has wanted to issue a variation of that threat to his bride, though the possible consequences have deterred him. Even in his terror, he takes some satisfaction from the fact that although Inga remains as restive as a rattlesnake caught in a gaffling noose, she speaks not another word.

The widow Hawk asks about the ampules containing the various kinds of command mechanisms. If she has his project files, she might as well have samples of the finished product. He says, "They're in one of the Sub-Zeros in the kitchen, top shelf."

Concealed behind six-foot-wide, floor-to-ceiling bookshelves, the safe has a voice-recognition lock that responds to two commands. As sheet lightning pulses through the day and flutters quick shadows through the room, Bertold says, "'Things are as I think they are,'" and the shelves swing open, revealing a stainless-steel panel, after which he says, "'and say they are on my blue guitar,'" to make the panel whisk into the ceiling.

26

STRAIGHT-FALLING RAIN drummed the roof and the skylights, a fateful funereal drone, as the rayshaw ascended fast, dodging left to right, right to left, which was the closest that he could get to a serpentine evasion on a staircase. The killer couldn't have shot accurately while staggering upward in such a fashion; but it was odd that he didn't shoot at all, that he came as if with no intent of conquering but with every intent of dying.

Dougal rose from behind the sideboard, fired the shotgun, the recoil knocking bone on bone in his shoulder.

The climber took the blast in the chest and abdomen. He dropped his pistol and went to his knees without a scream, not as if he had been hit, but as if he were instead a penitent seized by a sudden need to kneel and pray. At once, impossibly, he clambered to his feet, still coming although with diminished energy, staying to the inner curve of the staircase and against the railing. Maybe he wore a light bulletproof vest under his clothes, enough to spare him from most of the buckshot, or maybe he felt neither fear nor pain.

Rising higher above the sideboard, Dougal fired a second round, and the attacker was flung backward, headless, his body tumbling step to step like the straw-stuffed shape of a scarecrow wind-shorn from its crossed staves and blown to ruination.

Under cover of the first assailant, a second had raced upward, this time not bothering to attempt evasion. Staying to the outward curve of the stairs, passing the collapsing corpse, he could have squeezed off a few rounds while moving, to lend himself cover and with a greater hope of accuracy, but he held his fire.

Dougal rose higher still as the would-be killer drew near, and the third shell in the three-round magazine had such wicked impact that there was no kneeling and getting up this time, only a wild and final plummet.

Into the echo of the shotgun roar came the rattle of a fully automatic weapon. A third man, from whom the first two had meant to distract Dougal, assumed substance out of the half light in the living room, wielding an Uzi, chopping stair railing and sideboard barricade and Dougal, who dropped to the floor in a white flare of pain that bleached away the scene before him and that receded to a pinpoint of light in a great darkness, as he heard himself say his lost sister's name, "Justine?"

27

AS JANE INSTRUCTED, THE Shennecks remained in their chairs while she went to the open safe and found the clear plastic box containing the six flash drives in six labeled slots. She believed she had what she needed, because it was beyond unlikely that the scientist had labeled blank flash drives to trick her in expectation of her invasion of his home. Besides, this would-be maker of a new world, who was a man of stone and steel when planning the deaths of thousands, proved in the heat of action to have a spine of butter.

The safe also contained stacks of cash, as had Overton's safe in Beverly Hills, plus plastic numismatic cases containing one-ounce gold coins, hundreds of them, and the recorder that stored the video taken by the house security cameras. She ignored the cash and coins, but confiscated the disc from the recorder.

She thought that the words with which Shenneck had used the voice-recognition system to open the safe must be lines of verse, but she wouldn't give the bastard even the small satisfaction of asking. At the same time that he was a mass murderer by remote control, he was a perpetual adolescent fond of jokes and little games, and she could imagine him preening as he explained why he'd chosen that poem and poet.

As she tucked the flash drives and the disc in a jacket pocket, a shotgun blast silenced the rain for an instant, and then another, a third, followed by the chatter of automatic weapons' fire. Shenneck cried out in alarm, and his wife slid off her chair to huddle behind it in the corner.

Jane hurried to the hall door, which stood open. When the gunfire ceased, she crouched and looked out there, to the right, where Dougal sprawled at the head of the stairs, as still as a man who needed casketing.

She could allow herself grief in modest measure, but not yet anger. She retreated to the study, stepped to the side of the open door, her back to the wall. Fished a disposable phone from an inner jacket pocket. Entered the number she'd memorized. Pressed SEND.

Standing by at Valley Air, Ronnie Fuentes answered: "It's me."

Jane kept her voice low. "Bad weather."

Another gunshot, just one this time.

"No wind. Still can do," Ronnie said.

"He's down."

"All the way?"

"Don't know."

"Six minutes max."

They disconnected.

She wondered if that last shot had been one of the rayshaws administering the coup de grace to Dougal.

She pocketed the phone.

Still with her back to the wall, she held the gun in two hands, muzzle toward the ceiling, waiting for what would come next.

Bertold Shenneck watched her, walleyed.

Having deduced the meaning of Jane's side of the telephone conversation, Inga Shenneck rose to her feet in the corner. "So you're alone now."

"Park your ass in that chair," Jane whispered savagely.

Inga did as told, but facing the room rather than the corner, and with a smile as thin as the curved blade of a mezzaluna.

28

STREAMING RAIN, PROCEEDING from the trashed family room into the front of the house, as dead-eyed and grim as a forcibly drowned victim risen from a watery grave and bent on supernatural revenge, Nathan Silverman left his duty pistol holstered and instead drew the untraceable .45 Kimber from his belt. He stopped behind the man, the hollow man, who was wielding the Uzi, and just then the automatic carbine spat out its last round.

The hollow man lowered the gun and ejected the spent case and stood staring up at the head of the stairs as he fished a fresh magazine from under his jacket. He slapped it into the Uzi and chambered a first round.

Silverman shot him in the back of the head. He stepped around the gunman, leaving the Uzi on the floor. Seven bullets remained with which to finish the job that Booth Kohl—Randolph Hendrickson, Booth Hendrickson, Randolph Kohl—had given him when his phone had rung minutes earlier, as he'd stood among the dead at the front gate.

Silence settled over all, but for the restless rataplan of rain. The house seemed to be submerged and under great pressure, as if it were a submarine exceeding the maximum depth for which it had been designed. The light came watery and gray through the windows, and the shadows appeared to undulate like kelp leaves stirred by lazy currents. As Silverman climbed the stairs, the air felt thick, and thicker with each inhalation.

29

JANE IN SHENNECK'S STUDY, her back to the wall, the open door to her right. The genius at his desk with his face in his hands, like a child who believes the monster emerging from the closet will leave him untouched as long as he doesn't look at it. Inga in the corner, watching with feral interest, mane of pale golden hair like that of some stone-temple goddess half human and half lioness.

The lightning seemed to have passed, and the thunder. But for the thudding of Jane's heart, the only sound was the million-footed rain jittering across the roof.

From the hallway came a voice. "FBI. FBI. It's over now. Jane? Jane Hawk? Are you here? Are you all right?"

Three thousand miles from Quantico, four months from the life of which she had been stripped, she heard Nathan Silverman and felt relief and stepped away from the wall. Then she warned herself that, in the quick of action, reason must rule over emotion, and she took back the step she'd taken, pressing against the wall once more.

Nathan appeared in the doorway and looked at her, and she had never seen him more solemn, gray-faced and tight-lipped. "They're all dead," he told her. "The hollow men and all the agents with me. All dead. Are you all right?"

He had a pistol with a three-inch barrel, not a traditional duty gun, and he carried it at his side, aimed at the floor. He proceeded past her into the room. "Bertold Shenneck? Inga Shenneck?"

Turning in his office chair, the scientist made the mistake of lowering his hands from his face, and Nathan killed him with one shot.

Inga bolted to her feet, kicking aside the chair that penned her in the corner, and Nathan needed two rounds to put her down.

Regardless of the desperate nature of the situation, there was no Bureau protocol that allowed for the killing of unarmed suspects.

As Jane brought up her Heckler & Koch, Nathan turned with his pistol in a two-hand grip, and they stood face-to-face, less than six feet between them.

Seven years of respect and admiration, years of friendship, restrained her finger on the trigger, though the only one of them who had a chance of surviving was the one who fired first.

The rain rushed down the day, the house resonated with it, the seconds passed, then half a minute, until both the moment and the man became too strange for her to bear.

He said, "They were not needed anymore."

She waited for him to explain.

After a shorter silence, he said, "There are others to carry on Shenneck's work. Others less flamboyant, more reliable."

No doubt that he was Nathan Silverman, her section chief, the genuine article, not a doppelganger. He was the husband of Rishona, the father of a son and two daughters, as well known to Jane as anyone else in the world. But she was pressed now to the conclusion that he had sold out, gone to the dark side ... unless something worse had happened to him.

"How is Jareb?" she asked, inquiring after his son.

His face remained expressionless, and he did not reply.

"How's Chaya? Does she still like landscape architecture? She has such a talent for it."

His eyes were as dark as the muzzle of his pistol. They were locked on her eyes in something more than a staring match.

"Lisbeth?" Jane asked. "Have she and Paul set a wedding date yet?"

His mouth moved, tried to shape itself around his thoughts, but no sound came from him, as though he might have spoken if he hadn't known that he had come to a place where words no longer could redeem the past or shape the future. And still he searched her eyes as if he had lost something that he might find in her.

"My boy . . . Nick's boy and mine, our boy is five," she said, struggling to keep her voice steady, failing in the struggle. "You remember Travis. He wants a pony. My little cowboy."

His gun tracked away from her. Separate from the crash of the shot, she heard the whisper-whine of the bullet inches from her left ear, the crack of dry wall punctured, and she almost shot him then, restraining herself only because the miss was clearly intentional. He fired again, still inches off target and slightly higher, but then the muzzle tracked down and toward her, until that single eye, ready with the wink of death, regarded her.

Whatever he'd become, his control mechanism was of a different kind from the one that had commanded Nick to kill himself. That way out was denied to Nathan Silverman. At last his rigid face collapsed in an expression, clenched in anguish, his eyes but pools of misery, and he found a word to speak, the word a name, the name *Rishona*.

Something tore within Jane when she did what needed to be done, what he was asking her to do that he could not accomplish. If such a hateful thing could be an act of love, it was an act of love on her part, that she should release him from the hell of slavery, from being used to do the vicious work of men not fit to speak his name. In the instant between the motion and the act, she saw in his face the real-ization and relief that she would grant him what he wanted. At a terrible cost to herself, she shot him twice, and when he fell to the floor, she shot him a third time, to be certain beyond all doubt that the web spanning his brain and the weaver who crawled the web could not rule him even one moment lon-ger.

Over her raw sounds of grief, she heard the heli-copter coming.

30

AT THE HEAD OF THE STAIRS, BE-hind the bullet-chopped sideboard, Dougal Trahern lay bleeding and unconscious, his pulse too quick and too weak, but still alive.

Jane shoved the sideboard out of the way and

raced down the stairs, between the buckshot-ravaged dead, not allowing herself to consider upon what she was treading in her frantic descent.

She unlocked the front door, threw it open, and stepped outside as the helicopter cruised in low from the southwest, its rotary wing whisking the rain, wipers flinging fans of water off the advanced glass cockpit. The twin-engine medium-size craft could have carried nine passengers if the configuration of its interior had not been customized for the air-ambulance service that Valley Air contracted out to several area hospitals.

If the rain had been accompanied by stiff wind, the helo might have been grounded, although Ronnie Fuentes himself was piloting it and determined to do whatever his father's favorite sergeant needed. If neither Jane nor Dougal had been badly wounded in the raid, the helicopter would never have been called to the ranch. Now it landed not just with Ronnie aboard but also with his older sister, Nora, a pilot herself and a former Army medic, who was a partner in Valley Air.

Dougal was a big guy. Stabilizing him and getting him out of the house, into the helo, required Jane to assist Nora and Ronnie. If the carnage in the residence shocked the Fuentes siblings, neither gave any indication of it, maneuvering around the dead men as if around misplaced furniture.

When Dougal had been loaded aboard, as Nora tended to him, she looked out through the open door at Jane standing in the rain. "Did it all go to shit?"

"No. We did what we came to do."

"Maybe I don't want to know what this is about."

"You don't."

"Are you okay, girl?"

"I will be. I hope to God Dougal is."

The twin engines fired up in sequence, and the rotary wing chugged into action, and Nora closed the door.

Jane backed away to watch the helicopter lift off.

They could not take Dougal to a hospital, where he would sooner or later be connected with the bloody melee at Gee Zee Ranch. That would be putting him at risk of murder charges. Worse, he would be brought to the attention of David James Michael, the billionaire who funded Shenneck and perhaps now funded others who embraced the same mission.

From Valley Air, Dougal would be spirited to Nora's house, where she hoped to keep him stable until the nearest discreet and trustworthy doctor, Porter Walkins, arrived by car from Santa Rosa, nearly fifty miles away. Walkins, an Army doctor who had retired from the military to a private practice, had been given both Jane's and Dougal's blood types; on short notice, he could obtain, without attracting notice, enough blood for a significant transfusion.

Jane stood in the rain as the air ambulance churned off the lawn and skyward, wondering how it had happened that the world had slid so far into the present darkness. So far into it that there were people like Fuentes and Porter Walkins—once trusting in the law and still hopeful of its full restoration— who recognized this new and ominous reality and who would participate in a kind of underground resistance when called upon.

As the helicopter accelerated southwest, Jane hurried back into the house.

31

IN THE LIVING ROOM, SHE picked up the Uzi. She checked the magazine and found it fully loaded. This was a radical weapon, but these were radical times. Although she hoped never to have a need for the gun, she kept it.

She took a decorative pillow from one of the sofas, zippered open the case, stripped out the foam core. She went up to the second floor, returning to the dead genius's study, though she would rather have gone directly to the Gurkha and retraced the route by which she had driven to the ranch. But in this new world, you could seldom afford to do what you'd rather do instead of what you must.

She didn't look at the three bodies, but made her way directly to the open safe, where she stuffed the empty pillowcase with banded packets of hundred-dollar bills. She threw some gold coins into the makeshift bag as well. She was in a war now, and wars were damn expensive.

Downstairs, when she stepped into the kitchen, she found that it had been invaded by coyotes.

32

COUSINS TO WOLVES, THEY would have been beautiful in the wild, just doglike enough to charm the eye. Prowling the kitchen, however, stepping gingerly through broken glass, they were lean and ragged in their rain-sodden coats, lantern-eyed in the storm gloom, taking inventory with their flared nostrils and lolling tongues, like revenants out of Hell unleashed for Armageddon. When they caught sight of her, their black lips skinned back from teeth that could crack bones to get the marrow, and they greeted her in voices that were half menacing growls and half purrs in anticipation of their hunger satisfied.

She dropped the decorative pillowcase and took the Uzi in two hands and squeezed off a burst well wide of the Gurkha, by intention killing just one of the coyotes, hoping they would be wise enough to recognize superior power and sufficiently frightened by gunfire to be chased out by it. In fact, they scrambled over one another—five, six, seven of them—away into the family room and out through the opening where a wall of glass had been.

When she and Dougal had sprung from the armored vehicle to confront the Shennecks, they had left the doors open. She picked up the pillowcase, walked around to the passenger's side, put the money on the seat, and closed the door.

Out in the backyard, the coyotes sounded as if they were in ferocious combat with something, and she kept a wary eye on the archway to the family room as she went to the driver's side of the Gurkha. When she opened the back door to stow the Uzi, she came face-to-face with a lingering beast that had earlier invaded the vehicle.

She swung the Uzi up, not to fire it but to use it as a club, and the coyote sprang at her not to attack but, in its terror, to scuffle past her and escape. The impact of the creature staggered her backward, and she heard its teeth snapping hard against the barrel of the weapon, felt its feet clawing at her coat, smelled filthy fur and pungent musk and blood-soured breath, and then it flailed off her and bounded away.

Shaken and gasping for breath, wondering if the moment had turned supernatural, if Ground Zero Ranch might be fated to be her burial ground, she wanted to get out of there fast.

But she had to locate the ampules containing the control mechanisms. They were in the second refrigerator, on the top shelf, as Shenneck had said they would be. There were sixteen large ampules slotted in a foam-lined container, each neatly labeled.

She had to keep them cold.

The furious combat in the backyard continued. Her imagination drew for her an image of the coyotes contesting with a grizzly bear, though there were no grizzlies in California anymore.

How to keep the ampules cold?

Shenneck would have had to keep them cold when he brought them here from the lab in Menlo Park. Perhaps in a Styrofoam cooler, a picnic cooler, something like that.

Alert for the return of the coyotes or for whatever they might be fighting out there, she found the cooler in the pantry and filled it with ice and nestled the ampules in it.

She put the cooler and the Uzi in the back of the Gurkha, slammed the door, swung in behind the wheel, slammed *that* door, started the engine, and reversed out of the kitchen. She battered the tank-like SUV through ruined furniture and drove out of the house, across the terrace, onto the yard. No grizzly bear. The coyotes were savaging one another in the rain. Two of them were feeding on one of their own that they had killed.

If the entire world had not gone mad, this piece of it, this getaway property where life was meant to be a holiday, was surely mad, with predators eating their own, nature corrupted by the people who once had lived here, just as the people themselves had been corrupted.

She drove off the lawn and into the wild grass and up the long slope to the crest where she and Dougal had studied the house with binoculars. There she braked and looked back. The coyotes had not followed her; they were in a war of all against all.

She noticed then the blood on her right hand. She had not felt the sting of the scratch. Now she did. It was about two inches long and shallow, and she could imagine only that it had been inflicted by the coyote, the flick of a scrabbling claw.

She stared at the laceration for a long, still moment. There was nothing to be done about it just yet.

It was shallow. Bleeding very little. Not a major wound.

Using the disposable phone, she called Ronnie Fuentes once more. The helicopter had landed at Valley Air. They were in Nora's Range Rover with Dougal, just then pulling into Nora's garage.

"Call Dr. Walkins," Jane said. "If he hasn't left Santa Rosa, if he's still getting the blood for Dougal, tell him also to bring a complete course of postexposure rabies vaccine."

"The sergeant was bitten? By what?"

"Not Dougal. Me. And it's just a scratch."

After she had found her way back through the rolling meadows and open woods to a paved road, she got out and replaced the license plates that she and Dougal had removed on the way to the ranch.

The rain withered to an end as she finished the

task, and the waning day came to an early twilight under the wrung-out clouds.

Entering the county road, switching on the headlights, she thought she heard a shrill wailing. When she put down her window, the sirens were piercing in the washed-clear air. She supposed she knew where they were headed, but she was not concerned, because she would be going a different way from them.

33

VALLEY AIR, ITS HANGARS AND landing pads, was less busy on a Sunday than on other days, less busy on a Sunday of rain than on other Sundays, as quiet as a mausoleum in the lingering wet and deepening dark of a night such as this.

In the bathroom adjoining Ronnie Fuentes's office, Dr. Porter Walkins watched as Jane gently but thoroughly washed the scratch on her hand. Although she had cleaned it earlier, Walkins insisted she do so again, under his direction, first with soap and water and then with povidone-iodine solution.

In a tweed sport jacket with elbow patches, a pinstriped shirt, a hand-fashioned bow tie, and pants held up with suspenders, wearing a pair of half-lens reading glasses pulled down on his nose so that he

could look over them, Walkins seemed less like a
doctor than like a college professor of poetry, circa
1960.

"You should be with Dougal," she said.

"He's stable. He's conscious. He'll make it. Blood
loss, yes. But no evident organ damage. Nora can
manage till I get back to him. Okay. Clean enough.
Pat it dry."

With a hypodermic syringe, he administered
human rabies immune globulin, infiltrating much of
it around the wound in her hand, using the remaining volume for an intramuscular injection in the
upper part of that arm.

"Now another injection. Human diploid cell vaccine. In your other arm this time."

The vaccine felt hot as it diffused through the del-
toid muscle.

"You need to repeat the vaccine. It's essential.
Three more times. Wednesday. Again next Sunday.
And the Sunday after that. I'd rather administer
them myself."

"Not possible, doctor. I have too much to do and
too little time to do it. I'll have to self-inject."

"That's not preferable."

"I know how."

"I'd already left Santa Rosa. Then Ronnie called
about this. I got this course of treatment from a physician here. The vaccine is nearing its expiration
date."

"But I'm not," she said.

"We all are, Mrs. Hawk. See me Wednesday. For fresh vaccine."

"There's no reasoning with me, Dr. Walkins. I appreciate the risk you're taking. But I'm a stubborn bitch. I'll self-inject with what you've got."

He gave her a Ziploc bag containing three ampules of vaccine and three hypodermic syringes in sterile packages.

As he taped a gauze pad over the wound in her hand, he said, "Do you know the symptoms of rabies?"

"I'll bet you've written them down for me."

"There's a list with the vaccine."

"I may not even be infected."

"Doesn't matter. Just so you give yourself those injections." He picked up his physician bag. "I'm told I'm not making a mistake with any friend of Mr. Trahern's."

"I hope that's true in my case, doctor. And may I ask . . ."

"What?"

"Why do you risk this off-the-record work?"

"I watch the news, Mrs. Hawk."

"That'll do it," she said.

As Walkins departed, Jane shrugged into her sport coat and joined Ronnie in the adjacent office, where on the walls military helicopters flew in wars eternal.

He handed her a bottle of beer. She took a long, cold drink.

"Dougal asked about you first thing when he came around."

"He once said someone was blessed to have me for a daughter. Tell him I'd have been damn proud to be his."

Ronnie helped her carry her suitcases, the bag of autopsy reports, and the leather tote containing sixty thousand dollars. They loaded everything into the Gurkha.

As she drove away, she checked the rearview mirror. He watched her until she reached the end of the Valley Air approach road and turned out of sight.

34

AT THE FIRST TRUCK STOP ON Interstate 5, she refueled and bought a turkey-and-cheese sandwich and a screw-top bottle of cola. Sitting in the Gurkha, she took apart the .45 Heckler & Koch, with which she had killed Robert Branwick, William Overton, and the dear soul who had once been Nathan Silverman.

She loaded the Colt .45 that she had taken from Overton's safe on Friday night, which would now be her duty weapon. She would need to find a safe place to shoot and go through a couple hundred rounds until she understood the gun.

She drove south through the vast and lonely San Joaquin Valley, remembering Dougal in his pre-confession surly silence as they had come north less than twenty-four hours earlier, before she'd ever heard his sister's name, Justine.

Every fifty miles or so, she stopped alongside the road and, when no traffic was near, threw a piece of the dismantled pistol into a field, in one case into a pond.

At the last of these stops, she found that she had left the overcast behind. The wide valley was crowned with stars, and the westering moon glowed with the promise of tomorrow's light. Night air of crystalline clarity carried on it the distant lights of one farmhouse and another, of tiny communities where people lived out lives that the movers-and-shakers considered tedious if not squalid. All of it was grand beyond her powers of description, full of wonder and potential, all of it precious, all of it worth dying for.

Past midnight, not far from Buttonwillow, she exited the interstate to another truck stop, parked, bought fresh ice for the cooler, and then slept on the backseat, safe behind tinted windows. She dozed off with the soapstone cameo in her hand, and still held it hours later when she woke in morning light. If because of the cameo's protection she could not say, but though she had earned a thousand nightmares, not one had troubled her sleep.

35

IN HIS IMMENSE GARAGE IN Malibu, the actor helped her transfer everything from the Gurkha to her Ford Escape.

She said, "We thought it would be taking a lot of gunfire, but it never took a single round. Though it was still nice to have the bulletproof windows."

If he found the Uzi more curious or more interesting than the suitcases, he did not remark on it. He was happy to know that his old sergeant was alive and would likely sell back to him the armored SUV, but he did not ask from what life-threatening injury Dougal was currently recovering.

When Jane was ready to leave, the actor said, "First, I've got something you have to see and someone you have to meet."

"I have a heavy schedule," she said.

"Humor me, Mrs. Hawk. You owe me a little humoring."

She couldn't disagree with that assertion, and she accompanied him to a home theater that seated twenty-four in an elaborate re-creation of an Art Deco movie house. She did not sit, but stood in the opulent darkness as he played for her a recording of a story from the morning news, sized up to the big screen. She saw herself with long blond hair and then as she looked now, and she heard herself labeled a rogue FBI agent, a ruthless outlaw accused of terrible crimes, suspected of two murders.

When Nathan Silverman had walked into Shenneck's study in Napa Valley, she had known that something like this might be coming. By now she had thought through the means by which she might stay free long enough to get at David James Michael.

Nothing about the story surprised her, except that no reference was made to a violent event at a ranch in Napa Valley. Perhaps they felt that tying the death of Bertold Shenneck to her would wake a sleepy news media and lead them to make connections between Shenneck and Far Horizons, between Far Horizons and David James Michael with his billions, until eventually someone looked back to the innocuous story about regimented mice and saw in it more sinister potential than the value that brain implants might bring to animal husbandry.

When the news story ended and the theater lights came up, she said to the actor, "Yeah, that was something I had to see, sure enough. Now please tell me that the someone I have to meet isn't going to arrest me."

He regarded her with the solemn gravitas that he could bring to a role as a prosecuting attorney or a wise counselor of a superhero. "Whatever you've got to do, you're not done doing it yet, are you?"

"No."

"And you're not going away to Mexico."

"No."

"You seem to have a world of good guys chasing you, but they're not the good guys, are they?"

"No."

"Do you have an honest idea of what your chances are?"

"Near zero."

He fixed her with a long stare from which she did not glance away, and at last he said, "You need to meet my sister."

36

THE MOVIE STAR'S SISTER, CRES-sida, owned a chain of high-end beauty shops and a successful line of cosmetics, but she claimed, with a laugh, to have no background in law enforcement, other than being, for a short time in her youth, on the wrong side of it.

In a guest bathroom, with an array of chemicals and what she called "industrial-quality appliances," she stripped Jane's hair of its brunette dye, colored the blond tresses auburn, and added just enough curl to fool the eye into thinking this was a different woman.

Later, in the garage, beside her Ford Escape, the actor gave Jane a pair of horn-rimmed glasses.

"I have twenty-twenty vision," she said.

"And you'll still have it when you put them on. It's a movie prop, just clear glass for lenses. Get different hats and wear them. Not always the jeans and sport coat, a varied wardrobe. Think of different characters, roles you can play, and costume each one consistently. It takes only little things, like the glasses, to prevent people from recognizing you as the Clyde's Bonnie they're seeing on the news." He gave her a card with his cell-phone number. "I can only offer you frivolous advice. I've played an FBI rogue, but I've never been one. You have money?"

"Yes."

"Enough money?"

"More than enough."

"You understand you can come back here anytime?"

She understood too well that people didn't always know why they did what they did, that even when they knew their true motives, they often lied to themselves about them. Nevertheless, she had to ask, "Why are you doing this? You have so much to lose, why risk it?"

"For my old sergeant."

"Is that really all it is?"

"No. Not all."

"Well, then?"

"When you've played the good man who shows up at the right time in enough movies, there comes a point where you either have to try to synchronize your real life with the make-believe—or else admit that you're one of the biggest phonies who ever lived."

At last he flashed her the famous killer smile. This time she saw in it the faintest edge of sadness, which she realized was why his smile made millions swoon but also why it broke a million hearts.

37

SHE PARKED IN A SUPERMARKET lot in Santa Monica, where she used a disposable phone to call her father's unlisted line. She was sent to voice mail, as she expected to be. She had not spoken to him in a long time; and now she left a message that she was sure he would be quick to share with authorities.

"Sorry if all this bad publicity affects ticket sales for your current concert tour. But that's the least of your worries. We both know the truth of what happened long ago, and we both know that in what little time I have left, there's nothing I need to do more than bring the hard consequences of that night straight home to you."

Sometimes the only way to reassure your real quarry of his safety was with a bit of misdirection like this.

She dropped the phone through the bars of a storm-drain grating.

38

ON THE ROAD AGAIN, USING another disposable phone, she called ahead to Gavin and Jess Washington, to let them know that she was coming, but also to warn them that she had no time to visit. Her life was now a thousand-mile toboggan ride, a downhill course so treacherous and steep that Olympic luge stars would beg off the race. She did not want to disappoint Travis with a one-hour visit, which would only sharpen his longing for a permanent reunion.

Well after darkfall, Jane parked at the head of their long driveway, shielded from the sight of the house by the colonnades of California live oaks. At 9:40, Gavin walked out to the car to tell her that the boy was sound asleep. Together they returned to the house, where Jess waited in one of the rocking chairs on the porch, the dogs at her feet.

Jane went alone into the house.

As before, he slept by lamplight. Such innocence in a time of such corruption. So small, so vulnerable in a hard world ruled by the aggressive use of force.

When she had carried him from conception to term, she had never imagined that by the time he was five, the world into which she had delivered him would grow so dark. Children were the world as it was meant to be, and they were a light within the world. But for every light, there seemed to be someone bent on extinguishing it.

They said that if someone harmed a child, it would be better for him if instead he were hanged about his neck with a millstone and drowned in the depths of the sea. In spite of how she had been hardened by the task that had been put before her, Jane still had the capacity for tenderness, a storehouse of love to pay out when given a chance, an imperative need to mother this child and, for that matter, all children in his name. To be separated from him was a deep-heart sorrow. In spite of all the death, any day that ended with the chance to see this boy was a good day. She hoped that it was not the *last* good day. But whatever might be coming, she would meet the threat, for it had fallen to her, through no choice of her own, to fashion the millstones and hang them around the necks of the damned.

Please turn the page
for a special advance preview of
the next Jane Hawk novel from
#1 *New York Times* bestselling author

DEAN KOONTZ

THE
WHISPERING
ROOM

1

CORA GUNDERSUN WALKED through seething fire without being burned, nor did her white dress burst into flames. She was not afraid, but instead exhilarated, and the many admiring people witnessing this spectacle gaped in amazement, their expressions of astonishment flickering with reflections of the flames. They called out to her not in alarm, but in wonder, with a note of veneration in their voices, so that Cora felt equally thrilled and humbled that she had been made invulnerable.

Dixie, a long-haired dappled-gold dachshund, woke Cora by licking her hand. The dog had no respect for dreams, not even for this one that her mistress had enjoyed three nights in a row and about which she had told Dixie in vivid detail. Dawn had come, time for breakfast and morning toilet, which were more important to Dixie than any dream.

Cora was forty years old, birdlike and spry. As the short dog toddled down the set of portable steps that allowed her to climb in and out of bed, Cora sprang up to meet the day. She slipped into fur-lined ankle-high boots that served as her wintertime slippers, and in her pajamas she followed the waddling dachshund through the house.

Just before she stepped into the kitchen, she was struck by the notion that a strange man would be sitting at the dinette table and that something terrible would happen.

Of course no man awaited her. She'd never been a fearful woman. She chastised herself for being spooked by nothing, nothing at all.

As she put out fresh water and kibble for her companion, the dog's feathery golden tail swept the floor in anticipation.

By the time Cora had prepared the coffeemaker and switched it on, Dixie had finished eating. Now standing at the back door, the dog barked politely, just once.

Cora snared a coat from a wall peg and shrugged into it. "Let's see if you can empty yourself as quick as you filled up. It's colder than the cellar of Hades out there, sweet thing, so don't dawdle."

As she left the warmth of the house for the porch, her breath smoked from her as if a covey of ghosts, long in possession of her body, were being exorcised. She stood at the head of the steps to watch over precious Dixie Belle, just in case there might be a nasty-tempered raccoon lingering from its night of foraging.

More than a foot of late-winter snow had fallen the previous morning. In the absence of wind, the pine trees still wore ermine stoles on every bough. Cora had shoveled a clearing in the backyard so that Dixie wouldn't have to plow through deep powder.

Dachshunds had keen noses. Ignoring her mistress's plea not to dawdle, Dixie Belle wandered back and forth in the clearing, nose to the ground, curious about what animals had visited in the night.

Wednesday. A school day.

Although Cora had been off work for two weeks, she still felt as if she should hurry to prepare for school. Two years earlier, she had been named Minnesota's Teacher of the Year. She dearly loved—and missed—the children in her sixth-grade class.

Sudden-onset migraines, five and six hours long, sometimes accompanied by foul odors that only she could detect, had disabled her. The headaches seemed to be slowly responding to medications— Zolmitriptan and a muscle relaxant called Soma. Cora had never been a sickly person, and staying home bored her.

Dixie Belle finally peed and left two small logs, which Cora would pick up with a plastic bag later, after they froze solid.

When she followed the dachshund into the house, a strange man was sitting at the kitchen table, drinking coffee that he had boldly poured for himself. He wore a knitted cap. He had unzipped his fleece-lined jacket. His face was long, his features sharp, his cold blue stare direct.

Before Cora could cry out or turn to flee, the intruder said, "Play Manchurian with me."

"Yes, all right," she said, because he no longer seemed to be a threat. She knew him, after all. He was a nice man. He had visited her at least twice in the past week. He was a very nice man.

"Take off your coat and hang it up."

She did as he asked.

"Come here, Cora. Sit down."

She pulled out a chair and sat at the table.

Although a friend of everyone, Dixie retreated to a corner and settled there to watch warily with one light-blue eye and one brown.

"Did you dream last night?" the nice man asked.

"Yes."

"Was it the dream of fire?"

"Yes."

"Was it a good dream, Cora?"

She smiled and nodded. "It was lovely, a lovely walk through soothing fire, no fear at all."

"You'll have the same dream again tonight," he said.

She smiled and clapped her hands twice. "Oh, good. It's such a delightful dream. Sort of like one I sometimes had as a girl—that dream of flying like a bird. Flying with no fear of falling."

"Tomorrow is the big day, Cora."

"Is it? What's happening?"

"You'll know when you get up in the morning. I won't be back again. Even as important as this is, you need no hands-on guidance."

He finished his coffee and slid the mug in front of her and got to his feet and pushed his chair under the table. "*Auf Wiedersehen*, you stupid, skinny bitch."

"Good-bye," she said.

A twinkling, zigzagging chain of tiny lights floated into sight, an aura preceding a migraine. She closed her eyes, dreading the pain to come. But the aura passed. The headache did not occur.

When she opened her eyes, her empty mug stood on the table before her, a residue of coffee in the bottom. She got up to pour another serving for herself.

2

ON A SUNDAY AFTERNOON IN March, in self-defense and with great anguish, Jane Hawk had killed a dear friend and mentor.

Three days later, on a Wednesday when the evening was diamonded with stars that even the great up-wash of lights in the San Gabriel Valley, north of Los Angeles, could not entirely rinse from the sky, she came on foot to a house that she had scouted earlier by car. She carried a large tote bag with incriminating contents. In a shoulder rig under her sport coat hung a stolen Colt .45 ACP pistol rebuilt by one of the country's finest custom-handgun shops.

The residential neighborhood was calm in this

age of chaos, quiet in a time characterized by clamor. California pepper trees whispered and palm fronds softly rustled in a breeze fragrant with jasmine. The breeze was also threaded through with the malodor of decomposition that issued from one gutter drain and then another, perhaps from the bodies of poisoned tree rats that earlier had fled the sunlight to die in the dark.

A for-sale sign in the front yard of the target house, grass in need of mowing, a Realtor's key safe fixed to the front-door handle, and closed draperies suggested that the place must be vacant. The security system most likely wasn't operational, because nothing remained in the residence to steal and because an alarm would have complicated the task of showing the property to prospective buyers.

Behind the house, the patio lacked furniture. Breathing out the faint scent of chlorine, black water rippled in the swimming pool, a mirror to the waning moon.

A stuccoed property wall and Indian laurels screened the back of the house from the neighbors. Even in daylight, she would not have been seen.

With a black-market LockAid lock-release gun legally sold only to law-enforcement agencies, Jane defeated the deadbolt on the back door. She returned the device to the tote and opened the door and stood listening to the lightless kitchen, to the rooms beyond.

Convinced that her assessment of the house must be correct, she crossed the threshold, closed the door behind her, and engaged the deadbolt. From the tote, she fished out an LED flashlight with two settings, clicked it to the dimmest beam, and surveyed a stylish kitchen with glossy white cabinets, black granite countertops, and stainless-steel appliances. No cooking utensils were in sight. No designer china waited to be admired on the shelves of those few upper cabinets that featured display windows.

She passed through spacious rooms as dark as closed caskets and devoid of furniture. Although draperies were drawn over the windows, she kept the flashlight on low beam, directing it only at the floor.

She stayed close to the wall, where the stair treads were less likely to creak, but they still announced her as she ascended.

Although she wanted the front of the house, she toured the entire second floor to be certain she was alone. This was an upper-middle-class home in a desirable neighborhood, each bedroom with its private bath, though the chill in its vacant chambers gave rise in Jane to a presentiment of suburban decline and societal decay.

Or perhaps the dark, cold rooms were not what fostered this apprehension. In fact, a persistent foreboding had been with her for nearly a week, since she had learned what some of the most powerful people in this new world of technological wonders were planning for their fellow citizens.

She put down her tote bag by a window in a front

bedroom and clicked off the flashlight and parted the draperies. She studied not the house directly across the street but the one next door to it, a fine example of Craftsman architecture.

Lawrence Hannafin lived at that address, a widower since the previous September. He and his late wife never had children. Though only forty-eight, twenty-one years older than Jane, Hannafin was likely to be alone.

She didn't know if he might be an ally in waiting. More likely, he would be a coward with no convictions, who would shrink from the challenge she intended to put before him. Cowardice was the default position of the times.

She hoped that Hannafin wouldn't become an enemy.

For seven years, she had been an FBI agent with the Critical Incident Response Group, most often assigned to cases involving Behavioral Analysis Units 3 and 4, which dealt with mass murders and serial killings, among other crimes. In that capacity, she'd killed only twice, in a desperate situation on an isolated farm. In the past week, on leave from the Bureau, she'd killed three men in self-defense. She was now a rogue agent; and she'd had enough of killing.

If Lawrence Hannafin didn't have the courage and integrity that his reputation suggested, Jane hoped that at least he would turn her away without attempting to bring her to justice. There would be no justice for her. No defense attorney. No jury trial.

Considering what she knew about certain powerful people, the best she could hope for was a bullet in the head. They had the means by which to do much worse to her, the ability to break her, to scrub her mind of memories, rob her of free will, and reduce her to docile slavery.

3

JANE TOOK OFF HER SPORT coat and shoulder rig and slept—not well—on the floor, with the pistol near to hand. For a pillow, she used a cushion from the window seat at the end of the second-floor hall, but she had nothing to serve as a blanket.

The world of her dreams was a realm of shifting shadows and silver-blue half light without a source, through which she fled malevolent mannequins who had once been people like her, but were now as tireless as robots programmed for a hunt, their eyes vacant of all feeling.

The wristwatch alarm woke her an hour before dawn.

Her limited toiletries included toothpaste and a brush. In the bathroom, with the dimmed flashlight in a corner on the floor, her face a hollow-eyed haunt in the dark mirror, she scrubbed away the taste of dream fear.

At the bedroom window, she parted the draperies a few inches and watched the Hannafin house
through a small pair of high-power binoculars, her
peppermint breath briefly steaming the window
glass.

According to his Facebook page, Lawrence Hannafin took a one-hour run every morning at dawn. A
second-floor room brightened, and a few minutes
later, soft light bloomed in the foyer downstairs. In
headband, shorts, and running shoes, he exited the
front door as the eastern sky blushed with the first
rose-tinted light of day.

Through the binoculars, Jane watched him key
the lock, after which he safety-pinned the key in a
pocket of his shorts.

The previous day, she had observed him from her
car. He had run three blocks south, then turned east
into a neighborhood of horse properties, following
riding trails into the undeveloped hills of brush and
wild grass. He had been gone sixty-seven minutes.
Jane required only a fraction of that time to do what
needed to be done.

4

ANOTHER MINNESOTA MORN-
ing. A slab of hard gray sky like dirty ice. Scattered
snowflakes in the still air, as if escaping through the
clenched teeth of a reluctant storm.

In her pajamas and fur-lined ankle boots, Cora
Gundersun cooked a breakfast of buttered white
toast dusted with parmesan, scrambled eggs, and
Neuske's bacon, the best bacon in the world, which
fried up thin and crisp and flavorful.

At the table, she read the newspaper while she
ate. From time to time she broke off a little piece
from a slice of bacon to feed to Dixie Belle, who
waited patiently beside her chair and received each
treat with whimpers of delight and gratitude.

Cora had dreamed again of walking unscathed
through a fierce fire while onlookers marveled at her
invulnerability. The dream lifted her heart, and she
felt purified, as if the flames had been the loving fire
of God.

She hadn't suffered a migraine in more than
forty-eight hours, which was the longest reprieve
from pain that she'd enjoyed since the headaches
had begun. She dared to hope that her inexplicable
affliction had come to an end.

With hours to fill before she needed to shower
and dress and drive into town to do what needed to
be done, still at the kitchen table, she opened the

journal that she had been keeping for some weeks. Her handwriting was almost as neat as if produced by a machine, and the lines of cursive flowed without interruption.

After an hour, she put down the pen and closed the journal and fried more Neuske's bacon, just in case this was the last chance she would have to eat it. That was a peculiar thought. Neuske's had been producing fine bacon for decades, and Cora had no reason to suppose they would go out of business. The economy was bad, yes, and many businesses had folded, but Neuske's was forever. Nevertheless, she ate the bacon with sliced tomatoes and more buttered toast, and again she shared with Dixie Belle.

5

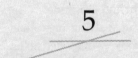

JANE DID NOT CROSS THE street directly from the vacant house to the Hannafin place. Carrying her tote bag, she walked to the end of the block, then half a block farther, before crossing the street and approaching the residence from the north, considerably reducing the chance that anyone would be looking out a window long enough to see both from where she had come and where she had gone.

At the Craftsman-style house, cut-stone steps

bordered with bricks led to a deep porch, at both ends of which crimson wisteria in early bloom cascaded from panels of lattice, providing privacy to commit illegal entry.

She rang the bell three times. No response.

She inserted the thin, flexible pick of the LockAid into the keyway of the deadbolt and pulled the trigger four times before all the pin tumblers were cast to the shear line.

Inside, before she locked the door behind her, she called into the stillness, "Hello? Anyone home?"

When only silence answered her, she committed.

The furnishings and architecture were elegantly coordinated. Slate fireplaces with inset ceramic tiles. Stickley-style furniture with printed cotton fabrics in earth tones. Arts-and-Crafts lighting fixtures. Persian rugs.

The desirable neighborhood, the large house, and the interior design argued against her hope that Hannafin might be an uncorrupted journalist. He was a newspaper guy, and in these days when most newspapers were as thin as anorexic teenagers and steadily dying out, print reporters, even those with a major Los Angeles daily, didn't command huge salaries. The really big money went to TV-news journalists, most of whom were no more journalists than they were astronauts.

Hannafin, however, had written half a dozen nonfiction books, three of which had spent several weeks each on the bottom third of the bestseller list.

They had been serious works, well done. He might have chosen to pour his royalties into his home.

The previous day, using one of several patron computers at a library in Pasadena, Jane easily cracked Hannafin's telecom provider and discovered that he relied on not just a cellphone but also a landline, which made what she was now about to do easier. She had been able to access the phone-company system because she knew of a back door created by a supergeek at the Bureau, Vikram Rangnekar. Vikram was sweet and funny—and he cut legal corners when he was ordered to do so either by the director or by a higher power at the Department of Justice. Before Jane had gone on leave, Vikram had an innocent crush on her, even though at the time she'd been married and so far off the playing field that it might as well have been on the moon. As a by-the-book agent, she had never resorted to illegal methods, but she'd been curious about what the corrupt inner circle at Justice might be doing, and she had allowed Vikram to show off his magic every time he wanted to impress her.

In retrospect, it seemed as if she had intuited that her good life would turn sour, that she would be desperate and on the run, and that she would need every trick that Vikram could show her.

According to phone-company records, in addition to a wall-mounted unit in the kitchen, there were three desk models in the Hannafin house: one in the master bedroom, one in the living room, one in the study. She started in the kitchen and finished in the master bedroom, removing the bottom of each phone casing with a small Phillips screwdriver. She wired in a two-function chip that could be remotely triggered to serve as an infinity transmitter or a standard line tap, installed a hook-switch defeat, and closed the casing. She needed only nineteen minutes to complete that work.

If the big walk-in closet in the master bedroom had not suited her plan, she would have found another closet. But it was all right. One hinged door, not a slider. Although currently unlocked, the door featured a keyed deadbolt, perhaps because a small wall safe was concealed in there or maybe because the late Mrs. Hannafin had owned a collection of valuable jewelry. It was a blind lock from within the closet, with no operable thumbturn on that side. A stepstool allowed the higher shelves to be reached with ease.

Hannafin had a lot of clothes with stylish labels: Brunello Cucinelli suits, a collection of Charvet ties, drawers filled with St. Croix sweaters. Jane hid a hammer among some sweaters and a screwdriver in an interior coat pocket of a blue pinstriped suit.

She spent another ten minutes opening drawers in various rooms, not looking for anything specific, just backgrounding the man.

If she departed the house by the front door, the latch bolt would click into place, but the deadbolt wouldn't. When Hannafin returned and found the deadbolt wasn't engaged, he would know that someone had been here in his absence.

She exited instead by a laundry-room door that connected the house and garage, leaving that deadbolt disengaged, which he was more likely to think he had failed to lock.

The side door of the garage had no deadbolt. The simple latch secured it when she stepped outside and pulled it shut behind her.

6

ONCE MORE IN THE DESERTED for-sale house, now that morning sun provided cover, Jane switched on the lights in the master bathroom.

As sometimes happened these days, the face in the mirror was not what she expected. After all that she had been through in the past four months, she felt weathered and worn by fear, by grief, by worry. Although her hair was shorter and dyed auburn, she looked much as she had before this began: a youthful twenty-seven, fresh, clear-eyed. It seemed wrong that her husband should be dead, her only child in jeopardy and in hiding, and yet no testament of loss and anxiety could be read in her face or eyes.

Among other things, the large tote bag contained a long blond wig. She fitted it to her head, secured it, brushed it, and used a blue Scünci to hold it in a ponytail. She pulled on a baseball cap that wasn't emblazoned with any logo or slogan. In jeans, a sweater, and a sport coat cut to conceal the shoulder rig and pistol, she looked anonymous, except that during the past few days, the news media had ensured that her face was nearly as familiar to the public as that of any TV star.

She could have taken steps to disguise herself better, but she wanted Lawrence Hannafin to have no doubt as to her identity.

In the master bedroom, she waited at the window. According to her watch, the runner returned sixty-two minutes after setting out on his morning constitutional.

Because of his name recognition from the bestselling books and the audience he drew for the newspaper, he was free to work at home from time to time. Nevertheless, hot and sweaty, he would probably opt to shower sooner than later. Jane waited ten minutes before setting out to pay him a visit.

7

HANNAFIN HAS BEEN A WID-ower for a year, but he still has not fully adjusted to being alone. Often when he comes home, as now, by habit he calls out to Sakura. In the answering silence, he stands quite still, stricken by her absence.

Irrationally, he sometimes wonders if she is in fact dead. He'd been out of state on an assignment when her medical crisis occurred. Unable to bear the sight of her in death, he allowed cremation. As a consequence, he occasionally turns with the sudden conviction that she is behind him, alive and smiling.

Sakura. In Japanese, the name means *cherry blossom.* It suited her delicate beauty, if not her forceful personality. . . .

He had been a different man before she came into his life. She was so intelligent, so tender. Her gentle but steady encouragement gave him the confidence to write the books that previously he only talked about writing. For a journalist, he was oddly withdrawn, but she extracted him from what she called his "unhappy-turtle shell" and opened him to new experiences. Before her, he was as indifferent to clothes as to fine wine; but she taught him style and refined his taste, until he wanted to be handsome and urbane, to make her proud to be seen with him.

After her death, he put away all the photographs of the two of them together that she had framed in silver and lovingly arranged here and there about the house. The pictures had haunted him, as she still haunts his dreams more nights than not.

"Sakura, Sakura, Sakura," he whispers to the quiet house, and then goes upstairs to shower.

She was a runner, and she insisted that he run to stay as fit as she, that they might stay healthy and grow old together. Running without Sakura at first seemed impossible, memories like ghosts waiting around every turn of every route they had taken. But then to stop running felt like a betrayal, as if she were indeed out there on the trails, unable to return to this house of the living, waiting for him that she might see him and know that he was well and vital and staying true to the regimen that she had established for them.

If ever Hannafin dares to speak such thoughts to people at the newspaper, they will call him sentimental to his face—maudlin and mawkish and worse behind his back—because there is no room in most contemporary journalists' hearts for schmaltz unless it is twined with politics. Nevertheless . . .

In the master bath, he cranks the shower as hot as he can tolerate. Because of Sakura, he does not use ordinary soap, which stresses the skin, but he lathers up with You Are Amazing body wash. His egg-and-cognac shampoo is from Hair Recipes, and he uses an argan-oil conditioner. All this seemed embarrassingly girly to him when Sakura was alive. But now it is his routine. He recalls times when they showered together, and in his mind's ear, he can hear the girlish giggle with which she engaged in that domestic intimacy.

The bathroom mirror is clouded with steam when he steps out of the shower and towels dry. His reflection is blurred and for some reason disturbing, as if the nebulous form that parallels his every move, if fully revealed, might not be him, but instead some less-than-human denizen of a world within the glass. If he wipes the mirror, it will streak. He leaves the steam to evaporate and walks naked into the bedroom.

A most amazing-looking woman sits in one of the two armchairs. Although she's dressed in scuffed Rockports and jeans and a nothing sweater and an off-brand sport coat, she looks as if she stepped out of the pages of *Vogue*. She's as stunning as the model in the Black Opium perfume ads, except that she's a blonde instead of a brunette.

He stands dumbstruck for a moment, half sure that something has gone wrong with his brain, that he's hallucinating.

She points to a robe that she has taken from his closet and laid out on the bed. "Put that on and sit down. We have to talk."

About the Author

DEAN KOONTZ, the author of many #1 *New York Times* bestsellers, lives in Southern California with his wife, Gerda, their golden retriever, Elsa, and the enduring spirits of their goldens, Trixie and Anna.

deankoontz.com
Facebook.com/DeanKoontzOfficial
@deankoontz

Correspondence for the author should be addressed to:

Dean Koontz
P.O. Box 9529
Newport Beach, California 92658

Join Dean Koontz
on social media!

Facebook.com/deankoontzofficial

@deankoontz

Instagram.com/deankoontzofficial

Visit DeanKoontz.com
and sign up for Dean's e-newsletter!